The Silver Currant

A Gaslamp Trinkets Novel

Book Two of the Luella Winthrop Trilogy

By Kenneth A. Baldwin

EBURNEAN
BOC

T0204614

To Kelly, who loves me even though.

The Silver Currant

A Gaslamp Trinkets Novel

Book Two of the Luella Winthrop Trilogy

By Kenneth A. Baldwin

Published by Eburnean Books, a trademark of
Emberworks Creative, LLC.
www.eburneanbooks.com
www.emberworkscreative.com

Chapter One

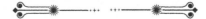

The Iron Greyhound

The moment immediately preceding a kiss—and I mean a truly sincere and anticipated kiss—is one of the longest and most sudden moments that exists. The subtle mix of longing, anxiety, elation, and vertigo would fill the shelves of pubs all over the world if it could only be bottled. But even if you could bottle it, I can't imagine it would keep long before spoiling.

But, the longer a moment like this stretches on, the easier it is for the more unpleasant emotions to taint the experience. Where once grew anticipation, instead sprouts doubt. Many a couple perished prematurely because one or both parties hesitated in this ever so important moment.

And why hesitate? Why pause if both want the same thing? Why question the shared experiences that rendered mutual affection all but certain? And what on earth should prevent two lovers from renewing such affection?

In other words, Edward had not kissed me since Fernmount.

I watched him across a smoky pub where he talked in low tones with a man etched with dark tattoos. Edward looked laughable, if such a thing were possible, adorned in false bushy eyebrows and a beard. As if this would disguise him from anybody who knew him.

The tattooed man eyed him warily.

I remembered our first lunch together at Doug's Fish and Chips Pub in Dawnhurst-on-Severn. The owner of that pub had been rough and tumble as well, and Edward had got along with him famously, but that was because Edward couldn't hide his sincerity. He didn't have much skill in deception or trickery. No matter. What he lacked in stealth he made up for with money to buy a lot of beer.

Here, in a rowdy Reading tavern lightly adorned with aged Christmas bobbles, we were repeating the same strategy we'd used at pubs across southwest England. First, find someone who might know about the not entirely law-abiding employees of the peculiar carnival we chased. Second, buy them enough beer to impair any ability they might have to see through Edward's disguise. Finally, glean what information we could from their drunken ramblings.

Unfortunately, until now that had just meant a lot of free alcohol for a lot of scoundrels in a lot of taverns.

A lumbering buffoon stumbled by my corner table, bumping my shoulder. I pulled my hood lower to cover my face.

"Sorry," the man grunted. I did not reply, opting instead to stare into my tumbler of brandy, still untouched. I wasn't much of a drinker.

When the Lord returns to the Earth to vanquish the devil and cast out evil, I wonder which He might burn first. Brothels or pubs? I suppose I should be grateful to have a traveling companion who was not interested in either.

Edward stood up and coughed twice before making a zigzag route to my table. He sat himself down with an overly dramatic plop.

"A bit more grace suits you better," I whispered out of the side of my mouth.

"I'm playing the role," he replied.

"What role is that? I grew up on the east side of Dawnhurst. I've seen a lot of wretched people, but never one quite like Mr. Pendles."

I let his false name drip from my lips dramatically.

"Well, some of us have traveled beyond Dawnhurst, and we've seen more wretched fellows than you have."

"It's not a competition."

"I'm simply stating—"

"Never mind all that. What did that man have to say?" Even now, when it would completely blow our cover and he was being difficult, I longed to reach out for his hand. If only we could run off together instead of chase empty leads.

I had closed that door on myself, though. Edward kept his distance from me because I had requested it. I was so stupid sometimes.

I reminded myself that his lack of affection was for the best. He asked me to marry him, and I said no for more than one reason. He still grieved his father. I was still infected with a magical illness.

If our romance had cooled, maybe it was meant to.

"He told me he's friends with someone who worked the fair, an impossibly large man in a bowler hat," Edward said.

My mouth fell open. After many weeks, this might be the most solid lead we'd uncovered. His steely grey eyes sparkled in the lamplight.

"That must be Gerald," I said. "He was friends with Bram. I met him many times." It was becoming difficult to keep my voice at a whisper. I never thought that Gerald, the big, hairy, hat-wearing guerrilla, would set my heart racing. "Did he say where Gerald is now?"

"That's proving to be more difficult," Edward replied, touching his false eyebrows tenderly. "I don't think Gerald appreciates being found by strangers."

"We must do something. This is the best chance we've had since we left your estate."

"Quite right, Miss Primrose." He winked at me, stood and pretended to be put off, gesticulating as though I'd refused an advance from him. If only. I wouldn't refuse an advance, even if the alias he had invented for me made me sound like an escort. "Sounds like I need another pint."

He signaled to one of the pub keepers, some grimy freckled man who still looked like a boy of twelve. I flexed my fingers, wishing I had something to do. Edward insisted that people went to pubs to drink by themselves and sit motionless in corners more often than I thought. I never spent much time in pubs, so I was forced to believe him.

If the tattooed man knew Gerald, we would really be on to something. One step closer to finding Bram. And, if we found Bram, we'd be one step closer to finding a cure for the supernatural malady that ailed me.

Even thinking of it caused my fingers to twitch. I had suffered from its effects for long enough now that it was difficult to remember life without it. I felt a low, budding anger inside of me at all times. I was irritated easily, and occasionally, when my feelings boiled to overflow, I was prone to terrible fits. The worst part was feeling that I was not my own. When the fits came, it was as though I was watching my body through a window.

I had once berated my sister, lashed out at my elderly neighbor, and physically assaulted my best friend. I had even almost done harm to Edward's mother during our first and only dinner together.

I took a small sip of the brandy. It burned going down my throat, but at least it broke my train of thought. I could not afford to have such a fit in this pub.

A nasty-looking man stared at me from another table. His cheekbones looked like shoulder joints covered in grease, and he had a front tooth missing. I could tell because of the perverted smile he sent in my direction.

I prayed he would not come toward my table.

I looked over at Edward, who was just sitting down to a game of cards. I couldn't interfere. Who knew what the presence of a woman might do to his inquiry about Gerald? Then again, if I was reading this hobgoblin correctly (and men can be so easy to read) and Edward turned to see said hobgoblin next to me, there was no telling what would happen.

The whiskery ball of grease finished his pint, wiped his mouth on the back of his hand, and stood up.

That was that. I made a direct line to Edward. I hoped his acting wasn't as poor as it was last time. When he turned, his eyes went wide with alarm. He looked past me and saw the man waiting at my abandoned table.

"I've reconsidered your request," I said to him, in a coquettish voice.

"My request?" he stammered. There were three other men at the table, and they all eyed me like a Christmas turkey. I had a chance to see our tattooed informant up close. Three dark lines stretched from his ear down his jawline.

"Yes. I'll sit next to you here and we'll see if I can bring you good luck, after all." I sat down next to him and put a hand on his arm. I squeezed it hard, and he finally turned back to the table.

"Looks like you blokes are at a disadvantage," he said. At least he knew to play along. Two of the men, our new inked friend included, rolled their eyes. The third had dark hair and a pale blind eye. He narrowed his gaze at us, searching for something.

I tried to ignore him, focusing instead on the game, but after a round or two he started to smile.

"That does it for me, gents," he said. Then he was gone, out the door. I stared after him, uneasy. Or maybe I was still queasy from the sweaty human ball of hair that had chased me from my seat across the room.

The other man grimaced and complained that a three-person game wasn't to his liking, and soon we were left alone at the table with just the three-stripe man and a couple of empty pint mugs for company.

"Miss Primrose, was it?" Edward asked. I resisted an audible scoff and nodded. "This is Scott."

"Pleased to make your acquaintance, Miss Primrose." He stood and made an off-balanced bow.

"Scott, you have to tell the woman about your big friend. Miss Primrose, you won't believe the tales Scott's been telling me about this louse named Gerald."

"Veritable giant he is," Scott said, tipping back a mug in an attempt to collect its last drops of beer. "One time, I watched him lift a horse."

Gerald was large, but this was an obvious lie.

"A horse?" I echoed playfully and giggled. This was demeaning. What was I?

"There we were, standing on the corner, when a buggy comes by. It must have been hot as the devil that day, and the buggy came to a stop in a bit of shade. The horse just lies down right there, heat exhausted. The driver tried everything he could think of to get it back up, but nothing worked. Finally, Gerald walks over, crouches down, wraps his arms around the beast's chest, and lifts it up off the ground. Truest story I ever told."

I tried to imagine how long Gerald's arms would have to be in order to wrap around a fully grown horse.

"There you go, Miss Primrose. Didn't I tell you? Crazy stories," Edward said.

"Mr. Scott—"

"Please, just Scott. That's what me mother called me, me mates call me, and me lady friends as well." He cocked an eyebrow at me as if to suggest there might be an opening in the last category. I'm sure there was.

"Scott. I don't know if I can believe a story like that. The man must tower over the rest of us."

"Aye. He does."

"It can't be true."

"Are you calling me a liar?"

Edward tensed next to me.

"I don't know what you are, but I wouldn't believe a story like that unless I saw the man myself. A girl can't trust everything she hears."

Scott looked perplexed and adjusted his belt. Then he lit up with a brilliant idea.

"Then you'll have to do just that," he said. "I can take you to him."

"Take us to him?" Edward gaped. "Haven't you been telling me he's not a sociable man?"

"He'll make an exception for a pretty face like this one." Scott nodded at me. "But I never said anything about you coming along."

Edward's mouth twisted.

"I'm not going unless Mr. Pendles accompanies me," I said, placing a hand on Edward's. It wasn't necessary, but it felt nice to touch him.

"Oh, come, now—"

"I won't have it, Scott. Mr. Pendles will you agree to be my chaperone?"

"I'd be glad to, Miss Primrose. Though, I depart from the city soon on business."

"We could see him tomorrow morning."

My pulse quickened. Finally, this pathway might lead us to some answers.

"This better be worth our while," Edward said in his overly affected dialect.

"It'll be worth it. It's not every day you get to meet a giant like him. Besides, if you like my stories, wait 'til you hear his. Running around with a ruddy carnival, there's no telling what he's seen. Meet me at St. Mary's tomorrow at ten, near Castle Street," Scott said, scratching his cheek.

"Tomorrow at ten," I repeated. "In the meantime, you will excuse me. I'm afraid I'll catch a chill unless I can get to bed. Mr. Pendles, will you escort me back to my lodgings, so I make it alright?"

"Of course," Edward replied. "I'll pay my bill, and we can be on our way."

We exchanged a handshake with Scott, and Edward went to the bar. I stood a small way off from him, doing my best to look occupied. However, some morbid curiosity got the better of me, and I shot a glance back to the little imp that had been waiting for me.

He noticed me looking and made his way over.

I panicked and considered sitting down at Scott's table before deciding it would be better to join Edward at the bar. But my indecision cost me dearly, and the man had closed the gap.

"What's a pretty 'lil thing like you doing here?" he asked, trying to smooth back his thin locks of hair.

"I'm here with my fiancé," I spat out. That was my go-to lie of late. I'd used it enough that I almost forgot it wasn't true.

"That's a fancy French word," he said.

"The man I'm going to marry. There, at the bar. So, if you'll excuse me—"

"You don't seem like the marryin' type the way you curl your lip and flash those pretty eyes like you do. Come on, why not go for a walk with me?"

The anger bubbled inside me, my magical malady searching for an excuse to erupt.

"I think you've had too much to drink," I said, clenching my teeth. My fingers twitched.

"I think I've had just enough." He grabbed my arm. My hand flew as if on its own and slapped him hard across the face. My nails left a small gash on his cheek. The patrons immediately near us halted their conversations, gifting me an eery quiet. The dark magic inside of me stirred like a child waking from sleep.

The greasy little man rubbed his cheek gingerly.

"You're feisty. I think I deserve an apology." He reached for me with more than playful intent. I tried to slap him again, but he caught my wrist in his hand. He squinted at me ravenously and pulled me toward him.

I felt a pang of fear before Edward tackled him to the ground.

"You should tend your manners better," said Edward, struggling to hold the man down.

"You her handler, then?" he asked with a devious smile.

Edward punched him hard across the face before standing up.

"Are you hurt?" he asked me.

"Edward!"

The greasy man had found a wooden chair. He swung it clumsily against Edward's back. Edward took the blow with a grimace, but I knew it would take more than a drunken bumbler to injure his broad shoulders.

Edward turned, grabbed the chair, and tackled him again. Unfortunately, by now they had attracted a good deal of attention. Two other men grabbed Edward by the arms. Edward kicked one of them in the knee, eliciting a roar of pain.

The other took the opportunity to punch Edward in the jaw. That's when Scott jumped into the fray, and I lost track of any logical sequence of events.

"Stop it! Knock it off!" I cried, a mix of concern and fury. Edward would blow our cover if that stupid false beard came off.

The barkeep placed a gentle but firm hand on my shoulder.

"It's best if you just stay out of this one, miss," he said, his freckly face glossy in the firelight.

I considered taking his advice and walking out the door when I heard the chilling sound of police whistles. Several officers of Reading's Police Force entered the building, batons in hand, and before I knew what happened, they had the brawl broken apart.

I immediately noticed a difference in the demeanor of the Reading Police Force compared to the one at Dawnhurst. At home, Sergeant Cooper and his band of officers worked comfortably and personally through the cases of our small city. I couldn't deny that even if they now hunted me. But the officers before me now looked mechanical, like gears in a clock.

"Cut all that out," said a tall, muscular man. "Come now, gents. Let's not forget it's almost Christmas." He had jet black hair that stuck out neatly under his constable hat. Sarcasm dripped from the word Christmas like water from an icicle.

I glanced at Edward. His fake beard hung halfway off of his face, which smarted with a sizable bruise.

"What have we here?" the dark-haired man continued. He strode toward Edward with a sense of foreboding, his hands clasped behind his back.

"That's the one, Inspector," said a man near the door. I turned and saw the pale eye that had dismissed itself from our card game not long before. He grinned deviously.

The Inspector held out a baton to lift Edward's chin. He looked all a mess, and his disguise, which may have worked on drunkards in the dark light of taverns, would be obvious to a practiced policeman. I winced in embarrassment as the Inspector gently tore the rest of Edward's beard off. I told him he should have grown a real one.

"Well, boys," the Inspector called to his men, "Christmas has come early. This, here, is Edward Thomas."

Chapter Two

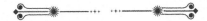

Inspected

I much preferred the Dawnhurst police station to the one in Reading.

It may have been prudish of me to like things from my home village, but the Reading station lacked personality. To bring a criminal here would be a severe sentence, indeed. The officers mulled about quietly, efficiently, and with little expression on their faces. All the lamps were lit, and bright fires burned in the occasional hearth, permeating the room with a nearly uncomfortable heat.

I sat near one such fireplace now, my hood laid across my lap, waiting to be dealt with. I still wore my outfit from the pub, a conservative flannel skirt and bodice and an oversized linen blouse beneath that tried to stay on my shoulders. I had insisted to Edward that, if we were going through pubs, I needed to look the part.

It wasn't long before the Inspector exited his office and marched over. He sat down with excellent posture. My mother would have been proud.

"Whatever you're thinking, you have it all wrong," I said quickly.

"The trustworthy and reputable Edward Thomas has been missing for weeks. He missed his own father's memorial, hasn't been seen at his place of employment, and left his household in a state of chaos. Then, we found him here at the Iron Greyhound, in Reading, brawling while wearing a false beard and consorting with a mysterious woman. Excuse us our assumptions."

"Where is he now?" I asked.

"In my office," the Inspector replied. He stared at me with dark piercing eyes until I squirmed from discomfort. "What is your name, Miss Primrose?"

"Sarah Primrose."

"Your real name, please."

"Can I speak with Mr. Pendles?"

He sighed and flexed his fingers, standing to pace.

"What am I supposed to do with you?" he asked. "I don't believe you're a prostitute, but I can't believe you're only friends with Lieutenant Thomas, either."

I straightened my spine, suddenly aware of how I slouched in my chair.

"And why ever not?" I asked, my voice bitter. I was tiring of paranoia.

"Edward Thomas?" he asked, scoffing. "Edward Thomas of Fernmount, son of the great Luke Thomas? The rich boy who donated his life to police work." His voice was laced with sarcasm and derision. It turned out not everyone had the esteem for Edward that his former comrades shared.

"No, you're not a lady of the night, and you're no lady of the day, either," he continued. "Even if the Prince of Police liked you, his mother wouldn't approve."

I opened my mouth to protest, but he happened to be correct. Edward's mother detested me. To her, I symbolized the death of her son's prospective future. I sullied their family name by association.

The Inspector threw a black and white portrait on a desk beside me. A younger Edward stared up at me, looking clean and pristine in a police uniform. It reminded me of the first time I met him. He looked like a toy soldier.

"Every police station in every city south of Manchester has one of these. Now, how many police lieutenants do you think have even one portrait like this? How about twenty portraits? They aren't cheap."

I studied the portrait, the meticulously combed hair, the spotless uniform, the clear, unmarred gaze...

"Be honest. What are you doing with Edward Thomas?" The Inspector stared at me, unflinching. He was so unlike Edward. Edward's eyes were gentle and kind. The gaze that looked at me now believed people, deep down, were weak and devilish. They stared right through me, and I felt afraid. Was it possible he knew about the rage I carried?

He almost got the truth out of me.

"Am I under arrest?" I asked.

"Do I have cause to arrest you?"

"Then I take it I'm free to go?"

"It appears that way." He didn't move.

"And Mr. Pendles?"

"Call him by his true name."

"Mr. Thomas, then. Is he under arrest?"

"I'm still deciding. He was in a brawl at The Iron Greyhound. Drunkenness. Assault. Disturbing the peace. That's enough to keep him overnight, at least. Besides, I'm sure his mum would be happy to know he's safe."

I bit my lip. I wanted to scream. I wanted to hit this man who looked so smug and condescending. My fingers twitched, a symptom of magical illness, eager to see me come undone. But I held no power here. Fear flooded through me, smothering my anger. I needed Edward. Without him I was penniless, lost, and unconnected.

If he were arrested, or worse, if his mother found him...

"Can I talk with him?" I asked, trying to keep my voice steady.

"No," he replied. "But we can."

He strode toward the other room without hesitation or comment. I followed, coming up with at least ten terrible insults by the time we got to the door of his office. Stupid man was one of them. I missed writing. I was out of practice.

The office was spartan and exact. Everything was excruciatingly neat and organized, stacks of paper looking like the blocks of wood they were cut from and books too well-kept to have ever been read. Everything was a different hue of old, well-cleaned paint. Edward sat in a chair next to the desk, his false beard crumpled in his hand. Traces of smeared, dried blood congealed under his nose. When I walked in, his face lit up with concern.

"Mr. Pendles," I cut in, "have they treated you well?"

"He's been treated like a prince," the Inspector said. "Let me lay out how this little chat will go. If either of you talks out of turn, Edward will spend the night in a cell. Here are the rules. I've already spoken with each of you. I will ask one of you a question. If your answer doesn't match what the other has already told me, I'll incarcerate Edward. If you refuse to answer, I'll incarcerate Edward. Who would like to start?"

I didn't answer. It was an interesting interrogation tactic. Edward and I had created a back story weeks ago, but it had never been truly tested. Then again, if he already spoke to both of us, he would already know whether our answers coincided or not. Did he just want to make us squirm?

The Inspector had us cornered in ways he didn't realize. We weren't trying to avoid a jail cell. We were trying to avoid detection altogether. The only way to win this scenario was to finish the conversation and discreetly walk out the door.

"Very well, let's start with the Prince of Police."

I winced at the way he mocked my—well, my friend, Edward.

"Edward Thomas," the Inspector began, "what is this woman's name?"

Edward looked at me and stared hard into my eyes. He had given me an alias, but he didn't know whether the Inspector had learned my true name. To avoid incarceration, Edward's answers would have to resonate not with the truth, but with what he believed I held out as the truth.

"Miss Sarah Primrose," he responded. I sighed. If I was this nervous over such a basic question, then we were in trouble.

"And tell me, Lord of Fernmount, what did this woman think your name was?"

"Mr. Charles Pendles."

"So far so good. Now, let's go a bit deeper, shall we? Miss Primrose, what is the nature of your relationship with Mr. Pendles?"

The Inspector turned towards me with a blank expression. I imagined he reveled in his line of work but wouldn't be caught dead admitting that to anyone. He knew exactly which questions would make me squirm. The nature of our relationship? I wanted to know myself.

What had Edward's answer been? I was confident that he hadn't divulged the truth—that I was the woman responsible for tangling in some dark magic that led to his father's death, whom he now accompanied to track down a carnival worker.

Not likely.

I doubted Edward would have suggested a more immoral relationship either. I had insisted that traveling with a mistress, although morally reprehensible, was all too common. He had refused. Sternly.

Then what? We had been at the Iron Greyhound several nights now. How would I explain that? How had Edward explained it?

"It's an unfair question," Edward piped in.

"Quiet, this is a warning," the Inspector replied.

"Miss Primrose can't respond because I've bound her to silence," he said.

"Bound her to silence? How?"

"How else might the Prince of Police bind someone to silence? With good money. I've paid her not to divulge our arrangement."

"So, unbind her so I can see if her story matches yours." He frowned at the corner of his mouth, displeased at Edward's interference with his game.

"If you wish. Miss Primrose, I release you from your vow of confidentiality for now. Be as open as you wish with the Inspector about our relationship."

I fought back a smile, understanding Edward's meaning. His words signaled that he had not provided an answer to this question. I had carte blanche.

"I'm his fortune teller," I spat out, instantly regretting it. I had carte blanche. I chose a fortune teller?

"His fortune teller?" the Inspector asked, incredulously.

"Why do you look so surprised?" I replied, leaning into the story. "This poor man recently lost his father. It's not uncommon for someone in his position to seek communion with those that have moved on."

He surveyed me up and down before clasping both of his hands behind his back.

"Forgive me miss, but you don't exactly look like you know how to conduct a seance."

"You are an expert on the subject, are you?" I asked, pointedly. "Tell me Inspector, have you ever been to a seance?"

"I've interrupted my fair share. They attract a certain variety of criminal," he replied cooly. I cursed myself. Of course, a police inspector would have seen a seance.

"Let me guess," I continued, "some woman wearing a satin sash and big earrings or a gentleman with a turban on his head usually conducted them?"

The Inspector didn't respond, only stood there curling his lip.

"Those are the imposters," I explained. "The only thing they can conjure is a heavy dose of disappointment. Parlour tricks and sleight of hand. They don't know about real magic."

It all came out fluidly. I should have been surprised, but truth be told, the only lie in my words was about my relationship with Edward. I had grown arrogant about magic. A byproduct of my mystical condition had been a feeling that no one else understood magic the way I could. Human nature is infinitely resourceful at making arrogance out of affliction.

"And is it typical for seances to extend over several nights?" he asked.

"No. It is admittedly unusual. We've had trouble connecting to Edward's father."

The Inspector sat down behind the desk.

"Edward," he said after massaging his temples. "Is Miss Pendles from Reading?"

"No," Edward replied without hesitation. "We traveled here in secret."

"And where is she staying?"

"The Boar's Head."

That wasn't true. It was a unified story we took into the pubs with us, but its blatant, verifiable falsehood had me biting my lip. I expected the Inspector to jump up and call us out, but he merely sat there. Edward took the silence as an invitation to elaborate.

"We traveled here in secret because of my mother," he said, sighing. Edward was mixing lies and truth, as I had. "She believes that so-called magic is the tool of the devil. If she heard that I had hired a mystic to communicate with my late father... Well, I'd rather work for the Reading Police."

"How quaint," the Inspector replied with a curt smile. "And why did you feel the need to commune with your father so soon after his death? You missed his memorial, did you not?"

Edward fell silent. I picked up the trace.

"All of us have our own forms of grieving, do we not?" I asked, swishing my words the way I had heard fortune tellers do at Bram's carnival.

"I wasn't asking you, gypsy, was I?" the Inspector retorted. I scoffed. I looked nothing like a gypsy. "Aye, Thomas? It's not like you to abandon your duty, father passing or no."

Suddenly, the Inspector's meaning dawned on me. Did he believe that Edward was trying to contact the dead to gain context about his father's death? Such a desire may betray a son's belief of foul play.

Given that I caused Luke Thomas' death, this was not a line of inquiry I wanted the Inspector inspecting. Edward seemed to have come to the same conclusion. I saw him looking for another answer that might satisfy our interrogator, but the man was shrewd and discerning.

"You're looking for answers," the Inspector said. "Why?"

"Wouldn't you be searching for answers?" Edward replied. "If a father who you assumed to be content took his own life?"

The Inspector shook his head.

"You come from a family that doesn't believe in mysticism. You've just said so about your mother. And you're a detective. Leaving before your father's memorial would hardly give you time to investigate before leaping into the unknown of the supernatural. Drastic choice, Thomas. Why make it?"

"It's as I've told you," Edward said. I bit my tongue, the paranoia seeping in. This man could discover us. He could hold us until Sergeant Cooper and the Dawnhurst Police Force found me. They could put me on trial as a murderess, or a witch. I needed to get out of that police station. My fingers twitched.

"Do you have any more questions for us, Inspector, or are we free to go?" I asked. "It's late, it's cold outside. I'm not looking forward to my walk back."

"Just one more, and I apologize for it in advance, but the truth must out," he said. "Are the two of you romantically involved?"

My mouth fell open in tandem with Edward's. The nerve! The sheer arrogance and nosiness! It surpassed anything my old gossip of a neighbor, Mrs. Crow, might have ever done, and that was an accomplishment.

My fury was only amplified by my inability to answer him honestly. I looked dumbly at Edward as we both made half consonant noises back and forth at one another.

"I understand," the Inspector said, looking at me with mock sympathy. "You may go."

I scrunched up my skirt and did my best to hold my chin high. All I wanted was to get out of that station to continue our search for Bram and hopefully a cure for the unnatural feelings that swelled inside of me at that very instant.

"I'll be reporting you to your superiors, Inspector. Shall we, Mr. Thomas?"

"Oh, I said you may go Miss Primrose. Lord Thomas will stay here tonight."

"You just said—"

"I gave you several reasons for which I would incarcerate Edward, and you came through on all of them. Two schoolboys caught bullying a new boy could have done a better job. Miles!"

I wanted to protest. I wanted to fight back. I hadn't been separated from Edward like this in over a month. My anger flared.

A long-faced man with drooping eyes entered and stepped to attention.

"Please escort Miss Primrose back to her inn. Which was it again?"

"The Boar's Head could not confirm her stay, sir. Poor William had to inquire at three different inns before finding record of Sarah Primrose at The Hare and Hounds," Miles replied, stiffly.

"Well, it's at least close to the Boar's Head. Somewhat. Just down on London Street. You won't be far from your employer, Miss Primrose, and I promise we will take care of him."

"You can't—"

"Please, don't trouble yourself. We're not throwing him in Reading Gaol. He is a fellow police officer, after all. We'll give him a room in the dormitories. I'm sure the boys will be thrilled to house the Prince of Police."

I saw Edward's shoulders slump, and before I could collect my thoughts to form an argument, Miles had whisked me out the door, replaced my hood, and swept me out into the December night air toward the Hare and Hounds.

Chapter Three

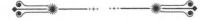

Through the Onyx Door

After a cold walk, Officer Miles bid me good night in front of the black and white facade that dressed The Hare and Hounds. I hadn't said a word during the walk, and the officer didn't try any conversation. He was likely cold and interested in getting back to his dormitory.

Stirrings of fear and fury chased each other around inside of me. I hadn't been alone since the chain of events that forced my exile from Dawnhurst-on-Severn, and I was afraid to face whatever I might find in solitude. Regret. Longing. The deep, fresh absence of my sister's abandonment.

I'm not sure what I feared most in my dark room in The Hares and Hound, myself or my magic. The hunger gnawed at me, distracting me from reality. I didn't recall the words Officer Miles used as he left me, but I spat something out in return, some form of etiquette that operated like an involuntary muscle.

Somehow, I got to my room, but when I lit the candles and closed the door behind me, long, ghostly shadows danced on the wall. It felt like walking into the local graveyard. The cold draft in the room sharpened my senses. I stalled in the doorway and strained my ears. I couldn't shake the terrible premonition that someone waited in the room for me, but I heard only the whistling winter wind and the settling creak of the inn in the night, heavy wood moaning with age.

Still, I knew what waited. My emotions had been building since my encounter with the greasy man at the pub. Since then, as Edward and I were interrogated, my temper slowly simmered to boiling. Even thinking about the Inspector now infuriated me.

My entire life infuriated me.

I braved steps forward and searched for the iron grate that let heat from the ground floor furnace. I didn't think it so late that the stove would be cold, but scant warmth filtered up.

My temper flared.

The stupid grate. The idiotic innkeeper. Did he think of nothing but himself?

The magic inside of me clawed at my mind, begging me to lash out at something, tear the grate from the floor, dash the window out with it. My hands shook with the want of it, the desire to just give in to the fury.

I turned from the grate and sat down on a wooden chair near a small writing desk, breathing in and out through my mouth.

So, here was solitude. An old friend returned with a vengeance. Since leaving his estate in Fernmount, Edward kept a watchful vigil over me, especially at night when I dipped into sleep. On bad nights he slept in a chair in my room, otherwise standing guard on the other side of a wall, never out of earshot.

Knowing that he was near helped me manage my symptoms. It was difficult for my anger to start at all with Edward attending to my every need. Not that the magic didn't try, but too many other emotions drowned it out. Edward Thomas was the type of man many little girls dreamed of marrying: attractive, noble, wealthy, and, for some reason, he believed he was in love with me. We had kissed on a midnight balcony. Even the memory of that night left me nervous, anxious, and dizzy.

I had asked that we postpone those feelings as I completed my journey. I thought they would be a distraction. Of course, I didn't know then Edward was coming along.

As we journeyed together, my resolve on this front weakened. I found myself hoping, wishing that he'd hold my hand or kiss me goodnight. What madness to feel so fortunate one moment and so needy immediately after?

The fits, when they came, preferred the evening. The first time after we'd left Fernmount was traumatic. Edward had paid a farmer to let us spend the night in his house. I locked myself in my bedroom when the magic bubbled to unbearable levels. Edward tried to break in, but thankfully, the lock held. When I woke the next morning, I had vandalized the room, and my fingernails were chipped and bleeding in some places.

It cost a fortune to make amends and keep the man quiet.

I rubbed my wrists. Since then, Edward had come up with a rudimentary and crude way to keep the attacks at bay. Each night, he would bind me in leather belts and cords from my shoulders to my knees. It wasn't comfortable, and I didn't sleep well, but it prevented the awkward reimbursements at inns for damage to their property or the need to wrap my hands like a pugilist.

I looked at the scars on some of my fingers. I was a volcano, just waiting to erupt. I feared every day that an outburst lay just below the surface while I was with another person.

I laughed bitterly as my fingers twitched of their own accord. To think, not six months before I was engaged to my editor, Byron, and writing silly articles about etiquette for rainy days. I had never meddled in magic, wandered into strange carnivals, or used allegedly magical artifacts.

But I could not rewrite my history. I met a man named Bram. He offered me use of a pen that turned fiction to fact. Using it had infected me. My weakness led me to use that magic in a way that led to the death of Luke Thomas.

Edward's father. I had his blood on my hands. I wanted to know why. I wanted to stop the anger simmering in the pit of my stomach all the time. I wanted to call out for help.

Tonight, I was on my own.

I found my way into a nightgown, clambered into bed and clumsily fumbled with the leather straps. Here was a feat. I would love to see a reverse escapologist at a traveling show one day. Instead of wiggling his way out of chains, he would have to find a way into them securely enough to satisfy a jailer.

I tugged at the straps, fumbling awkwardly with their small buckles.

To fasten them tight, I gripped them at awkward angles and pulled with my teeth. Even alone in my room, the actions humiliated me.

I blew out the candle, and the darkness overcame me.

I stood on a rocky shore, watching the moon dance on the tide as foamy waves came crashing in. The inky water slithered through softly polished rocks and over my bare feet.

I had always dreamed of a holiday at the sea. As a girl, my father promised me that one day we'd go to a little shack near Dover, a place he'd visited with his own dad.

The sea whispers truth if you listen between the sound of the waves. My father used to say that. You can hear it if you have the right ears.

But I never saw my father in my dreams. Not truly. A monster made of fog would appear as my father, distorting my most cherished memories in an effort to manipulate me. It had fooled me before, but it never would again.

I stared at the waves and listened. I wished my father taught me the language of the sea. Instead, the tide crept toward me, slow and unstoppable.

I took a deep breath and a few steps backward.

Luella.

Something whispered behind me, as subtle as a breath of wind, but it pulled every hair on my neck upright. I knew that feeling. I knew the sound, and it turned me around like an insistent lover.

In the rock face behind me, blanketed in algae and shimmering moonlight, stood a heavy door made of black wood.

Next to it stood what-was-not-my-father. His eyes were dark where the color should have been, not black, but several shades darker than natural. He stared at me.

"Luella! There you are!" he said, jovially, falsely.

I didn't respond, instead turning to walk away from him. There had to be some other direction available to me, but cliffs, tide, and fog closed in from all sides.

"Why do you run from me?" the phantom asked.

"Why do you still impersonate my father?" I retorted. "I see what you really are."

"And what am I?" Its question sounded like a thunderclap, freezing me, as if someone had suspended me in the air with a meat hook.

"You've been avoiding me," my father said, falling back into a gentle voice that sounded so close to my girlhood memories.

"And yet, you've made contact," I said, unconsciously touching my fingertips together, probing where I had injured myself scratching walls like a lunatic.

"You are an enigma, Luella. I didn't expect to find a person like you."

"Oh, now you're a charmer?"

"It's not flattery. It's truth."

"Excuse me if I don't take your word at face value."

The waves lashed against my legs, so frigid they burned. My father faced the door, his hands in his trouser pockets, looking as unassuming as a Sunday stroll in the park.

"Why won't you open this door?" he asked.

"You mean the ominous, black door unnaturally situated in a rock face? I don't know. I suppose I'm just waiting to make sure another, more exciting door doesn't come along."

"You make light of what you don't understand. Aren't you curious?"

I didn't answer. Gentle thunder rumbled in the fog and clouds around me, muted balls of light firing off menacingly.

"If you're so curious, why don't you just open it?" I asked.

"I cannot."

This surprised me, but the slightest twinge of empowerment seeped into the corners of my mouth.

"Why not?" I replied.

"The handle will only turn if you will it."

"If I will it? You've infected me down to the core. I don't will the fanatical episodes I suffer. I didn't will Luke Thomas' death. You did that despite me. Why is this door so special?"

I blinked, and the image of my father closed the gap between us in a split second. It talked now with a low, gravelly voice. The surrounding fog stirred.

"Don't blame me for your choices. You assume I cause these episodes. I want to empower you. You smother your true desires when they're just within reach." He beckoned toward the door.

I furrowed my brows, trying to make sense of the phantom's words. I didn't trust its words. It wore my father's face like a costume. The waves were at my heels, and I could not retreat. The fog closed in. Soon, the only shelter from the storm would be behind that sturdy impenetrable door. Or else I might drown, as I had done in similar dreams on similar nights.

"You vilify me," my father went on, "but I did not tempt you down this path. You walked into the Meddler's tent of your own accord."

"I didn't know what I wanted. I didn't realize the cost," I replied, stepping forward to retreat from the advancing tide. Despite myself, the phantom's words aroused my desire for any illumination on my condition.

"What is cost and what is coincidence? You blame yourself for the death of Luke Thomas, and yet you cannot prove you caused his death. You play with powers you don't understand."

This was dangerous and addicting tonic. If the phantom was telling me that perhaps I did not cause Luke Thomas' death, my heart wanted to believe it.

"I used Bram's pen. I wrote the story about his suicide. The pen brings my words to life."

"The Meddler held more than a few secrets from you."

My cheeks burned. Bram had withheld much from me. I resented him for deceiving me, manipulating me.

"There are things I also wish to learn," the phantom went on, as though reading my mind. "Together we could learn an impressive deal." He turned back toward the door.

I stepped forward again. I could let the water take me. It would end the dream, but there was no telling what damage I would cause myself and my surroundings. I was so tired of going through that cycle. What if behind the door lay another route? What if behind the door lay answers?

"You know what lies behind you. Your search for the Meddler is all but fruitless."

"We just found a lead, if you care to know," I spat back.

"You've found leads before," it replied.

I despised how well the phantom could read me. It exposed my deepest doubts. I hoped this lead would be different, but his invitation called to me. Why not open the door? I was closer to it now than I'd ever been before. I'd never seen something so black. The waves kept pace behind me.

"Go on, Luella." I flinched when it used my name. "I'm yours, remember? Bid me do, I will obey. I'm only interested in your potential."

I gritted my teeth. I didn't believe him. It made me nauseous to see my father lie to me so boldly, but I grabbed the handle, anyway.

I turned my head over my shoulder to see the water rolling in. A colossal wave sped toward me, picking up momentum and sucking the fog up underneath it.

"Choose now, Luella!"

I swung the heavy black door open, rushed inside, and closed it behind me, blocking out the wave and blocking out the ghostly visage of my father.

My heart raced. I expected to wake up in a cold sweat, but I just felt warm. The ground beneath me was familiar, dirt covered by straw and decorative rugs. The walls were canvas.

I was in Bram's yurt.

My breath caught in my chest as a rush of hope swam in.

"Bram!" I called. Could he have been here all this time? Had he left some connection between us?

There was no response. I called his name again and again, but all was quiet.

It was all exactly as I remembered it. The bed and small dresser on one side across from a writing table, the fire in the middle, the old carnival posters hanging up. But I noticed two differences.

The old, sickly plant that rested near where the entry flap was gone. Instead, the door I had just come through sat there, rooted into stone. Directly across the tent, another black door, nearly identical to the first, stood like a mirror.

Most peculiar of all, I was alone. Bram was not here, and I saw no trace of my false father. Instead, the only movement was the flickering fire and the flapping pages of a notebook, as though touched by a gentle breeze, on the writing desk.

I approached the desk. Next to the notebook sat a crimson inkwell. I looked for the wretched enchanted pen that had been the root of so much evil, but it was not there. I cast a glance toward where Bram's chest of magical trinkets should have been and noticed that it, too, was missing from this version of the yurt.

I sat down and reached out to touch the crimson inkwell when everything went black.

When I opened my eyes, a winter morning light squeezed through the gaps in the window shutters.

Instinctively, I reached for the leather straps I had tried to bind myself with. But they were gone.

Anxiety and panic struck. What had I done to the room? To myself? I shut my eyes, not daring to look, but up and down my arms and hands where sores and blisters usually resulted from my episodes, I felt nothing.

I opened my eyes and surveyed the room. Everything was in its proper place. Nothing was out of order. It looked as though any normal person might have spent the night there in peace.

Except I noticed the leather straps folded neatly and lying on the dresser.

Chapter Four

Forbury Gardens

The dream left me deeply unsettled. Despite my best efforts, I couldn't decide on how the leather straps ended up on the dresser. The logical part of my brain insisted I'd sleepwalked, but I'd never sleepwalked before. I had damaged things in my sleep, I supposed.

But I had locked my door from the inside, and it didn't look like something had disturbed it. Who knew about my situation, let alone cared enough to risk arrest sneaking into my room to untie me?

I put off the obvious explanation. There was a question of magic.

This was a whole different kind of magic, though, and that made me uncomfortable. At Fernmount, I had seen a shimmering trail of particles leading me off on this journey. In Bram's yurt, I saw floating fireballs.

But magic that would so directly interact with my immediate reality? I shivered.

I checked my bag for my two most prized possessions. The letter from my sister sat there, undisturbed, as did the inkwell Bram left me, looking just as it had in my dream. For weeks, I had clung to it protectively, but I never really believed it was more than a trinket.

Now it scared me.

I dressed quickly, thankful that Edward had insisted on buying me some winter clothes. "A winter spent traveling isn't like a winter at home," he had said. Now, I wore a reddish dress made of wool under a warm black cloak. It was a practical garment, buttoning up to my neck. My blouse ruffled out at the collar and wrists.

My favorite bit of clothing he'd bought me, though, were a luxurious pair of gloves made of black leather and lined with the softest fur I'd ever felt.

I dined quickly on a few baked buns from the innkeeper's wife. They tasted hearty but made me miss Mrs. Barker's bakery in Dawnhurst. Soon it would be Christmas. My sister and I always made sure to have some of Barker's buns on Christmas morning… well, all right, any morning we could afford it.

I wondered where Anna was now. I hoped she found happiness with Jacob. Perhaps they already married. It would have been a lovely ceremony.

I set off into the crisp morning air and quickly picked my way back to the station. I needed to talk to Edward. He excelled at plotting our next steps. Hopefully, after spending a night in the barracks, they'd let him go, and we would meet Scott at St. Mary's church.

I entered the stark stone building a little disoriented. It reminded me of the first time I had entered the police station in Dawnhurst to drum up stories for my magazine. At least there, the Sergeant had been a friend of my father's. Here, I had no friends, just an Inspector who already thought I was lying to him.

"Miss, please step aside," said a severe-looking man at the front desk. "This isn't a social hall. It's a workplace."

"I'm—I'm here looking for someone," I stammered. Brusque. I shouldn't have been surprised.

"Name?"

"Edward Thomas."

"Not accepting visitors," the man said without pause.

"I'm not a visitor—"

"Are you his wife?"

I shook my head, displeased to have the issue brought up again.

"No visitors. Please, on your way."

With a wave of his hand, he summarily dismissed me. I wanted to protest, found no words for it. I surveyed the station, but from the front desk I saw mostly walls and closed doors. Through a window in one of these doors, the Inspector stared at me. He raised a cup of tea and nodded.

The message was clear.

I left through the front door and ducked down an alley before collapsing against the brick wall. An embarrassing sense of panic came on.

I was alone. I had no way of connecting with Edward. What would I do without him?

I took several deep breaths. I hated this. Regression had snuck up on me. Between my reliance on Edward's resources and the constant weight of my condition, I no longer respected the woman I'd become.

I'd lived without Edward my entire life. Did my feelings for him inspire such dependency or my own deficiencies?

They had to let him out, eventually. He was Edward Thomas, and he'd done nothing wrong except get into a small bar fight.

The frosty air hurt my teeth as I breathed it in, a reminder that the very world was against me. These were lessons I learned years ago. Nothing is handed to you. Scrape what you can of the life you want. I used to be confident facing the world, but that was before I knew the truth of it. There are monsters in the shadows and demons in the mirrors.

Still, if I sat idle, I'd lose the only lead we had towards finding Bram. What would Edward do if he were in my position? I doubt he'd sit around moping.

What was the time? I could still meet Mr. Scott at St. Mary's. I was sure of it. Then we'd be off to Gerald and perhaps answers. Finally, answers.

After an animated walk, I found myself in front of a Roman-styled facade that I assumed was St. Mary's. Horses sloshed through the snow on the streets behind me, and passersby had to dodge around me as I stared at the building.

I made my way up its steps and found Mr. Scott leaning against one of the pillars, both hands stuffed into the pockets of a sooty pea coat.

"I was beginning to think you wouldn't come," Mr. Scott said flatly, without an introduction.

"You do me so little credit," I replied, still out of breath.

"Where's your Mr. Pendles?" He grinned ironically. I was sure Edward's blown cover at the pub didn't escape this man's notice. Yet, he showed up all the same.

"It's just me." Just me. I hoped he couldn't hear how feeble I sounded, but I was scared. Even having Mr. Scott with me eased my anxiety, and I could not even vouch for his intentions.

"He's not the first bloke with a fake name I've met in that pub. Though, looking back, I can't believe that false beard fooled me. I hope discovering his true identity didn't disturb you much. A wretched thing to deceive a woman."

I paused. Scott had no reason to assume I was aware of Edward's deception. I nodded solemnly.

"Let's not dwell on it," I said. "Now, I hear you have a veritable giant to introduce to me. You said he was here on Castle Street?"

"He was, yeah, but he kept going on about some new statue in the Forbury he wanted to see. A lion. He always has loved animals. One time he lifted a horse right off the ground."

I resisted the urge to roll my eyes.

"We'll have to meet him there. I hope you're up for a quick walk, Miss Primrose. It's not too far."

I nodded again. Scott looked me up and down before extending his arm.

"Chivalry, now?" I asked.

"Even paupers deserve to act like knights sometimes."

I took his arm. Scott was easy company, happy to talk away any awkward silences. I was grateful, afraid that too much time to myself would drag me back to my dream last night.

It took us no more than fifteen minutes to reach the Forbury Gardens. Scott was in the middle of recounting a story in which Gerald had lifted two horses at once when I saw a tall figure in front of a massive sculpture of a roaring lion.

Gerald.

Tears sprang to my eyes, unbidden. The sight of him chased away a doubt that had secretly lodged itself in my subconscious. As Edward and I had labored without success to find Bram, I feared that inexplicably I had invented the carnival at Dawnhurst altogether. Now, evidence that I was not crazy stood in front of me.

"Oi! Gerald! There's someone I'd like you to meet," Scott called. Gerald didn't turn around. He stood still, large square shoulders facing the lion. Scott had exaggerated his size, but Gerald was a formidable figure even so.

"It's not all that larger than a real lion," he said, admiring the statue. "I like the way it's roaring."

"I always wished you had a lion at the fair." I unhooked my arm from Scott's. "As much as I enjoyed the turtles with the bejeweled shells."

At the sound of my voice, Gerald turned.

"Luella?" He gaped at me. "I didn't think to see you again, least of all in a place like this."

"Luella?" Scott asked. I ignored him.

"You mean out of Dawnhurst?"

"I mean out of prison."

"What's going on here?" Scott took his hat off and scratched his head, shoulders tense. "Gerald, you know this woman?"

"I'm surprised you don't. You've brought me a wanted fugitive."

So, Gerald knew the Dawnhurst police were pursuing me. My name must have made the papers. I'd have liked to read that article. It would have taken a creative journalist to find enough credible evidence to link me to Luke Thomas' death.

"Fugitive? For what crime?"

"Murder," Gerald said, matter-of-factly. Scott's face turned gray, matching this coat. He snorted out a sound of disbelief.

"Is that what they're saying," I asked. Gerald nodded.

"Word travels fast among a certain ring of society. You may realize that not every member of a traveling circus has enjoyed a strictly lawful adulthood. When the bobbies are on the search, we use some names and hide others. Wouldn't be much of a show if the police could take away half the performers."

"Do you believe it?" I asked. Gerald barked out a seedy laugh.

"What, that you killed Luke Thomas by hanging him in his office?" He laughed again, which grated on me. Phrased so plainly, the story sounded implausible, but I didn't appreciate his nonchalant parlance on something so gruesome.

"Tell me," he continued, "when you hoisted a full-grown, heavy-set, still-living man off the ground did you use just your arms, or did you brace yourself against something and push with your legs?"

"You've made your point," I said, eager to shut him up. "I appreciate that you can see the idiocy of the investigation."

Scott shifted uncomfortably in his shoes.

"You've broken poor Scott's heart here, Luella." Gerald nodded over to his friend. I turned and saw him awkwardly tapping his feet.

"Will he tell the police?" I asked Gerald.

"I don't suppose I will," Scott said. "Not if Gerald thinks you're innocent."

"Innocent of murder, yes," Gerald said. "But she may be guilty of some other misdeeds." He leveled his eyes at me, playfully. I shrunk under his gaze, searching for my courage somewhere on the ground. I had dropped it during my conversation with the Inspector last night.

"Can we walk privately?" I asked.

"Wait a minute here, Scott," Gerald barked.

"If it's all the same to you, Miss Primrose," he spat out my false name, "I'll take my leave of you." I nodded, and he was off without another glance.

"Do you think he's lying?" I asked. My paranoia rose like a lump in my throat, and I resented Gerald for spilling my secret so openly.

"Who cares?" Gerald asked. "Scott weaves tall tales. Did he tell you the one about the horse?" He motioned with his hand toward the gravel walking paths that wound through Forbury Gardens. Each of his steps crunched heavily down and left recognizable imprints behind him. I followed, trying my best to leave no trace in the gravel.

"What are you doing here, Luella?"

"I'm looking for Bram," I said.

Gerald's step faltered, and he raised his bushy eyebrows in pleasant surprise.

"Have a change of heart, then?" he asked.

"Change of heart? No—wait, what do you mean?"

"I've known Bram for a while. It was easy to tell that when you two parted ways, he was sore over something."

I remembered our farewell in Bram's yurt. He had asked me to leave Dawnhurst with him. He had promised to find a cure to my magical condition and tenderly help me through my symptoms in the meantime. Should I have agreed? Was my refusal akin to turning down a doctor's care? No. I refused him because I sensed more than a Hippocratic interest. Going with him would have meant something very different, indeed.

"He has something of mine," I managed. After all this time looking for someone like Gerald, a connection to Bram, how had I neglected to come up with what to say?

"Taking back a token, then?" Gerald grinned. "That doesn't seem too good a reason to tell you where he is. Let him have it, eh? At least something to remember you by." He nudged me with his arm. I pursed my lips.

"You're being very difficult."

"What can I say? I'm aiding and abetting a murderer. If a convicted fugitive asked you where your friend was, would you tell?"

Gerald was just as I remembered him. The first time we met, he had his fun at my expense, insinuating that I was romantically involved with Bram. As I became more familiar with the carnival, he and I had occasion to become better acquainted. He seemed to know everyone in that carnival, and he treated most of them the same, drawing close to his friends through brusque jokes and games.

"Is my lot that bad? I have heard nothing from Dawnhurst since I left."

"When was that?"

"The day they tried to arrest me, right after the carnival left the city."

Gerald stopped and drew some circles in the gravel with his foot.

"I'd probably give it some time before heading back there. Unless you had some good proof you were innocent."

"It was that bad, then?"

"I've been all over her majesty's country. A fugitive woman escaping the police after being accused of murdering a top financier is big news anywhere, let alone Dawnhurst."

My heart sunk. It would have been in all the papers, my name dragged through the mud. It would scandalize everyone who knew me.

No. That wasn't true. My proper friends tried to protect me. Rebecca. Mrs. Crow. Doug.

But I also had friendly neighbors. The journals would seduce them into believing the worst of me. Mr. And Mrs. Barker. What about my sister? Had she read about my illicit behavior in the newspapers?

The evil inside of me reached out like tendrils smoking up from my gut. It would love nothing more than for me to give in to the despair that gnawed at me now.

I needed to put all of this behind me. I needed Bram, and to get him, I needed Gerald to cooperate.

"Well, to clear my name, I need to find Bram," I lied. It was almost true.

"That's classic Bram for you. He's always getting himself mixed up in things he shouldn't."

"You'll take me to him, won't you?" I stopped and clasped Gerald's big hands. Coarse hair patched the back of them.

"Luella, like I said, I doubt your guilty of that man's murder. If there's a way I could help you, I would. But I don't know where Bram is. He's slippery, that one. At times, I'd talk with him in his tent, leave for a second, and come back to empty air, just his weird books and gaudy decor in his wake."

I deflated like empty bellows. Defeated again. This was another dead end. I couldn't accept it.

"I thought the carnival traveled together," I stammered.

"It does when we're in season. Notice that in the winter you don't see a lot of groups like ours. True, most of us still roam city to city so that when it's time to perform again, we can just pick back up, but Bram left."

A bitter flavor came to the back of my throat, like biting into a rancid chestnut. I felt deluded, disappointed, and furious—with myself, with Edward, with Bram.

"That beast of a man. I was just some type of experiment to him, and now he's off doing who knows what to another poor woman."

Gerald put a hand on my arm.

"I wouldn't judge him so harshly," he said. "He rarely keeps company with women."

Lies. What was more cliché than a man lying for his mate?

"I'm sure. I was a one of a kind experience." I sneered.

Gerald now used his other arm to grab me firmly.

"I'm not joking. It's easy to thinkin' he gallivants with his pick of partners, what with his devil-may-care looks about him, but he just doesn't. You're the first I've seen him show any interest in for a very long time."

"Why?"

"That's not my secret to tell. You'll have to ask him if you ever find him. And, if you do, tell him I'm still expecting those ten pounds he owes me for watching something for him."

He let me go and headed back toward the large lion statue.

"Oh, and Luella, we'll be moving on soon, but until then, I like to take walks here in the gardens."

He walked away, leaving me furious, aimless, and speechless.

Chapter Five

Shifting Alliance

I returned to the police station that afternoon, eager to talk with Edward, but I found disappointment again. Nor could I gain any audience with the Inspector. He was "otherwise occupied" according to the man at the front desk.

Instead, I wandered, getting tea in a small shop on Castle Street and trying, vainly, to occupy my mind.

My road had to come to an end. There were no more leads. What better chance would I have at locating Bram if even his traveling companions did not know his whereabouts?

I should have gone with him when he asked me. I loved Edward, but Bram held the keys to unlock my shackles.

I put my teacup down, fingers burning from holding it too long.

I couldn't give in to this. I searched my bag and found Anna's letter.

I had re-read it hundreds of times. Why not a hundred more?

By the evening, I'd wandered all over the city, but I failed to refresh my spirits. The resistance to my magical illness hung by a thread. Another night alone might break me. I wanted Edward near me. I needed his steadying presence that somehow kept so many of these feelings at bay.

I found myself at the front desk of the Reading police for the third time that day. A man I hadn't seen before with wavy blonde hair sat behind the desk. Hope sprang in my bosom. Perhaps this man would be more lenient.

"I'm here to see Edward Thomas," I said, sheepishly.

"Name?" He grabbed a sheet of paper and looked at it.

"Luella Winthrop," I said. What point was there in lying anymore? If they imprisoned me, so be it. Perhaps that would be safer for everyone, anyway. Besides, I doubted this man received instructions not to admit Luella Winthrop to see Edward Thomas.

The man squinted at me, glanced at the paper, and squinted again.

"I'll see if I can find him," he said. "Come with me."

I was so surprised that I almost forgot to move.

He led me to a windowless room with a small table where he instructed me to wait. I sat and tried to be patient.

After an unbearable wait, the door opened, and Edward walked in. It had only been a day, but he looked different. Some cuts and bruises marked his face from the bar fight, but they had been tended. It was something else.

I stood and started across the room to embrace him, but he cut me short with a brusque shake of his head. He sat down quickly.

I sat down across the table as if I'd been reprimanded.

He doesn't love you. The words formed in my head. Doubt? The fog creature?

"Miss Primrose, thank you for coming," Edward said.

"Edward, they know. They wouldn't let me see you. I tried several times. Tonight, there was a new man at the desk, and I gave him my real name. I think they have instructions not to admit—"

"You what?" Edward hissed. I leaned back in alarm.

"I told them my true name."

"Why would you do that? After everything I've done to keep Dawnhurst and Sergeant Cooper from finding you, you thought it wise to share your name with the Reading Police?"

I stumbled for words.

"I just—I needed to see you." Could he not discern my weakness? I needed him. I didn't need an argument.

"We're a day's ride from Dawnhurst," Edward said, leaning in. "How can I protect you when I'm in custody? I need you to stay sharp."

He sat with a rigid spine. Stress and nerves coursed out of him. Even if I weren't cursed, it'd have been easy to become defensive.

"It's my name. I'll do with it what I please."

"This is no time to argue. We need a new plan. Hide here in the city —"

"What's the point, Edward?" I said, red in the face. "I met Scott today."

"And?" Edward's eyes stretched wide. "Did you see Gerald?"

"Yes. It's a dead end."

"What do you mean a dead end?"

"I mean he doesn't know where Bram is, either." Hearing myself say it out loud brought tears to my eyes.

"That can't be right." Edward wrung his hands, staring at the table. "You must not have questioned him correctly. Once I'm out of here, we can go back—"

"He doesn't know, Edward. No one from the circus knows. Bram took off as soon as their group left Dawnhurst. He's gone. He left me. I'm—we—"

Edward clenched his jaw so firmly that its muscles bulged in his cheek.

We both sat in silence for a long minute.

"Then our hope of finding Bram's magical remedy is extinguished?"

I nodded. He swallowed.

"Then, perhaps it's time we try to find our own remedy."

I blinked.

"What are you talking about?"

"Why don't we dive into the research on our own? If Bram discovered this magic, surely someone else can."

"Bram studied and searched for years. He had a team of explorers."

"But he didn't have the resources we have at our disposal. We could hire professors, researchers, archaeologists—anyone we need."

I shook my head slowly.

"What would your mother think of that?"

"I am Lord of Fernmount now."

The door swung open with an ear-splitting creak. The Inspector stood in its frame, the man from the front desk looking very poor behind him.

"You are resourceful, Miss Primrose. I'll award that to you, but I'm rather certain that if you were Luella Winthrop, this man would not be associating with you."

They escorted me out without another word.

I walked back to the Hare and Hounds with a new appreciation for the phrase 'hidden in plain sight.' I swept up the stairs to my room, ignoring the management's questions on whether I'd eaten. I wasn't hungry, anyway. I slammed the door behind me, furious, fed up, and embarrassed.

I locked the door behind me and fumed. I ripped off the heavy coat Edward had bought me. Seeing him had done nothing. He still thought he maintained some control over the situation. He would not beat this. He didn't know how.

Helplessness overwhelmed me. I was weak, pathetic, and Edward was losing interest in me. I could see it in his eyes.

No. I tried fighting back against the negativity, but it was like holding back a river with a serving platter.

The darkness called to me, begging to come in. There had been a door in my dream of Bram's yurt that I hadn't opened yet. I could open it, explore the darkness. Why not explore in the absence of hope?

The magic churned, making me nauseous. After all the emotional let downs of the day, I crumbled under its force.

I glanced around the room, seeing signs of the damage that I had already inflicted on some furniture from previous episodes. Fingernail scratches in the bedpost. Lightly cracked wood from thrashing on the bed frame.

Where did this road lead?

I stumbled to the desk and set my bag on it.

Where was Anna? Rebecca? Mrs. Crow?

Even Edward had abandoned me.

Where was that trail of moondust I had seen on Edward's balcony?

Unconsciously, I toppled the items from my bag. Perhaps Anna's letter could bring me back to my senses.

But the inkwell fell and landed upright, staring up at me the same way it had in my dream the night before.

I stared at it and remembered the rush I used to experience writing my stories with Bram. Before I could catch myself, it was in my hands unstopped. I couldn't find a pen, so I dipped my little finger into the ink, hoping my nail might work like a quill.

I scratched out the first words that came to me on a loose piece of paper.

"Where is the moondust trail?"

My hand shook as I held the paper above a candle. The flames licked at the edges, catching, heating the tips of my fingers closest to the flame.

I threw it onto a metal tray and watched the paper vanish, smelling the fire as it burned itself out. Then I waited.

My heart pounded quickly as I waited for something to happen. Bram had once told me that magic camouflages itself, and the pen I used wouldn't work to affect my life directly. He was wrong. Besides, I wasn't using the pen. I was using his ink.

It seemed so clear to me now. For what other purpose had Bram left the inkwell to me?

I sat on the bed and hugged my knees, glancing around the room. The moondust might appear anywhere, anytime. But, as I sat waiting for the effect of my attempted divination to manifest, I felt nothing. I saw nothing.

I must have sat for an hour before realizing the futility of my attempt.

If Bram had meant me to find him by using the ink, he would have told me. If the crimson inkwell had any magical properties, fumbling with it in a desperate frenzy was no way to discover it.

My lot remained unchanged. Bram hid somewhere beyond. My relationship with Edward was crumbling. My condition was getting worse.

Exhausted, I fell back onto my pillow, praying that leaving the leather straps on the desk was no mistake.

When I closed my eyes, I found myself again at the Forbury Gardens. It looked almost exactly as it had earlier that day, except the colors glowed more richly, and the sounds and smells of the place seemed more distant. The conversation of other passersby sounded muffled, and I hardly detected the crisp smell of winter, replaced with—if I wasn't mistaken—the perfume of old books.

Gerald stood in front of the lion sculpture again. I approached as I had before.

"Are you posing as Gerald now as well?" I asked. Perhaps the fog creature finished imitating my father, opting instead for more immediate relationships. If it mimicked and distort my recent memory

—that would get confusing.

Gerald didn't respond to me. In fact, he didn't move at all. I moved closer and gasped.

He was carved from stone, an eerily lifelike sculpture. I looked up, half expecting the statue of the lion to be living in his place, but it stood still.

As I looked around, I noticed no movement anywhere. The whole Forbury was a sculpture. The trees and grass, the birds in the branches, all of it.

I sat down on a bench near a granite hedge, wondering what my dream meant.

"I'm proud of you," a voice behind me said. I turned, and dread poured into me. What-was-not-my-father stood there.

"Leave me alone," I said. He walked through the stone and sat next to me on the bench.

"You've realized by now that your search is pointless."

I didn't respond, just stared a hole into a marble tree across the path.

"You look different," he continued. "Calmer, despite your impending failure."

"What do you want from me?"

"Companionship."

"Companionship? If you wanted a standing appointment for tea, you didn't have to infect me like this."

"Don't blame me for your condition."

"Don't blame the evil mystical being that haunts my dreams?" I scoffed.

"An ally, then," he said. "What did you find on the other side of the door, Luella?"

"You don't know?" My eyes went wide. To think I had a secret beyond this creature's reach...

"That's the whole point." As he looked at me, a cloud rippled through his face beneath the skin.

"Your fog is showing," I said, pointing.

"You have not answered my question," he went on.

"Nor do I have to." I stood. "Why all the stone? Is this a trick? The next stage of my illness? You push me into madness by blurring what's real with what's dreamland?"

The fog creature did not respond, but another ripple spread across his chest, revealing the rough petrified wood behind him.

"Your attacks will get worse, but they don't have to," he said.

"Now you're worried for me."

"The Meddler will not save you, but I could teach you how to remove the side effects."

He was lying. If he wasn't lying, it was a trap.

"Why would you do that?"

"I would like us to align our interests. Tell me what lies beyond the door, and I will show you how to gain control of the magic that corrupts you."

Desperation caused many people to do many things they would never normally consider. On one hand, what harm might come from sharing what was behind the black door? After all, it was just an empty shell of Bram's tent. But I had a secret from the creature. There was power in that.

It was as I weighed these considerations that I noticed it. There in the stone Forbury, far in the distance and barely visible around a cut rock shrub, rested a dog frozen mid-stride. And, if I wasn't mistaken, it had the familiar gait of a pointer I knew. Hope blossomed in my chest.

I turned to the fog creature with a sense of indignant revulsion.

"I will never tell you what was behind that door. I don't know how long you exist, but you'll spend the rest of it knowing that I kept this from you."

The clouds in its eyes swelled tempestuously. Fear and empowerment battle inside me.

"I never want to see you again. You've ruined the image of my father. You think I'd want to be your companion? I hate you. You may ruin me, but you'll never know what was behind that door."

I watched as my father burst into thick billowing fog that rushed out angrily at me and filled all the gardens.

My eyes shot open. The morning winter sun shone peacefully through the window. My room was untouched.

Chapter Six

Lady of the House

I sat at the police station, fiddling with the cuff of my sleeve. I felt guilty about the way I'd reported my disappointment over Gerald. I had pulled the hope out from under him and lost my temper when all he'd only ever helped me.

The station was quiet. A few officers, fluid as clockwork, filed in and out, checking paperwork or grabbing a bite to eat from some room to which I wished I had access. I had eaten little in the past day and a half.

Edward was right. I was foolish to use my real name. I put him at risk as much as I did myself.

As for dreams, the strange stone version of Forbury stuck in my mind. I'd said bold things to the fog creature, angered it. I didn't look forward to our next visit.

Still, it felt so good to know I had something it wanted but couldn't take by force. For the first time, I might have some leverage. It said it knew how to manage my symptoms. Maybe I was too rash to dismiss the offer. If it told the truth, maybe we didn't need Bram.

The Inspector came through a door and approached me.

"Miss Primrose, should we bring a mattress, so you don't have to bother going back to your inn?" He smirked a great smirk.

"That won't be necessary. I doubt you would recognize a suitable mattress. You must sleep on the bare ground to be so uptight all the time."

"You are in high spirits. I wonder how that will change."

"Spirits are everywhere. Just because you've been possessed by an evil one doesn't mean we all have to mope around."

"I will say," he said, taking an ominous step toward me, and putting a hand on the back of the chair I sat in, "you are curiously devoted to Lord Thomas for being a fortune teller. Are you interested in his looks or his wealth?"

"True wealth is in friendship." I smiled tartly.

"Well, I'm curious to see how your friendship withstands what comes next."

"What do you mean?"

"This is out of my hands now." He smiled crookedly, the only crooked thing about him. I didn't have long to stew on his words. The door near me swung open, and Edward walked out.

"Edward!" I cried, standing and running to greet him. He again shook his head, a signal to restrain my warmth. His face was white. "What's wrong?"

The Inspector clapped him on the back.

"He's just embarrassed his mother came to rescue him from the Reading Police."

Lady Thomas, looking disheveled and angry, stepped from behind her son.

I almost ran away.

"You just left," Lady Thomas said, her mouth looking tiny from the way she pursed her lips. "Left! Edward! Your father had just died, and you took off with some frump of a woman you dragged home."

"Mother—"

"You may not speak yet," she said. The word frump seemed a little rude, but I understood. We sat in her carriage, which smelled as though her perfume had been riding in it for some time.

"Do you have any idea what your actions put me through?"

Edward stared at the floor like a little boy being chastised over a stolen bun.

"I had to organize your father's memorial all by myself. A grieving woman! To make matters worse, what do you think all the guests asked me after they expressed their condolences?"

She waited, and while Edward realized she wouldn't go on until he answered her.

"I imagine they wondered about my absence," he said, folding his arms.

"Wonderful. You worked it out." She fumed and fanned herself despite the winter cold.

I stayed as quiet as possible. In fact, I wasn't exactly sure why she had invited me into the carriage at all. Perhaps I would get my own reprimand once she finished with her son.

"Did you tell our guests how father died?" Edward asked.

"Your father had an unfortunate work accident. I've been spared the details because of my delicate sensibilities."

"A work accident? For a banker? Well, mother, I'm not sure why you're so upset. You were already lying about one thing, why not another? What excuse did you provide for me?"

She stopped fanning herself and looked at her son as though he had just asked the most foolish question of his life.

"You were ill on your deathbed at Fernmount," she said. A patch of red flushed under the aging skin on her neck. The woman despised me, but given how she explained her situation, I instinctually pitied her.

"The scandal," she bemoaned, seeming to talk now more to herself than either of us. "My unwed son, running off with a woman."

"I'm not the only man to have a secret relationship with a woman," he quipped. This stopped his mother in her tracks. I suspected that he may have been referring to his father.

"That's not what you've done though, is it, Edward? You haven't just had a fling with a tartlet holed up in a city apartment. You've gallivanted for months with someone, holding yourselves out as what —married?"

"As his fortune teller, ma'am." What courage filled me adequately to chime in here, I know not. I regretted it immediately. If possible, the phrase fortune teller made her go even whiter than when she considered me a tartlet, whatever that was.

"She must be lying. My son, tell me she's lying."

"It made sense, mother. I recently lost my father. What would be more natural than a man seeking some connection with the afterlife? Eccentric? Perhaps. But it would inspire pity, not condemnation from those who heard it."

She glanced back and forth between Edward and me, considering his explanation.

"She doesn't even look like a fortune teller."

Edward rolled his eyes and stared out the window.

I felt very exposed. Attempted fortune telling was rather innocuous, but the truth would ruin her. I used evil magic and accidentally killed her husband. Now, Edward and I traveled all over the south of England, trying to find the only man I believed capable of curing that magic's negative side effects. We also hid because the Dawnhurst police thought I was a murderer.

It wasn't exactly what I had hoped to disclose to a potential mother-in-law.

"I've been looking for you ever since you left. I called in discrete connections. I've been staying in Oxford of all places, just hoping to get word back that you would surface somewhere. I mean honestly, Reading?"

Lady Thomas took a breath and exhaled slowly.

"Edward, find lodging for us. Proper lodging, not whatever hole you've been hiding in. I came from Oxford early this morning and doubt I can make the trip back today. Some place with good food is preferable, but you should know that already."

Edward hesitated, considering the risk of leaving me alone with his mother. On one hand, he knew I was prone to magical, violent outbreaks. On the other, his mother was having a violent outbreak of her own.

"It's Reading, mother, not Cornwall. There will be adequate space —"

"Go find it, Edward," she repeated, immovable as a brick wall.

He looked at me, haltingly, but I nodded. He sighed and left the carriage.

"First and foremost," Lady Thomas began, "are you truly a fortune teller?"

She asked this with a grave severity, leaving no room for doubting what she thought of such a profession.

"I am not," I replied.

"Oh, thank heavens," she said, leaning back into her seat and fanning herself again. I tried not to smile. At least, I wasn't a fortune teller.

"Was it you or my son who insisted on running off as you did?"

Perhaps I lacked courage, but I told the truth.

"When I chose to leave Fernmount, m'am, I insisted Edward not accompany me elsewhere."

She nodded resolutely.

"I assumed as much. Men are filled with so much bravado. He tries to act as though his father's death does not weigh on him, yet here he is making decisions only his father would make."

I nodded, though not eagerly. Lady Thomas put her fan away and assumed an attentive posture.

"Miss Winthrop, I fear our last meeting was not indicative of how I would like our relationship to proceed."

I'm not sure what I expected to hear after Edward left, but it wasn't an apology. The last time I was alone with Lady Thomas, she had basically called me rubbish from the gutter, and I almost assaulted her with cutlery.

"I think we both said things we didn't intend."

"I was under considerable stress with the passing of my husband. I wasn't myself."

"Of course," I said, eager for a chance for a positive relationship. "I can't imagine I would be in my right mind after losing someone so close to me."

"Then you agree that Edward was not in his right mind when he brought you to Fernmount?"

That crafty snake. She had me.

"Undoubtedly," I said, in part to myself. I had wondered the same thing hundreds of times. In Dawnhurst, he had spoken so resolutely about his affection for me. After he found out I was responsible for his father's demise, he did not waver. He had even acknowledged his impaired judgment on the issue.

But, since we left Fernmount, Edward had renewed none of the affection he pledged me then. His mother's comments kindled all the doubt that had been building since we began our search for Bram.

Were his feelings simply grief's byproduct?

"I can see that you care for him," his mother said. "And my son seems to take some interest in you. Please help him see reason. Help him get through this arduous time. Why don't you both come back to

Oxford with me? We can collect my things and head to Fernmount where we will figure all of this out together."

What could I say? I had a fool's chance of finding Bram in Reading, and an evil fog creature was trying its best to make me go clinically insane.

Why not try Edward's plan of starting our own research or try to make a deal with the fog creature? I could do all that at Fernmount, and perhaps it would re-inspire Edward's romantic feelings toward me.

If we were careful, I doubted the Dawnhurst police would find me there. I might even find a way to reach out to my sister.

I smiled sadly. Maybe it could be that simple.

"I'm sure that would be up to Edward," I responded.

She tsked me.

"I need not tell you the effect a woman's opinion has on a man. At any rate, we don't have to decide right now. I would like a cup of tea and something sweet. Perhaps you should go collect your things. Where have you been staying?"

"There's a tavern nearby. We have two rooms there. It isn't far. Please, though, I must insist that while you and Edward should find lodging together, I remain at my current lodging. Edward and I stayed well-hidden until now, but publicly boarding with you might not be prudent."

She looked pleased as a fox.

"Very well, but you will at least spend the day with us. Even if it isn't prudent. I can't imagine Edward agreeing to anything different."

I agreed and begged leave to stretch my legs, deciding that a quick dip into the winter air would do me good.

I left the carriage and promised to return in a half-hour.

After my dream last night, I had an itch to return to the Forbury Gardens and compare its natural state to the stone sculpture version in my dream before. The past couple of days had been a whirlwind. Although the outcome was not what I had hoped for, I'd woken that morning with a peculiar calm that even Lady Thomas didn't chase away.

The world was beautiful, in its own wintry way. Christmas was just around the corner, and for the first time, I noticed the occasional evergreen wreath on the doors of the shops and residences. A man stood on the corner, asking for alms to care for beggars. Small evergreen branches were tied to an occasional lamppost, and I smelled the delicious scent of pastry dough and autumn spices from the eateries nearby.

The season turned my thoughts to my sister. She must be looking forward to a wonderful Christmas—the type of Christmas I had never provided, filled with roasted duck and warm, ample indoor rooms filled with friends and well-wishing.

She would be in heaven.

I was in the gardens before I realized. My ears had not noticed the subtle difference between the crunch of snow and the crunch of gravel. I glanced around. Everything was as I had dreamt it. What a peculiar thing. Why stone?

I saw the bench I'd sat on. I saw the topiary, twiggy and hewn of wooden branches. The lion stood proudly in its iron costume, not the polished stone I dreamed the night before.

The only thing missing was Gerald. Everything else was here.

Even the dog.

My hands dropped to my side. I had nearly forgotten about the dog in the anxiety of seeing Lady Thomas, but there it was. A very familiar looking Burgos pointer. If I remembered correctly, I saw in its fur the same spots I had pet many times near Dawnhurst's riverbank or in Bram's tent.

But it couldn't be Bram's pointer.

I feared to investigate. I had just discovered the sweetness of surrender. If I'd allow myself to give up, there were things to look forward to. Wonderful things.

But if this was Bram's dog…

My legs carried me forward, faster, and faster.

"Cyrus?" I called.

The pointer stopped sniffing the rotting remains of a weed and perked up to look at me. Did it respond to its name or just because I yelled?

"Cyrus?" I called again, holding out my hand in invitation.

Cyrus looked at me, tilted his head, and scampered in the opposite direction. I found myself sprinting after.

It's not every day you see a woman sprinting through the city streets chasing a dog. I still can't understand why all the idiots that stopped and stared couldn't be bothered to help me catch the dog.

He bounded down sidewalks, passing food stands without so much as a sniff. I did my best to follow, but matching the speed of an exercised pointer proved impossible. When he arrived at a street corner, he sat and waited for me to get within a reasonable distance before bolting in a different direction.

Cyrus was playing with me. At least he was for the first couple of blocks. Play turned into torment as I realized how quickly I ran out of breath in the cold.

Then it hit me. He was leading me somewhere.

"Oh Cyrus! Good boy! Good boy!" I called. Perhaps Bram was in Reading after all. I could think of no other explanation for why his dog might be here. This jaunt through the city might lead me straight to Bram.

It puffed like I had run for miles by the time Cyrus finally turned into an alleyway with no exit. He pranced to the back corner of the recessed alcove, behind a large stack of boxes. The alcove smelled like fish and spoiled meat. Cyrus seemed pleased by that.

I followed, my heart racing from the exertion and the excitement. Bram might be behind these boxes. Maybe he was hurt or trying to keep a low profile. What if he was dead?

When I rounded the crates, Bram was not sitting against the bricks. It was just Cyrus, breathing rapidly. He jumped, putting his forelegs onto my stomach and tried to lick my hands.

There was no doubt as to the identity of the dog, but Bram was nowhere to be seen. Wherever he was, his faithful pup had either run away or Bram discarded him. I petted him between the ears, in a disappointed, albeit relieved gesture of thanks.

He jumped down, sniffed the ground, and picked up something dirty from beneath a newspaper.

To my surprise, he dropped a book in my hands.

"Poems from the Wanderer?" I said, reading the title. I raised an eyebrow at the dog.

Cyrus barked.

Chapter Seven

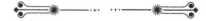

Three Is a Crowd

I didn't have time to speak with Edward privately for most of the day. As soon as he was back, his mother asked him about leaving Reading. When Edward expressed his unease, she insisted she was just voicing a possibility and looked at me. I played the obedient soldier and commented that it might not be an awful idea. I figured it was the least I could do, considering I came back from my walk with a stray dog in tow.

Cyrus wouldn't be left behind. Edward eyed him quizzically when I told his mother it was mine but kept quiet.

He found a lavish hotel toward the south of the city, and after dropping off her things, we lunched in a nearby restaurant, decorated richly with evergreen trees dressed by strings of nuts and candles waiting to be lit for Christmas.

I hadn't appreciated the Christmas season. Being discovered by

Edward's mother was like having a veil pulled from my eyes. I saw it everywhere now in decorations, food, and the excitement lighting the eyes of even beggar children who found well-to-do passersby slightly more generous than normal.

I furrowed my brows. There were years Anna and I had relied on similar generosity.

The dishes came out one after another. Apparently, purchasing a title had not diminished Lady Thomas's motherly urge to overfeed her son. The food was hearty and rich, though not extravagant. I sampled several dishes, savoring the cheese on a plate of Welsh rarebit and even daring to try to the spice-filled kedgeree.

"You are brave, my dear," Lady Thomas noted. "I can't abide that foreign flavor. From India, is that right? You won't even find me appreciating anything too French."

As we ate, Lady Thomas filled us in on all the excruciating details of the memorial, despite Edward's protests that the event was nonsense and a discredit to his father's name.

"Certainly, your father deserved remembrance," his mother said.

"Yes, but we don't have to make excuses for him. The tripe you've been sharing around about an accident is rubbish."

"Don't take that street police language with me. I raised you better."

"It's obvious. Either father took his own life or—" Edward stopped himself. I nearly choked on a bit of Cornish pasty.

"Or what?" his mother asked, putting down her teacup. I wondered the same. He stopped himself but couldn't hide the distress in his voice.

He chewed on a bit of beef and stared tiredly at a Christmas tree across the room.

"Nothing. I just—I don't want to believe that he would kill himself. There must be another explanation."

There was another explanation, an explanation he told me never to discuss with his mother. If Lady Thomas ever discovered that her husband's death was linked to magic—and that it involved me no less —I shuddered at the outcome.

She reached out and grabbed her son's hand and gave it a squeeze.

"I know, dear. It makes you afraid, doesn't it? I fear there may have been more to your father than we knew."

For not the first time in our company of three, I was an unwelcome fly on the wall. This poor woman grieved her husband and wanted only some time with her son to manage their tragedy. Meanwhile, here

I blocked her every access point.

I blushed. I couldn't make sense of my emotions today. One moment I felt so light, the next guilty. Doomed. Hopeful. Disappointed.

I wiped my mouth with a napkin. I had lost my appetite.

"I'm sorry I wasn't with you," Edward said to me later in the bar of his mother's hotel. She had gone upstairs to lie down. "I worried for you all night."

I rubbed my wrists where I wore the leather straps two nights previous. No fresh scars or scratches.

"I managed," I replied.

"Did you have an attack?"

"Not the way you may think."

He leaned back in his chair and put a hand through his hair in apparent defeat. With the afternoon light highlighting his silhouette, he looked so tired. His face was still bruised from the brawl, his shirt torn in places, and he had bags under his eyes. His hair sprouted defiantly through his fingers as he tried to smooth it down.

I had to be honest with him, but I didn't want to. At Fernmount, before we left on this journey, I told him I'd share the truth about myself with him piece by piece. He was due another. I asked so much.

"Edward, I think my relationship with the magic is changing." I expected him to rise from his chair, alert and interested. Instead, he slouched back in his seat.

"How do you mean?"

"While you were incarcerated, I had a dream. The fog creature came to me again."

"Where were you this time?"

"On a beach. Near a cliff. There was a black door."

"You've had similar dreams before," Edward said, finally rising off the chair's armrests.

"I opened it."

"You what? Isn't that what the monster wanted from you?"

"That's correct."

"So, you gave in to its demands?"

"I broke down. What was I supposed to do? You were locked up. I had no idea when I'd see you again. It's not easy to be strong when you're—well, when I'm all by myself."

He massaged his temples. He looked perturbed—not angry, at least not with me, but certainly frustrated. I didn't blame him, but he would have reacted differently before we left Fernmount. This journey took its due from both of us.

"What happened?"

"I went through the door, and I ended up in Bram's tent from the fair."

Edward clenched his jaw. I had not yet shared any details with him about the extent of my involvement with Bram. Jealousy was bitter, sticky, and unseemly.

"His tent?"

"More a yurt, really. It was quite spacious, decorated with rugs and furniture. I saw the crimson inkwell on his writing desk. That's how it worked back then. I wrote a story with Bram's pen and ink, then we tossed it into the fire. Then it would just happen. I don't know how else to explain."

He turned to hide the heat flushing his face. I imagined him trying to avoid the inevitable lines of inquiry that sprouted from his curiosity. I took his hand.

"Edward, nothing happened. We wrote stories, we talked a great deal, but nothing happened between us."

He looked at me, his head off-kilter as if trying to decide whether to believe me.

"You mean to say you never had any romantic relationship with the man we've been chasing?"

He had never asked me so bold a question. In some ways, it was a relief to hear he was human and prone to insecurity. I wished he asked a long time ago. Perhaps if he had, I would have told the truth.

"Nothing romantic," I said, staring him in the steely gray eyes. Lying is a peculiar phenomenon. In no other circumstance can one so consciously feel the skin covering one's face.

Slowly, Edward squeezed my hand, a sweet reward for my white deceit. The relief of his returned affection smothered my guilt like a blanket over a candle. His question was inconsequential. He had no right to know my unvoiced feelings from the past. I hadn't chosen Bram in the end, had I?

"You saw the inkwell then?" he asked. "Maybe, we should give it a closer inspection."

"I used it." The realization dawned on me as the words came out. "I asked for something."

"You what? You've always told me that using the magic caused your condition from the start."

"It does, but I was hopeless after talking to Gerald. What did I have to lose if there were no cure? I asked for a sign, a trail to point me in the right direction. Then I found Bram's dog."

Edward let go of my hand.

"And the book of poems." He couldn't keep an edge of cynicism out of his voice. "You're sure this is the same dog."

"I'm certain. He led me to the book. Bram meant me to find it. It happened like my stories used to."

"And does this book have any clues to Bram's whereabouts?"

"Not a first glance. It's filled with amateur poetry," I admitted. He took a deep breath in. "I wanted to find some quiet time to study it in greater depth, but every moment I've had has been monopolized by your mother."

He coughed and winced, holding his ribs, apparently still sore from his bar fight.

"Luella, I think we should go back with my her," he said at length. "It's possible that this book may contain some fresh lead, but we've been at this for months, and we're no closer than before. Even if we find a trail, there's no telling how much longer this road will stretch. At Fernmount we can keep you safely hidden, and if this book doesn't turn up answers, we could start on our own research."

I fingered the leather cover of Cyrus' book. I refused to leave it in the carriage. There had to be a clue in it somewhere. Why else would the dog have brought me to it?

"What other road do we have?" Edward asked. Part of me wanted to remain in Reading in case I discovered something else here, but the city felt like a looted chest already. I doubted it could offer any more hint of Bram's whereabouts.

Besides, I could always study the book while traveling.

"Very well," I said. "Let's go to Oxford, then home."

Edward closed his eyes and let out a breath. I smiled.

"But the dog comes along."

Chapter Eight

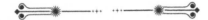

Unexpected Visitor

The sheer history of Oxford made felt like walking through knee-deep water.

We had arrived in the late evening, and I had no chance to explore, even though a fresh snow illuminated the city streets. The cobbled roads and old buildings looked like they stretched on in every direction. As our carriage rolled in, I wondered if someone might take a wrong turn and just vanish into a beautiful stone-constructed past.

Some facades appeared to look at me with disinterest. What was a woman from Dawnhurst to a city that had seen so many generations come and go?

I woke late the following morning, weary from travel but well-slept. This marked three nights in a row that I had not experienced some nocturnal episode. In fact, I hadn't dreamt at all.

Edward's mother had an appointment with a man at the university and insisted Edward accompany her.

"Even if you plan to abandon the task to me now, you can't avoid managing Fernmount forever. This man lectures on the economy of agriculture. Yes, it sounds dreadfully boring. Yes, that's why I want you to learn about it," she said as we breakfasted in the dining room at the MacDonald Randolph hotel.

Edward looked at me as though he marched toward to a torture chamber, but I wasn't about to liberate him. If I wanted to improve my relationship with his mother, I would have to insist that he find opportunities to spend time with her.

The hotel's luxury made me feel self-conscious. The lavish decor distracted me at every angle. Looking out the window, I imagined there might be some place I could enjoy a cup of tea while I researched the book. Cyrus could probably use a chance to stretch his legs.

But, it turned out the pointer took quite well to a life of luxury, and I couldn't coax him off of a large cushion in our rooms. Evidently, I was on my own.

It didn't take me long to find a decent tea shop where (the proprietor assured me) I could read for a spell in peace.

I dived right into the book, first examining its aged leather cover. The title had all but worn off, but not from excessive use as with a beloved volume. No. This book looked weather-worn. Pages suffered from brittle edges, perhaps having seen their fair share of rainy days. The typography was a little too cramped to read the prose quickly, and the author's name was nearly illegible on the title page from grime, stains, and inkblots. Michael Harris. I'd never heard of him.

Still, I eagerly leafed through it and found pages and pages of odd and often poorly written verse. Some poems were aggressively nausea-inducing, filled with gushing lines about love. Anna may have liked it. I riffled the pages, giving myself a whiff of musty paper, looking for any handwritten scribbles from Bram. But there was nothing.

No poem indicated a specific location, though I found at least one with a motif about searching.

I don't know where the wind comes from
Or where trees hide in seed
The origin of the running stream
Is mystery to me
I can't explain the pendulum
That undulates the sea

But at least I know to find you
Where dreams meets memory.

Wonderful. Maybe I could find Bram where dreams meet memory. That sounded like the stupid, vague way he liked to talk.

Perhaps the book was a puzzle, and a secret compartment or secret message hid somewhere in its binding.

In any case, I'd need at least another cup of tea to get through a section of poetry entitled *Her Hair is like the River*. Perhaps a few biscuits as well.

I raised my arm to catch the attention of the staff.

"Yes, miss?" the woman said.

I opened my mouth to respond, but surprise unlatched my jaw. Entering the shop at that very moment was none other than Brutus, my most regular critic.

"Miss?"

"Yes," I stammered. "I—could I trouble you for a few scones."

"Well, of course, dear. You needn't seem so shy about it. Wouldn't be a tea shop if we didn't have scones at this hour, now would we? Don't have to look so shocked neither, dear. They're scones, in the end. Mind you, scones don't win any fancy awards, but they're mildly pleasant, and that's the point of scones, isn't it? Oh, hello Mr. Evans!"

She nodded at Brutus, who tipped his hat in turn, and she scurried off behind the counter. I unconsciously tried to shrink into the lace table runner beneath my teacup. What business did Brutus have here?

I'd never given him a good look-over before. In the past, I had always avoided his gaze, out of either fear or spite. He was gaunt and pale, with dark brown eyes and a hooked nose like a vulture's beak. I wondered if the winter coat he wore could make up for his lack of natural insulation. Unlikely. I imagine he liked the cold, having a frozen heart and all.

He turned toward me, and recognition lit up his face.

Oh, no.

He approached my table, and I was trapped. The only door to the shop lay behind him, and I had nowhere to hide now that he'd seen me. This man came from Dawnhurst. His approach could mean anything. He might believe me a criminal. A murderer. I could melt into a city like Oxford if I had to.

He arrived without a word, and I looked up, speechless and angry. I hated that face. I spent so many recent years despising this man.

He took off his hat and sat down, calm as if I had invited him. I failed to get any words out, though there was plenty I'd have liked to say.

After my tea had assuredly gone cold, he spoke.

"Did you really kill Lucas Thomas?" he asked. I'd never heard his voice before. It differed from my imagination. I had always imagined a whiny ferret of a man speaking his written work in my head, but he would have comfortably sung the bass part of a Christmas choir. I smirked. I doubt he sang.

It was poor timing for a smirk. He raised two curious eyebrows at me.

"What are you doing here?" I asked.

"A friend of mine is lecturing at the university."

"A lecture?"

"Yes. There's a gaggle of young writers that want to do some oafish things with grammar."

"I suppose you have a firm opinion on the issue."

He leaned back and crossed his spider legs.

"It didn't take me long."

"What didn't?"

"To uncover your secret," he said with a tight mouth. My heart jumped to life.

"What secret?" What could he know? He leveled his gaze at me as if I had belittled him.

"Travis Blakely?"

"Who?"

"Your pen name." He looked like a child tattling on his sibling. "I saw through it in an instant."

An undue tide of relief melted me in my seat.

"My pen name."

"I critique writing for a living. Did you really think I'd fall for Travis Blakely's articles on etiquette, fashion, and how to treat women? It wasn't a man's voice. Obvious from the first sentences."

"You never said a thing." Hopefully, he'd gloat for a minute, then leave me alone.

"And why should I have? If Byron Livingston wanted to publish a woman under a man's name, why should I spoil his fun?" He raised his arm to signal for a cup of tea, apparently content to stay awhile.

"And how is Byron?" I surprised myself by asking after him. He may have turned me in, but we'd still been engaged at one point. Even damaged emotional ties do not come undone so smoothly.

"As well as you might expect for a man whose fiancée ran away after being accused of murder. You may be interested to know that he's tried to defend you."

"Has he been explaining to the entire city about my psychological instability then?"

"Heavens no. He's raised logical issues with the police's theory, your unclear motive, for example."

I sipped my tea to drown the knot rising in my throat. I did not think I could feel gratitude for Byron after his actions. He was naïve in some ways for a man his age, but he had truly cared about me. I never doubted that.

"Can we discuss the looming presence in the room?" he asked.

"I thought we already had. What? Would you like congratulations for seeing through my pseudonym?"

"Come now. You know that's not what I'm referring to."

"Then what?" I gripped my book more tightly, wishing that Cyrus was here. I wondered if Cyrus had any value as a protector. I had only ever seen him lazing about.

"You do make a man work for it, don't you, Miss Winthrop?"

"Perhaps too many men believe things should come freely."

His wiry lips spread into a smile.

"One moment, Travis Blakely wrote stories about drapery and manners. The next, I pick up a copy of Langley's Miscellany to read about monsters, ghosts, canine burglars, and who knows what else."

"Yes. I remember how fondly you appreciated those stories." Brutus' cutting remarks about my them had sent me into my first debilitating magical episode.

"Nonsense."

"It was true," I replied.

"Then let the gossips share the news. Be honest with me, why did you shift your subject matter?"

"You can't be serious." I gaped. "You don't mean to tell me you preferred my articles on street etiquette."

He rolled his eyes and drummed his fingers on the table.

"I hoped you might understand," he said.

"You wanted Byron to drop me. He told me so."

"I wanted Byron to drop you because he was in love with you." He whispered the word love like someone might overhear him. "His feelings made him incapable of helping your writing. Despite what you think, that is my job at the end of the day."

I crossed my arms and sat back. What a peculiar conversation to be having today of all days? Brutus was being so candid. He might answer a million questions for me, and to be honest, sitting here talking about my writing made me feel, well, normal.

"You called my work forgettable. You wrote about your indifference."

"And if I was so indifferent about articles on street etiquette from an obscure writer at a small publication, have you wondered why I'd bother with a review in the first place?"

He had me there. I had wondered that frequently. I thought he'd drawn the short straw and was given his publication's least favorable assignment.

"In my humble opinion," he continued, "writers need boring topics before they deserve the exciting ones. Your articles were drab, yes, but you put so much of yourself into them that I identified your gender."

I wasn't sure if I should have been insulted or flattered.

"Then, you got all these fantastical topics." He harrumphed. "Sure, the first one wasn't so bad, what about that detective and all, but these other trifles? They were children's books."

I folded my hands tightly over the book of poetry.

"I see. So, my original stories were boring, albeit formative for my writing, but my latest stories were complete rubbish. Your charm never ceases to amaze me."

"Why can't you see this for the compliment it is? I'm telling you that if you didn't abandon your own trajectory, you were on your way to something brilliant."

"That being?"

"Becoming a formidable literary voice, a candidate for Dawnhurst's Golden Inkwell."

I smiled sadly.

"What a paradox you are, sir. Though you didn't like my fantastical tales, I can't see Travis Blakely winning the Golden Inkwell off of street etiquette articles, even if he were the best writer in the world."

"Opportunity favors those prepared," he said with a conspiratorial grin. He looked almost evil with a smile like that on such a thin and peaky face.

"Why are you smiling like that?" I asked delicately.

"Byron showed me your last article, Luella."

Blood rushed to my face.

"Which article?"

"The one chronicling the dramatic demise of Luke Thomas."

I must have gone white as the snow outside. I had written that article before Luke Thomas had died. It was the single most damning evidence possible against me. If Brutus had pieced the timeline together...

I shakily took my teacup to give myself something to do, and for the first time in days, demon picked up momentum inside me.

"Byron wasn't to show that to anyone," I said after taking a long sip.

"I'm not anyone."

What could I feel but paranoia? I considered my next statement as though I were tiptoeing through a room lined with porcelain saucers. Yet, he didn't have the trapper's look about him—that sadistic satisfaction from snaring prey. Instead, he looked excited to share something, leaning forward like I was about to open a Christmas gift.

"And what did you make of it?" I asked.

"It was your finest work by leaps and bounds." He thumped the table.

My stomach turned in knots as I wrestled with conflicting emotions. It didn't seem like he thought I was a murderer, or else I must have taken his comment as congratulations on killing Luke Thomas. That was absurd. I wanted to smile. I had sought this man's approval for so long, and I had predicted he might appreciate the article in question. Yet, I hardly had a claim on the craftsmanship given that I was in a magical stupor when I wrote it.

"I can't understand why you wouldn't let Byron publish it."

"It was complicated," I said, looking distractedly out the window. Strangers walked by wearing large scarves. "I was too close to the story."

Brutus nodded.

"Every woman deserves her privacy. I will not insist on knowing the specifics."

"Have you not read the papers?" I asked, snapping back to attention. "I hear the specifics are all over the city. I am accused of his murder, am I not?"

He sighed. "Yes, there is that."

"Let me connect some more details for you. Luke Thomas was the father of the Steely-eyed Detective."

Brutus' eyes grew wide.

"It didn't seem appropriate for publication."

"Why do they suspect you?" he asked.

"From what I can tell, Sergeant Cooper is following a gut reaction. Edward Thomas is a dear friend and under his command. After his father's death, I—I admit I was furious over how the Sergeant was treating Edward, and I gave him a piece of my mind. Cooper knew Luke Thomas personally and discarded a suicide as unrealistic. Between my errant behavior and his hunch at foul play—it probably didn't help that I fled the city either."

This was the account I would have told a jury had I been forced to.

"Why did you run?"

"Do you have so much faith in our system of justice that you'd allow yourself to stand trial for a murder you didn't commit?"

This quieted the critic. It was partly true. I knew the courts to produce erratic outcomes, but that wasn't really why I ran.

Still, there was therapy in explaining myself.

We sat quietly for some time, avoiding eye contact and sipping tea before he broke our silence.

"Is it an enjoyable volume?" he asked, nodding toward my book.

"I hope so," I replied. "Truth be told, I'm finding it rather difficult to immerse myself."

"May I see it?" he extended a hand, and an unusual wave of protective energy washed over me. I hesitated, not wanting him to touch it, but had no excuse to refuse. Instead, I awkwardly put it on the table in front of him, using my own hands to riffle through its pages on his behalf.

"The text is rather foppish, and I'm having a hard time connecting to the words."

Brutus pored over the pages professionally, before I withdrew the book. This snapped him out of his trance, and he smiled as warmly as his fatless features would allow.

"I've read my fair share of gushing text, regrettably," he said.

"Any advice?"

"Dive in and don't give up on the author." He grabbed my hand and gave it a quick congenial squeeze, filling me with more affection than it deserved, then looked at his pocket watch. "Well, our happy encounter must come to a close. This has been my pleasure, Miss Winthrop."

"I'm surprised to say the pleasure was mine, if you don't mind my honesty."

He smiled, warm and wiry.

"I imagine I won't get the chance of reading another Blakely article until this is all cleared up."

"I imagine you're right."

"Well, when he returns, I wouldn't be bothered if he went by the name Winthrop."

He settled his bill and left through the front door after giving me one last encouraging glance. I stared after him, wondering if at any moment I might not wake up.

Chapter Nine

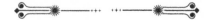

Battlehardened

"What do you mean they took the dog?" I paced the floor back at the hotel.

"What did you expect?" Edward asked. "The proprietor doesn't want drool all over his silk pillow covers. It's understandable."

"So, they just came right in here unannounced? Where is he now?"

"The proprietor?"

"The dog!"

I slumped onto the couch.

"He's being treated like royalty. There are some kennels on the ground floor where the chef keeps his dog."

I folded my arms.

"What good is going to an expensive hotel if you still have to follow all the rules?" I asked.

"In my personal experience, the more expensive a thing is, the less you can do with it," he replied.

I hadn't been able to concentrate for an instant after my conversation with Brutus, nor bring myself to enjoy the mildly pleasant scones at the tea shop. I came back to the hotel hungry right before the Thomases. Edward's mother awkwardly insisted she needed some rest before escaping into her bedroom, leaving Edward and me alone.

"Did you discover anything this morning, apart from your dislike of the hotel management?" Edward asked.

"Nothing." I pouted. "I found a local tea shop and tried to dive into the book, but I came up empty."

"Nothing out of the ordinary?"

I almost told him about Brutus' visit but thought better of it. After all, nothing had come of it, and Edward would worry over it for no reason.

I shook my head.

"And what about your condition? Have you noticed the magic lately?"

"I felt something earlier, but nothing as strong as before."

He sat down next to me.

"I was so worried about you while we were apart."

His concern made me blush.

"Tell me about your trip with your mother."

"I'd rather not."

"It can't have been that bad," I said, grabbing a pillow and pulling it toward me. It was wet. The proprietor may have had a point about the dog drool.

"Well, it began with a lecture about maturity," he started.

"Maturity? You're a police officer."

"She brought that up. Apparently, gallivanting around beating up on criminals is a young man's game, and sooner or later, I need to think about either leadership in my current role, or pivot and find something more suitable for my future."

Poor Edward. Since his father died, his life was full of others who thought they knew better. I monopolized his efforts since we left Fernmount. Now, his mother tried to do the same.

It chilled me to think his mother and I might not be all that different.

"And what did she have in mind for your future?"

"What would you expect?" He stood up and crossed to a tall window. "She wants me to find an agreeable woman to settle down with and manage Fernmount."

Marriage. What more could a mother want for her son? The way Edward said the word though, heavy as the drapes on the windows beside him, made it sound as if dreaded the prospect.

Months ago, he had proposed, and I had refused him. He was grieving, and I was in no condition to give all of myself.

Through all this time, nothing had changed.

"Is that the life you want?" I asked, fiddling with the tassels on my pillow.

"It might be if I were with the right woman," he responded. He didn't turn his head, just kept looking out the window. The sun was setting behind the old roofs of Oxford's skyline.

I rose and stood beside him at the window. Something twisted in my stomach. It wasn't magic, at least not the fog creature's magic. I tried to will him to hold my hand. Why was it so hard to talk about my feelings?

"What is the right woman like?" I finally asked.

"According to me or my mother?" His voice was dispassionate. If I had read his comments to be an invitation to rekindle something between us, I had misunderstood the conversation. My shoulders fell.

"I take it a girl from the east side of Dawnhurst isn't what she has in mind for you."

"I've never been able to understand. I wasn't born into wealth. I don't know why my mother feels this prejudice. She keeps going on about how much good we could do if we can strengthen our position."

He looked at me expectantly. I struggled to find a comment.

"Charity may often camouflage greed," I said.

"That's just it," he said, walking away from the window. "I don't know who is selfish and who selfless. Life is so much easier when you're chasing down criminals. I could never be a judge. Do I misunderstand marriage? I thought my mother suffered in her union with my father, but the way she goes on it's like she lost her true companion."

It was strange for me to hear this. I wanted to renew his affection, to let him know that I would withstand a difficult mother-in-law. Instead, my courage failed me. What if his feelings toward me had changed? He had already done so much. He owed me no more.

"And," he continued, "here I am looking for Bram and hiding you from the authorities. Life is strange, isn't it?"

I timidly took his hands in my own, staring up into his gray eyes, trying to show him what I could not say. He looked back at me, but I did not recognize the Edward I knew months before.

I wanted to kiss him. I wanted him to know that all of this was for us, for him. The search for Bram, the months traveling, the hiding, the secrecy, the false identities…

But though he brought a hand up to caress my cheek, his eyes remained empty.

"I told my mother that she should grow accustomed to having you around," he said.

I tried to smile.

Dinner was quiet and awkward. Lady Thomas, who had been full of trivialities the previous evening, chewed and swallowed her food in silence. I tried my best to make conversation, inquiring about the history of Oxford or what types of agriculture sustained Fernmount, but without success.

That evening, I found myself alone in my room, wishing I had Cyrus there for comfort. A new breed of loneliness plagued my mood. Edward's vacant stare haunted me. Without his support, I had no one.

I rustled through my things and found my sister's letter. I read and reread it, but her words just reminded me she was not here. I had failed her. My choices left her with no action but to leave me.

I missed her so much it hurt, and not just her. I missed our mother. I missed Mrs. Crow. I missed Rebecca Turner, the best friend I never deserved.

The magic started swirling inside of me, taking advantage of my weakened defenses. My fingers twitched. It was back. It would always come back.

Edward had allowed me to commandeer one of his heavy coats, and I wrapped myself up in it. In the past, the feeling of him I found in that coat had been enough to distract me from the magic. But despite its blanketing warmth, my anxiety and nerves clawed their way out of me.

I grabbed Poems from the Wanderer and flung it open, reading desperately. I needed to escape myself, my thoughts, this place—all of it.

I tried to read, but the look in Edward's eyes struck my mind like lightning.

I tried to read, but the memory of Mrs. Crow's haggard hands clutching Anna's letter rushed me.

I tried to read, but I saw Rebecca's flushed face insisting I get in a carriage and leave Dawnhurst.

I tried to read, and my father's face laughed at me. Distorted. Wrong. All wrong.

"Enough!" I cried.

I slammed the book shut, and my hands clapped together painfully. I looked down. The book was gone.

So was my bed. So was my room.

I looked around and almost screamed again.

I sat under a willow tree on top of a grassy hill. The hill descended into a small meadow that disappeared into mist. Bluebells and snowdrops dotted the field, but they looked deeper and less colorful than they should have. A heady breeze blew by, making strands of my hair dance on my forehead. I wrapped myself up in Edward's coat. Was this a dream?

The surrounding mist felt different from the fog in my previous dreams. It hung lighter, purer, more like the mist around Fernmount where I had last seen the moondust trail.

My yell had set startled several birds. They took wing gracefully and colorfully. I watched them and hardly believed my eyes.

I recognized a few of the breeds. There were dusty-winged sparrows and a crow or two. But among those, dancing in between the shafts of sunset breaking through the clouds, were a variety of other birds, all looking foreign and exotic.

Where was I? I'd been in my hotel room a moment ago. Now, it didn't feel like winter at all, and I had a hard time believing this was Oxford.

A chill ran through me. Maybe my condition had worsened. Was this the next stage in my symptoms? First, I dreamed up the Forbury Gardens made of stone, now I woke up to a world that belonged in a fairy tale. At any moment, I expected the fog creature garbed in my father's body to appear, but I waited and waited, and he did not.

I found my courage and tried to explore. Behind me, the hill sloped lightly into a dense wood, the start of a foreboding forest that poked through the mist. It curved around me in a great arc, a natural and impassible barrier.

If I squinted, I could see another hilltop in the distance, topped by a stately oak tree. I walked down the hill and took a deep breath. Somehow, the air felt fuller, each lungful satiating and rich.

As I traversed the meadow, I discovered a body of water hidden among the tall, rustling grass. It stretched out into the mist and vanished, beautiful and serene.

Then I felt it. Freedom. Deep inside of me, where the magic lay, I detected nothing, no trace of it at all, not just dormancy but complete remission.

I laughed, disbelieving it, but even in the laugh I sensed the truth of it. Joy and relief swept over me. I couldn't explain how or why, but I was suddenly sure that my magical malady was gone.

In a burst of excitement, I ran through the field like a little girl. For a moment, it didn't matter that I didn't know where I was or how I got there. I was free. It was like flying.

After a few minutes of celebration, I collapsed, heart pounding steadily, onto the grass. I connected to the fullness of the earth. If I laid still long enough, perhaps the grass would just grow over and consume me.

I don't know how long it took for me to come down from my state of euphoria, but the first thoughts to rouse me were fears I'd be torn from this place and desires to find a route back.

How did I get here?

One moment I had been reading in the hotel at Oxford, then—

Cyrus' book. Where was it now? I sat up and looked all around, but it was nowhere to be seen. I tried retracing my steps, trekking all the way back up the hill to the willow tree, but I didn't find Poems from the Wanderer anywhere. I looked curiously up at the sky. It looked almost as if I was in a massive cathedral, and high above my head a roof stretched— a roof made of clouds, wool, and parchment...

But that wasn't possible.

I twisted the grass between my fingers. It felt real enough, even if the color was off, more vague somehow. I even found a thistle thorn or two in my stocking from running across the field. I wasn't dreaming. It was all so tangible. Time passed too normally. Undreamlike mundane moments were everywhere.

Then, I heard a faint commotion in the mist. My curiosity drove me to investigate. I descended again from the hill and walked into the clouds.

As I pushed forward, I discovered farmland brimming with crops from different seasons, all in different stages of maturity. Spring peas and asparagus looked plump and ready for harvest beside winter squashes and summer squashes alike. Then there were crops I was completely unfamiliar with, brightly colored fruits growing from well-manicured trees.

Small acres of wheat and other grains lay beyond them, and I finally saw man-made structures. There were farmhouses, hewn of rough stone with thatched roofs beside neat Georgian-style plantation homes.

I spotted a dirt road winding through them and gasped as I discovered these farm buildings formed the outskirts of a developing village made of an eclectic mix of architecture from different time periods and cultures.

The buildings grew more varied as I wandered into the village.

I found a bizarre temple made of blackened wood fit together in intricate patterns. The roof formed a thin, tapering spire. In other places were paved squarish buildings, huts made of straw, and traditional Danish cottages. Above me, I noticed the familiar silhouette of a smokestack pitched on top of a small factory.

It looked as though the history of the world had moved in together.

Movement caught my eye. I blinked, and a figure ran past me with a curious bow and quiver of arrows slung over his shoulder.

It was a man clad in armor made of mirrored panels, more resplendent and reflective than any looking glass I'd ever seen. The effect rendered him brilliant one moment, and a mix of reflections the next. The last rays of the setting sun bounced off the panels, casting bright reflections on the buildings he passed.

"Excuse me!" I cried, but the man either didn't respond. I rushed after him through an alleyway that spit us out into a round courtyard boasting a beautiful and spacious fountain. Above us loomed another hill with what looked like a small castle perched atop it. But what really took my breath away were the scores of other men in similar sets of mirrored armor rushing toward one road beyond the hill. Sounds of metal and glass reverberated off the stone as they united into a solid unit. Watching that many mirrors at so many angles put so closely together had a dizzying effect, as though I was following a wall of moving fragments of the world.

"At the ready!" a husky female voice shouted. I turned the corner of a sharply slanting roof that connected all the way to the ground and found lines of soldiers beside a heavy-set wood gate, dressed in iron and situated between stone towers. A stone wall stretched out in either direction. Atop the tower, the woman paced like a tiger. Unlike the rest of the soldiers, she wore a mask made of the same brilliant mirrored material as the rest of her armor.

My blood ran cold as I realized I'd somehow stumbled into the middle of a battle.

The mirrored army had weapons as various as the birds, crops, and architecture I'd already discovered. There were pistols, longbows, short swords, scythes, morning stars, and a collection of other weapons I did not recognize.

Two exceptionally large soldiers stood in alcoves built into the parapets of the wall at enormous wheels.

"On my mark!" the woman shouted. "Three, two, one!"

The men in the alcoves furiously turned their wheels, and the large wooden gates swung open.

I screamed when I saw what was on the other side. It looked like someone had tried to piece together soldiers from whatever living things they could think of. There were normal men and men with legs like lions. Some had giant horns on their heads, and others had wings sprouting from their arms. And then there were creatures that weren't men at all, bulls with scales instead of fur, and stags with antlers that moved like the legs of a squid.

Nearly all these monsters were void of color altogether, just different shades of white, gray, and black. They were there and not quite there all at once, flickering in and out of my vision like a mirage.

I ran as fast as my legs allowed to the nearest cover, something I assumed was an overturned fruit stand. I pinched myself repeatedly. This had to be a dream. A moment ago, I never wanted to leave this place. Now, fear paralyzed me.

The noises of the battle raged behind me. Clanging metal, the thumping of feet, bodies, and hooves beating the earth interspersed with rifle fire and splintering wood.

It went on and on, and as I tried desperately to slow my heart and breathing, I realized I needed to get further away from the gate. If the soldiers failed, I would be in the direct path of danger.

I pushed my back against the wooden fruit stand and found the strength to peer over the top. It took me only a moment to become transfixed by the terrible beauty of the fight.

Reflections and ghostly mirages clashed ferociously. The mirror-paneled garrison fought swiftly, but as they landed killing blows with their brilliant weapons, the bodies of the mirage monsters faded away altogether, leaving nothing behind.

When Anna and I had lived on Dawnhurst's east side, I'd seen many things I hoped to forget, but never anything like the heat and intensity of two mortal forces coming together with the sole purpose of violence.

The terror hypnotized me, rooting me to the spot.

The casualties were heavy on both sides, and as I watched a lion-wolf with a spike like a unicorn stab through a mirrored soldier, I noticed that beast seemed to gain a small bit of color, as though he had won a greater hold on reality through his kill.

The captain with the mirrored mask moved quickly through the ranks, a whirlwind of deadly skill with her curved sword.

The battle ended quickly, and it couldn't have been more than an hour before there was clear momentum for the mirrored army, but for all of their conquests, theirs were the only bodies remaining in the courtyard, the bodies of the fallen beasts having disappeared entirely.

From the stories I read about King Arthur, Caesar, or even the Duke of Wellington, I expected the ending of the battle to ring through the hills with cries of victory. Instead, as the masked captain stabbed her sword into the chest of a colossal bear, the mirrored army quietly leaned against their weapons or sat down and rested. I didn't see them speak to one another. After a few minutes' rest, they checked the surrounding bodies, presumably to see if any life remained in their friends.

Mirrors mourned mirrors.

I expected to be more affected by the loss of the soldiers' lives, but as yet, I wasn't entirely sure they were human. I'd only heard the voice of the captain. The rest maintained a machine-like coldness and efficiency.

"Drycha!" A voice behind me cried. "Come and report."

I shrunk deeper into the shade of the awning over my fruit stall and closed my eyes as the masked captain strode nearly directly beside my hiding spot. Although I sympathized with the mirrored army, I did not understand if their motives were any more pure than the odd creatures they fought against.

"Moderate casualties, commander," The captain named Drycha said.

"How long will it take us to get the gate repaired?" A voice to my left asked.

"I'll have the unit on it right away. By morning, I would say."

"Have it done by midnight, captain."

"Yes, commander." The captain turned on her heels, and I let out a sigh of relief. I was still undiscovered for now. After waiting a few minutes, I decided it was safe to creep forward to search for a means of escape.

An iron-clad hand gripped my arm.

"Commander," the captain said. I winced in pain. I looked up at my captor, but instead, I saw a frightened, haggard woman from Dawnhurst in her mask's reflection.

"What is it?" asked the commander. I was too afraid to speak.

The captain dragged me into the street and pushed me to my knees. My kneecaps jolted against the stones. I buried my gaze in the ground, afraid to look up.

The commander put a cool hand under my chin and turned it up to assess me. His dark blue eyes penetrated me to the very soul. Under his helmet, it looked almost as though his skin had too many shades of blue in it, like a robin's egg. Whatever he saw in me, he did not like it.

He snarled to himself and stood back up. I dropped my gaze back to the ground, willing myself to come up with some plan of escape.

"You lied to me," he said out of view. "Take care of this. Now."

"If you'd just let me—"

"You cannot. I'm not talking to you about this here. Take care of it."

My head was spinning. My arm was hurting where the masked soldier held me.

But I didn't lose my breath until Bram knelt beside me.

"You arrived faster than expected," he said, with a pitiable smile. "It's all right, Drycha. You can release her." Though he said little, his eyes were filled with warmth. I could have sworn he reached out and embraced me.

A thousand words blew past me, and I couldn't seem to grab even one. He wasn't wearing mirrored armor like the others, just his old ratty coat. Drycha roughly released my arm.

"I'm sorry about this." He produced a small bottle from his pocket, dabbed it on his wrist, and rubbed it forcefully against the other. Then he put his hands gently on either side of my head. I recognized the strange aroma from the carnival where we'd met. My eyes drooped as though from drowsiness, but rather than the blackness I usually found on the inside of my eyelids, I saw my room in the hotel.

I fell asleep to a new waking in a new place, alert as the morning, the book in my lap, no hills, armored warriors, or Bram in sight.

Chapter Ten

Inside an Armoire

I rushed to Edward's room as quietly as possible. It was late, all the lights in our suite had gone out, leaving just the moonlight reflecting off neighboring rooftops to filter through some windows.

My heart raced. Bram. I had seen Bram. It all made terrible sense now. What a magnificent piece of magic! Cyrus had led me to the book because Bram hid inside the book!

I got to Edward's room, situated uncomfortably close to his mother's, and tried knocking softly.

"Edward," I whispered. Silence.

I tried again, increasing the volume as much as I dared. I could only imagine the conversation I'd have with Lady Thomas if she found me at her son's door in the middle of the night.

There was still no response. Where could he be? He'd always been ready to hop to my aid before, despite the hour. I'd burst if I couldn't tell him the news. All this time searching, and I finally found Bram!

I knocked again, louder this time, and heard footsteps. But to my dismay, the footsteps sounded from behind me. I was just about to tiptoe back to my room when Edward's door opened.

"Luella?" he asked, hair disheveled.

"Your mother," I managed to whisper. He pulled me inside quietly and closed the door, right as his mother's room creaked open.

"The armoire," he mouthed to me, and before I knew it, I'd balled myself up inside a dressing cabinet, trying not to breathe too noisily. I suppressed a giggle, still so excited about finding Bram and what felt like a romantic adventure. Edward Thomas was hiding me from his mother as if we were two teenage children.

A crisp knock rapped at the door. Edward put a finger to his lips and closed the armoire before answering.

"Mother?"

"What are you doing awake?" I heard Lady Thomas say.

"I couldn't sleep," he said.

"Could you not sleep a little quieter, perhaps?"

"I'm sorry I didn't think my footsteps would wake you."

A pause.

"Edward, can I talk to you for a moment?"

"Can it wait until morning?"

"Seeing as we're both up, I wanted to take advantage of your undivided attention."

I heard her walk into the room. A few candles cast their light through a crack in the armoire, obscured momentarily as she passed in front of me. I held my breath unconsciously.

"I wanted to finish our conversation from earlier about the woman you brought home."

"Please, mother. I am tired and—"

"I deserve an explanation. I understand you disagree with me, but put yourself in my shoes. Your father died, and your son comes home immediately after with a nameless woman."

"She has a name."

"Oh, yes. Sarah Primrose, was it? Don't insult me. I've been looking for you for over a month. You think I didn't start at that little town you work at? It's all over the papers there. The police are investigating your father's death. A prime suspect is a woman named Luella Winthrop."

Crippling paranoia filled the armoire, smothered my giddy euphoria. One of my greatest fears had been realized.

"She did not kill father," he said flatly.

"Then why are the police looking for her?"

"Because they need to save face. You know old Cooper was friends with dad. It wasn't easy for him, finding the great Lucas Thomas hanging on a rope in his own office, inexplicably and without warning? Does that sound like a homicide to you, mother? You can't believe a woman that size forced a man into a noose and hoisted him up in the rafters."

The bed creaked as Lady Thomas sat on it.

"How can you speak about it so coldly? It's barbaric. It's morbid."

"I'm a police officer. I have to look at the facts. It simply doesn't make sense. Cooper is beside himself with grief."

"Why run if she's innocent?"

"The same reason people do anything. She was scared, and I don't blame her. You should have seen Cooper that day, all but frothing at the mouth. Once he got it in his head that she was tied up in something untoward..." Edward sighed. "I've long had my disagreements with the man, but I would not stand by while he arrested an innocent woman."

I leaned my head back against a panel in the wardrobe, allowing a few of Edward's hanging clothes to brush across my face. Edward spoke directly to me as much as his mother. But he was wrong. I wasn't innocent. I may not have been guilty of murder, after all I didn't intend to cause his father any harm, but I was foolish and reckless. I carried the weight of culpability.

"I want to trust you," Edward's mother replied. "You can see how I might doubt her innocence, even if you're convinced."

"I can't see it. As far as I'm concerned, if you suspect her, you suspect me. After all, I helped her escape the city."

Silence stretched long and thin, and my breathing grew louder. Unbidden, I remembered Lieutenant Edward Thomas as I first met him. His eyes had been so clear. What had I done to him?

"It's late, mother. Why don't we both get some rest? In the meantime, please give this woman a decent opportunity to show her true colors?"

The bed frame groaned again, and Lady Thomas walked to the door. The wind whistled outside the window.

"Goodnight, Edward." The door opened, but Lady Thomas hesitated. "What is that book on your desk?"

Quick footsteps crossed the room.

"Oh, it's nothing."

"Tell me you are not reading those books again. Edward, now of all times. I thought her fortune teller act was just a ruse."

"It's just a novel. I read it to unwind. Please, mother, I insist you sleep."

The door closed, and the candlelight shone bright as Edward opened the armoire. I stared at him, helpless. I would never unhear that conversation. His mother's grief had become more real to me in the past few minutes than I'd ever thought possible.

"I'm sorry you had to hear that," he whispered.

I shook my head.

"I'm the sorry one." He helped me out of the cabinet, and I found a seat near the bed. "Edward, how can you forgive me for what I've done to your family?"

He leaned against the cabinet. He was handsome, even out of uniform. Under an evening robe, his Henley shirt lay sloppily across his torso, all but ignoring a pair of well-worn braces.

"Why not tell me why I found you at my door in the middle of the night," he said, ignoring my question. "You look like you've just gone out."

"In some ways, I think I have." The memory of the otherworldly battle came back to me, although with less enthusiasm after the sobering conversation. "I found Bram."

"Here? In Oxford?" The timbre of his voice amplifying more than prudent. His arms dropped from his chest, and he grabbed a bedpost. "When?"

"Not in Oxford exactly." In my hurry, I had given little thought to how I would explain my trip into the book. His expression was merited. I'd be confused as well.

"What are you talking about? Where have you been?"

"It's the book," I whispered. "He's in the book."

Edward sank to the bed, scrutinizing me.

"After dinner, I was reading in my room, and before I knew it, the book vanished from my hands, and I just—well, I just—I woke in a field."

He gave me a dumb nod.

"It was beautiful, with a sky full of clouds, and the entire thing world felt like a big room. And then these mirrored soldiers went to battle against these monsters that just disappeared when they died. Then after the fighting stopped, the captain found me, and she didn't seem pleased to see me, but Bram came around, and he made me smell his cologne, and I blinked and was back in my room."

I hadn't written a story in months, and it showed.

"You mean to say," Edward replied after a bloated pause, "that the book is magical?"

"Yes." It had to be.

"I mean, it doesn't contain text about magic or alleged spells, but that the book itself is magical?"

"I can't see how else it would have transported me. Don't you see? Cyrus led me to the book, and when I read it, the book led me to Bram. I was following a trail of breadcrumbs all along!"

It's an ugly thing, telling something important to someone you care about and knowing they don't believe you.

"You're sure this wasn't one of your dreams or the fog creature trying to deceive you?"

I hadn't considered that the fog creature might have fabricated the whole thing. It had impersonated my father. Why not Bram?

But no, in dreams with the fog creature, I never escaped the gnawing heat of a nightmare. Even when I feared for my life in the middle of the battle at the gate, it had felt different. Besides, I'd been freed from my magical illness. That never happened in my dreams.

"When I was there, I didn't feel my condition at all. I hadn't felt so free in—well, since—"

"Since our lunch at Doug's Fish and Chips?" His smile looked far away somehow. Our lunch at Doug's seemed years ago. I had been so happy that afternoon, watching Edward and the pub's proprietor swap stories. They were like family.

I nodded.

"Can you show me?"

In a moment, I had skulked back to my room and returned with the book. I thought it pulsed with energy in my hands.

"Here it is," I said, tucking my feet under me on the bed next to Edward. I put the book down and opened it. "I was reading it like this. One moment I was here and the next I wasn't."

"Can you do it again?" The mattress dipped when he leaned to look at the book, pulling me toward him. It was likely unintentional, but distracting, nonetheless.

"I—I haven't tried it yet," I said, ignoring the scent of him. I had only sat on a bed with a man once before. It hadn't seemed as momentous with Bram. Being next to Edward, I felt suddenly conscious of my hair.

"Why not now?" He turned the book toward me.

"I'm not sure. They sent me back. I don't know if they want me there again."

"What do you mean they sent you back?"

"Like I said, Bram used this cologne or smelling salts or something. He said he was surprised I arrived so quickly."

"So, he won't help you?"

He looked at the book threateningly, like he would force Bram to cooperate with a stern look from a different world.

"Let me try it." I gathered the book in my hands, trying to recreate my pose from before, and started reading. My eyes flew over the text, searching desperately for that magical hook. I flipped through pages, trying to find the poem I read in my room.

I found the page with a rush of exhilaration and read it through, but nothing happened.

Edward looked at me expectantly, and I nervously started over, but couldn't focus. Perhaps there was some code I had inadvertently deciphered, or maybe I was looking at it too closely.

"Is it working?" Edward asked after several minutes.

"It's just taking some time," I said, flustered. Last time I didn't have Edward Thomas next to me. It was difficult to concentrate.

"Did it take this long last time?"

"No. I mean, yes. I can't remember."

He leaned back in a way I considered dismissive, which hurt me more than was reasonable. I searched frantically for an explanation, my mind quickly losing any semblance of order. Anxiety and panic barreled toward me. My fingers began twitching.

Evidently, wherever my illness had gone while inside the book, it was back now.

"Perhaps they've closed the door."

"What do you mean?"

"Bram sent me back. What if he closed the door to make sure I didn't return immediately?"

Edward stood up and crossed to his desk. I felt the distance between us like an empty stomach.

"Then we are back to where we started—further back, in fact." He picked up a tumbler and weighed it in his hand. I couldn't believe what I was hearing.

"What are you talking about? We found Bram."

"He is refusing us. This was my greatest fear. Finding a man is hard enough, but coercing him to cooperate is not easy or pretty."

"We won't have to coerce him," I stood. "He wants to help."

"His actions speak otherwise."

"He's just not ready! I know he wants to. If you had only seen the way he looked at me—" As soon as the words were out of my mouth, I regretted them. Edward tried to mask his reaction, but it was clear even in the dimly lit room. "He looked friendly. Happy to see me."

Once, back in Dawnhurst, I had carefully danced around my wording to convince Byron Livingston, my old fiancé, that I had no feelings for Edward. Now, I said a similar thing to my new fiancé— hopefully fiancé. Had I changed so little?

Edward grabbed a bottle from his desk and poured a bit of Scotch into his tumbler. He didn't drink it.

"Luella, you once said you wanted to show me the truth about you, piece by piece. I've followed you, protected you, and I've tried to understand. You've talked to me about a dark door in the dreams that haunt you, but I've had a dark door of my own, one I haven't opened but is ever-present."

"Edward—"

"Now, it's as if it's opening on its own, and I'm straining from holding it shut."

He had cut me open. My history was a chasm in our relationship, and nothing pained me more.

"Edward, can we talk about this at a different time? We're both excited."

"What was the nature of your relationship with him?" It is shocking to see how vulnerable even courageous men become when reduced to affairs of the heart. "I've chased him with you for months, and now at the end, I ought to have some explanation."

My mouth hung open, and I aborted half-formed words. I had hoped he'd be happy that our effort wasn't wasted. Edward was granite, a sculpture carved from principle and unfailing loyalty.

"You're jealous," I said, as much to understand myself than for him, "worried."

He pursed his lips and considered the glass.

"I don't blame you," I said. "I will keep my word. I'll tell you anything. But, please, with your mood right now, can't we talk about it when we're more rested?"

"When will that be? Your road to recovery will be long and

difficult."

"You don't know that."

"You're right. I don't know anything. I can't tell my mother anything. I have to pretend this is all something different with no explanation. And now—"

He trailed off.

"And now?" I pressed. He kept silent, avoiding eye contact. "And now?"

An edge grew in my voice, and it scared me. I clenched my fists.

"Now, you're saying a book transported you to a magical world."

He took a drink, but it was my throat that burned. I gripped Poems from the Wanderer more tightly than comfortable.

"You—are you saying you don't believe me?"

He looked like a phantom, silhouetted as he was in the light of a candle.

"You said yourself that the fog creature has been changing its approach, that perhaps it wants to distort your view of reality."

"This was different."

"It may have seemed different, but how can you be sure?"

Having no answer made me angry and afraid.

"You think I'm losing my mind?"

"I didn't say that." He stepped toward me, and I recoiled.

"I'm sorry. I shouldn't have come until I had something more definite. Until I had proof."

"Luella," he said. "Wait—"

I left the room furious and tried to quiet my steps as I went down the hall, but it was a struggle to care. So what if his mother woke up? Who cared about her at all?

My thoughts turned to a memory of Anna and Byron at Bunbury's restaurant what seemed like ages ago. She'd endured hardship but hadn't fallen to pieces until we'd found the privacy of a carriage. I could get back to my room.

I closed the door behind me while a volcano erupted in my chest. I wanted to shred the linens with my fingernails and tear the furniture apart.

Please. I didn't want this.

A soft knocking sounded behind me

It was hard to focus, to walk. I fumbled toward the dresser and set the wretched book down before I ripped it apart. I tore into my purse and searched for Anna's letter.

I read it while trembling on the floor, missing my sister fiercely, trying to be brave for her though I didn't even know where she was. I'd always done hard things for her. How was this different?

The knocking persisted. The doorknob rattled. Had I locked it?

Edward didn't believe me. He never had. He never loved me. He was just under a spell. I wasn't worth it. I wasn't worth anything.

I looked at the book. Had I dreamed the field? Was anything true?

I closed my eyes and saw Bram looking down on me. Even he had turned me away.

The next thing I knew, I was standing in an open doorway. Edward gaped.

"Do we still have the leather cords?" I asked.

Chapter Eleven

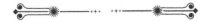

A Stroll Through Oxford

If I had been dreaming up that eclectic village with the mirrored soldiers, I didn't that night. Nor did I enjoy a coy conversation with the creature parading around as my father. I blacked out.

When I came to, it felt like fog and waves had buffeted me all night long. My ribs ached like they had been bruised all over, and the leather straps had rubbed angry sores through my nightgown on my wrists, forearms, stomach, and legs.

This was the ugly, familiar aftermath of one of my attacks.

I turned my head and saw Edward asleep under his coat in a chair across the room.

"Edward," I croaked. He woke before I had finished his name. "Is there water?"

He put a finger to his lips and silently brought a glass of water to mine. I drank, but the water hurt my throat.

Outside the door, I heard footsteps pacing and knocking on a room down the hall. Silence. Then more unhurried footsteps scuttled across the suite, and the front door closed.

"Your mother?" I whispered. He nodded.

"I left her a note saying I'd gone out for a ride around town early. She'll be headed to breakfast downstairs."

"Edward. I hurt. Everywhere."

He put the glass on the dresser

"You didn't thrash about as violently as usual, but it was steadier, more—"

He cut himself off and started untying me.

"My attacks are getting worse."

"They're not getting better." He hadn't changed his clothes. His trousers were wrinkled from sitting in the armchair all night long.

"I'm sorry," I whispered.

He pulled the chair closer and sat down.

"I need to show you something." He produced an old leather tome from the desk.

"What is that?" I asked.

"I was serious when I said we should start researching our own solutions. I found this book in the Oxford library. It might be a fit place to start. It turns out they have several books on the occult sciences in their collection. The librarian that helped me wouldn't touch this one with his bare hands. I figured it would be—"

"Have you lost your mind? We can't just start rummaging through books about dark magic." I sat up and rubbed at my wrists.

"I need to be honest with you, Luella. I'm afraid the fog creature is winning. If that's true, we need to prepare you to deal with the side effects. It can do what it likes to unhinge your mind, but as I see it, that's a consequence not a cause. If Bram can't help us, then—" He struggled over which word to use next.

I pitied him looking so desperate, clinging to a book that contained heavens knew what nonsense inside. I knew we were closer than ever to securing Bram's help, but Edward was right that he'd turned me away inside the book. Edward's eyes implored me. He was just trying his best, and he had given so much. Couldn't I at least try one of his ideas?

"I understand," I said, "but I still question your book selection strategy. Why don't I accompany you back to the library, and we can see if any titles resonate with both of us? We can start there."

"Are you up for it?"

I gestured toward the pitcher on the dresser. Edward poured me another glass.

"If possible, I'd like to delay your mother's thinking I am crazy for as long as possible. What if I'm on a sickbed all day? She already thinks I killed her husband."

"If she thought that, she would have told the police already."

"I don't know, Edward. There is strategic timing to things. She may fear she will lose your affection if she swoops in to have me arrested too early."

He coughed out a sarcastic laugh.

"Then maybe we're just lucky that my mother had a complicated marriage."

I tried to stand, using a hand on the bedpost to steady myself. Edward rushed to my aid.

"Her mourning seems earnest enough." I winced.

"She's going through the proper motions," he said. "Come along then. Can you dress yourself?"

"What alternative is there?" I shot him a suspicious glance, eliciting a blush and grin, a bright spot of levity to fuel me through the morning.

Edward left the room, taking his dusty tome of magic with him. I changed into a dark green striped skirt and jacket and wrapped myself up in a warm cloak. The corners of the window had iced over, and I had no interest in adding a chill to all my other aches and pains.

Edward found a serving lad to bring up some cheese and sausage, and we ate quickly before departing. The climb down the stairs left me exhausted, and I had to lean on the bannister to rest for a moment. Edward went ahead to find a cab.

"Are you all right, dear?"

I nearly jumped from my stockings. Lady Thomas swept towards me. A young hotel employee with overly large sideburns carried several large parcels behind her.

"Lady Thomas, you startled me." I tried to recover, but my face flushed. Somehow, I was instantly afraid she knew her son had slept in my room the night before.

"Poor dear. Edward mentioned you weren't well, and yet here you are looking ready to venture into the cold. What a lovely cape. Where were you taking it?"

The man behind her awkwardly adjusted a parcel to rest on his knee and started lowering another to the ground.

"Now, now, Jansen, let's not get too comfortable. I'll only be a moment," Lady Thomas said without looking at him. He picked the parcel back up with his free hand, a feat considering he had another parcel tied over his shoulder and another tucked under an arm. Sweat beaded his brow, and he wobbled under the weight like a drunkard on his way home from the pub.

"I was just getting some fresh air," I said. "Clear my lungs."

"Well, you won't mind if I join you. I'd love a chance to talk, just the two of us."

She folded her hands in front of her as polite as a schoolgirl, and I could think of no legitimate reason to refuse her.

"Of course," I said haltingly. "I could use your expertise on a good walking route."

"Don't be silly. I haven't walked anywhere in years. It will be a fun new adventure. Jansen, take those up to my room, and be careful. Do not damage them. Oh, could you fit this one as well?"

She searched for a place to put a bag she had in her hand. Jansen nodded and extended an index finger as a hook. She hung the bag on his finger and turned away without a second glance. She took my arm and led me through the doors. I searched for Edward with no success.

"Have you seen Edward this morning?" I asked, trying to keep my inflection casual.

"I can never keep track of my son. He's always out and busy—similar to his father in that respect."

I nodded.

"Let's see, which way shall we go? Toward the university, perhaps?"

We turned and set off down the street. As we were leaving, I finally caught Edward out of the corner of my eye.

"Oh, there he is," I lifted my hand to wave. He saw me and, while masking a look of surprise on his face, approached us.

"Now, now, you wouldn't deny me the opportunity for some time to speak as ladies. Men are so boorish from time to time, yes—even my son, going on about police work and duty and politics and all that."

Lady Thomas waved a dismissive hand at Edward without stopping our walk. He stopped in his tracks and looked at me.

Evidently, Lady Thomas had something she wanted to discuss, and I was quickly learning that she was not a woman easily refused. I inclined my head at Edward. A pained expression sprouted on his face.

We walked in silence for several minutes, dodging busier

pedestrians and casting lazy glances about the aged architecture.

"To be honest, I would like to unburden myself," she began with no preamble. "I have some troubling thoughts that won't seem to leave me alone."

Her conversation with Edward the night before rang in my memory. I wondered which of those thoughts she would divulge here and how.

"Your son has been so kind to me. If I can repay him by lending an ear of counsel for his mother, it is a small token."

"Counsel? Oh, please, don't misunderstand. To imagine, I'd seek counsel with a child." She patted my hand, which threaded through her arm. Had she called me young, it would have sounded a compliment, but "child" was a bit much. "Edward is quite taken with you, but I hardly know you at all. Such is the curse of motherhood, I fear. You care so much for a son only to see him leave you for a stranger."

I thought about my sister's engagement to Jacob Rigby. Now, she was just a pleasant daydream, a relative living far away.

"It's difficult to watch the ones we love develop relationships that change things," I said.

"Well listen to you, a female John Locke. No. You may have noticed that I am spoiled. I often find a way to realize my desires, and I don't want to lose my son. It may sound trite, but I really would enjoy gaining a daughter."

I couldn't help but taste a small swill of resentment on my tongue. Was she purposefully duplicitous? This conversation contradicted the sentiments I heard the night before.

"You speak as though Edward and I were engaged," I said.

"Are you not? I know that formalities are often culminating, not initiatory events. I've never seen him take another woman traveling, you see. Why do you look so drab? I thought you'd appreciate the assumption you weren't a trollop."

"Your son is still grieving his father," I said, clenching my jaw.

"And he always will." She looked stoically forward, chin held high. "I've had friends who lost husbands. Some became rich widows, others poor. I always wondered if the money would ease the passing."

"And?"

She stopped abruptly. "What a beautiful store."

She looked at the window of a jeweler's shop by the name of Foxword's. It didn't advertise necklaces or rings. In its window lay all kinds of pocket watches, cravat pins, and snuffboxes. As I peered into the store, I found swords and pistols on display as well.

"I must confess, with all the excitement lately, I haven't even considered a Christmas present for Edward. Come. Help me choose something."

Something in me resisted as she pulled on my arm. I wasn't sure I trusted Lady Thomas, and going into a weapons shop with her seemed unwise. If she entertained even a notion that I killed her husband, I wasn't sure I'd come back out.

But it was a silly thought. Lady Thomas would not murder me using a piece of merchandise in the middle of an uppity downtown store.

Edward would be furious.

I followed her in, and a warm, polite man dressed in tweed and a tightly trimmed beard greeted us.

"A most cordial welcome to Foxword's Jewelry. What brings you in today, my lady?"

"How do you do? I'm afraid I've been neglectful of my motherly obligations in finding my son a Christmas gift."

"Fear not, ma'am. Perhaps a pocket watch or a signet ring? We could stamp your family's crest in a matter of days."

He brought us in and produced several pieces of men's jewelry. Each of them was worth more money than my father would have earned in a year. There were shining gold cuff links, beautifully jeweled rings, and cane handles with intricately carved details. After a while, I couldn't tell the difference between one and another. It was all a blur of shine.

"I'm not seeing something that would suit him. Do you have anything more adventurous?"

"Adventurous?" the shopkeeper asked.

"My son is quite sporting, you may say."

"Of course. Right this way." He gave a knowing glance and led us to a different corner of the shop where the beautiful swords and pistols hung on the wall, gleaming with danger. My thoughts flashed back to the battle I had witnessed inside the book of poetry.

"They are all so beautiful," Lady Thomas said, clasping her hands together. "Might I see that one?" She pointed to a pistol with a long snout and a hammer carved into a wolf's mouth.

"An elegant choice, my lady. You have a keen eye." He displayed the pistol on a counter nearby, a cloth draped behind it. Lady Thomas had an almost wild look in her eye. I had to remind myself that the pistol wasn't loaded. "Over a hundred years old. Lost by a French aristocrat during that madness across the channel."

Lady Thomas touched the weapon gently.

"Would you give us just a moment?" she asked. The man hesitated. "Oh, don't worry. I won't shoot anyone."

They both laughed. I didn't. He busied himself elsewhere in the store. Meanwhile, I started plotting escape routes.

"Have you ever shot a gun?" she asked me.

I stumbled, trying to respond. Was this why we were here? Was she going to interrogate me about her husband's murder? I had to give her credit. Edward never considered that I may have forced his father to hang himself at gunpoint. I wondered what type of man would prefer the noose to the firing squad.

"No," I said.

"Never? Surely, you've held a pistol before, though."

I shook my head.

"The working class has little access to such a weapon. Nor would I have a reason for such access."

"The working class," she echoed. "I remember. It seems like a lifetime ago. I was so desperate to leave that life. Luke and I both were. I never considered the problems that come with advancement." She turned to me. "Would you like to hold it?"

When she insisted, I reached out and felt the cool metal and smooth wood of the gun's hilt in my hand. It was heavy and powerful. It would have made an effective club, if not a firearm. To think that lethal force could burst from a tool even a woman like me could hold in my hand—it filled me with reverence and fear all at once.

Out of the corner of my eye, I noticed Lady Thomas staring at me with a fierce intensity. She tracked my hands, my facial expressions, even the way I shifted my shoulder to heave the thing.

"You are a delicate thing," she said, more to herself than to me. "I hear when you fire one of these weapons, the force of it knocking back into you can leave a nasty bruise. Earlier pistols could break an arm."

I put the weapon down on the counter.

"I can imagine. Have you had occasion to experience such kickback, Lady Thomas?"

She shook her head.

"Though, I will say I'm not a poor shot with a bow." She beckoned to the shopkeeper. "It's beautiful. My son will love it."

"Of course, my lady."

"Deliver it to Edward Thomas at Macdonald Randolph's with a

message! Do you have a pen?" The attendant brought her a small parchment. "Not to open until the twenty-fifth. Happy Christmas, with much affection." She signed her name. "Won't you sign as well, dear?"

"I couldn't. It's your gift."

"You helped pick it out. Come, come. Don't make an issue of it."

Lady Thomas was clever—much more clever than she let on. This was the second time in days that I had been outwitted. How was I to sign this card, in the awkward improvised hand of Sarah Primrose or the natural flow of my true signature?

I narrowed my eyes. It was my turn to do something surprising.

I took the pen and boldly signed my name as she watched on.

Luella Winthrop.

I was afraid to look at her. I had just confirmed her suspicions that I was the woman suspected of her husband's murder. As the man left us to package the pistol, she clutched my arm.

"It's nice to meet you, at last, Miss Winthrop," she said.

Chapter Twelve

Goodbye Miss Primrose

We sat in a carriage that did not move. From what I could tell, Lady Thomas hired it for the sole purpose of this conversation. She sat across from me, our knees almost touching. Steam formed from her breath as we waited for the chamber to warm up.

"It's refreshing to be treated like an adult," she said.

"I never intended to deceive you."

Since the shop, I fluctuated between fear for my person and confusion at the pleasure she took from discovering the truth of my identity.

"When I came to Fernmount, I was still in such a daze," I continued. "I had never left Dawnhurst before, and to do so without warning in such circumstances shook me deeply."

It was liberating to speak even partial truths to her.

"All Edward told me was that he was bringing a woman home who had been publicly attacked because of a progressive article she wrote. I didn't even get a name until the note he left me before chasing after you. Primrose. I thought you were a prostitute."

She sighed and looked out the window.

"So, what now?" I asked.

"What, indeed. I'm sitting in a carriage with the woman accused of killing my husband."

"But you don't believe it, do you?"

"Edward doesn't. He seems to think it's impossible that you could have forced Luke into that noose. I had thought perhaps at gunpoint, but given how you handled that pistol. Pathetic."

The compartment was getting warmer now. I was getting uncomfortable in my winter clothes, though I suspected that wasn't just from the temperature in the carriage.

"There's no point in asking you outright, either," she said. I let out a breath of relief upon hearing this. If she had asked me, I didn't know what I would say. "It wouldn't be the first time that old Sergeant Cooper messed something up. If you knew half the stories Edward has told me, you'd second-guess a thing or two about that city of yours."

She studied me shrewdly. The way her bonnet framed her face made her look like a hawk.

"Why won't you defend yourself?"

"Would it sway your opinion one way or the other?"

"Absolutely not." She leaned back against her seat and straightened out as though about to make a formal announcement. "Very well. Listen carefully. If my son wasn't so taken with you, make no mistake, I would turn you into the authorities, doubts be damned. But, if Edward believes you're innocent, I will force myself to share his conviction at present."

I could not have asked for a better Christmas present. It must have showed on my face. I choked back a few tears of relief.

"I'm not finished," she said, sticking a finger in the air. "Just because I'm giving you the benefit of the doubt does not mean I'm prepared to bless your union with my son."

I opened my mouth to protest.

"And don't tell me that the two of you aren't engaged. That is the most ridiculous thing I've ever heard. What is the formality of an engagement compared to such a flippant disregard for the morality of our society? Your innocence is only the most basic prerequisite to associating with my son. What it earns you is a clean slate. I would like to get to know you the same way I would become acquainted with any other suitor."

I was crying now, quietly, and with no small portion of shame attached.

"Oh, wipe off those tears. Women should cry only when useful. You'll join me at the theater tonight, and we shall try to get acquainted the appropriate way."

"Tonight? I—"

"Not a word. It's not up for discussion. And Edward isn't coming, either."

It was a fair exchange for her not reporting me to the authorities. I planned to pore over Poems from the Wanderer again that evening in an attempt to enter its magical world again. If anything, I needed to prove to myself that I hadn't conjured the whole thing up. The book would be there when I got back from the theater, though.

"I have nothing to wear," I said.

"That is easily remedied."

The package I saw the poor hotel employee lugging up to our room had apparently been for me. When Lady Thomas opened it, my jaw dropped.

This was the second gown the Thomas family purchased on my behalf. Edward bought me something on our way to Fernmount. When I saw its dark green fabric and daring cut, in all honesty, it felt sensual. The thought that he picked out for me, imagined me in it...

A dress chosen by a prospective mother-in-law does not invoke the same feelings.

But it was beautiful.

The crimson bodice swept up into sleeves accented by soft white mink. The skirt trailed in dramatic folds to the ground. It was all set off by a pair of white velvet gloves and a heavy deep green cape. Thankfully, it covered each area of my body that still bore the sores from my episode the night before.

"I thought that it was a bit ostentatious, but that's what youth is for," Lady Thomas said. "Besides, it's close enough now to Christmas that it will be appropriate. It's a fitting theme anyway for Handel."

Christmas. Although it surrounded me in shop decorations and hidden underneath the chill of winter, it still seemed worlds away.

I always was fond of Christmas. Even after my parents died, Anna and I always made a special effort to make the holiday meaningful.

Truthfully, some years it didn't take much to make the day special. A batch of iced buns when we'd gone a long while without or a new ribbon or bonnet was enough.

I found it odd that God refused to be ignored at Christmas. The local churches busied themselves with double their normal efforts to remind all about the mystery penned by the apostle Luke, a man with the audacity to claim a virgin conceived and bore a child.

Perhaps it was the cynic in me, but I always resisted such a message. Then again, before this year, I never believed in magic either. For the first time in my life, I felt a human pity for the saint.

As I stared in a looking glass, I wondered how different things might have been if a less malevolent magic had possessed me. Would I be so despondent if a magical creature made of Christmas cheer haunted my dreams? Mr. Dickens' ghost of Christmas present seemed merry enough.

"Mother, I hope you didn't-" Edward froze few paces from the door of our suite. His eyes drunk me in like hot cider. It made me feel warm all over, and I instinctively turned away, shy and giddy to learn that perhaps I still had some allure for him.

"I'm sorry. Excuse me." He stuttered.

"What is it, Edward?" Lady Thomas asked with a knowing smile.

"Miss Primrose and I were just making plans for the evening."

"Miss Primrose—plans? Where are we going?"

"You are going anywhere you like, other than the Sheldonian. It's time your friend and I became better acquainted. Handel's Messiah is playing, and you know how I love music, even music written by Germans."

Lady Thomas put a hand on my back and pivoted me gently toward her son. I stood facing opposite him with nowhere to hide. His gaze landed on me and sprung away to anything else in the room. I was flattered but also aware of a peculiar summation that I was serving out one of Lady Thomas' little tests. She probed and observed incessantly. In some ways, she reminded me of my old neighbor, Mrs. Crow. They were both information gatherers. Mrs. Crow did it to gossip with the baker. Lady Thomas, perhaps, enjoyed more ambitious motives.

"Mother, I wanted to—I was going to invite her to my own activity."

"An activity, were you? Well, it is a shame you've arrived in second place, then," Lady Thomas said. "Heavens, this morning really was rather eventful. So much walking. I'm going to go and lie down for a few hours. Edward, dear, would you ask the management if they won't have some lunch brought up?"

She put a hand to her back and winced as she trailed off to her room, leaving Edward alone with me, still dressed for an evening out.

"She's toying with you," I said when I heard her door close.

"My mother has toyed with me my entire life." He shook his head. "I about passed out when I saw her whisking you off this morning."

"I was afraid, too," I said. "There's no telling how a woman may behave when she believes someone guilty of murder."

"She doesn't believe that."

I shrugged my shoulders. "It was good that we went out. I told her my true name."

Edward gaped at me. And not because of the flattering gown.

"That was bold," he said.

"She knew it, anyway. If I want her to trust me, I have to open up to her."

"Open up to her? Are you prepared to tell her everything then? About the magic? About the fact that you really—" He trailed off, pursing his lips.

"That I really killed your father?" I finished his sentence for him. It gave me a terrible churning in the pit of my stomach that resurrected my aches from that morning. "Do you believe that, Edward?"

He ran a hand through his hair, disrupting its usual orderly maintenance.

"I believe you continue to do things without consulting me that may result in drastic consequences. And now... now..."

"Now what?" My voice came across more stern than I wished it. My frustration was mounting. We had danced around this issue for too long. I just wanted him to be honest with me.

"Now you look like that," he said, face flushing pink. It was not what I expected him to say.

I fumbled out several failed responses before managing an awkward "Do you like it?"

Edward rolled his eyes and headed back to the door.

"Where are you going?"

"To the library," he called over his shoulder. He turned back toward me to steal one more glance before he left.

With my entire evening planned by Lady Thomas and Edward storming off in a huff, I found myself alone with an awkward few hours to spend. I took some time to check in on Cyrus. He looked at me longingly through his cage, as though I dropped him off to play with a much younger sibling. He avoided with disdain the other dogs, which wrestled primitively around the kennel.

I spent the rest of the afternoon wishing I'd gone with Edward to the library and waiting for the performance that evening. I had slipped out of the evening gown, and into a pale linen dress. To ward off the chill, I wrapped myself in Edward's heavy coats. It didn't take long to dive into the book of poetry again.

I found Anna's letter lying in its pages like a bookmark. Edward must have put it there after I dozed off the night before. I pocketed it and picked up where I'd left off.

Had I dreamed the whole thing? The hill and the town and birds and the battle... it all seemed so real. So did the brusque discomfort of being manhandled by the masked captain.

I tried reading a poem.

Mr. Badger, Mr. Badger
  Come out from your den
  Why do all my efforts fail
  When I try to be friends?
  I look inside but I can't see
  You hiding round the bend
  I guess I'm left to wait and want
  till you emerge again.

I blinked. Michael Harris was an... unusual poet. One moment his verse was deep and cryptic, the next, it was nonsensical and childish.

I couldn't concentrate, anyway. I ruminated over Lady Thomas, our shopping trip to purchase a pistol, and her resolution to give me an audition, for lack of a better word, for her son.

I turned the page.

Then there was my exchange with Edward and the way he looked at me. He hadn't gazed at me like that since Fernmount. I wasn't sure if he was furious or if he wanted to wrap me up in his arms and kiss me.

I turned another page.

Our relationship had soured. I needed to admit that, but I kept finding brief moments, glimpses of something more than him honoring his word. There was desire there, affection. Perhaps he experienced the same longing I did. Why couldn't I just talk to him about it?

I turned another page and found it blank. It just sat there, white and empty in the middle of the book.

I flipped it back and forth, wondering if the writing had worn off with age or if it was left intentionally blank. It took me so much by surprise that I glanced around as if to check whether anyone else had seen it. But that was ridiculous. I was the only one there.

There was no one to inhibit the curious idea that took shape in my mind.

I scrambled to my writing desk, found a pen, and brought the crimson inkwell back to the diary.

For some reason, I wanted to fill in the page with a poem of my own. I dipped the pen and wrote the first thing that came to my mind. The words came from a song my father sang to me as a girl, a song I'd all but forgotten.

There was once a songbird
  dreamed of travelin'
  All around the earth
  To share her ballad
  With all who felt
  That they had lost their worth
  Oft, she sang
  And oft discouraged
  By who refused her song
  But I count the winter
  Days until
  I'll listen summer long.

I don't know why I got the impression that this page was left for me, but I put down the pen and smiled tenderly, uncovering this treasure from my memory. As I'd written the words, I was swept up in a euphoric vision of my father, tucking me into bed beside my sister Anna.

When I lifted my head, I sat on a rock beneath a tall oak tree, overlooking a marshland that disappeared into a blanket of mist. The surrounding colors were muted not in the hues of dormancy but separation, like someone forgot to rinse a garment in dye enough times. Above, the sky's parchment-textured sky loomed with clouds.

It looked just as I remembered it.

I was glad to be wearing Edward's coat. Although it wasn't cold, a breeze blew through my linen dress that made me feel vulnerable. I wrapped the coat around me like a blanket and found Anna's letter still in my pocket, a stowaway in this world of gray bluebells poking through the grass.

I expected to experience a thrill upon reentering the world. Instead, it felt more like taking a breath of fresh air. I stretched my limbs and fondly found the aches I experienced all day had vanished, as did the constant weight of my building dark magic.

As a smile spread across my face, I ruminated again over how wonderful it would be to live in this place free from the pains of the real world. But even as I basked in that lovely carefree desire, I sensed something behind me. It felt like one of my episodes was coming on but from somewhere outside of me, distant, getting closer.

Although I arrived on a different hill this time, the dark forest stretched around me in a similar rounded border as it had on the hill with the willow tree.

Something about the wood drew me in and frightened me all at once. It was shocking how quickly the light died away under the trees. The canopy must have been very dense. I walked toward the edge of the trees and peered into the darkness.

Eerily, it reminded me of the dark door from my dreams, and though no fog creature urged me onward, the dark had an attraction of its own. An impending, magnetic dread came from deep inside that wood, where the dark was so deep one might touch it.

I almost did.

Instead, the faint sound of horses' hooves distracted me.

I found I was panting and had the strange epiphany that the forest seemed upset I changed my mind. The sensation frightened me. I stumbled back from the trees.

Meanwhile, the horses crested the hillside and swooped in like lightning. They thundered in on thick flanks in thick woolly coats. I watched blankly, noticing how very similar they were to the horses I was used to, but feathers trailed behind their legs and gathered on their chests, all in marvelous blues, greens, and silvers. They were colors I'd seen before in riverbeds.

On them rode the mirror-paneled soldiers from the night before. At their head, the masked captain led them boldly, sun glinting brightly off her armor. They stopped several paces from me.

"Miss Winthrop, come with me," she said from atop her mount. In the reflection of her mask, I saw myself staring up at her like a child.

"I'd like to see Bram," I said.

The captain nodded to her soldiers, and I heard the terrible sound of weapons being drawn.

"I am not on your timetable," she replied. "Come with me, or I'll be forced to drag you behind me." With two quick gestures of her hand, two members of her company dismounted and threw me on the back of the captain's saddle before I could protest.

She didn't have to issue a command. The party took off at once. We galloped through the mist, past the hill, through the swampland, and into the town.

Chapter Thirteen

The Netherdowns

We trotted through the streets of the town, giving me a chance to confirm all that I had noticed previously. The architecture of the city and its surrounding landscape were an eclectic mix of different pages from a geography or history book. We passed through a street lined with brick storefronts and scampered up the hill in the middle of town. The castle I'd seen on my last visited loomed above us.

At various checkpoints on the way up the hill, I saw disparate groups of soldiers running through different drills and training routines. Looking at them now, I could not identify any racially distinctive features. If anything, they embodied physical characteristics stemming from many countries.

They gave us no heed as we galloped past. The captain's horse brought us straight to a tall stone tower. She got off and helped me down before heading directly through the main wood door without waiting for me to follow.

I got the impression she wasn't often disobeyed.

When I set out to find Bram, I never imagined the search would lead me inside a book, let alone a book like this one. Yet oddly, the fantasy of my surroundings didn't shock me. Perhaps the dreams that came with my condition had desensitized me to unusual realities.

I hesitated before entering, but the captain turned to hurry me along. Again, I saw myself in her mask. It was easy to read the fear in my eyes.

Inside the tower, a massive table stretched across the middle of the room, textured with topography from the surrounding area. Hills and mountains rose from its surface, and a large body of water bordered one edge. Beams of light came through from small windows high on the wall, and lit braziers stood in the corners of the room, but for what little light there was, the space was lit strangely well. I found myself searching for another light source.

Behind the table, with both hands on the map, stood the man with the robin's egg skin. To my great disappointment, Bram was nowhere to be found.

The commander looked at me and uttered a sound of disgust. He turned to a small table along the wall next to a rustic wooden chair and poured himself a drink.

"That will be all, Drycha," he said, sharply. The mirrored captain clicked her heels together and retreated from the room with a curt bow. When she left, I felt an innate sense of danger fill the room. I had no idea who this man was. Being left alone with him could yield any number of outcomes. Not only was the door closed behind us, an entire army stood at his command outside. It was smothering.

Despite the soft color of his skin, there was something about him that exhibited the impression of power.

"What are you doing here?" he asked without looking at me. He set his goblet down and strode back to the map on the table.

"I'm sorry. I'm looking for Bram," I said, obediently truthful. I had no courage to play coy.

"Yes, but we sent you back last time you came, and you returned here a day later." His voice was like a minor-keyed melody. I swallowed. "Why?"

"I'm sorry," I said. "I'm just in trouble, and I think Bram is the only one who can help me. To be honest, I'm not even sure how I got here." I backpedaled. I felt like a glass figurine around this man, transparent and easily breakable.

"There's only one way into the Netherdowns. I doubt you took it by accident." He picked up a wooden figure off the table and moved it to the end of the map. I screwed up my courage.

"Where is here, exactly?"

He unbuckled a sword belt and placed the weapon on the table before turning to me.

"How did you find it? The book, I mean." He started walking up a stone staircase that wrapped around the circular room. I followed hesitantly, assuming it was the right thing to do since he had just asked me a question.

"Find what?" I called after him.

"The Mystic Diary."

"You mean the book? Poems from the Wanderer?" A jolt of excitement coursed through me. Hearing another person acknowledge the book took a weight off of my shoulders. That the person giving me such validation lived inside said magical book was not lost on me, but I chose to ignore it.

"Is that how Bram bound it? Poems from the Wanderer? Nausea-inducing."

"I found it in Reading. A dog, Bram's pointer, led me to it." I said, climbing the steps with belabored breath. "Do you know where Bram is?"

"Cyrus? I thought he'd have had more sense than that."

"Bram?"

"Cyrus."

"You know Cyrus?"

"Do I know Cyrus?" he asked quietly to himself, mocking me. His pace up the stairs was impressive, and he didn't slow down for my benefit.

"Please, it's a tall tower, I'm struggling to keep up mister... mister..."

He stopped suddenly and turned to me.

"Bram never mentioned my name?"

I put a hand on the wall and pretended not to pant. I shook my head.

"He told you to come here, but never bothered to mention me?"

I searched for a response. No one enjoys being the accidental bearer of unwelcome news.

"That's typical, isn't it? Just typical. You think you mean something to a person." He shook his head, ruefully. "Who did you leave the diary with?"

"Leave it with?" How many questions could this man possibly have that would leave me sputtering so stupidly?

"Yes. When you came here, who did you leave behind to watch the diary?"

"No one." I stuttered.

His face went tight.

"It's just laying out, then? Anyone could walk up and read it?" He let out another derisive scoff and redoubled his efforts up the stairs. I pumped my legs to follow him. The tower didn't look so tall from outside. How long had we been climbing?

"I don't understand what the problem is. I found it unguarded in Reading."

"Lies. Cyrus was guarding it. He always guards. Bram must have cast some misguided enchantment on the animal," He called over his shoulder.

"The dog? You can't be—"

"I'd trust the diary with Cyrus before I would Bram."

Finally, we reached the top of the stairs. The man with robin's egg skin led me through a wooden door, and I immediately lost my breath. The whole world stretched before me. I had never been so high above anything.

He stood near the edge of the tower ramparts, standing with his arms crossed. I walked up beside him and took in the town below us, laid out like a piece of paper.

"How high—"

"About thirty stories by English standards."

"Thirty?" My head spun. I had seen the tower from several angles and didn't believe it was that tall. I certainly hadn't climbed thirty flights of stairs. "But the tower looked four stories at most."

"It's beautiful, isn't it?" He placed an open compass on the wall.

I couldn't reply. It was the most beautiful and peculiar thing I'd ever seen. Here, high above the mist, I saw miles in every direction. Jagged mountains dusted with snow stood like titans to the north and south. To the east, a turquoise ocean with white sea caps buffeted a rocky and impassible shoreline. The dark forest nearly encircled the town and its surrounding hills and farmlands before reaching past the western horizon in a blur of green.

A childlike part of me wanted to venture out and explore them, but there was only one road that stemmed out from the town. It led through the front gates where I'd seen the mirrored soldiers battle last night.

It was as if the territory had carved out a hole for itself in the middle of a sea of trees.

"Miss Winthrop, welcome to the Netherdowns."

"What is this place?"

"My own personal hell."

"I beg your pardon?"

"It is easy enough to navigate, though. You can see three hills at the cardinal points of south, west, and east, each marked with their own tree."

"I've seen the willow and the oak," I said. He stopped and peered at me, annoyed.

"How nice for you. The third is a walnut. They are the entrances. When you read the diary and enter the Netherdowns, you arrive at one of those hills. We have tired old sentries keeping an eye on them most of the time, but we've never had a visitor before. Just Bram's occasional comings and goings."

"It's extraordinary." So this was how birds must view the world. My gaze swept across the map and landed on the man beside me. "And what is your name?"

He looked at me with a raised, scrutinizing eyebrow, reminding me of Rebecca, Sergeant Cooper's secretary and my first proper friend in likely a decade. I wondered where she was now.

"You're infected, Miss Winthrop. It was a gamble bringing you here. I tried to say as much, but Bram is more than a little stubborn."

"Where is he?"

"I told him I needed to meet with you alone. I need to assess your intentions and your condition."

"Are you a doctor or something?" I asked.

"Or something," he replied. He walked back to the staircase door, reached inside, and produced a stool.

"Sit."

I cautiously obeyed, and he grabbed me roughly by the chin. He brought his face inches from mine, staring intensely into my eyes.

"What are you doing?"

"Diagnosing you. Stay still."

I snorted. "I hardly think you can diagnose someone just by looking at them."

He let go of me and pulled back.

"You're very intelligent, aren't you?" He curled his lip, stood up, and headed toward the stairs.

"Well?" I called after.

"Well, I think you should go. Bram does not understand what burns inside of you. I'm not about to set it loose on my home."

I ran to him and put a hand on his arm. He looked at it like I'd just insulted royalty.

"Please, I know there's something wrong with me. That's why I came here in the first place. Bram is the only one who can cure me."

He plucked my fingers from his sleeve.

"Bram cannot cure this," he turned his back on me, and my heart sunk.

"There must be a way."

He stopped again and turned back to scrutinize me, a judicious eye assessing me all over.

"Please, help me. Or do you support Bram's malicious interference in the life of a wretched woman?"

These last words moved something behind his eyes. I don't think he appreciated being compared to Bram.

"We can start small. At least tell me your name," I said.

"You may call me Hirythe."

"Hirythe," I echoed. It was safe to say he was the first man of that name I'd ever met. "I'm Luella."

"I know," he said.

Whatever progress I was making was severed instantly by the sounds of screams below. He ran past me to the tower's edge.

I fear those sounds may never leave me. An unseen force dragged me back to the edge beside him. There, far below us, Hirythe's troops scrambled to arm themselves as what looked like a giant, terrible cat swept its razor claws through their ranks. It was at least three times the size of any lion or tiger I'd read about, and its coat rippled in a sheer pattern of white, gray, and black just as the monsters from the night before. When I looked into that coat, I wanted to curl up inside of it and fall asleep.

"Drycha! The nets!" Hirythe called down with an uncommonly loud voice. He whirled around and ran back into the tower.

By the time I got to the stairs, he was already on the ground floor, an impossible feat except that I saw the tower now only had three stories. I descended as quickly as I could. The surrounding stone failed to keep the sounds from outside at bay. The hissing roars of the cat mixed with the wails of injured and dying soldiers in a terrible chorus. I didn't want to exit the tower, but it seemed so wrong to cower inside of it.

I burst through the door, my heartbeat throbbing in my ears from taking the stairs so quickly. The cat was even more monstrous now, its coat even more alluring. Hirythe's troops had mobilized sharpened staves and tried to surround the beast. The cat spat wildly, seeing sharp points on all sides. Hirythe stood behind a group of men with a large barbed net. Drycha led the advance, a portion of the netting in her hand.

Then, to my horror, the cat lifted its arm and swept three armed soldiers into its coat. There were some shouts and then nothing. They were simply gone, swept into the dark pattern. No weapons, armor, or any portion of their bodies remained.

Drycha wasted no time. She tied her end of the rope around a stone, sprinted forward and hurled it over the creature's back. Soldiers on the other side caught it and heaved mightily. The cat roared and hissed as it felt the barbs of the net close in on its back, but slowly the cat collapsed on its stomach.

"Mark its tail," Hirythe cried too late. The beast's tail lashed out like a tentacle and swept a soldier under the net, where he vanished into the creature's coat like his comrades.

The mirrored fighters gave the tail a wide berth after that, and the violence seemed to be over. We were left with a terrifying and massive creature that growled menacingly under the net.

I stepped forward, and the beast acknowledged me, locking its eyes with mine.

"What is it?" I asked aloud.

"I might ask you that question." Hirythe's voice was biting.

"Me?"

"You're the one that brought it here. Take her," he called to his soldiers. Several hands grabbed me by the arms. I didn't struggle. What would be the point? This outfit had just subdued an unholy monster. They could easily manage me.

Besides, the cat continued to look at me, unblinking.

Drycha came forward and thrust a gloved hand into the pocket of my coat. I protested by instinct.

"Get your hands off that." I glared, trying to menace her, but I had no threat against a woman like that. She produced Anna's folded letter and held it up.

"What is that?" Hirythe asked me.

"A giant cat."

"Check your cheek, woman. What is this?" He took the letter from his captain and fluttered it in my face.

"It's nothing. A letter from my sister." A hot flush crept up my neck. For some reason, I didn't want him to read it. He unfolded it anyway, his eyes moving furiously.

"Where is she?" he demanded.

"You just read it. What. Do you think?"

He looked up at me slowly.

"You can't stay here. Drycha, go fetch the bottle."

"Please," I said, trying no invoke whatever womanly sympathy I could conjure. Hirythe walked toward me, crumpling the letter, and stuffed it back into my pocket.

"Do not come back this time, Miss Winthrop. If you do, we will have no choice but to fire on you."

"Kill me?" I gasped. None of this made sense. The soldiers let me go, withdrew a pace, and drew arrows. I heard the creak of bowstrings. Adrenaline shot through me.

"What about Bram?" I yelled. "I need him to cure me!"

"Then he can do it in the real world," Hirythe said.

Drycha surfaced again from the tower with a bottle covered in markings that reminded me of the pen I used to write our magical stories.

"When will that be?" I asked.

"If I have it my way, quickly."

I panicked. All of this was so strange. This place couldn't exist. And what? Bram was hiding somewhere inside of it? He would have come here for a reason. I refused to be helpless anymore. I wouldn't be forbidden to return and find him.

I looked at the hissing cat, at the surrounding soldiers. I felt the crumpled paper in my pocket and my anger building, not a dark magical anger, but a wounded, sad realization. For the first time, I was angry with Anna.

She had left me when I needed her most. I knew she was younger, but I was her sister. On many occasions, I had clung to that letter as my only means of warding off the darkness, but the darkness had taken me, anyway. And now, when I was finally making strides toward righting my condition, somehow, her letter sealed my expulsion.

I walked past Hirythe and ignored the weight of fifty pointed arrows tracking my movement. I found the closest torch and lifted the letter to the flame.

The hesitation came too late. It was already ablaze, and the flames licked down the paper hungrily, singing the tips of my fingers. I let it fall as tears worked their way to my eyes, but I refused to cry today.

When I looked back to the commander, his soldiers had lowered their weapons, and Drycha stood next to him.

"Well, commander, she's not all that stupid," she said.

Chapter Fourteen

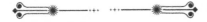

The Phantom Battalion

"It seems like just yesterday Bram told me about you for the first time."

Hirythe sat across from me in a beautiful study. We were in a stone house beside the fountained courtyard I saw the night before. The interior was decorated in a very masculine sort of way with swords and pistols adorning the walls, dark smoking-room colors, and a heavy emphasis on naturally finished wood, brick, and stone. Heavy rugs blanketed the floor, and rich muslin curtains hung over the tall windows.

Hirythe sat, legs crossed, behind a large executive desk, beside a few curious instruments I imagined were for nautical navigation. He had discarded his mirrored armor and paid the weather no mind in a linen shirt and moleskin breeches.

"I tried to convince him to leave you well enough alone." His jaw clenched and unclenched. Drycha, dressed similarly to her commander except she had not removed her mask, poured several cups of tea at a small bar cart by the bookshelves. The linen shirt outlined a surprisingly slender form, given her athletic prowess in battle.

"But that always was Bram. He suffers from the same condition you do, though it's a much more dire case."

I took the cup from Drycha, who retreated to lean against a wall by the door, gracefully sipping her own tea.

"Bram is addicted to magic?" I asked. Hirythe rolled his eyes.

"I'm addicted to magic. It's taken Bram like a parasite. There is a fine difference between an addiction and an unbridled dependency."

He stood and produced sugar, honey, and some treacle from a drawer in the desk. He added all three to his tea. "Would you care for some?"

I nodded and accepted two spoonfuls of sugar.

"Bram entertains several magical entities. I believe he has given up any hope of being rid of them."

My heart sank. I was relying on him to find a cure for me. If he couldn't treat his own maladies, how could he help me?

"The poor wretch," I said. The teacup was warm in my hands. "Here I am struggling with just the fog creature."

Hirythe nearly spit out his tea.

"The what?" he asked.

"The fog creature."

"Bram said you were a writer."

"I am—was—what does that have to do with anything?"

"You ran into the most extraordinary occurrence of your life, and the best name you can conjure is fog creature?"

I blushed.

"Well, what do you call it?" I said with a sour expression.

"It's proper given name."

"It has a given name?" I asked.

"Everything has a given name if someone gives a name to it."

"If you're done being petty, maybe just tell me."

"Sraith," Drycha chimed in. "Its name is Sraith." The name sounded so melancholy on her lips. She stared at the table as she took another sip of tea.

"That's one of its names," Hirythe replied. "It comes from an old Irish word meaning chain."

I understood why.

"For bondage," I nodded.

"You're wrong. Though it's not a poor peripheral. Sraith is a monster that feeds on the feelings of people like you. It's not interested in binding you. It wants you to feel more so it can feed more."

I bit my lip. "Everything turns to fury inside of me. I assumed that it eats my positive feelings and replaces them with anger somehow."

"Not everyone gets angry, though most get hostile. It depends on the person."

"Well, why does Sraith make me so angry?"

Hirythe stole a glance with Drycha.

"It amplifies what's inside of you."

I fought against the implication. I was not an angry person deep down. I wasn't.

"I don't want to believe that," I said, shaking my head.

"That must be hard," he said, taking a long draught from his cup.

I clenched my fists and remembered all the moments my emotions had overwhelmed me. They felt natural. They had started small. I hadn't even noticed something was wrong until it was too late.

"I see you're not an angry person at all," Hirythe said, motioning to my balled fist and iron grip on my teacup. I blew out an exasperated sigh.

"What will happen to me?" I asked, fearing the answer What was the finish line? Would this monster, Sraith, slowly eat away at me until I was nothing but anger? "Am I going to lose my mind?" My voice broke.

"You'll have to manage your symptoms," Hirythe said casually.

"Manage symptoms? You mean the symptoms of violent outbreaks? The life I've been living the past six months? No. I can't."

"Outbreaks? What? Have you run out of ink?"

"Ink?"

"Yes, ink. Bram told me he left you an inkwell full of it. Haven't you been using it to ward off the attacks?" Hirythe looked at me like I was a foolish girl refusing her medicine. I visualized the crimson inkwell sitting on the table in my room.

"You mean to tell me that the ink would have warded off my attacks?" I tried to slow my breathing. The idiot. The absolute idiot.

"Why else would Bram have given it to you?"

I threw my head back and stared at the iron chandelier above me. The inkwell hadn't been a romantic gift. I might have killed him were he in the room. I had guessed the true magic behind my stories lay in the ink for some time, but to imagine it was an antidote...

"Bram told me using the magic would increase my dependency," I said.

"Well, sure. But compared to how much you were using to write your stories, we're talking about a negligible amount. Most medicine is just poison in small, careful doses."

I buried my head in my hands, sensing the sores around my wrists where the leather straps had worked to constrain me. All of this pain...

I knew what he said was true. Hadn't Bram used the ink to calm one of my episodes in his tent? And, just the other day, I had inadvertently done the same after entering the dark door in my dreams and finding the inkwell.

How did I miss it before?

"I will kill him," I said.

"There's a queue," Hirythe replied. "It's a shame that he developed such feelings for you. I can't imagine a sloppier way to integrate someone into magic."

My head reeled. I had been looking for answers for so long, and Hirythe just spat them out like the seeds of an apple.

"This book was in his chest of magical trinkets," I said dumbly.

"Among other things," Drycha chimed in. I had almost forgotten she was there.

"Why didn't he tell me anything?" I asked. I blinked back tears, remembering when I inquired about the chest, how he waved it in front of me and yanked it away.

"Because he's a fool." Hirythe said. "I think he wanted to impress you. I don't know how this whole courting thing works. I've seen birds build nests. Deer grow antlers. Why he thought this would woo you is beyond me."

"Bram believes that human beings can quickly become seduced by an abundance of knowledge in this topic." Drycha cut in, shooting a dirty look at her commander.

"Still a fool. Rather than allow others to make informed decisions, he prefers to withdraw the opportunity to decide for themselves." Hirythe stood and walked to a polished stone globe. He spun it gently and traced his finger across its surface.

I gawked at him.

"Those are tall words for someone who refused to tell me anything an hour ago," I said.

He rolled his eyes.

"I knew you would say that. I hoped that we had avoided whatever nasty things you brought into the Netherdowns. I was wrong."

"The cat? I brought in that cat?"

"Yes," Hirythe said.

"Most likely," Drycha corrected.

He eyed his captain for a moment and stopped the spinning globe.

"Drycha, I'd like to speak with Miss Winthrop alone if you wouldn't mind."

Despite her mask, I detected the briefest flash of annoyance, but she swept it away quickly. She put her cup down and left through a sturdy wooden door. Hirythe's gaze followed her, and he waited until we heard the door close behind her downstairs before talking.

"Should I be frightened?" I asked him with an unamused look on my face.

"Yes, but humans never embrace fear. That's what makes you so predictable."

"Humans?" I echoed.

Hirythe strode to a desk, folded his fingers, and sat down, "Do you know where you are?" he asked.

"Inside the book. The Mystic Diary, as you call it."

"Yes, but have you put together what the Netherdowns is?"

He leaned forward over a desk covered in newspaper clippings, small frames, and glass bell jars.

I shook my head.

"We made this world as a refuge." He turned a frame around, revealing a torn photograph. I studied it. A group of five people stood on the deck of a ship. I saw Hirythe standing in a smart jacket and waistcoat, a terse expression on his mouth. Bram stood next to him, his coat slung over his shoulder and his arm around a beautiful dark-skinned woman. I looked closer.

Her dark hair was done up under a military-style cap, long wavy trails escaping down her shoulders. She smiled brightly. A man's shirt was tucked into a gray skirt.

"Bram looks so happy here," I said.

"He was," Hirythe nodded, grimly.

Beside the woman stood a large athletic man with a square jaw and beard, his shoulders and chest bursting from his vest. For some reason, he looked familiar, though I couldn't place why. Beside him was an Italian, if I had to guess. The photograph was torn beside him, leaving only a slight hint of another figure beside them.

Letters were scribbled in pencil along the bottom. H under Hirythe, O and L beneath the woman, B and L below Bram, R and R under the Italian. N and E under the large man, and J and E along the tear. I presumed they were initials.

Unbidden, something Bram had told me about his magic pen and ink came to my mind. Several friends had died to find it.

"What is this photo?"

"We called ourselves the Phantom Battalion. We were dedicated to locating and hunting down objects of otherworldly power." He spun the photo back around to study it himself. "It was Bram's idea. He was always convinced life was filled with phenomena neither he nor any member of the human race could explain. When he met me, I proved him right."

He put the glass ball down.

"How did you do that?" I asked.

"I explained them to him, and I'm not a member of the human race."

I should have been surprised. From the faintly wrong hue of his skin to his air of arrogance about the weakness of others. The way he flaunted it now seemed almost like he was begging me to ask him about it. Out of spite, I refused.

Instead, I took the photo from the desk and found myself looking at the woman again. Beside her, Bram smiled, younger and lighter than I'd ever known him, despite the time I'd spent with him this past autumn. The man in this photo looked more like a brother than the vagabond himself.

"What did you explain?"

"I told him that magic was as real as the stone in the ground. There are different kinds, and it doesn't fit neatly into any packages. However, you can follow traces to sources of such magic if you manage to find some that humans haven't already tainted or eradicated."

He stood and strode lazily over to a spent fireplace flanked by mounted taxidermies.

"You mean there are ways to find maps? It's a bit like treasure hunting?"

"It's not treasure."

"Call it what you will." I moved from my seat by the desk to a tufted leather sofa. "Where did you find my magical trinket, the ink?"

He fingered a pinecone he found on the mantle and looked past me, his mind anywhere but in the room.

"We didn't. We found the magic. Bram was the one who bound it to the ink. For all of his flaws, he is resourceful. The ink, and any other trinket he collected, finds power from a magical principle."

"So, what magical principle powers the ink?"

"Cause and effect." He tossed the pinecone into the hearth, and it burst into a healthy, warm fire. I grabbed a patterned tartan blanket from the back of the couch and pulled it close.

"You mean to tell me the ink is a distilled manifestation of cause and effect?"

"Yes, though oddly, we haven't found many accounts of people describing it as a fog creature. You must have quite the case. Most people try to ignore it altogether, and their relations gradually look down on them as they spiral into narcissism and madness. They don't realize it's magic. Humans rarely do. For all the progress your scientists make in medicine and industry, they decimate the foothold that magic has held against humanity for thousands of years."

"Are humanity and magic at war?"

"Magic doesn't share such ambition. But, like a forest felled for lumber, magic is exploited to benefit your lifestyle. As your learned men unravel its secrets, magic's power decreases and crystallizes."

He looked up at a taxidermy lion mount.

"Even the echo of the magic suits your purposes. You don't realize you only have the frozen husk of what was once a living thing."

He paced slowly across the room. I shook my head.

"Please, forgive me. I'm struggling to understand."

He stopped by a standing suit of armor.

"Take something like electricity. What once ruled the skies and sparked fires across forests is now managed by nothing less crude than a metal bar on top of a building. Not only that, it's been dissected and replicated to be a more efficient version of fire. And there's no telling how it will be used in the future."

I picked at the wool in the blanket.

"But surely every time science progresses it doesn't sound the end for another magical principle," I said. "One day there wouldn't be any magic left." I tried to imagine a world devoid of magic. It was a world filled with Luella Livingstons.

"I don't fear magic's eradication," Hirythe said, taking the sword from the armor beside him and hefting it experimentally. "For one, humans are too lazy. There are so many ways to accomplish one thing.

Why go to the trouble of a new magical discovery if they could just bend something science has already unraveled to a similar end? Besides, some types of magic are stronger and more elusive than others."

My head spun. Hirythe's suggested view of the world was breathtaking and arduous. How could one choose between magic and science when one was so beautiful and the other so necessary?

"It's about time for you to go. Your presence endangers the Netherdowns."

"You said that, but I still don't know how."

"Bram created the Mystic Diary. Can you suppose what magic he used to do so?"

I bit my lip.

"Well, what is the diary's purpose?" I said after puzzling for a moment. "What's the purpose of this world at all?"

Hirythe smiled.

"You're starting to ask the right questions. Bram created the diary to hide important things. If you had to hide something where no one could find it, a place locked to all others, where would you put it?"

I couldn't think of any place like that. Surely even the greatest vaults have means of being opened.

"Let me put it another way," he said after seeing me struggle for an answer. "What do you cherish most?"

The words tumbled out as a hoarse whisper.

"My father."

He smiled again.

"Where do you keep your father?"

"My memory."

"Welcome to the Netherdowns, Miss Winthrop," he said with a broad sweep of the hands, "where every stone, tree, and blade of grass is forged by memory."

I looked out the window and saw the varied architecture outside. I thought about the flocks of mismatched birds and the forest made of trees I didn't recognize.

"Bram made all of this from memory? How can one person remember so much?" I wondered aloud. I knew Bram roamed with the carnival, but I never imagined it would travel so far and see so many things.

"One person did not," Hirythe said, hitting me with the bottom of a drape to get my attention. "He is crafty. He convinced me he was using a different principle to create the book, so I lent him a portion of my own magic. It was much too late before I realized what his true intentions were."

I knitted my eyebrows and considered the mirrored soldiers, the feathered horses, and the army of mirage monsters.

"Your memory, too?" I asked. He nodded.

"Bram combined our memories to make a world of safekeeping. He didn't foresee that some things exist in our memory even if we can't or choose not to recall them. The memories of a twenty-five-year-old human are one thing, but when he added mine..."

He shook his head sadly out the window.

"You've seen real trauma," I suggested. He turned to me. A grim shadow covered a part of his face.

"I've seen terror incarnate."

Instinctively, my hand rose to his shoulder to comfort him. He ducked away, graceful as a cat, and went back to the desk.

"Now you are here," he said. "Which poses significant problems. It's possible, somehow, that you could inadvertently, or not so inadvertently, add your own influence to this diary."

Visions of the giant cat whose coat consumed soldiers like quicksand flashed through my memory.

"The cat was me?" I gaped.

"A part of you. You brought it in on the back of that letter."

"I'm so sorry," I said, remembering the felled soldiers. "I didn't know!"

He sighed and leaned back in the large, throne-like chair behind his desk.

"That's enough for now." He rubbed his temples as if he had a headache.

"Enough?" I said. "This is just the beginning. I thank you for telling me about the inkwell, but there's only so much ink in there. I can't hold off the fog creature forever."

"Sraith."

"Whatever its name is."

He stood.

"Seeing as I can't seem to keep you away from the Netherdowns, on your next visit, we can sit down with Bram and figure something out. For now, Drycha will send you back."

"What if I don't want to go—"

"Enough!" Hirythe spoke softly, but the power from his voice sent a shock wave through the room. My hair swept behind me as if a large gust of wind blew by. Papers ruffled into the air, the fire sputtered, and the photo of the Phantom Battalion fell on its back.

The merry cadre stared up at me as Hirythe breathed heavily.

"Please. Not all cats can be trapped in a net."

I nodded meekly and turned. Drycha waited outside the study at the bottom of a narrow staircase.

"Would you like to sit or stand?" she asked.

I sat down on one of the stairs, and she dabbed a piece of cotton with the scent in the bottle, the strange aroma from Bram's carnival.

"Drycha, please before I go." She paused, and I nodded behind me. "What is Hirythe? How does he know so much about magic, and why does he look so empty?"

Drycha's shoulders fell as she considered my request.

"Commander Hirythe is the last living fae," she said at last.

When I arrived back in my room at the hotel, a tear trailed down my cheek.

Chapter Fifteen

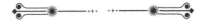

Thomas Family Magic

Melancholy accompanied me back to the real world, and as I pushed it down my throat, I found my dull anger ready, as always, to flare up as soon as I lowered my guard.

I looked around the room for the crimson inkwell. I finally had a weapon to fight my condition. It sat on a small writing table next to a chair, on which lay my beautifully festive green gown—

I jumped off the bed.

What time was it? I had completely forgotten about the theater with Lady Thomas. No. That wasn't fair! I had finally unearthed answers about my condition, about the fog creature. Why did those have to come at the expense of any semblance of a relationship with my possible mother-in-law?

I threw my coat off and practically jumped into the dress, doing my best to make it fit the way one of the hotel maids had that afternoon. I managed to tighten the corset a fraction of the proper amount. It would have to do. I spun the heavy cape around my shoulders and left the suite, one glove on the other.

It's amazing how much a determined woman in a beautiful gown can get accomplished if she speaks directly. I did my best impression of Lady Thomas, and I was in a carriage bound for the Sheldonian in a matter of minutes.

How was I so stupid? She was going to give me the benefit of the doubt. She needed me to show that I could be a proper match for her son. Did I really blow off her invitation before the sun set?

The carriage briskly rounded cobblestone corners. The driver sensed my urgency, and soon the theater came into view.

Even amid my frantic anxiety, it took my breath from me. A beautiful octagonal building jutted up from the ground like a marvelous wedding cake. It was surrounded by a cast-iron gate, heads of important men carved in stone on pillars all around. A central tower rose like a lighthouse from the roof, calling all those who appreciate the arts, storytelling, and culture.

I swallowed my emotions. My father had taken me to the theater a handful of times as a girl, but it wasn't even Dawnhurst's finest. They were small houses with amateur performers, usually halfway or fully inebriated. Still, I loved the plays we saw there together.

The full weight of Lady Thomas' invitation struck me. Not only had I neglected her, I missed the opportunity of a lifetime. To pull up to the theater as an important guest, to be her evening's exclusive companion. It was a station I had never dreamed of.

I stepped out of the carriage and immediately heard a muffled choir chanting angelic choruses through the walls. Theater attendants escorted me to the front and asked to see my ticket.

"I'm here with Lady Thomas. I'm afraid I am a bit late," I said sheepishly. My first public affair and already I had to make excuses. Who knew what the theater attendants thought of me?

"Of course, my lady," a portly man in a shirt with hard-working buttons told me.

"Oh, I'm not—"

"Just wait here one moment."

He left me standing outside at the door at the sound of enthusiastic, albeit well-mannered, applause, presumably to check with Lady Thomas for my invitation. I waited, wringing my hands and fiddling with the cords of my purse, trying to pretend it wasn't as cold out as it was.

Soon, he reappeared.

"Lady Thomas has a seat beside her. I will escort you at the next break in the music."

"Thank you," I gushed, more audibly relieved than was dignified. At least she hadn't abandoned me altogether. I waited, listening to the sound of a beautiful soprano warm the air.

There were shepherds abiding in the field,
  Keeping watch over their flocks by night.

When the solo ended, the portly man motioned with two fingers, and I followed.

When the doors opened, my mouth dropped, and my heart sank. Hundreds of eyes fell on me. Apparently, the doors at the Sheldonian were located directly behind the performers. The stage didn't have curtains or much of a backstage area. I imagined it was most likely intended for musical performances or other presentations that didn't require behind the scene workings the audience was not intended to see. Instead, seats stretched in a large arc around a circular performing area.

I entered facing the audience directly, and they got the full view of the woman not quite filling out the green, almost overly festive, gown, walking in late.

Some of us have an overabundance of luck.

My ears burned as I followed the man who shamelessly directed me to my seat. Thankfully, the music continued without a misstep, and soon I was bumping knees with several concert-goers to arrive at my seat next to Lady Thomas. A positively wicked smile stretched through her lips, and I realized she had allowed me to enter late to teach me a terrible lesson.

Still, I was in the wrong, and all I wanted to do was apologize, even though I had no idea what excuse to provide. Unfortunately, when I leaned toward her after the next chorus, she repositioned her body to send a clear signal. I would not drag her into the faux pas of chatting in the middle of a concert. I exhaled.

Instead, I examined the venue. I wished I knew how to forge locations out of memory like Bram because I wanted to show this memory to my sister one day. Beautiful cream-colored walls with practically golden swaths of light enveloped the room. The ceiling above was faintly visible, painted in a heavenly ring of beautiful fresco, punctuated with figures I didn't recognize but reverenced all the same.

I must have looked like a little girl gaping at everything. Beauty was everywhere and, being everywhere, rubbed off even on the perception I had of myself.

The music was so heavenly, the performance so masterful, and the words so encouraging, that I dared to believe in something. Though I was tainted by something dark and unholy, the angels painted above did not impose shame. Instead, I felt hope.

Perhaps I could beat Sraith. Perhaps I could earn the love of Edward's mother. Perhaps Edward and I could correct the course of our relationship.

Perhaps.

Soon, the audience was standing and applauding. The musicians bowed graciously. This went on for some time, which to me, seemed only just. Why shouldn't exquisite talent receive such high praise? I clapped exuberantly with the rest.

Lady Thomas gave me a curious look, and soon the entire audience was shuffling toward the open air where a line of carriages waited.

She offered her hand to several men and nodded across the room to many women. I saw all of their eyes roll slowly and politely to me. "Who was the woman by the side of Lady Thomas?" I almost heard them wonder.

To some, she even introduced me.

"How are you holding up?" an older woman with an heirloom around her neck asked. "What a tragedy. And where is your son this evening?"

"Edward was not invited. I insisted on a night out with my friend, Miss Primrose."

I curtsied awkwardly more than once. Despite the repetition, my form did not improve. It took us nearly an hour to get from our seats back to the carriage, and by then, I was nearly exhausted.

It wasn't until the door closed, and we started clattering back to our hotel when I received the dreaded treatment I had almost hoped was not coming.

"Well," Lady Thomas said through pursed lips, "are you going to explain yourself?"

The way she phrased the question insinuated I tried to avoid explaining, which wasn't fair at all. I tried to talk to her several times, but I was unequivocally shushed.

"Lady Thomas, I am so sorry. I hardly know what happened. I lost track of time."

"Where were you? Not out with that son of mine, I pray. I checked your room, and you weren't there."

"I wasn't?" I had wondered what happened to me when I entered the book. Part of me thought I just stayed where I was reading it, but my consciousness slipped into the Netherdowns. Apparently, that was not the case.

"Don't take me for an idiot. This isn't a game, Luella. I'm very upset. I arranged a wonderful evening for us, and I was looking forward to a chance to get to know you better. Perhaps I did."

I opened my mouth to respond.

"Save your excuses," she said, cutting me off with a wave of the hand. "I don't want to hear them. Let me make myself clear. This will not happen again. Are we understood?"

I nodded dumbly like a girl of sixteen.

"That's a good girl. Now, on to the important matters."

In minutes, I understood that the night out at the theater had very little to do with the performance and an awful lot to do with who was there and where they were sitting and with whom they arrived and left. Lady Thomas prattled off names, reminding me I shook so and so's hand, and that it was very good of me not to sneer at a certain man who had fallen out of practically everyone's favor, but then how was I supposed to know about that, and did I see the ghastly outfit of one Lady Drow?

By the time we were back at the hotel, I was dizzy, unsure even of my own name. Luella. That's right. Lady Thomas kept using it to snap me back to attention.

She boldly swung the door to our suite open, and Edward, who had a small pile of almost rotting books at the dining table, nearly jumped.

"A bit of warning wouldn't hurt anyone," he said to his mother as he collected his books and escaped to his room. He emerged a moment later.

"Aren't you reputed to be a tough police officer?" She needled him. I couldn't determine if her tone was playful or derisive. "He's back at those books again," she whispered to me. "If you are a long-term installment, do me a favor and don't let him slip back into his boyhood habits."

Boyhood habits? Had a young Edward taken a fascination with old books?

"Perhaps no criminal in Dawnhurst-on-Severn is quite as intimidating as my mother after attending the theater," Edward said as he returned from his room.

Lady Thomas looked at me.

"Do you see how terrible he can be?"

"Oh mother, don't feign a turtledove. I'm sure she knows you well enough by now to see right through it."

She raised her eyebrows.

"Am I so transparent?"

I didn't respond. I was still in reprimand for being late, and I didn't want to push my luck.

"A stained-glass window," he countered. "They have dinner waiting downstairs."

"And now you'd give me a stroke? I just arrived upstairs. I'm not some athletic tennis player, Edward. Have something brought to my room. I'm going to bed."

He sighed. "Just as well. Luella?"

"Dinner sounds lovely."

"Thank you for accompanying me tonight, Miss Winthrop," Lady Thomas said formally. It felt like a handshake for my ears.

"The delight was mine," I said with a curtsy. "Next time, I hope my company will be more enjoyable."

"It undoubtedly will be." She swept down the hall into her room.

"I'm sorry I stormed off earlier," Edward told me, between bites of his steak and kidney pie. "I just feel so out of control of everything. My own feelings included."

"We're all a little beside ourselves," I replied. I finished a turnip and potato mash and eyed a helping of glazed carrots hungrily.

"I'm happy to report that my trip to the library went well."

"It looked like you found a mountain of volumes," I said, trying to flavor my words with some encouragement.

I wiped my face with a napkin. I wanted to tell Edward about the Netherdowns, all about the magical details I learned from Hirythe—that I even met Hirythe, but something held me back. The last time I'd told him about the Mystic Diary, he made me feel so foolish. He'd said he believed me, but I couldn't erase the belittling doubt I'd seen in his eyes.

I had nothing to show for my expedition except an unusual name for my condition. There was the truth about the inkwell. I wondered how he might respond if I told him Bram's parting gift to me was also a treatment for my side effects. He was so insecure about Bram already. Perhaps it was not to drag Edward into the magic, if it were possible.

His enthusiastic leap into unknown research about the arcane made me uncomfortable. His mother's comments about his boyhood hobbies reminded me I knew less than I thought about Edward Thomas.

"I found a new librarian, and he was quite helpful. More courageous, though I never thought I'd have said that about a librarian."

"A life's devotion to books is very courageous," I countered.

"In any event, I think I found something important. It came about —"

"Edward," I cut him off, "please, let's finish our dinner first. Then, if you'd allow me to get out of this gown and into something more comfortable, we can discuss your findings in a less public place."

He nodded and washed down his impatience with a cup of cider.

When we returned upstairs, I changed into a linen skirt and blouse. I enrobed myself with Edward's large coat, more for modesty than warmth. Then I quickly found the inkwell.

Hirythe referred to it as a medication but didn't prescribe dosage or procedure. Still, I had used the ink before, albeit accidentally, for this purpose, and it worked well enough.

I was dying to test it, but I wanted to use no more than absolutely necessary. If this was my medicine, it needed to last as long as possible.

I dipped a quill into the ink and scribbled out the word "hope" before holding the paper to a lit candle. I watched the flames lick up the paper before dropping it into the candle tray below. I may have imagined it, but I thought I saw the flames form into a small fireball before snuffing out.

I sat on the bed, waiting for the liberating effect of the ink to soothe my mood, but I only became more sleepy.

Perhaps I had used it improperly.

A gentle knock sounded at the door.

"Luella, are you decent?"

What a question.

"Come in, Edward."

He poked his head through the door, sniffed the air, and fixed his gaze on the trail of smoke rising from the candle tray.

"Is everything all right?" he asked.

"Never better." I smiled at him. "Now, let's talk about your discovery."

"Right," he said, sliding over a chair and side table to display one of the old books he found. The book was ratty, and the leather binding was flaking off in dirty brown flecks. It smelled musty.

"From my reading," he continued, "there are distinct forms of enchantments or hexes."

I nodded like a governess hearing the alphabet from her student.

"Some of these enchantments revolve around accidental disturbances of magical items or failures to abide proper tradition. In the north, for example, it's customary to leave out offerings from a harvest to appease magical beings that might otherwise disturb them."

He flipped a page in the book. The text was handwritten in some pages, and it was a miracle the binding kept the thing together. Edward took a deep breath like he was preparing for something.

"In other cases, an individual enchants or hexes someone else. I found this passage about those instances."

He handed me the book. I held it gingerly. It was heavier than it looked. I read aloud.

"When witches or warlocks adequately bind a victim to such a scheme, remedies are difficult to find and harder to replicate or effectuate. However, based on folklore and first-hand accounts conducted through villages in all corners of Europe, some enterprising individuals thought to fight fire with fire. This researcher has managed to track down a spell, reportedly purchased from such a witch or warlock, that would unbind the tether between enchanter and enchantee."

My condescension toward Edward's research waned. I looked at him with concern before reading on.

"Skeptics are right to treat such claims with derision, but I cannot discredit this spell in such an offhanded manner. I found the same words, though translated, written on parchments owned by poor, uneducated, and illiterate individuals in countries across the continent and in different languages. Some owners of such transcripts admitted they did not understand what the writing on their scrap of paper said but were reticent to part with it all the same. Such independent creation is enough to silence my inner critic. Caution is to be urged, however. This spell is not to be trifled with and must only be used when one is certain its target is indeed an enemy, for great bodily harm or even death can result from the surge of its resulting power."

I stopped. Edward continued to explain.

"The author even has the nerve to name the spell after himself, Dr. Rupert's Uncantation. It's a silly play on words if you ask me—"

"Edward, why did you show this to me?" I asked carefully.

He straightened.

"I'm just sharing some of my research."

"Are you suggesting that I use this spell on Bram?" I stared at him, trying to decipher my emotions. I felt afraid and morbidly curious. Edward was my stalwart knight. Could jealousy tempt a man so far?

"Luella, it's not like that, and you know it. This is a tool, and there are many ways to use a tool."

"Such as?"

He sat next to me on the bed.

"Such as a bargaining chip. You said Bram refused to see you inside the book. If that's true, perhaps by wielding this spell, you can coerce him to do the right thing."

I furrowed my brows.

"In the event he chooses not to cooperate? What then?"

Edward put his hands nervously on his knees.

"Then you'll do what you think is right."

I shook my head.

"I can't believe what I'm hearing."

"My father is dead," he said, throwing his hand in the air and standing up. He paced the room. "I can accept that his death wasn't your fault. I can't imagine how you could have ever truly had a hand to play in it. But he's dead the same. Someone must be at fault, and if it's Bram, I don't think it's fair that he can escape justice."

I set the book aside, fearfully.

"So, we take matters into our own hands? Weren't you the one just telling me you never wanted to be a judge?"

"I don't want to be a judge. That's why I'm giving you the spell."

My hands trembled. This was not Edward. It was an impersonation, a distortion like Sraith's version of my father.

"This is vengeance, Edward. You know that."

"I don't know what it is, Luella. I trust you to do what's right with this spell. All I know is that you've told me there is no future between us until we've dealt with this. I just want to move forward."

His voice broke on the last word.

"I just want to move forward," he repeated, eyes glittering in the candlelight. "Forward."

I rushed toward him and embraced him, understanding sparking to life. With this journey, I had stolen Edward's chance at grief. It had built up inside him, compounding the pressure for weeks, months. I held him close.

"Edward, it's all right," I said, stroking his hair.

He buried his face in my shoulder and shook, struggling to swallow tears. We stood there as he attempted to regain his composure, and my heart ached for him. I wanted to erase his pain, to gather him in my arms and smother the hurt.

He pulled away from me and placed his forehead on mine. His arms flexed and gripped me tighter, pulling me closer. My breath caught, and I stared into his eyes before we both lunged into a desperate kiss.

I lost myself in him with a furious passion. The kiss wasn't sweet like it had been at Fernmount. I felt an impatience, almost an anger, emanating from both of us, as if we both believed fate had robbed time from us, but we would spite it.

I stepped backward, not sure if I was leading him or he was pushing me. I fell backward on the bed, still a captive of his embrace, still hungry for his kiss.

Then all at once, we reached a crossroads, and he took his lips from mine to look at me. I stared back, wide-eyed. I can't explain what I felt in that moment. I was concerned for him. A protective instinct swelled up in my heart so intensely that I couldn't predict what I might do or allow next.

But as Edward Thomas looked at me, I saw shame take root in him. His eyes, filled with raw, vulnerable emotion a moment before, faded into downcast shadows. He mechanically took his arms from around me and sat up on the bed.

I sat up next to him and put a hand on the back of his neck. We sat in silence, both of us boring holes into the ground with blank stares. At length, he turned to the crumbling tome on the table and tore the page containing Dr. Rupert's Uncantation out of it. He stuffed it in my coat pocket, squeezed my hand ruefully, and left the room.

Chapter Sixteen

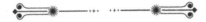

Stowaway

I woke early the next morning after tumultuous sleep. I kept dreaming about Edward, the moment on the bed, our kiss, and the spell he placed in my pocket.

I rolled out of bed and wrapped myself in a blanket before plopping down in a chair next to my window. I cracked Poems from the Wanderer open in my lap. Had Hirythe told me that Bram made this book into a portal or wrote the book himself? If the latter, I had to admit to some curiosity as to his inspiration for some of the poems.

I was eager to get back to the Netherdowns. I found myself missing the place, although I'd only ever been there twice. There was something sweet about walking through a world made of memory, even if the memory wasn't my own.

I was starting to understand how to use the book. I could almost feel the magic tug at me as I lost myself in the words. It was just as Brutus told me in that tea shop. Who knew his advice would work so well.

I blinked and closed the book. If I was going to the Netherdowns again, why would I go wearing a nightgown?

I quickly changed into what I considered practical clothes for traveling the countryside. Somewhere amidst my Sarah Primrose outfits and the gown Lady Thomas bought me, I found the trousers that I'd worn to escape Dawnhurst-on-Severn. I smiled. I had used them on an occasion or two as Edward and I traveled in disguise.

I put them on quickly, as well as a white blouse, a waistcoat, and Edward's heavy coat. I reached my hand in the pocket and clutched the spell. Perhaps Edward was right. Maybe I could use it as a negotiation tool. Shouldn't I be honoring Edward's request?

Then again, Anna's letter had summoned an enormous, vicious cat. But Anna was my sister. I had a deep emotional connection to that letter. This was nothing. A trifle. It probably didn't even work.

Catching a glimpse of myself in the looking glass wearing such masculine clothes made me feel ridiculous. Why not also wear a top hat? And a monocle?

No matter. Equipped as I was, I sat down and started reading again.

The transition wasn't as alarming as it had been during my two previous visits. I found myself on the hill with the walnut tree this time. The same forest I almost wandered into last time lay quietly foreboding behind me.

I looked into the trees again but didn't let my gaze linger. Memories of the mirage monsters skulked through my mind. I had no desire to discover what other evils lived in the depths of the wood. I wondered why there weren't fortifications here on the forest's edge.

I walked away from the tree line, trying to remember what pathway the feathered horses had taken to arrive at so quickly in town. I wished I had such a beast now.

I had made it just about to the bottom of the hill before I heard a horse's hooves. She was like a warrior angel on splendid horseback. Drycha's mirrored mask glinted in the light despite what I considered typical Netherdownian cloud cover.

She nearly jumped off the horse when she was within speaking distance.

"You came back quickly," she said.

"I'm eager to get to work."

"Finding Bram?"

"Yes," I said. She nodded her understanding.

"I am to go with you," she replied.

This was a surprise. The last time I saw her, she had hardly said two words.

"Hirythe sent you to escort me to Bram? He didn't come himself?"

She surveyed the trees.

"He has other things occupying his mind. One of our lookouts saw another group of nightmares approaching the gates. He has to prepare our company for another attack."

"Another? It hasn't been long since the last one."

"They're sporadic here. It turns out when you make a world out of memories, one of its favorite ways to fight back is to bombard you with terrors you wish you could forget."

I thought back to the gate battle. The monsters vanished from sight when they died. The soldiers did not.

"You mean to say Hirythe is fighting bad memories?"

"His. Bram's. Mine. Possibly yours now as well." She swung her legs over her horse again and held a hand out to me. "Bram is waiting for you at Hollow Lake."

I nodded, wondering if it was the body of water I'd found on my first visit. I still wasn't sure what I would do to Bram, but as the opportunity to speak with him drew near, Dr. Rupert's words made too much sense in my head. What if he was right? What if ridding myself of Bram would sever my enchantment?

Gooseflesh crawled down my arms.

I grabbed her hand, and we were off. The wind lapped my face and hair, my coat trailed behind me like the tail of a comet, and I clung to the captain. We rode through the mist, but occasionally the sun poked through the clouds, illuminating the land's unnatural and eery beauty. We were on the outskirts of the town, past the farms, and the landscape reminded me of the northern highlands—or at least what I'd read about them. As we traveled past the hills, our surroundings fulfilled all of my dreams of seeing Scotland.

I noticed streams running down the hilly landscape, forming waterfalls off of craggy outcroppings, and I wondered where the water came from. I still failed to orient myself with the abundant diversity of natural life. Evergreens stood beside elms, fruit trees, and exotic shrubs. I even found a copse of bamboo here and there. Irish moss encroaching on bamboo is a sight.

Occasionally, a river stretched by us, its water shining sharply and emanating cool air. It made me thirsty.

"Drycha, might we stop for a drink from this river?" I asked, breaking the traveler's silence.

"I thought ahead," she said as she handed me a waterskin. I did my best to smile and take gulps amidst the gallops, but it wasn't easy. I ended up coughing and sputtering.

For the first time, I wondered in earnest about the woman in front of me. I knew little of her. She was formidable, even outside of battle, and she had dropped few clues about her character or identity. Somehow, I got the impression she wasn't like the rest of the soldiers. Hadn't she just said that monsters were made of Bram's, Hirythe's, and her memories?

The road narrowed and became rockier.

"We're getting close," she said, bringing the horse to a stop. I waited.

"Well, are we going to proceed?" I asked. Drycha fidgeted and started checking the joints of her armor.

"Of course," she said haltingly. Then she dismounted. "We should walk from here." She offered me a hand down. I puffed out my chest.

"I can manage."

She withdrew her hand, and I made my best attempt at sliding gracefully off the saddle. I landed with a thump, but without falling from my feet.

The horse turned and found somewhere to graze without instruction. Drycha looked at me.

"It was smart to dress so sensibly."

"Thank you," I replied, unsure if she meant it sarcastically. She had already started steadily up the trail. I hurried to catch up.

"How much further is the lake?"

"Not far," she said, glancing over her shoulder toward the village. "This way."

She ducked behind a group of rocks and proceeded quietly. I didn't understand why we were trying to sneak around.

"So, how did you end up in the Netherdowns?" I whispered.

She exhaled roughly.

"That's none of your concern."

I let out a breath. Apparently, Drycha wasn't much for conversation.

"I get the sense that Hirythe isn't thrilled to be here," I continued.

"Would you be?"

"To be honest," I said through labored breath, "the Netherdowns seems a bit like paradise, apart from the monsters, of course."

She snorted.

"Paradise and prison are relative."

"Well, what do you think?" I was determined to learn more about the woman behind the mirrored mask.

She stopped abruptly and turned, her eyes burning into mine.

"I hate it."

A wave of hot embarrassment made me aware of the sweat under my collar. The Netherdowns was beautiful in a ghostly way. Nearly every tree and stone inspired a delicious melancholy. But I hadn't considered what it would be like to live day in and out within someone else's memory.

"I'm sorry. I meant nothing by it."

She shrugged and continued. After an awkward silence, I turned behind us to mark how far we'd traveled, but I couldn't make out any of the features we'd passed already. In fact, it looked as though we hardly traveled from the Walnut hill.

"Is the landscape an illusion?" I asked. "We've been traveling for at least a half-hour, but it hardly looks as though we've gone a half-mile."

"Such is the curse of memory," Drycha replied. "It never lies still, does it? So long as Bram lives, this land will continue to change."

"What about Hirythe?"

"He knows how to stabilize his thoughts. It must be a gift that comes with old age."

"How old is he?"

She smiled.

"How old are you?" she asked.

"Closer to thirty than I care to say," I replied with a blush.

"He's older than that."

As she finished the end of her sentence, an overwhelming force took hold of me around the waist and pulled me backward.

"Much older and much wiser." Drycha stumbled over in surprise at hearing Hirythe's voice. "What are you doing, Drycha?"

She avoided his gaze.

"I'm just escorting her to Bram."

"Is there a reason you did so in secret?" His eyes were piercing.

"I just wanted to see him," she said.

"You have seen him."

"See him without you chaperoning me," she replied quietly into the dirt.

"Drycha, you can't. You know you can't," he said.

"But what if he finds a cure for her? What if it could work for me as well?" she asked.

Hirythe shook his head.

"You know our rules. This is for him. Don't chase dead ends." The fae folded his arms in front of him, and Drycha's shoulder slumped forward.

"Very well." She looked wistfully up the trail where it vanished into the mist and stalked back toward the village. I watched her curiously until she vanished around a bend of rock. What rules? Did Drycha suffer from her own magical illness?

"I told you not to return so quickly," Hirythe scolded.

I knit my brows.

"If he wants to see me, you should let him. Or is he a hostage of some kind? The faster he can rid me of Sraith, the faster you will be rid of me in turn."

Hirythe ran a hand through his hair and exhaled impatiently.

"Coming into the Netherdowns this often is dangerous. He didn't design the diary for traveling back-and-forth at this frequency."

"You're afraid it will break?"

He sneered.

"I'm afraid people are listening."

We stared at each other, the steady trickle of the stream accompanying us like a harp.

"Is he close?" I asked, sobering. Meeting Bram would not be the joyous reunion I'd hoped for. Edward was suffering. If I wanted any hope of a future with him, I needed to get all of this sorted. If Bram knew a cure, I wanted it. If he didn't... I wasn't sure I had the courage to try the spell, but what other choice would I have? This was survival. I swallowed hard.

Hirythe nodded toward the mist. I started forward with Hirythe on my heels.

"You're coming?" I asked.

"Do you have to ask about something that is so obvious?"

I bristled, protectively putting a hand over my pocket. I didn't want to imagine what he might do if he learned about the spell in my pocket.

"You don't need to get defensive," he said.

"I'm not defensive!" I hissed.

Hirythe and I walked side by side as the mist cleared. We reached the lakeside in no time at all.

Chapter Seventeen

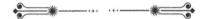

Dr. Rupert's Uncantation

The lake was pristine and crystal clear, shining unusually bright, considering the overcast sky. Here, the water sparkled of its own accord. Lush vegetation sprung from the banks.

The mist retreated from the waterfront, and my eyes followed the shoreline until I saw a shack sheltered by a small wood and a large grouping of tumbled boulders lying against a hill, the remains of a rockfall. Water trickled from these boulders into the lake.

Standing next to the shack was Bram.

He was wearing a heavy tweed coat that gave him an almost scholarly aesthetic. In his hand were a pen and notebook. He looked over the lake and methodically scribbled in its pages.

There was nothing to separate us but a gentle stretch of soft dirt and a grumpy fae.

I'm ashamed to say I fell to my knees where a sob escaped me.

I felt like I had been searching for years. I'd traveled to a whole different world to find him. Even the comforts of Edward's attention had turned sour. All for Bram.

All for this.

At first, he didn't notice us, just kept to his observations.

Having Dr. Rupert's spell in my pockets seemed to fill my legs with a heavy, muddy dread.

Could I possibly take another man's life, even if it meant my own freedom? Even if it meant avenging the family of my betrothed. Well—almost betrothed. Was Edward right about Bram escaping justice?

I walked forward, reaching my hand into my pocket, fingering the old paper with its dark, handwritten lettering. Edward's face looked like a ghost in my mind, his severity, his intent.

I needed to at least give Bram a chance to heal me. My father would have wanted that. My real father. He wouldn't encourage me to harm another person preemptively.

When those you love point you down different pathways, what's right and what's wrong?

I wanted to creep up quietly, ease into things. Apparently, Hirythe had other ideas.

"Hullo! Bram! Have you found your silver currant, yet?" Hirythe shouted.

Bram looked up at me. His eyes were honey, his smile fresh water.

"You can stop whining. Here she is," the fae called out. Then he whispered to me. "He's been absolutely unbearable."

"Luella Winthrop," he said, looking at me sheepishly. "How is Cyrus?"

"He's well," I spit out. "Being well cared for at the MacDonald Randolph in Oxford."

"Oxford? I left him in Reading with the rest of the fair workers."

"I found him in Reading. I brought him to Oxford."

"I left you in Dawnhurst."

I pursed my lips and let the implications of his sentence settle.

"Those were poor words," he said. "Damn. I've looked forward to this moment for so long now. I would be fated to ruin it, wouldn't I?"

He tucked his notebook into his pocket and stepped toward me. For some reason, I retreated a step. To an outside observer, I may have appeared afraid, and I was—but not of him. I was afraid that despite everything, despite how much I despised what he did to me, how he ruined my life, there was a small something inside of me begging to reach out and embrace him.

"Well," Hirythe said, "this is going better than I thought."

"How are your symptoms?" Bram asked.

"You might have told me you left an antidote," I replied, letting myself fall into the tart attitude I planned before arriving.

"Tell you? I showed you."

"When?"

"That night in my tent, when you had an attack. I used it to calm you. Don't you remember?"

I looked at Hirythe for validation.

"Don't look at me," he replied. "I already told you he's terribly stupid."

"You consider that adequate instruction?" I said, bristling.

"Why else would I have left you the inkwell?" He looked puzzled. Did he honestly believe he had adequately instructed me on staying my attacks?

I walked forward and punched him hard on the arm. He winced. I did it again. Hirythe applauded.

"The last time I used that ink, a man killed himself! I wasn't about to start experimenting. How could you be so stupid? A note. A letter. Would that have been so hard?"

He blushed. He actually blushed.

"I just—I meant to say more, but the last time we met, I got distracted. I wanted you to discover it on your own. There's a good reason—"

"Distracted by what?" I was shouting now. He tilted his head and massaged the back of his neck with one hand.

He didn't want to say, and I was left searching my memory of that night in his tent. We had argued. He told me he would find a cure. He had invited me to go with him. I refused.

There it was.

I began a sentence or two, awkwardly. He was distracted because I had just rejected him. The stream trickled from the boulders with gentle lapping noises.

"So, the attacks have continued, then?" Bram asked.

I threw my hands in the air and turned around.

"Luella," Hirythe said, "he's trying. You have to forgive him. He can't help but put his foot directly into his mouth."

Bram took a heavy breath and approached me.

"Well," he said, "on the bright side, you should have plenty of the ink left still. I worried you'd run out soon. Then we'd really be in trouble."

"Can't you make more?" I asked, tucking my hands again into my sleeves. He looked embarrassed. He was acting so differently than how I remembered him. It gave off the impression that he rarely reunited with old acquaintances. He was overly warm.

"Well, no, not really. Yes, but no."

I closed my eyes and massaged my temples.

"Technically, I could make more, but it's a complicated process and requires no small sacrifice—"

"Can you heal me?" I asked. This conversation was getting off track. The spell in my pocket was like a hot coal. I couldn't lapse into the familiar back and forth I enjoyed back on the Severn River in autumn. If he couldn't heal me, I had to try an alternative. If it came to that, I shouldn't make it any harder on myself.

He stretched taut lips across his face.

"That, too, turns out to be a little more complicated than originally contemplated. I—"

He didn't finish. A bull burst through the rock where water had been trickling out. Shards and fragments of stone shot in all directions as the bull landed in a steaming, angry stance. Its hide shared the unforgettable sheen of the mirage monsters and the cat that attacked Hirythe's camp.

It looked like I didn't have to use the spell. I might have just killed Bram, anyway.

Bram jumped aside as the bull charged past him, shaking its horns all the way. It turned with unnatural agility and charged Hirythe. My breath caught in my throat, but Hirythe dodged the beast with chilling nonchalance. The bull slammed into the rocks behind him, splintering the rock face behind.

Bram got to his knees. Papers from his notebooks were strewn everywhere.

"What have you done?" he called. I tried to answer, but the bull finally connected with his torso, tossing him across the ground. He groaned loudly.

"Bram, get up! Don't let it trample you," Hirythe shouted.

I did this. This violence came from me. I had not read the spell Edward gave me, but as sure as Anna's letter brought the cat, the paper in my pocket brought the bull. I was so stupid, so arrogant, to think it would be different.

And it had all happened before he told me what progress he'd made toward finding a cure.

"Stop!" I shouted at the bull. Instinct took over. In my heart, I knew I didn't hate Bram enough to watch a monstrous bull gore him to death. The animal's hide shimmered menacingly, triggering memories of the soldiers who had vanished in the cat's fur. Did Bram face a similar danger?

The bull reared its head and turned on me, eyes like the cat before. I was this beast's master.

I was wrong.

Where the cat found docility at the sight of me, the bull snorted angrily and scraped the ground. I was running before my mind told my legs to move.

"Luella!" Bram's voice called to me. I quickly slipped between two sturdy tree trunks, trying to get something between me and the charging beast. A moment later, one of the trunks splintered like a fractured pencil.

"What did you bring in?" Bram called. He started shouting and waving his hands to distract the animal, which repeatedly butted the trees.

"You brought something else?" Hirythe called. "Didn't you learn anything after the cat?"

I considered retreating deeper in the forest, but I didn't see many trees thick enough to slow the beast down.

"Luella, what is it?" Bram shouted.

"It's a spell!" I shouted. Even with the adrenaline, I blushed admitting it.

"A what?" I heard a stone hit the tree trunk, and Bram grunting from the effort. The bull turned and stared at him. Bram tossed another rock before taking off his coat and holding it up like a Spanish matador.

He couldn't be serious.

"A spell!" I repeated.

"On paper?" he shouted. The bull charged him, coursing through the shallows of the pond, kicking up water in its wake. Bram tried to pull his coat away, but the bull's horns snagged into it. The force pulled Bram from his feet.

"No, Bram, she brought in some ancient inscribed pottery!" Hirythe jeered. He had climbed on top of the boulders and now watched Bram struggle below. Every matador needs an audience.

"Yes, paper!" I cried. I had to think. Before, when I had burned Anna's letter, it cowed the cat. Perhaps, if I destroyed Dr. Rupert's Uncantation.

"Do you have it memorized?" Bram choked out. He wheezed from exertion. The bull tried furiously to rid itself of the coat on its horn.

"No!" I called, mustering my courage to leave the cover of the trees.

Coughing on his knees, he pointed at the water. The bull shook the coat off, and Bram scrambled again to his feet.

"I think he wants you to waterlog it," Hirythe called to me.

The beast was relentless, focused like a hot iron on Bram.

I ran from my cover, the spell in hand, and knelt by the lake. Waterlog it. Destroy it another way. It made sense.

I paused. Without the spell, without the bull, would there be any way to sever myself from Bram in the case he could not heal me? I saw Edward's defeated face.

"What are you waiting for?" Bram asked.

I chewed my lip, shooting glances at the bull, Bram, Hirythe, the spell, and the water. The fae looked at me, curiously.

"Are you trying to kill me?" Bram asked. He sidestepped the bull as it charged him. I heard his shirt rip. Hirythe raised his eyebrows, as if he, too, wanted an answer to that question.

The bold-faced accusation was enough to conjure up a healthy dose of shame and righteous condemnation. I plunged my hands into the pond and set to ripping the spell up under the water. The aged paper fell apart like pieces of old bread.

I would not kill Bram. What had come over me?

As if on cue, the bull shook its head, took a final, threatening look at us, and stamped off into the mist.

Bram gasped heavily, gulping in air, again on his hands and knees. My heart raced. I practically sensed every vein in my body. I ran to him.

"Are you all right?" I asked, checking him for bruises.

"Sure," he replied. Hirythe slid down from the rock and strode forward. "No thanks to you," Bram said to him.

"Don't get too excited," Hirythe said. "I wouldn't have let the beast kill you. What would become of my home?"

As we sat there, letting our nerves calm, the cold came. Chilled breezes wafted over from the surface of the lake. My shirt and the tips of the sleeves on my borrowed coat were wet from destroying the spell.

The silence waxed awkward.

"Bram," I started, "I'm sorry. Please, I didn't intend—"

He waved a hand dismissively.

"You couldn't have known."

"She should have known," said the fae. "She already brought one terrible monster in here. I believe the cat was loneliness. Tell me, what emotionally charged missive found its way into your pockets this time?"

I sneered at him.

"It depends," Bram said.

"What?" I puzzled.

"Whether I can heal you." His breathing was still heavy. "It depends."

I gaped. The bull had hardly fazed him at all. Nothing had changed for him, not even the topic of conversation.

I looked around at the ravaged earth, kicked up by the bull's furious hooves. The pile of stone looked like someone had used a stick of dynamite. I glanced back at the woods where I had taken cover. The trees had splintered into unrecognizable heaps of kindling.

"I hate magic," I said, shaking my head. I sat down, rested my arms on my knees, and hung my head.

In a moment, Bram sat beside me, a muddy mess. He shouldered me, congenially as he sloppily organized some mud-drenched papers from the notebook.

"I don't blame you for saying it, but you don't mean it," he said. "You're a bit wet."

I looked up at him. He produced another pen, touched it to his tongue, and began writing through the mud. His face was scraped, and his neck bruised, but he acted like he had survived a lecture by a boorish professor, not an attack by a magic bull.

I laughed. He eyed me curiously. I laughed more.

Soon, it was beyond my control. I couldn't help it. I hadn't laughed in so long. My whole body shook with every momentous burst from my diaphragm.

"You look ridiculous," I said, between breaths.

"Me? I've never seen you wear pants before."

This only made me laugh harder.

"I escaped the police in these pants." I laid back in the mud, looking up at the Netherdowns' peculiar sky.

I found him. I had finally found him.

Chapter Eighteen

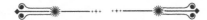

The Meddler and The Fae

"It occurred to me that despite all the time we spent together in Dawnhurst, I knew very little about your illness," Bram said as he gingerly washed a cut on his side with a linen cloth. I sat up to help him.

We had retreated to the small shack beside the lake. Although it looked simple on the outside, I was surprised to find many of the amenities one might appreciate in a city.

"I didn't think you could get hurt in the Netherdowns. After all, aren't you its creator?" I asked, carefully dabbing at his wound. The cut looked worse than it was. Blood had dried around the opening, but the lesion itself wasn't as deep as I feared.

"Because it was made from memory?" he asked, wincing.

I nodded.

"Most people die from the effects of memory," Hirythe said. He had been sitting at a table across the room, meticulously dissecting a tree branch.

"Most people die from the effects of disease," I corrected. My father had. I applied a bandage more roughly than I meant to. Bram grimaced.

I turned away from his wound, and he pulled down his shirt. It made me uneasy how comfortable I was dressing a wound on his bare torso.

"I'm afraid the Netherdowns is much more dangerous than you may believe," Bram said. "It's not just a pleasant dream. I fear some places here as much as I would any neighborhood in London."

"Ah yes, the almighty London," the fae quipped. He leaned back, and I was surprised to see that he had managed to disassemble the branch in perfect separate pieces. The bark looked undisturbed, but the extracted wood lay naked and split in two as evenly as a carpenter's saw.

Bram took a bottle from a cabinet by the sink and took a sip. Its contents were nearly as thick as syrup.

He squinted hard as if he'd sucked a lemon.

"Balsamic vinegar," he said with a far off look.

I carefully wrapped the bandages we didn't use and stowed them in a wooden box by the bed. The shack was small. The kitchen was also the bedroom, which was also the dining area.

Bram handed the bottle to Hirythe and plopped himself down on a bed in the corner. Hirythe took a long swig.

"What are the monsters? Just bad memories?" I asked.

Hirythe wiped his mouth.

"Why do you say it so dismissively? Reflect on your life. What is the powerhouse of your free will? What drives you to do the things you do? Memory is your future."

"Some memories are quite dangerous," Bram added with a less condescending tone. "When we created the Netherdowns, I wasn't—I didn't know how many terrible memories Hirythe had."

"I'd have told you it was a bad idea if you had consulted me." Hirythe stood and looked out a small window at the lake.

I sat down next to Bram on the bed, as if we were in his yurt at the Dawnhurst fair.

"It's easy to dismiss this place as merely symbolic. But I made it to protect Hirythe. If we had made it from shadow and smoke, it could be penetrated just as easily. So, the memories were made physical."

"From what or who are you trying to protect Hirythe?"

Bram and Hirythe exchanged a glance. I got the sense that Bram was asking for permission to share. Hirythe turned back to the window.

"We had a colleague who turned against us."

"You mean from the Phantom Battalion?"

Bram nodded.

"I saw a photograph on his desk, torn on one side."

"You have sharp eyes, Luella. Is that your training as a reporter?" Bram asked.

I blushed unwillingly when he used my name.

"We tore the photograph so there would be no trace of him inside the diary. We thought if his image existed in the Netherdowns, he might find it somehow."

I fiddled with a pinecone I found on the windowsill.

"What about your memories of living people?" I asked.

"The only way for a living thing to get into the Netherdowns is through the diary," Hirythe said. "Everything you see around you has passed on, except the plants. Bram managed to replicate the plants. Their souls aren't quite the same as more sapient beings."

I crossed my arms. My blouse was finally starting to dry out, but even with my coat, it was cold in the shack.

"And why would a former colleague want to do you harm?"

"No valid reason," Hirythe said stonily.

Bram's face darkened, and he turned to build a fire in the hearth. "I don't think his vendetta justified, but only because the blame is misplaced. He lost his brother."

"His brother lost his brother." Hirythe curled his lip.

"That's terrible. How?"

"We were on an expedition. I had traced down an old rusty sword, which I believed to embody a strong, albeit dark, magic."

I pulled a blanket from the mattress and wrapped myself up.

"Darker than the ink you had me use?"

"Much darker," he said.

"Only certain types of magic are comfortable carving a home for themselves inside weapons." Hirythe remarked. He turned and watched Bram struggling with the fire. "I shudder to think of what magic will one day reside inside a cannon or rifle."

"The ink is dark enough for me." I shook my head. Bram and Hirythe shared a knowing glance as I continued. "It's inspired me to harm others. I lashed out at my best friend. I almost tried to write

Edward's mother into illness."

The fire crackled to life, and Bram resumed his place next to me, trying to grab a share of the blankets.

"Absolutely not," I said, pulling them tighter. He stared at me.

"Your lines of propriety bewilder me. You're in the middle of a world made from memory, in the middle of the mountains, in a shack. I'd never try my way with you, but you still won't share a blanket?"

I glared at him.

"Are you so magical that you can do away with a woman's sense of dignity?"

"Please, for my sake. I'll be sick if you continue," said the fae.

Bram sighed, got back up, and found another scratchier-looking blanket before taking a seat by the fire.

"That brings me back to my earlier point," he said. "For all the time we spent together, I know very little about your illness. You asked if I can heal you, and I told you true. It depends."

"Depends on what?" I sat forward.

"The ink you've been using comes from a very particular type of magic. It belongs to the phenomenon of cause and effect."

"How can anything belong to cause and effect?" I stared.

"It's as I explained to you before," Hirythe said, leaning against the wall. "Humans move forward in the name of science. As they do so, they crystallize whatever magic they exploit to do so."

He was speaking absolute nonsense, and it must have shown on my face. What did any of this have to do with him healing me?

"Take this fire," Bram went on. "Would you say that humans have done an adequate job of harnessing fire for our own purposes? After all, we use it for light, energy, cooking, heat, weaponry... By studying it, we've killed all the magic right out of it."

"So, the more we understand something, the less magic it has?" I said, trying to dumb down his theory.

"The more you think you know something, the less you believe there is to discover," Hirythe corrected. How was he so derisive all the time?

"The lesser magic forces have all but gone away," Bram continued. "Things like fire, water, ice. Now, electricity is losing its power."

"But we don't have complete control over those things," I said, despite myself. "Fires still get out of control, ice breaks through cobblestones and destroys crops."

"Oh, Luella, do you hear yourself?" Hirythe rolled his eyes. "Even your examples are all about you. Cobblestones. Fires destroying your property. Your domesticated plants. How small a consolation prize those trophies are for the raw power those elements possessed before being relegated to human measurement."

I leaned back on the wall.

"If those used to be so powerful, what is the higher magic?"

He smiled like I had just asked a professor to explain his research paper.

"They're much more interesting," Bram said. "Cause and effect is just one such high magic."

"How so?"

"Despite all the best efforts of our greatest minds, we can't truly understand it. Or, at least, we can't make it practically reliable. If a dove somewhere in the orient eats a bug, could we ever trace the effect of this action to its completion? And if so, would we comfortably attribute the resulting action to that dove? Say that bug carried a disease that infected the bird, and the resulting spread of that disease reached an emperor, resulting in his death. Would you say the bird took down an empire?"

"I suppose, in a silly kind of way. It's a bird. It's ridiculous."

"It's ridiculous in terms of human sensibility," Hirythe said, "and yet, the trail leads us there."

"Then why not look back even further? The bird surely had a mother, and that mother bird must have had a mother bird," I added.

Bram smiled deviously.

"Now, you've got it. Everything can be connected, and we act according to the blame or credit we take for certain decisions. If you eat in the morning, it's because you believe the action will quell your hunger, and it does. Cause, effect."

"Please, can you get to the point? What's magical about any of that?"

He sat back down on the bed.

"Don't you find it interesting that we get to arbitrarily decide where we get involved along this chain? It's not regulated the way fire is. Something is on fire. We put water on it. It's done. Cause and effect are different. We attach blame and responsibility to it wherever we like. Wherever the dictates of our conscience decide."

"Your legal scholars have come up with convoluted doctrines to regulate it for the sake of criminal justice, but their theories are faulty and arbitrary." Hirythe grinned. "They can't even generate a healthy dose of consistency from one judge to another."

Bram's enthusiasm was making me uncomfortable. I had seen him lit up like this the night I had penned Luke Thomas' death. Worse, I didn't like what he implied.

I stood and paced across the floor.

"What is your point?"

"The ink tampers with cause and effect. You wrote stories that couldn't be true, and yet the next day they materialized," he said.

"Your condition, Sraith, results from this tampering. Since you've seen how fragile the system can be, your internal compass no longer points north," Hirythe said. "Now, when you're not sure how to feel about something, which is becoming more common, you default to anger, and it builds and builds."

I bit my lip and considered my past outbreaks. My swells of anger were set off by incidents that I normally might have handled with more maturity and poise. Had I reacted to those incidents as if they had the gravity of a much more grievous affair?

Mild annoyance turned to unbearable impatience. A slight by a reviewer transformed into a complete unhinging of my self-esteem. A mild paranoia from Rebecca's observations turned into a blind, survivalist rage.

It's like someone had held a magnifying glass to every one of my emotions and focused them into white-hot light.

"But wouldn't this affect my positive emotions as well?"

"You mean emotions like love and admiration?" Hirythe said with a wicked smile.

My blood chilled as I considered the implications. I had wondered how I'd fallen in with Rebecca, Doug, Bram, and Edward so quickly. Could I trust even my own heart?

The fog creature had once promised me it could make Edward love me.

"Bram, does this magic have the power to alter reality? It's one thing to say that it alters my perception of the natural chain of events, but can it actually change the world around me?"

"Or the people?" He nodded grimly. "Free will is a funny thing. Half the time, we don't use it, and if it's not occupied, what's stopping other forces from borrowing it for a while?"

I steadied myself on the rough wooden table behind me. Since Edward had first expressed his interest in me, I was afraid it was a lie. When I'd asked Rebecca Turner why she risked so much to help me, she dodged a response. Were those relationships counterfeit?

"You have to cure me," I said.

"That's the issue," he said. "I didn't understand why you needed healing in the first place. I've seen the effects of Sraith take hold of someone before. It doesn't happen as quickly as it did with you, not when you were using the magic in such small doses."

"This can be unpredictable, Bram. You know that. Like yeast that rises too unexpectedly in a loaf of bread," Hirythe said.

"I thought that at first, too," Bram said. "But, after talking to Hirythe, it hit me. Your timeline made little sense."

"What do you mean my timeline?"

"When we first met, I believed there were greater forces at work in Dawnhurst, but I should have realized sooner what that meant. I should have asked you about your illness, as a physician might have. When you told Hirythe about a fog creature, it all clicked."

"What do you mean?" I asked.

"When was the first time you dreamed about the fog?"

"Immediately after I interviewed Edward for the first time, when he told me about seeing the fog kill a man."

Bram took a seat directly across from me and stared intently into my eyes.

"You mean before we met?"

Gooseflesh crept up my back. That couldn't be right. I shook my head. Hirythe laughed and clapped his hands.

"Well done, Bram. I've missed how sharp you used to be," he said.

"Think carefully, Luella. When did you first dream about the fog creature? Was it before or after you used the ink for the first time?"

"It was before." The words sounded like faint echoes in my ears. How had I not noticed it before? I'd been blaming Bram all this time for everything that had gone wrong in my life. But the dreams had started the night after I spoke with Edward about his story. That night, I had seen the fog turn into the face of my father.

"Bram, what does this mean?" I asked, my pulse climbing. He hung his head.

"It means you're not infected by just Sraith," Hirythe said, excitedly. He looked like he just stumbled across a tricky game of chess.

"I believe someone intentionally infected you with another bit of dark magic," said Bram.

"Who would do that?" I asked, my whole mind rejecting the idea. "Before I met you, I swear, I didn't know anyone that claimed any type of magical knowledge."

Hirythe flipped a stool and sat down uncomfortably close to me.

"You never can tell who has a hidden penchant for mysticism locked away. A morbid interest in the supernatural, perhaps," Hirythe said as he rolled up his sleeves.

Instantly, my thoughts drifted to Edward. His mother had a powerful belief in the reality of the occult. He had been reading books in secret. Hadn't he been the one to hand me a spell that might kill Bram? I pushed the thoughts down. The implications were too much.

"But why would someone want to infect me?"

Bram shrugged.

"Now, Sraith comes about from repeated use of magic like the ink," Hirythe told me clinically. "The remedy is relatively simple. Stop using the magic, and eventually, your instincts will reset. At least it works that way while the case is still young. When Bram first told me he had left you an inkwell to continue using magic, I thought he was crazy."

He put his hands on my knees.

"Look at me now, and don't turn away," he said. He gazed in my eyes, and an eager vertigo clambered from his pale irises into my stomach. The world turned under me. My sight went black.

"I'm going to fall over," I said.

"Be gentle with her," I heard Bram say.

"You always think this is so much easier than it is. Let me work," Hirythe growled.

"It'll be harder if she can't even sit up."

Hirythe tore his gaze from mine just as I collapsed onto the bed. I laid there, waiting for my vision to swim back into focus as the room spun above me.

"Well?" Bram asked.

Hirythe's cheery, sarcastic tone of voice dropped. "This is grave," he replied. "This is very grave."

"Do you recognize it?" Bram asked.

"Not at present."

I sat up, steadying myself with a pillow. "What did you just do to me?"

"He just looked inside of you," Bram explained. "It's a fae trick."

I instinctively covered my chest with my arm. For some reason, the concept offended my sense of decency.

"You didn't want to ask first?"

"I was seeing if you had any marks from magic on you," Hirythe started. "Sure enough, there were some faint traces of Sraith."

"Well, we already knew that," I said, a little impatiently.

"And stronger markings by something else. They're well hidden," he finished. "I should have looked at you more closely last time. Bram was right, and that's unfortunate in the best of scenarios."

I eased myself up back on to the seat and squeezed the cushion against my chest.

"You can't heal me, can you?" I asked. The diagnosis was too much. It was hard enough believing I was infected with one type of magic, but two? I thought I'd been close. I thought there was a possible future with Edward.

I shook my head and wandered to the window. It was getting dark out. The trees outside were shadowy silhouettes. I stared out, becoming acquainted with the new guilt taking residence in my heart. I had blamed the wrong person. Could I still blame Bram for the stories I wrote? Was Bram complicit in the death of Edward's father? I struggled to come to grips with any of it.

"How am I supposed to endure this?" The toll the magic had taken on my life was abundant. What life could I lead now?

"There are two pathways forward," Hirythe said. "And both of them require knowing who infected you with this other enchantment. We can either kill that person and sever the magical tie that started this —that might help—or we determine what monster they let out of the bag, and see if we can come up with a remedy after that."

I stared at him.

"Oh, is that all?" I said saltily. Hirythe threw his hands up defensively.

"Don't blame me. I'm not the one who got you into this."

"I'll go back with you," Bram said quickly, "and we will find out who did this. I'll monitor the magic. Who knows, maybe with greater scrutiny we can determine what it is."

I put both hands on the windowsill.

"Absolutely not," I said.

"Luella?"

"Do you have any idea what type of mess that would cause?"

He screwed up his face in disbelief.

"Who cares about the mess? You have—"

"I currently live with Edward and his mother. How would I explain the sudden appearance of Bram—"

I paused and looked at him.

"I don't even know your last name!" I said, raking a hand through my hair.

"It's Lowhouse."

"Dutch ancestry," added Hirythe, "which explains a lot, in my opinion."

"It doesn't matter what your last name is."

Bram shuffled his feet.

"That's not the kindest thing you've ever said."

"You're not coming back with me. There must be an alternative."

He bit his lip and flipped through his notebook. The light in the room was a warm orange now that the fire in the hearth was its primary source. Seeing him in the fire reminded me of all the nights we had spent in his tent. His messy hair lit up to match his honey-colored eyes.

"I have an idea," he said at length, "but I'm not sure either of you will like it."

The fae and I looked at each other. Bram continued.

"Some high forms of magic are related. Memory, for example, has cousins in scent, music, nostalgia. Since high magic enjoys such close connections, I wonder if we might not use one to draw another out."

"Like a snare," Hirythe surmised.

Bram's words made my head spin.

"Are you saying that all of those are high forms of magic?"

"Some of the highest," Hirythe said. "Humans, despite all of their miraculous science," on the word science, he made quotations with his hands, "may never completely understand why or how music's power is so well connected to the human soul. I'm certainly not going to tell them."

"You mean, you know?" I asked, bewildered. He quieted me with a shake of his hand.

"How do you propose we set the snare?" he asked Bram.

"Well," Bram casually scratched his jawline, "I was hoping we might use a trace of your magic."

I am by no means an expert on faerie facial patterns, but if I had to classify the look Hirythe gave Bram, I'd say it was a mix of intense apprehension, guarded fury, and reluctant admiration. If a human could fit all that into a grimace, I've never seen it.

"You're a damn fool, Bram Lowhouse," he folded his arms and went to study the fire. "A damnable fool."

"It would be the most effective way. Traces of fae magic are so rare now, but nothing is stronger. If someone had purposefully enchanted Luella, whatever magic they used will resonate with it."

"It's also dangerous." Hirythe crossed menacingly to him. "Need I remind you that the reason I'm here in the first place is because my magic is too easily traceable? If we send some of it back out of the diary, it will give away our whereabouts."

"The diary is original and airtight," Bram countered. "Even if he finds it, there's nothing that would recommend it as an object of magical value. He'd walk right by it."

"You've always underestimated him!" Hirythe shouted. The fire in the hearth sounded furious, as though a strong wind fanned the flames. He turned and walked away, his hands on his head.

"Listen, I don't want to compromise the lives inside of the Netherdowns." I thought not only about Hirythe, but Drycha as well. "But if there's anything you can do, please, take pity on me."

Bram had a curious smile on his face, drilling his gaze into Hirythe's back. The fae sighed.

"He's right," Hirythe finally said. "It's an elegant and effective way to detect a magical residue. If someone hexed you, my magic should mark them as uniquely as a fingerprint."

"A what?" I asked.

"Never mind. It's risky, but I have to admit that a part of me hopes we're discovered. I'm tired of hiding."

The fire crackled in the heart, filling a wide gap in our back and forth.

"So how will this work, then?" I asked, changing the subject. Hirythe eagerly took the bait,

"We will keep it simple. I'll imbue a melody with a piece of my soul. Then, you can use that melody like a pair of glasses."

"How do I do that?"

"It won't be comfortable, at least not socially."

"I beg your pardon."

"You'll need to look your subject in the eyes, like I did to you a moment ago, and sing the melody to them. I recommend you do this with everyone who had an opportunity to enchant you before you met Bram."

Uncomfortable was an understatement. Bram stifled a laugh behind me.

"I have to sing to them?"

"It's one of the highest forms of magic," Hirythe explained, confusion manifesting on his face. I whirled on Bram.

"This is funny, is it" I spat.

He held his hands up in a sign of surrender.

"It's the best option. Scent was bound to get messy. Music is elegant, and you don't need to carry anything around with you."

I massaged my temples.

"Are you trying to tell me I have to find Byron Livingston, sit him down, gaze into his eyes, and sing him a song?"

"Would you prefer forcing him to take a large whiff of something? And I mean a large whiff." Bram looked at me as if he'd just offered an unbeatable argument.

"I might," I retorted.

"Is it acceptable or not?" Hirythe asked impatiently. "It's a risk, and it's not comfortable putting a piece of my soul into a melody."

"I suppose we should ask if you can sing in the first place," Bram said.

I scoffed. I hadn't tried in ages. I had distant memories of my father's low voice humming a lullaby or my mother singing to herself as she worked at the stove or the wash. I sang as a girl. I thought about the concert I had recently attended with Lady Thomas and swallowed.

"It depends on the song." It occurred to me that not all melodies were created equal. I couldn't sing like any of the soloists for Handel's Messiah. "Will it be difficult? High with lots of runs and scales and such?"

My question teased out a slight smile, even from Hirythe.

"You would prefer it otherwise?" he asked.

"I don't think I could manage if it's too complicated."

"Well, then maybe we can just borrow an old faerie tune. Those are simple enough, and it will be much faster than making something up."

"Wouldn't it be easier to weld some of your magic to a composition of your own?" Bram asked. He really was a know-it-all sometimes. Hirythe smiled sadly.

"Sometimes, you don't have to make up a song for it to have a part of you."

Hirythe took my hand and sat me down. His hand sent a jolt of something like courage through me.

"Are you ready?"

I nodded, my heart rising in my chest. He gazed directly in my eyes in a way that made me nervous.

"Listen closely." He still hadn't let go of my hand, and as he started a low humming, some connection formed through our fingers. It sounded something like a lullaby, haunting and moody. I stared, more transfixed than I had been at the concert in Oxford.

> *Do you hear the echo*
> *On the crags and in the meadow*
> *Do you see the moonlight mellow*
> *In the cracks and in the barrow*
> *But where have the hill folk gone?*
> *And where have the wood folk gone?*

As he sang, I closed my eyes, and other voices chimed in to sing with him. It sounded like a melancholy and well-practiced choir. They split into humbling harmonies stretching octaves below Hirythe's voice. I picked out undulating, pipe-like melodies sung by crystal clear altos, and the most delicate soprano notes I'd ever heard.

He finished and retracted his hand. The music faded immediately, leaving a great chasm and a sense of hopelessness. Tears dotted under my lids. When I opened my eyes, I knew the figure in front of me in a whole new way. The reclusive aura I picked up from his careless attitude before gave way to smothering sadness.

What happened to his people? I didn't ask him out loud, but I didn't need to.

"Sing that, and if you hear the voices, you'll know your subject has been touched by high magic. Can you remember that?" he asked.

"I don't think I'll ever forget."

Chapter Nineteen

A Hint at More

I surfaced from the Mystic Diary at the table in my room. It was already dark outside.

Exhausted, I lay back on my bed. I was too tired to fall asleep, and my mind raced and reverberated with the sound of faerie choirs. Hirythe made me prove I had the words memorized and test out the magic on Bram before I left. When I sang it to Bram, awkwardly gazing into his eyes, the voices sounded off as if they sang in the Sheldonian.

Apparently, high magic marked Bram in spades.

He sent me back soon after. I agreed that I would set to work trying to locate anyone who might have had an opportunity to infect me.

I made the list in my head. Byron. Cooper. Mrs. Crow. Mrs. Barker. Rebecca. Anna. Edward.

The list got more ridiculous the longer I went on. Who among these people would have cause to enchant me?

In the meantime, Bram and Hirythe agreed that they would see to further research in the Netherdowns.

"Insights can be gained here," Bram said. "Hirythe's memory is vast and scary."

That was my life now. Scary. Lost.

My stomach rumbled. I had forgotten all about eating. I entered the diary early that morning. Food is so often the ailment for despair. Perhaps if I found some scones or biscuits to munch on, I could approach it all with a clear head.

What I wouldn't give for one of Mrs. Barker's iced buns. Maybe she enchanted me through baked goods. In fact, I wouldn't be surprised if she stirred something into her iced buns that made them otherworldly delicious.

I crept out of my room without a candle. On the table in the sitting area lay the remains of an earlier meal, mostly untouched, awaiting the hotel staff's attention. It didn't take much for me to recognize them as Lady Thomas' cast-offs. She had a way of taking nibbles of everything and leaving the majority behind.

Lucky for me.

I munched on some Beef Wellington. Lukewarm gravy and peas sat in a white dish, and I took healthy bites from them as well. As the food hit my stomach, my thoughts felt stronger, more stable.

There was a writer from America that made his career off of macabre tales of mystery and the darker, baser motives of human nature. As a young woman, I found a battered copy of one of his books in an alley side bin. I snuck it home and spent hours daring myself not to be afraid. I had even read some to Anna. She didn't like it. Nor did my mother.

Little did they know, my life would one day become so much like one of those terrible stories. The pieces all fit together somehow, I knew they must, but I was lost as a detective in the Rue Morgue.

Someone had sabotaged me. I couldn't trust anyone. I either suspected them of wishing me harm or being magically persuaded to like me. If Sraith—or whatever this fog creature was called—wanted my grip on reality to slip, he had planted the seed long ago.

It suggested it could make Edward love me. Edward Thomas, whose judgment was already so suspect by the loss of his father, might have had his affection tampered with. Or worse, he might have intentionally—

The door swung open, and Edward's form, silhouetted from the hall's gas lamps, filled its frame. I started, and peas spilled off the table like a rockslide.

"Luella!" Edward ran to me and wrapped me up in his arms. I stumbled up off of the chair into him. "You're here. I was so worried."

His arms cradled me powerfully. He put a hand on the back of my head, and his embrace wooed me. I felt as though I might happily snuff out like a candle and dissipate into the air.

I hugged him back tightly.

"Of course, I'm here," I said into his ear. "Where else would I be?"

"I've been looking for you all day," he said, letting me go. "I thought Cooper had found us and taken you by night."

"You thought Cooper snuck into our hotel to arrest me?" I attempted playful sarcasm, but my desire to be near him rendered my tone emotional. Thoughts of our encounter last night tempted me into forgetting everything about the Netherdowns.

He let out a breath.

"When I hear someone else say it, it sounds foolish." He took my hands and sat us both down again. "But where have you been?"

"I was in the Mystic Diary."

"In the book? You returned then?"

I felt a stab of guilt. I had shared nothing about the diary since my first visit.

"Yes," I said.

"What wonderful news," he said, kissing my hand.

"Edward," I blushed, "you certainly are expressing yourself."

"Forgive me," he said. "If I'm being honest, the fear of Cooper didn't worry me. I was afraid that I'd chased you away after my indiscretion last night."

The darling man. I patted his face.

"There was no indiscretion, Edward. I hold nothing against you. I was just gone for the day."

"We just haven't been apart like that in so long. Even when I was in custody at Reading, I had a general idea of your whereabouts," he said.

I smiled. He was right. We had been separated, but not without a trace.

"I'm not complaining," I said, bestowing a kiss of mine on his knuckles.

"So, you can enter the book now at your will?" he asked. "Can you show me?"

"Not now," I said. "I'm exhausted."

He nodded.

"Perhaps tomorrow, then. I can accompany you."

My heart nearly stopped.

"No," I said too quickly. "I'm not sure that's a good idea."

"Why not?"

"What if something happened to the book while we were inside?"

He smirked.

"I hardly think that should be a problem. Didn't you find the book with a dog? If it is so fragile, it would have merited greater protection."

"He's an unusual dog," I replied. Edward laughed. I loved his laugh. We both basked in the freedom and happiness that came with clearing up whatever passed between us the night before.

"Let's postpone our joint holiday into the book, then. It's probably for the best, anyway. What with Christmas coming at the end of the week."

"Christmas is this week?" I asked.

"Yes, it caught me off guard as well. We've been at this for some time now, haven't we?"

I nodded, and the conversation lapsed. Edward looked at me, fixedly.

"Luella, what did you find in the diary? Did you find Bram? Did you use the spell? I'm almost afraid to ask. Are you free?"

Sages say that truth is always the simplest story to maintain, but something kept me from telling it to him now. How could I explain that all of our work was just the beginning, that now an even grander mystery lay before us?

Besides, Edward was a fixer. If he heard about a second magic in me, and that someone intentionally set it off inside of me, I didn't know how he'd react.

I wanted to surrender to the reality the fog creature had made for me. I wanted to bask in my affection for Edward Thomas.

Either way, I needed time. Sometimes, delay is wrapped in progress.

"I found Bram." I swallowed.

"You did? What happened? Did you use the spell?"

"I didn't have to." I detected the slightest sense of disappointment in him, but he covered it quickly. Perhaps it was just boyish curiosity, or perhaps he really had hoped that somehow it would be as easy as that to put all this behind us.

"Bram told me that using the pen created a magical disturbance in the power of cause and effect. As a result, my reactions to daily life spiral out of control. My episodes originate in pent up energy from these reactions." I don't know why Bram and Hirythe didn't explain it so succinctly.

Edward leaned back in his chair with a curious expression. His mustache, neatly trimmed since his mother joined us in Reading, twitched on one side of his mouth.

"Fascinating," he said, "and terrifying. Did he mention a remedy?"

"He said he knew of one," I said, choking down the half-truths I delivered. "It's a series of doses. I must go back into the book periodically to have them administered."

"You can't take them here?"

I shook my head.

"Something about the magic in the book. He was firm on this point." It was just a small lie, necessary even. I couldn't have Edward interfering with whatever I'd need to do to track down the person responsible for enchanting me. Technically, laughably, I supposed his name was on that list of suspects. Was that why I kept the truth from him?

"Did he say how long this might take?"

I also wanted an answer to that question. I shook my head and picked at a piece of pastry. Edward's shoulders sunk like a collapsing dirigible.

"But he sounded confident of success," I said. "Very confident. And, if he's so confident, I am as well."

He studied me carefully.

"What do you mean to say?" he asked. I swallowed. The pastry tasted dry without gravy.

"I mean, it's been wonderful getting to know your mother, and I hope I can look forward to more of the same. I mean for a long time." The sentiment tumbled out of me without censure. Despite my recent cause to distrust him, perhaps because of it, I wanted him to read between the lines. I wanted commitment to ward off insecurity, to double down and risk my heart.

I never wanted to sing Hirythe's song to Edward.

He started breathing hard, and he fumbled for words.

"Luella, I have tried my utmost not to make your journey more difficult by any means of distraction. I've found myself too weak on the days I indulged in lovely fantasies about the future. But, if you're telling me now that the journey is in hand, that victory is in hand—"

I grabbed his hands again and squeezed them. If I was to sink, let me sink in him.

"—and the feelings I've withdrawn for your benefit might from their exposure lift you up, I would so readily renew them."

Weeks before, these words would have fueled me like a steam engine. What wrong could there be in accepting Edward's affection? The damage could only be theoretical. The thought that Edward had something to do with my deranged state was laughable, impossible.

And, in the case Bram and I never discovered the true culprit behind my condition, this was my reality, and I'd learn to live with it. I would manage my symptoms with the magical ink. If the inkwell ran out, Bram would teach me to make more

I was sick. I had medicine to manage my illness. Surely other couples faced similar difficulties. Why would I block out a chance at happiness? I looked at Edward's steely gray eyes, shining in the darkness from the light in the hall. I nodded.

"Let's take it a step at a time, but yes. I think it's time to push our story along."

He kissed me, and it felt so different from the night before. Where that kiss had been surrender and defeat, this was triumph. I was back on the balcony at Fernmount, my shoulders quivering from cold and excitement. I let myself melt into the present and wrapped my arms around him.

I had waited so long for this, and I didn't want it to end.

I would not give it up for anything. We pulled apart, and the world came swimming back in, but I tried to lock my eyes on his. They glittered now with specks of joy, two life rafts for a drowning woman. This man could not have intentionally harmed me. Whatever test Hirythe or Bram came up with could not be more accurate than this moment.

I collapsed into his arms again.

"I am so happy," he whispered to me. "So very happy."

I squeezed his arm and let his words wash over me.

"I think it's time we left Oxford," he said.

"Leave? " I asked.

"Aren't you weary from traveling? Living in hotels and hovels?" He looked down at me and stroked a stray lock of hair from my face. "Wearing men's clothes?"

I blushed. I forgot I still wore a pair of trousers. I laughed to myself, thinking about his mother's reaction should she walk in on us.

"Where would we go?"

"Let's celebrate Christmas at Fernmount. We can get back in time for Christmas Eve."

I thought about the beauty of his family home, how it must look in the snow with large stretches of meadow and forests beyond. "Do you have memories of Christmas at Fernmount?"

"Of course," he said with a playful grin. "I'm afraid I gave you the wrong impression. Not everything about my father was as bad as I made it out to be. He was fond of Christmas. It was one of the few times during the year when we enjoyed his undivided attention."

Christmas at Fernmount with Edward would be a dream come true. Why not? I could bring the Mystic Diary along. Besides, if I went caroling to a few people in Dawnhurst, Fernmount was one step closer to home.

"Can Cyrus come?" I asked wryly.

"The dog?

"I'm not leaving without him."

"Well, I hope he likes fresh air and no shortage of sticks to chew on." He sighed.

I kissed him again and did my very best to forget all about the list of people in my head, the war in the Netherdowns, the crimson inkwell, the torn photograph on Hirythe's desk, and Bram.

Chapter Twenty

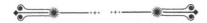

Reunited

Fernmount was even more beautiful than I remembered. I left it in a state of fog and decay. When the carriage pulled up now, a blanket of snow covered the landscape. Cyrus jumped up and put his paws on the small window in the carriage door.

"Must you have insisted we bring the dog?" Lady Thomas asked. The carriage was cramped with the three, or rather, four of us. We had taken our time traveling, stopping in a small town for the night, so we arrived right at midday, the perfect hour to make Cyrus drool over open fields ready to explore.

I didn't blame him.

The carriage wheels crunched the gravel as it went through Fernmount's gates, past the Celtic animal statues that looked so ominous the first night I saw them. Now they looked playful.

"Welcome back to Fernmount, Luella," Edward said. Even though

I'd only been here for a night, I enjoyed a sense of homecoming pulling through the gates. I supposed this to be the safest, most welcome place in England.

"Oh, I have a surprise I forgot to mention," Edward added. "We have some guests."

The carriage door opened, and Rebecca Turner stood on the front steps as resplendent and beautiful as I ever imagined her.

"Here to report a missing person?" she asked.

I sprang from the carriage and embraced her. In the grand scheme of things, it had only been a matter of months since I had seen her last. But the method of my departure and her great loyalty to me during my escape had rendered her absence excruciating. Apart from seeing my dear Anna at Fernmount House, this was the best Christmas surprise I could have hoped for.

"What are you doing here?" I asked, still breathless from shock.

"I thought it about time I came to visit the Steely-eyed Detective's uppity manor. After all, I put up with him long enough at the station."

Edward clambered out behind me.

"It turns out Rebecca needed a place to hide. I received a letter while in Oxford, forwarded from the house." He turned to offer his mother a hand.

"Hide?" My jubilation faltered. "My escape?"

She looped her arm in mine.

"It's the Sergeant. Listen here, Luella Winthrop. I have more respect for myself than to stick around working for some man who believes he is God. Your escape humiliated him, and now he's convinced more than ever that—"

She paused and eyed Lady Thomas. I put a reassuring hand on her arm.

"It's all right," I said.

"Miss Winthrop has many faults," Lady Thomas said as she gracefully dismounted, "but I don't believe she murdered my husband. Mr. Crawling, where are you? Will you unload things? Oh, and call Mrs. Toffer! My back is aching."

A few members of the house staff hopped forward to comply, adding a warm, albeit professional, "glad to have you home, my Lady."

"Well, that's a relief," Rebecca said, watching the servants like something in a museum. "I thought Edward's suggestion daft. Running from Dawnhurst to his home, with his mother, seemed like out of the fire and into hell. How did you manage it?"

"Don't look at me," Edward said. "I created a wholly separate identity for her. If she had cooperated, she might still be Miss Sarah Primrose."

Rebecca laughed.

"You jest, surely. A name like that? Was she disguised as an escort?"

"I'll tell you everything," I said, wrapping her in another hug. "We can talk through luncheon."

She smiled coyly.

"I hope you like fish and chips," she said.

The wealthier classes have strings of etiquette that solidify the formal relationships between them. This grants them power. Familiarity erodes the walls of the aristocracy, encouraging lapses in social convention.

But I wasn't a member of the wealthier classes. Nor was Rebecca. Nor was Doug Tanner.

When I found him popping in and out of the kitchens, barking orders at the staff as if it were his own restaurant, I nearly cried. He rushed over and hugged me so tightly my ribs grated against one another.

"Luella Winthrop," he said in his loud, gruff voice. "It looks as though you've managed the love quandary you were so worried about."

"Thanks to you." I kissed his big, scratchy cheek. "Your theatrical performance with Mrs. Crow was award-worthy."

"I'll be honest, the old lady and I had an unusually strong chemistry." He winked.

"There will be plenty of time to talk once you're done cooking," Rebecca said. "Doug insisted he welcome you all back with his fish and chips." She grabbed us both by the arm and led us toward the dining room.

"Not Christmas without fish and chips, now is it?" The old bear grinned.

"Doug, for you, it's not any day without some fish and chips," I replied.

Before long, we'd all gathered in Fernmount's extravagant dining room, Doug's specialty comically plated like a dish from a fine restaurant.

Lady Thomas crinkled her nose as she prodded it with a fork.

Edward did a very poor job of hiding his amusement.

"Customarily, it's eaten with your hands, mother," he said with a touch of sarcasm. "Not that you would know, seeing as you've never once had fish and chips before."

"I haven't eaten with my hands in years," she said. "Is this not that immigrant dish the Italians sell on the street corners?"

"Aye, the Italians try their best. You can use a fork if you like," Doug said with a dismissive wave of the hand. "Whatever makes you comfortable, lady."

"Doug, it's *my lady*, not just '*lady*,'" Rebecca whispered. Doug seemed large for his fine chair, and it gave the impression that the two of them sat very close together. Or was that just the two of them actually sitting very close together?

"My apologies, miss. My lady. Haven't met many ladies before."

Night decorated the dining room last I'd seen it. Now, shining daylight spilled through the large windows framed by rich curtains bound with silk ties. The winter scene outside looked its own type of magical, and the details that looked gloomy and foreboding in the dimly lit evening now looked beautiful. The large rug added warmth, the hearth crackled, and the table runner spoke merriment.

Lady Thomas failed to hide her enthusiasm for Doug's secret sauce. She first tried the fried fish plain to mild enjoyment, but when she dabbed it in the pinkish sauce, her eyes lit up.

"Very lovely," she said several times. Doug beamed. Now he could say his fish and chips cheered pauper and aristocracy alike.

"Well, well, Doug," Rebecca said, grinning. "That sauce might be worth a fortune."

"Don't start with me, Rebecca," he replied.

After lunch, Edward and Doug, thick as thieves, disappeared. It energized me to see Edward so light-hearted. He bragged about the horses in the stables and the collection of swords and pistols Fernmount claimed. Doug snorted with disbelief, and off they went, leaving me gratefully alone with Rebecca.

"Things seem to have gone your way," Rebecca said. "I was so afraid when I saw you last, dodging police and ducking into a carriage. Edward had insisted your well-being was his greatest interest. But you never can trust a man, can you?"

I hoped she was wrong.

We walked outside in the crisp winter air, bundled up in hoods. The sun warmed the heavy fabric on our back wonderfully.

Cyrus ran around us in circles, begging me to toss a stick he'd dragged from the fields.

"You were right to believe him. He has been a saint."

"And your condition?"

"Moving in a positive direction," I said with a smile. It was true in some ways. Seeing Rebecca warmed my heart, and yet some Bram-inspired logic prevented me from talking as openly with her as I once had. After all, she might be the one who enchanted me. I was sure she'd pass whatever test Bram came up with to determine such, but it was best to be cautious.

Besides, I didn't want to talk about my illness.

"Rebecca, what happened with Cooper after I left? I heard I was in the papers."

She took a heavy breath.

"Well, when you slipped through his fingers, he about had an episode. That a woman masquerading around in a man's costume to escape his police force was maddening."

I blushed.

"I suppose it impossible to have hidden it from the papers for long. But it fizzled out quickly enough, which made Cooper even more furious. Byron Livingston wrote an article defending you, claiming that Cooper should be removed from his post."

I stopped walking.

"You're lying." My ex-fiancé? Byron betrayed and turned me over to Cooper. Why would he defend me?

"I wish I were. It'd be easier to hate the man. But despite his faithlessness, he really cared about you. Perhaps he truly thought you'd just gone mad. He kept going on about how Cooper had no proof other than conjecture, and that begged the question why he was hell-bent on blaming a suicide on some woman from the east side."

I had worried for a long time that Byron would continue working toward my ruin. The most incriminating bit of evidence against me after Luke Thomas' death was the article I wrote for Langley's Miscellany. Byron held one of the few copies of that front page. If he came forward with it, I doubt I would recover.

But to discover he not only kept the story hidden but railed against my accusers was too much to accept. It made little sense.

Perhaps he was still in love with me, or maybe he hoped to cover something up. A part of me wanted Byron to be the one who had enchanted me. I had no semblance of a relationship left with him. He would be tidiest.

But I tried to imagine Byron poring over some evil spellbook. It didn't stick.

"What then? It must have escalated to a breaking point, or else you would not have written Edward."

"He had me followed one day when I took a step out for a bite to eat," she said with a sad smile. "After all my time in the service, he had me followed. When the officer saw Doug and recognized him as the theatrical lover from the day of your escape, it was curtains for us."

"You mean, he implicated you?" Guilt turned in my stomach.

"I didn't give him the chance. As soon as I sniffed out his intention, I didn't go in again. If he wanted to arrest me, I wouldn't make it easy."

"Arrested?" I scoffed. "He wouldn't dare arrest his own secretary."

"He intercepted my letters, Luella. I was corresponding with Doug. He had all the evidence he needed."

It sounded as though Cooper had transformed Dawnhurst into his own private city-state. Who could live with such paranoia? He was so unlike the man I remembered as a little girl.

Perhaps Cooper was the villain I sought. He certainly displayed signs of an affected character.

"I kept a shallow footprint for some time before Doug and I both knew it was time to leave. Go on holiday, you might say."

"You and Doug ran away together?" I asked, raising my eyebrows. Rebecca threw the stick for Cyrus and didn't look at me.

"Oh, come off it," she said.

"I am only asking a question." I noticed a suppressed smile creep into the corners of her mouth. "I can't imagine it was easy for him to leave the pub behind. That building is his cathedral."

"It wasn't easy," she said, her smile souring.

"Rebecca Turner, if I didn't know any better, I'd say you have a love quandary of your own."

Cyrus came back with the stick. When Rebecca tried to grab it, he didn't let go, sinking into his hind legs trying to coax her into a game of tug of war. She didn't fight him for long, and the pointer strode off, content to gnaw on his prize.

"What's wrong?" I asked. "The two of you make a fine couple."

She wrung her hands. We were now quite far from the house, approaching the tree line along an easy pathway. She glanced backward.

"It's just that, Luella," she said. "It wasn't easy leaving his pub. You know as I do why he clings to that place."

I nodded. Doug's pub was a living memorial to his late wife. He had fixed it up for her, and when she passed, her memory lived in its success.

"It's only natural he'd struggle to leave such a large piece of his history behind," I said, trying my best to console her. Her composure cracked. I'd never seen this side of her.

"I'm sorry. This isn't your trouble," she said, dabbing her eyes.

"Rebecca, nonsense! After all you've done for me, please allow me to support you."

"He's just still in love with his wife," she said. A tear leaked out of one eye, silently, gracefully, beautifully.

"But his wife passed away many years ago," I said.

"Not to Doug."

I put my arm around her shoulders.

"There, now. I'm sure that if he knew there was a match to be had with you—"

"I rejected him," Rebecca said flatly.

I gaped. "You did what?"

"We fled the city on his boat, and it was just the two of us. Things happened. He kissed me."

"That's wonderful."

"I didn't kiss him back. We haven't talked about it since. Oh, don't you see, Luella? Doug's not the problem. He's willing to move on, to start something new. It's me, and I hate myself for it. I can't understand how any type of affection could develop when he has a literal monument erected to his late wife. How can I judge the sincerity of his feelings? If she were still alive, he would never choose me over her, even if he had known me before they were married."

"Should that matter?" I asked.

"No," she sniffed, "and yet for some reason, it does. What am I supposed to do? Go there to work with him every day? See her at every table and floorboard?"

She wiped her nose on the inside of her sleeve.

"I hate this," she continued. "I feel like a teenage girl again."

I took her hands.

"Take that, at least, as a good sign. Love makes all of us young again." I put her arm in my mine and led her back toward Fernmount House. "Now, I don't want you to fret another moment over this at present. It's Christmas time, and perhaps a wonderful celebration can help your situation. Can you try to pretend like this issue doesn't matter, and see where it gets you? At least for the next few days?"

She laughed. "I can at least try."

"If I can do it, so can you," I replied.

And I did. Our time at Fernmount was paradise. Between the gentle walkabouts in the nearby wood through crisp snow, helping to groom the horses, learning to play cards, and eating delicious food, I wished it would have stretched on forever.

The four of us created a merry band, the variety of friends I could see lasting far into the future. Doug and Edward wrestled and swapped stories as if they had been boys at school together, leaving ample time for Rebecca and me to talk about books and go riding.

The night of Christmas Eve, we enjoyed an impromptu choral performance by the staff of the house, directed by Lady Thomas. They sang carols in home-brewed harmonies in the lounge while we listened. The melodies of familiar carols brimmed with nostalgia, taking me back to Decembers long forgotten. The face of my mother toiling over a modest goose came into focus, as I played with whatever toy my father had scraped together to buy as a gift from Father Christmas.

I leaned a head on Edward's shoulder, feeling the warmth of the fire behind us and the warmth of the music in front. Wonderful smells of chocolate drifted from the kitchen. I glanced over and saw Rebecca's hand resting on Doug's massive arm. I smiled. She caught my wandering eyes and shot me a look that reminded me of Anna.

If only my sister were here now. I wondered how she would celebrate this year. It was the first Christmas we had ever spent apart. I managed her absence by stuffing the pain down with gratitude for my friends.

After the concert came a puppet show, followed by dancing. It took me some time to get the hang of the steps, but I managed to find the rhythm and swapped partners in a dizzying cycle. I relished getting to know the staff better, but nothing was better than seeing Lady Thomas scold Doug for doing the steps as gracefully as an elephant.

Before bed that night, I took out Bram's inkwell, dipped a pen, and wrote out the words "thank you". I wanted nothing to ruin the next day, and the treatment seemed to keep my episodes at bay so far.

When we woke the next morning, I was surprised to find that Christmas parcels had materialized in the dining room.

"This is from Luella and me," Lady Thomas said, handing one to

Edward. He unwrapped the pistol she had chosen back in Oxford. His face lit up like a child, and he repeated his gratitude many times. The finest there could be, he said. Lady Thomas winked at me. Could she be warming up to a possible Luella Thomas?

Rebecca opened a lovely velvet hat. She modeled it stylishly. Doug was peculiarly complimentary.

"Here you are, Doug," Edward said, shoving a wrapped package across the table. "Something for the pub when you return, and you surely will. We used to play it at headquarters in the courtyard."

Doug unwrapped a round target with several small darts.

"I've heard of this game!" Doug said, beaming.

"It's been going around for some time. Look here. These different wedges count for varying scores."

"I'm sure I will beat you later," Doug barked, his contagious laughter ringing through the air.

"And finally, Luella, for you," Edward said. He put a big box before me.

"What's this?"

"You have to unwrap it," Rebecca explained, needling me.

The box came apart, revealing a shiny, brand new Remington typewriter.

I gasped.

"Edward," I said, searching for words. "I haven't, I mean, since everything—I couldn't—"

"How could I ever let you give up on such a beautiful part of yourself?" he asked. The typewriter was beautiful. It looked as fresh as the snow outside, keys gleaming, ribbon crisp and unused. I hugged him.

"Thank you," I stuttered. I gave him a generous embrace. "Thank you."

"Well, go on," Lady Thomas said. "Why not prepare a story for tonight? Maybe I'll want to arrest you afterward."

I wiped my eyes. A smile spread across my lips. No crimson inkwell on this one. This story would just be pure Luella Winthrop.

I filled the rest of the afternoon with the clacking percussion of typewriter keys.

Chapter Twenty-One

A Very Fernmount Christmas

My story was simple, but I hoped heartfelt and appropriate for Christmas dinner. After some prodding, I read it aloud before dessert. Even the serving staff poked their heads in to listen along.

It was a quick tale of a young boy, Richard, who wished his sister, Julia, wouldn't be so selfish around the Christmas season. Julia's continual nagging and whining for a present she hoped to receive on Christmas morning drove Richard mad. His irritation waxed sore as all his attempts to enjoy the season were sidetracked by Julia's obsession over what would be on the tree.

On Christmas morning, Julia opened her gift to joyous anticipation, much to Richard's disapproval. A shiny new whistle, the very gift Richard secretly wished to receive himself. Julia beamed, then turned to her brother and explained that despite her efforts, she couldn't scrape together a tuppence for Richard's gift. So, she'd done all she could to get a shiny new whistle. Then she gave it to her brother.

Richard was overcome, and whenever he blew the whistle, he remembered that it was impossible to discern the circumstances or hearts of others.

The applause made me blush, and I sat down quickly to enjoy some delicious sticky pudding. Doug, who had never heard one of my stories before, was enthusiastically gracious, but I noticed a peculiar gleam in Lady Thomas' eye.

As the gathering of staff, family, and friends dissipated, I watched Doug and Rebecca comfortably enjoying one another's company.

There are so many faces to love. Some look like infatuation and gooeyness, others like a gentle fistfight. I gave my friends ample space, satisfying myself by casting a few encouraging glances at Rebecca.

I sipped on some cider and settled into the happy, warm glow of the room. Edward begged leave of me for a moment to tend to the fire, and Lady Thomas had taken his seat beside me in an instant, the same strange expression painted on her lips.

"That was a lovely story, Luella," she said.

"Thank you. I'm glad that the quick deadline didn't take away from the effect."

"No. It was quite effective," she said, taking another sip from her glass. "I do miss my husband, you know."

"My lady?"

"Luke. I don't know what Edward has told you, but I did love him. I was furious with him most of the time, but I loved him all the same. I just never understood what justified the time he spent away from us. But oh, he loved Christmas."

Her eyes twinkled as she talked. The table had been cleared, but it still bore noticeable marks of after-dinner. The tablecloth lay askew at intervals, there were some crumbs that missed the sweeping eye of the butler, and half-drunk glasses of coffee and cider sat forgotten.

I traced the rim of my glass, wondering if she wanted me to speak.

"What should I think of you, Miss Winthrop?" she asked. "It's infuriating. In so many ways, you remind me of a younger version of myself. I went by Charlotte back then. I was so eager to chase the world, like it was a cat running off on me. I was afraid that one day I would die and be forgotten. No portrait. No lasting effect on my community. Just vanish into emptiness."

"Charlotte is a beautiful name," I said gently after a moment of silence. "How did you meet your husband?"

She waved my question away.

"I don't want to tell you that story right now. I want to talk about my son and his intended wife."

The foggy euphoria I had been lounging in gave way to alert focus.

"He told me that the two of you intend to announce an engagement soon."

I nodded sheepishly.

"I've never known a man as good and courageous as your son," I said.

"Do you love him?" she asked.

"I do," I said, smiling into my cup of cider. I saw him across the room. He laughed while trying to convince Doug to join him in a game of darts.

"I wish that mattered more than it does," she said. "To us, it matters. The women. The stitches that hold the seams of our civilization together. To the men, it's different. They aren't content with it."

Edward threw a few of the darts and laughed as they bounced off the fletchings that Doug had already sunk into the target.

"I want my son to be happy," she said, "but I'm not blind to his lineage. If he's anything like his father, the two of us will have to be close, as we may spend a good deal of time supporting one another."

"Lady Thomas—"

"To begin with, I wish you to call me Charlotte. And please, you're not obligated to say anything right now. Just know that if you're joining this family, I wish to be on your side. I have no interest in warring over my son's attention. So, when you say that you had nothing to do with Luke's death, you better well be telling me the damnable truth."

She took a deep draught from her glass and patted my hand.

"Edward and Luella," she said, weighing the sound of it in her ears. "It has a ring to it."

She stood and walked over to her son, planting a motherly kiss on his cheek before she left the room.

Rebecca filled her seat beside me in an instant.

"You look like you've seen a ghost," she said.

I swallowed and watched Edward demand a rematch.

"Not lately," I replied.

That night, I tossed in my bed uncomfortably kept up by Charlotte Thomas' words. What bothered me most was the realization that there were sides of Edward that I did not and could not know. I'd traveled with him for a couple of months now, more time than many couples courted before an engagement, and he had been consistently exceptional.

The idea of marrying him sent warm feelings through my entire body. But did I not have reasons to doubt his sincerity? Was he inhumanly good?

The truth of the matter remained. I still did not know who infected me or why. I couldn't take any of the suspects on my list seriously. I would wager practically anything that my sister was innocent. I would say the same for Mrs. Crow. Byron was a possibility, I supposed, though I wasn't sure why he would meddle in otherworldly things. He never professed to believe in the occult.

There was Cooper. He would have Rebecca's vote.

But what if someone had inadvertently done me harm? I didn't purposely kill Luke Thomas.

I sighed. I would not find sleep tonight. Cyrus, who lay snoozing at the foot of my bed, groaned as I slipped my feet out from under the blankets. I sat at the writing desk in my room and produced Poems from the Wanderer, or the Mystic Diary, as Bram and Hirythe called it.

I wanted to put off returning, but Lady Thomas had set something off inside of me that chased out the seasonal euphoria as readily as a hound chasing a fox.

I wanted a way out of administering Hirythe's test to each of my friends to see which of them betrayed me. I would prefer finding another way to cure my ailment altogether. Then, I could go on pretending that none of them wished me harm.

I put on Edward's wool coat, ensured the pockets were free of any emotionally charged document and dug into the reading. Oddly enough, I found a Christmas poem.

Packages, parcels wrapped in paper
Toil and work are saved for later
I wish the glow of yuletide bliss
Could wash away your promises
For though they weren't wrapped like rest
They were the presents I loved best
And knowing now they've all expired
Has laid mute the brightest choirs
Still, while I sit here by the tree

I pray you'll return to me
To realize all the simple deeds
The daily love you promised me

As usual, I didn't notice when the transition happened, but I found myself at the top of a hill in the Netherdowns. This time, a bright moon lit up the fields below me with a pale, silver light. It looked like a cosmic dew had settled over everything.

It took me a moment to orient myself. The willow tree branched above. Lights from the village flickered through its drooping leaves. As always, the dark wood stretched behind me, ominous as ever, but the sky was uncharacteristically clear.

As I made my way toward the town, I saw her amidst the swaying limbs. She looked like an angel, reflecting dappled moonlight off of mirrored armor.

Drycha stared at the sky, motionless. I didn't want to disturb her, so peaceful did she look bathed in a lunar glow. But I was drawn to her like a moth to a flame. Hirythe and Bram had been open with me about their presence in the Netherdowns. I believed Drycha to be the only other living soul here.

As I neared, I noticed something that almost made me stumble.

She had taken her mask off, and underneath I saw the face of the woman from the Phantom Battalion, the one beside Bram in Hirythe's photograph. I didn't have much time with it, but the woman's appearance had a magnetic aspect that imprinted itself on my memory.

Drycha was that woman, only caked in years of sadness.

"What's it like?" she asked when I was in earshot.

"I beg your pardon?" I asked, embarrassed to have been caught spying on her.

"Coming and going at your own pleasure," she explained. "What's it like?"

"It's disorienting. The more I'm there, the more I seem to think about here. And vice versa."

She nodded and continued looking at the moon.

"You're not wearing your mask," I said. "You have such a lovely face."

She turned that lovely face down on me to scrutinize every hair on my head.

"No one can wear a mask at all times, Miss Winthrop."

I put my hands deep into my pockets. "It's just nice to see who has been under there this whole time. I saw your photo on Hirythe's desk."

She nodded. "Those were joyous times."

"So, what is the mask for? Is it just standard uniform? I've noticed Hirythe's other soldiers don't wear them."

She looked at me again, hand on the hilt of her curved sword. Her dark brown eyes reflected brightly in the moonlight, like shadows on water.

"I don't know whether I can trust you, Miss Winthrop," she said at length.

Having the distrust of a fearsome warrior standing beside you is never comforting. I did my best to act unworried.

"And why should you? I've done nothing to inspire your trust. Perhaps we can start fresh. Call me Luella."

I extended a hand, the way men of business did when meeting. She slowly gathered it up in a firm grip but didn't speak.

"And you are Drycha." I filled in on her behalf to help grease the cogs.

"That isn't true," she said, "not when I'm without my mask."

"Then who are you without your mask?"

"Olivia."

When she told her name, I heard a distant rumble of thunder, which I found odd given the cloudless sky above us. There must have been a storm coming from over the sea beyond the wood.

"It's a pleasure to meet you, Olivia," I said cheerfully.

"Perhaps I should not have told you. Hirythe won't be happy."

"He doesn't have to know. Let's keep it our secret."

"He will, anyway," she said. "It's difficult to keep secrets from a fae when you live in his memory." She leaned against a tree and stared past the sweeping valley toward the tower in town.

"Why wouldn't he want me learning your real name?"

"The same reason he wouldn't want you to see my face," she said.

My questions were getting me nowhere, and it was frustrating. Drycha was a woman of action. I took a chance.

"You're being cryptic. It's all right if you don't trust me, but making me feel stupid is unkind," I said, calling her out.

She smiled. It was a tragically beautiful smile, straining under-used muscles in her face.

"Perhaps you have more of a backbone than I realized. Luella, I've gone so long without someone real to talk to. You've been told that everything in the Netherdowns is made of memory. I'm not. But I have to pretend that I am."

"What for?"

"Because Bram thinks I'm dead."

I wrapped my coat around my body a little tighter. A breeze was blowing past us, making our hair dance. My mind fluttered to the book of poetry that brought me here. I'd read no shortage of love poems.

"Why would Bram need to believe you are dead?"

"Do you love him?" she asked. She pushed off from the tree and pierced me with an intense stare.

"Who? Bram?" I stepped back. "No. Don't be ridiculous. He's much too... strange, I suppose. No, no. I'm practically engaged to a man named Edward. A detective."

"Ah," she said, relaxing her shoulders. "Well, let me ask you a hypothetical question. Which would you rather live with? In one scenario, you accidentally give Edward an incurable condition that eats away at his soul forever. In the other, Edward dies in an accident beyond your control."

"What a ghastly question," I replied. Considering her options drew my mind to Bram. He had, in fact, led me into a terrible condition. Is it possible that he wished I'd die in some accident?

"It's cruel," I said as I mulled it over, "but I'd prefer if he were dead at no fault of mine than to know I caused his ruin."

"I'm like you, Luella, except in one aspect. By the time Bram realized Sraith had infected me, any hope of a cure was well beyond our reach. I am in love with Bram. Back then, we didn't know about Sraith. He could not have known what our magical explorations would do to me, but that won't remedy his guilt."

She sank to the ground next to the trunk of the willow.

"Hirythe and I staged an accident to set him free. He thought I fell overboard on a voyage back to England from one of our adventures. Hearing his reaction tore me apart. I wanted to climb back up the side of the boat and tell him it was a trick. But when we realized I was losing control of my mind, it changed our relationship. I had lost him. He had lost himself. I needed to set him free."

I struggled for words.

"Don't look at me like that. It wasn't your choice to make. Don't judge me."

"I'm sorry. I don't mean to offend. I'm just taking it all in."

And it was a lot to take in. Drycha, Olivia, was telling me she was in love with Bram. And, given the way she told the story, that Bram was in love with her. And she was alive. How could she keep that from him while she was living in a place created from his memory?

"What would happen if Bram found out the truth?"

"There are times I can't bear it," she said. "I either want to find him and show him who I really am. Other times, I want to kill him. But it's not just that."

She walked over to her satchel on the ground near the tree and picked up the mirrored mask.

"If Bram saw me, there's no telling how he would react. What if he chose to spend all his time here in a halfway place? What if he never came back? What if realizing that I had tricked him turned our memories into dark, twisted things, more monsters for us to fight at the gate?"

She carefully put the mask back down. I felt a stab of pain for her. I was fully aware of the Netherdown's dangers. The bull that materialized from the spell in my pocket was real enough.

"It seems wrong that you're keeping this from Bram. Why not just leave the Netherdowns? Why are you all stuck here in the first place?"

"Safety. Perhaps you've experienced the same, but my condition doesn't bother me here. If I leave, what if I end up in an asylum? Besides, there is still a member of our old brigade that wishes harm on us."

I nodded. The first time I entered the diary, I felt practically weightless.

"Well, that explains you. Is Hirythe infected by magic as well?"

She looked at me as if I had just asked a very stupid question.

"You can't poison a viper with its own venom," she said. "Hirythe is magic. But that makes him easier to trace in the world out there. To keep him a secret from Jeremy, we've kept him in here."

"Jeremy?"

"He's the one who turned on us," she said.

"Bram told me that Jeremy's brother died on one of your expeditions."

She nodded.

"An accident. But when a loved one dies, emotions can be dangerous and illogical. He and his brother were aware of the danger, but Jeremy swore that we withheld information. Since then, he's made it his personal mission to hunt the rest of us down."

"There were five of you, then?" I asked. She shook her head.

"Six, but one of us didn't believe in the Netherdowns. One of our expeditions in Iceland spooked him. He didn't want much to do with magic after that."

I sat down beside her. I had so often wondered about Bram's history. He shared so little of it with me. Now, it came into focus in an ugly, plain type of way.

He was a treasure hunter. He and his colleagues tracked down traces of magic and gambled on the effects they might have. He was a fool, tampering with powers he didn't understand. I understood now why the fog creature had called him the Meddler.

"You're lucky he cared enough to expose you only to small, intermittent doses of the magic," she said. "Had you waded waist-deep into the magic as I did, you might be like me."

I found the courage to take her arm.

"I'm sure he cared for you. We can't begrudge our friends their ignorance."

She looked at me icily, and the breeze bit through my coat.

"If you tell Bram, I'll kill you," she said. I'd seen how agile she was with the sword at her hip. I didn't doubt her. "You may have perverted notions of true love or justice. This is not your decision to make. If you try to undo what we've done, I don't share man's tender outlook on the docile nature of women."

Her gaze was sharp, her features resolute, and I felt like I may have been staring into the eyes of an ancient warrior. Where did she learn such ferocity?

"I told you I wanted to earn your trust, didn't I?" I said. She nodded, put her mask back on, and shouldered her satchel. I heard a sharp whistle and the not-so-far off reaction of horse's hooves.

"How long have you been in the Netherdowns?" I asked. She sighed and slung her satchel over the feathered horse that now stood by her side.

"Seven years."

I gasped.

"All that time? Do you have no hope of leaving?"

She silently checked the belts and buckles of the horse's saddle.

"If we find a cure for Sraith, and we can permanently dissuade Jeremy from his desire for vengeance, there is hope." She looked at me, and I saw myself in her mask, arms crossed and moonlit locks of hair gently moving in the breeze.

"I wish I could promise you everything will be well," I said, sheepishly.

"No one can." She swung a leg over the horse and held her arm out to me. "Come on. I'm assuming you didn't come here to talk to me."

Chapter Twenty-Two

Dream Meets Memory

"I hope you're back to share some good news," Hirythe said, taking a sip from a teacup. He, Bram, and I were in his study, enjoying the warmth of a healthy fire in the hearth. I had to admit, there was something homey and inspiring about his choice of decor. I imagined great minds toiling away with all sorts of architectural instruments or writing great works. The way the hearth illuminated the tall-backed chairs we occupied framed our conversation like a philosophical debate.

"I haven't administered the test to anyone, yet, if that's what you mean."

Hirythe looked annoyed.

"Are you having trouble finding your possible enchanters?" he asked.

I buried myself in the chair.

"It's not that easy," I said elusively. He tsked me.

"It doesn't matter if it's easy for you or not. If you don't hurry, things might go sour."

"Look around," Bram said, gesturing to the office, "things are already sour. We're all trapped in a book. Relax, Hirythe, it's Christmas."

I swelled with gratitude for Bram's understanding and regretted I had not brought them gifts. Never show up to a party empty-handed, my mother would say.

Hirythe crossed to a stand on his desk and picked up a long, notched knife. He waved it in a motion of acquiescence.

"Luella, forgive me if I speak too plainly for your ever so sensitive ears."

I stared at the fire.

"What about you two?" I asked. "Have you discovered anything new regarding my condition? A part of me hopes that two brilliant minds like yours may rid me of the awkward responsibility of singing to my ex-fiancé."

"I've been very busy," Hirythe said dismissively. "We were attacked again earlier today. Nasty business. At this rate, I'm not sure how many more good memories we have left to fight the bad."

Bram cleared his throat and crossed to a standing slate board beside the fireplace. He picked up a piece of light blue chalk and began explaining.

"Fortunately, I'm not a part of the defense team, and I have made some progress. Let's sum up what we know. Luella is doubly infected," he said, scribbling on the slate like a professor. "At first, I thought it happened when she used the ink to write her stories for Langley's Miscellany. While that is true, the precautions I used to guard her from the effects of that exposure proved ineffective."

"Precautions?" Hirythe scoffed. "You've always considered magic like a disease."

"Well, in some ways it is," Bram retorted. "At least to us human beings."

"Not always," Hirythe muttered. I looked back and forth between them like watching two bickering children.

"As I was saying," Bram tapped the slate with the chalk, "I limited her exposure to the magic, but the effect we know as Sraith took root radically fast. We've also deduced that she had her first brush with magic before she even met me, let alone when she tried the ink for the first time."

"My dream," I said. I had that terrible dream of reliving Edward's case, filled with downy fog and the shocking view of my father's face. "It was the first time something otherworldly impersonated my father in a dream."

"And it impersonated your father since then?" Hirythe asked.

"Often," I nodded. "He would sit and talk with me, using my father's memory to influence my decisions. That's what pushed me to become more daring with the ink."

"You mean, the fog creature wanted you to dive deeper into the magic?" Hirythe asked, looking up from the knife.

"I suppose." I narrowed my eyes. "Did you just use the term fog creature?"

"It's merely a place holder!"

Bram cleared his throat.

"I propose that this other magic is working to multiply Sraith's effect. It's a catalyst."

"That explains why I can't see it clearly," Hirythe said. I furrowed my brows and picked at the sofa.

"Why do you say that? What's a catalyst?"

"A catalyst," Bram drew a circle on the slate, "is a form of magic particularly adept at hiding itself." He drew a little star in the middle of the circle. "It buoys up another type of magic and comfortably settles down in a little corner somewhere out of view."

The fae dropped his knife on the desk with a clatter.

"Drawing them out like that it makes it sound like we're discussing mice," Hirythe complained.

"This is the best way I can show it on a slate," Bram replied.

"Just say it practically," Hirythe placed a chair next to mine and took a seat. "Miss Winthrop, what he means to say is that your symptoms are skewed so it's difficult to identify exactly what the source is."

Bram sat on the edge of his own chair, surrounded by two men obsessed with differing theories.

"You have a distorted view of cause and effect," he said.

"I very much appreciate your summation," I replied, not so chuffed as he appeared to be.

"But seeing a creature that impersonates your memories is not typical of our findings about Sraith."

I slapped my hands down on my knees. "I understand already. You don't know what's wrong with me. But I can't help but feel like this is all preamble. Bram, you look too optimistic."

He crossed again to the slate.

"We need to collect more information about what's inside you. If we do that, then maybe, possibly, we can figure out how to fix things. So, I propose that you stop using the ink to treat your symptoms."

He tossed the chalk in the air as if he'd just solved an equation. My chin sunk to to my chest.

"This is your brilliant plan? If I stop using the ink, I'll have another outbreak." The idea terrified me. I thought of the rage-filled nights, the fear of not knowing what would happen when the lights went out.

"Exactly," he said. "Then as you are experiencing the attack, I will monitor what happens in an unbiased, objective way, and then, hopefully, we can figure out what is acting as our catalyst."

"Absolutely not," I said.

"He didn't even get to the part you will like most," Hirythe said with a sardonic smile.

"What?"

"We can't do it here," Bram said. "As you may have realized, your attacks simply won't occur in the Netherdowns. That was one protection we built into the diary. Whatever is combining with Sraith will have to wait outside."

"So the magic is just sitting there waiting for me to come back?" I asked.

"In very simplistic terms, yes."

I blinked before understanding what he was saying.

"No." I stood up. "No. No. No. I already said, you can't come back with me. There has to be another way to do all of this. How am I supposed to explain to Edward and his mother who you are and what you're doing at their home, in my room no less!"

"I'm not going on holiday with you," he said, stuffing his hands into his pockets. "I'll come out of the diary at night and be gone by morning."

"You are absolutely impossible," I said, pacing the length of the rug.

"Yet here he is," Hirythe said, "despite all reason."

"What if someone walks into my room?"

Bram mocked an injury to his sensibilities.

"And who, may I ask, are you admitting to your private bedroom in the middle of the night?"

I threw a book at him this time, a nice hefty one from the side table by my chair. This elicited bothered responses from both of them.

"Easy with that book. It's older than you are many times over," Hirythe shouted. Well, he never really shouted, but his voice rang with more presence.

"I won't do it. There must be an alternative."

"One alternative, despite Bram's insistence that only he can correctly record your episode, is to find someone you trust that can watch over you and write down their observations. Bram and I can be satisfied with a secondhand account. Isn't that right, Bram?"

Bram shuffled his feet.

"Well, why didn't you just say so from the beginning? Edward could —"

"No, not Edward." Bram jerked his hands out of his pockets. A dark shadow passed over his brow. Hirythe and I both stared at him in alarm.

"May I ask why not?" Hirythe voiced my question, though I suspected to know the answer. I wondered if Bram the Meddler considered jealousy a high or low magic. Would he be jealous if he knew Olivia breathed not far from where we were now?

"He is too close to you," he said. Was this true or merely a tactical retreat? "His observations will be tainted by his emotion for you. Concern will dot every I and cross every T. It will have to be someone who can look on with the objective eyes of a scholar."

Despite my suspicions, I couldn't argue with him. Edward had sat with me through many of my episodes, but each experience had been agonizing for him.

"Very well," Hirythe said slowly, as if we were both children. I supposed to him, we were. "Is there someone else, then? Someone you could trust?"

I stood and paced in front of the fire.

"Well, there's Rebecca, but I'm not certain that she didn't enchant me in the first place. It's unlikely, but possible. I met her before my first dream."

Hirythe crossed his legs dramatically.

"Miss Winthrop, I can only take so much offense. I literally bound my soul to a melody for this exact purpose. Is there a reason you throw that gift right back in my face, and on Christmas, no less?"

I bit my lip.

"I'm sorry. That must have been very hard for you, but you must understand the risk of going back to Dawnhurst to find the people I suspect. The police there want me for murder."

"I understand all that, but if this woman—Relcavitch did you say?" I stared at him.

"Rebecca."

"Yes, Rebecca. If she's available to monitor your evening attacks, she's available to hear a little song."

He was right, and I supposed of the people on my list, singing to Rebecca was more comfortable than Sergeant Cooper or Byron Livingston.

My shoulders fell.

"All right. I'll test Rebecca and ask her to take observations."

"Miracles do happen," Hirythe said with a dismissive wave of his hand.

"As soon as you have some observations from you friend, come right back and share them with us," Bram cautioned.

"I will," I said. "I promise."

Bram clapped his hands.

"Well, Hirythe, it looks like you'll be hosting me for a bit longer."

I bit my lip, realizing my refusal of Bram's plan effectively trapped him in the diary so long as I had it in my custody. He couldn't very well come out of it while the book sat at Fernmount.

"I'm sorry, Bram," I said. "If you want, I could leave the diary somewhere discreet so you could return to the real world."

He shook his head.

"There's no point. I'll need to come back anyway, and Hirythe's right. Too much back and forth might give us away if Jeremy can track the magic."

I nodded.

"Thank you for all of this," I said. It seemed so futile. I looked at Bram and considered our brief but deep history. "Especially if it's true what you say about me being infected before we met, I owe you a great deal."

"Happy Christmas," he replied with a sad smile.

Hirythe stood and looked out the window. He listened carefully for a moment.

"Enjoy the festivities, you two," he said. "It appears the terrible memories don't respect your holidays. Drycha will need me at the tower."

"What? An attack at the gate, now?" I asked.

"Hopefully, the gate and not the wood, or else none of us may survive the night." The fae swooped by a coat rack, tossed a heavy cloak over his shoulders, and was out the door. The fire crackled in the quiet after him.

I realized this was the first I'd been alone with Bram since he left Dawnhurst. For some reason, it felt awkward now.

"How is my dog?" he asked casually.

"Good, I think. As happy as a dog can be." I quickly added, "without its true owner, I mean."

Bram smiled and rested his head on the back of his chair.

"Likely happier."

There were so many questions I wished to ask him, especially in the wake of my conversation with Olivia, but they stuck on my lips. He wasn't just an obscure carnival worker, anymore. He socialized with fae, built a small world from memory, had a traumatic past... He had lived so much life compared to me.

"You're staring," he said. I jumped.

"I am not."

"You are. What is it?"

I took a deep breath.

"It's just—I mean everything—you built a world out of memories, Bram?"

He laughed.

"It seemed like a good idea at the time. I'm not sure I'd do it again. I find myself here much too often. It's hard staying away."

"After you left Dawnhurst, why did you come here? Was your only aim to consult with Hirythe?"

He leaned forward, gazing into the fire.

"Yes, and no. After I learned you were infected, I hoped to find something here to help you."

"In Hirythe's memory?"

"Or in my own. Luella, I have holes in my memory that shouldn't be there. People I should remember but can't, or at least I can't remember what happened to them."

My thoughts flew to Olivia.

"I don't know if I unintentionally blocked things out or if I was prey to an accident that caused these lapses, but I've always hoped they were in here somewhere." He looked at me. "Have you ever forgotten something you were sure was precious or important to you?"

His words reminded me of the song my father sang when I was a child. I hadn't remembered it until I wrote it in the diary, yet now the memory was so precious. How had I let it lapse?

"Somewhere in the Netherdowns, I want to find the pieces and put them back together," he went on. I furrowed my brow.

"Is that what a silver currant is?" I asked. He smiled. "I heard Hirythe shout it at you by Hollow Lake."

"Something like that. I've never found one, so I can't speak too accurately, but from what Hirythe has told me, a silver currant is like eating one of your purest memories. They come back to you in their truest form." He wandered over to the window. "If I could find one, I wonder what it would show me. My search for it in the village has been fruitless, excuse the pun, but I wonder if I were to explore the surrounding forest..."

I shuddered.

"You said there's no telling what's in that forest. It fills me with dread just looking at it."

"It does the same to me. But I'm starting to believe that to discover true insight about myself, I must be willing to face the darkest parts of my character."

Bram was an adventurer. He chased after treasures and unknown pathways, addicted to the thrill it gave him. We were so different in that respect. I had no intention of ever going near that forest again. I'd already had enough adventure for my lifetime.

All I wanted was to settle down into a cozy life with Edward. Let the adventurers search for their silver currants or their untamed memories. I was just searching for a way home.

Chapter Twenty-Three

A Test of Friendship

I didn't return from the Netherdowns until the early hours of the morning. After allowing myself the indulgence of sleeping in well past my usual hour, I woke up groggy and ached all over. I was getting too old to stay up so late.

I found Rebecca in the dining room reading a novel by Jules Verne, an adventurous French writer. When I entered, she set the book down.

"Can you possibly imagine what the world would be like so deep under the sea?" She asked without preamble.

"Is it your first time reading that novel?" I asked. She shook her head and laughed.

"Are you joking? It might be my tenth. But what an imagination the author has. I've read only one other writer with such creativity."

"And who's that?" I scooped some butter to scrape over her half-eaten slice of dark brown bread. I hadn't felt hungry, but fatigue had different ideas.

"Luella Winthrop," she smiled. "Do you remember that piece you wrote about the dogs' art heist?"

I waved the bread knife at her.

"Let's not bring that up."

She took a sip of her tea. Rose appeared from the kitchen and brought out a bit of breakfast reserved for me. She smiled at me sweetly. I'd tried to tell her I was no different than she was, but being connected to Edward as I was, she treated me as if I was born into nobility.

In any case, I had a dress to return to her. She set down my a full English breakfast and scuttled from the room before I could get two words in.

"So that typewriter was quite the gift," Rebecca said, a question laced artfully in an observation. She would have made an excellent reporter if she ever had the interest.

"It was very thoughtful," I said after a bite of roasted tomato.

"If I didn't know better, it's what I would call a husband gift."

"Excuse me?"

"Flowers, jewelry, those are new romance gifts. Dresses and clothing are gifts reserved for relationships a little more mature. But a typewriter? That is a gift from someone secure about the prospects of the relationship and can afford to invest in a woman's passions."

"You've given a lot of thought to this," I said, cutting into a bit of sausage. I didn't mind Rebecca's questions. In fact, I relished dangling something in front of her like this. Good news is like a showing off a successful garden.

"Come on, Luella. I've been here for days. I can tell something is going on. What are you hiding?" She moved to the seat directly beside me. "I shared my developments with Doug. Your turn."

"Have you? Our conversation before Christmas and your proximity the night after told two very different stories."

She blushed. It was so fun seeing Rebecca in my shoes for once.

"Christmas magic," she said. "I was only trying to do what you said."

"And how was it?"

She shook her head vehemently. "It's my turn for questions."

I smiled with closed lips.

"All right," she said, putting an arm on the back of her chair. "You're not as mysterious as you believe to be. Shall I explain what is happening?"

This was the Rebecca I knew. Confident. Clever. I inclined my head while I ate my eggs.

"You've agreed to be married, but you're afraid of his mother's opinion, so you're keeping it secret until you're ready to make a public announcement."

She crossed her arms as though she'd solved an equation. I put down my fork, exasperated.

"Rebecca, how am I supposed to enjoy anything if you're going to sniff it out on your own?"

"So, I'm right?" she practically stood out of her chair.

"Not exactly." I grabbed her hand.

"Well clear it up! What exactly?"

If I was to ask her to observe my attacks for Bram and Hirythe, I needed to know I could trust her. I would prefer if I could explain everything. I would like a friend I didn't suspect of betrayal.

"Do you trust me, Rebecca?" I asked. She leaned back.

"What kind of question is that? Have I not proved my loyalty?"

She had a point. Rebecca had undergone no minor sacrifice for my well-being. Of course, that's part of why somewhere I doubted her sincerity. I never had discovered why Rebecca showed me such loyalty. We bonded instantly. It was so easy. Was it too easy?

"I'm going to sing something to you now," I said, lacking any better explanation. "Is that all right?"

"Something unusual is about to happen, isn't it?" Her eyes widened. In Dawnhurst, I had told her about Bram's ink and pen. I admired how she took the news, reluctantly believing me against her better judgment.

"Don't be afraid," I said. "It's just a song." Was her fear an act? If she had enchanted me, she might know something was amiss. How would Rebecca act when cornered?

"Very well." She smiled. "I've never experienced magic before."

"Remember to breathe." It was odd to feel like I was in control of a magical experience. To Rebecca, I may as well have been a wizard. I looked in her eyes and started singing.

>*Do you hear the echo*
>*On the crags and in the meadow?*
>*Do you see the moonlight mellow*
>*In the cracks and in the barrow?*

But where have the hill folk gone?
And where have the wood folk gone?

She didn't turn away from me. She sat there, regal and solemn. As I looked into her irises, I strained my ears for the sounds of the voices that would identify whether she had tried to manipulate high magic.

But I could hear only my shaky voice. Rebecca's chest heaved in and out. Neither of us spoke for a good minute or two. The remaining eggs on my plate grew cold.

"Where did you learn such a song?" she said at last.

"It's an old tune," I said, "about the fae."

"You're not much of a singer, Luella."

I broke into a laugh. Rebecca was not my enemy. She never had been. To think otherwise was ludicrous.

"What? Why are you laughing?" she asked, but it only made me laugh harder. "Did you just perform some prank on me? I knew it! I shouldn't have believed you! Oh, you're awful! You are simply awful!"

"It's not that," I said. The laughter teased tears from my eyes. I squeezed her hand firmly. "I've missed you so much."

She hugged me, and we were both crying. She wiped her eyes.

"Now aren't we poetic ladies?" she asked sarcastically.

"I hope you didn't have plans this morning because I plan to monopolize its entirety." I filled her teacup and began in hushed tones.

I held nothing back. It was as though we were chatting away in Doug's Fish and Chip Pub. I'd forgotten how well Rebecca listened. She nodded at all the right parts of the story, gasped at others, and pressed for more information when needed.

When I told her about my shopping appointment with Charlotte Thomas, she nearly fainted. In fact, she seemed more stricken by that account than the giant cat or bull in the Netherdowns.

She made it incredibly easy on me. When I finished, she looked at the novel she'd been reading.

"If Jules Verne only understood how strange life truly is," she muttered.

"After everything I've been through, I don't doubt there is a giant creature at the bottom of the sea."

Rebecca put a hand to her head.

"To think all this time Byron Livingston infected you!" I almost spit out a sip of tea.

"That's not certain," I said. "Why would Byron purposefully unleash some evil power on me? How?"

"If it were so obvious, we would have seen it before," she replied. "How does the book work? To travel to the Netherdowns I mean?"

I paused. I'd never had it properly explained to me. Teaching my method to another felt clumsy.

"Have you experienced the sensation when you're engrossed in the words of a book? There's a moment where the world around you fades and you become absorbed to the point of distraction. Someone might need to say your name twice or three times to snap you out of it."

"Oh, I know all about that." She nodded enthusiastically.

"Well, it's like that. There's no shortcut, you must to get to reading, and when you dive in, truly dive in, you emerge in the Netherdowns on a hill under one of three beautiful trees."

I smiled to myself. I'd just discovered another type of high magic. That had to be as powerful as music.

Rebecca looked like she was trying very hard not to clap her hands in delight.

"What is the matter with you?" I asked.

"It's just—I'm sorry. It's created loads of problems for you, but it's real. I mean, it's all real. I dreamed of magic when I was a little girl. I can't remember at what age I shoved down the whispers inside of me. To know the feeling of a spring morning might hold more than time, or that the bonds of friendship might be more than etiquette."

She trailed off and looked outside as if this were the first time she'd ever seen snow blanketing the ground. I smiled. Magic had made my life infinitely more complicated. And yet, Rebecca was right. It had saved me. What if I had married Byron? What if my life were simply trying to fill a frame on a wall?

There was so much at stake, and the risk made living all the sweeter.

Rebecca's face darkened as her thoughts returned to the complications at hand.

"You have to test Byron," she concluded.

"Yes."

"The police in that city have claimed you're a murderer."

"That's right."

"I suppose Christmas is over. Have you told Edward?"

"No. And I don't want him to hear about everything in the Netherdowns."

Rebecca raised a signature eyebrow at me.

"You told me you were planning on marrying Edward," she said, tapping a finger on the table.

"I am. Oh, stop looking at me like that. He's already done so much for me. I don't want to concern him. I've already found a method to treat my symptoms. That was the only thing keeping me from him in the first place."

"How do you plan to explain why you need to go back to Dawnhurst?"

"I haven't decided yet." I sipped my tea. I had almost forgotten her uncanny ability at pushing me to ponder what was least comfortable.

"I'm afraid you're going in circles," she said. "Half a year ago, weren't you engaged to a different man, keeping different secrets from him?"

"That's not the same," I said.

"Why not?" she asked. I swallowed.

"I kept secrets from Byron because deep down I didn't love him. I'm keeping secrets from Edward because I do really love him."

She looked at me in that motherly way, and my insides coiled up like a defensive serpent. There was a reason I had mentioned none of this to Edward. There had been a time I wanted to tell him everything, share every part of my story with him. He told me he wanted the hard truths to come out slowly over the course of a lifetime. Now, I wondered if a lifetime might be too brief.

"You haven't tested him yet, have you?" Rebecca asked.

I bit my lip.

"I don't need to," I said.

"You didn't need to with me, either," she offered.

"That's not the same."

"You keep saying that."

"This time I'm right."

"I understand. You don't think it's him. If that's true, what harm is there in checking?"

"Rebecca, enough," I said, more forcefully than I intended. She sat back, startled, reminding me of the night I had once attacked her while under the influence of magic. I took a breath.

"For some things, you don't need magic. It wasn't Edward." It can't have been Edward. I wouldn't test him.

Even if I had seen the dangerous gleam in his eye when he offered me a spell. Even if his mother had a peculiarly strong disapproval of anything deemed supernatural. Even if his affection for me was all but inexplicable.

I snapped from my thoughts as I heard the rambunctious friendship between Doug Tanner and Edward Thomas approach the dining room.

"I won. There's no shame in admitting it, Lord Thomas," Doug called mockingly.

"I don't know how you inspired your horse to snap at mine like that, but in any civilized race it would be considered cheating."

They turned through the door frame, the bottom half of their pants spattered in mud.

"It's hard for races to be civilized when you're riding animals. Despite how fancy the riders' clothes are, they're still animals." Doug plopped down ungracefully next to Rebecca at the table. She looked at him with a disgruntled expression, evidently displeased they'd interrupted our conversation

"What's gotten into you?" he asked.

"You enjoy the gift of timing," she replied.

"You two look like you had a bad egg," Edward said. "Is everything all right?"

Rebecca and I had a quick tennis match, trying to communicate wordlessly how best to navigate this conversation.

"Doug, we should leave these two alone for a moment. Luella has to discuss something of great importance with Edward."

"Something important?" Edward asked. "I hope nothing is wrong."

"Come along, Doug," Rebecca grabbed him by the arm and dragged him out of the room despite his grumblings that he was starving. I shot Rebecca a nasty look as she exited, which she politely reciprocated. Game, set, and match.

Edward and I were alone

Chapter Twenty-Four

A Change of Plans

Edward called a miniature conference in the library that evening. The room was lit only by the roaring fire in the hearth. Edward had insisted it best not to illuminate meetings that ought to go unnoticed.

Somehow, I convinced him I needed to go back to Dawnhurst. It hadn't been easy, but I pleaded with him we should clear my family name. I didn't want him to be courting a fugitive.

I also told him that my treatment was ongoing, and a crucial factor for my eventual clean bill of health required a face-to-face intervention with Byron. He pressed me for details. I made something about retracing my steps and letting the magic unwind, like untangling a knot.

At least it was close to the truth. He hadn't liked it, stomping around in a rotten mood for a good portion of the day. He demanded to go into the Netherdowns and talk to Bram himself. It was outrageous! The risk was too high! It was simply impossible! Couldn't be done.

Etcetera etcetera.

I tried reminding him that the sooner we managed it, the sooner we had a clear and beautiful pathway to our union.

I even gave him the Mystic Diary, knowing that in his current state it would be impossible for him to get lost in the words and enter the Netherdowns. He pored over the text anyway, causing me no small degree of anxiety in the case I was wrong.

In the end, though, he got up in a huff and took a walk around the property. He came back with a clear head full of apologies and, ever the detective at heart, a plan of attack.

"So what's this about, Edward?" Lady Thomas asked over a glass of wine. "Why have you lit the room as if Jacob Marley were due for a visit?"

"We need to go back to Dawnhurst," he said, an elbow on the mantle, looking more dashing than was appropriate for the moment.

His mother puckered her lips as if someone swapped her drink for lemon juice. She shot a glance at Doug and Rebecca, who vacantly moved pieces around a chessboard.

"Are you sure that's wise?" she asked.

"Sergeant Cooper has lost his mind. We all know that," Edward said. "Everyone in this room is aware of his allegations against Luella."

"Edward!" his mother hissed.

"It's all right, my Lady," Doug said. "Rebecca here worked with your son to organize Luella's escape. Myself? I stalled the police force while she snuck out the window." He beamed as if this was supposed to calm Lady Thomas' worries.

I stifled a laugh, remembering how well Doug had played the part. His dramatic acting with Mrs. Crow was worthy of the Globe Theatre in London. Lady Thomas sunk into her chair.

"How very kind of you," she grumbled. The poor woman. She grabbed at every thread of propriety left to her. I was flattered. That she was trying to keep my secrets meant she acknowledged me as a member of the family, or at least close enough to her son to incriminate her should I be exposed. That was something.

Still, I hadn't forgotten her veiled threat from Christmas. She might play along, but I had not yet convinced her I was guiltless.

"To clear Luella's name, we need to expose how ridiculous Cooper's accusation really is."

"How do you intend to do that?" Rebecca asked. "There's been some criticism of Cooper in a few magazines, but it'd take something spectacular to make it go away entirely."

"I plan to remove him from his role as Police Sergeant," Edward said grimly. My mouth dropped.

"Remove him as Police Sergeant?" Lady Thomas asked. "Isn't that a little severe?"

"It's the only way," Edward replied. "If Cooper's gone mad, then he shouldn't have command, anyway."

I looked at Edward with a furrowed brow. He and I both knew that Cooper's suspicions in me had some merit. It didn't seem fair to penalize him for having an experienced instinct.

"It's the only way," he repeated, purposefully avoiding my gaze. "But it will take some creativity to convince a few of the city's lead publications to take the bait."

"Let me get this straight," Doug said, turning away from his chess game. "You want to get the papers to write incriminating articles on the Sergeant?"

Edward nodded solemnly.

"That's cold, but no more than he deserves." Doug folded his arms.

"It is cold," Edward agreed, "but it's less cold if we can stick to truth rather than make up fiction."

"Please," I said. My stomach churned as I imagined what my father might think about this plan. My anxiety started to build. My fingers began to twitch. I hadn't used the crimson ink since Christmas Eve. "We can't start inventing falsehoods about Cooper."

"So we just need to find some truth that can unveil Cooper's impropriety." Edward said. "Conflicts of interest, illogical conclusions."

"Cooper knew Luella's father," Rebecca said, shrugging. "It's not much, but some of the best stories start with a small kernel of coincidence."

"He admired my father," I protested.

"It's enough that they had a relationship at all," Rebecca countered. "Didn't you tell me your father would often go into the police station to talk his friends out of a jail sentence?"

"He did. But I don't see what that has to do with Luke Thomas' murder."

"All the better," Edward said. "Let the writers write. It will help with the second phase of my plan."

"Second phase?" I asked.

"Yes, after we've undermined Cooper's authority, we must bring in some credible voices to recommend action. And who would be more credible than some of Dawnhurst's influential families?"

He let his suggestion settle into the room.

"You mean you'd convince your rich family friends to speak up on Luella's behalf?" Doug asked.

"I mean, the grieving widow speaks up for Luella," he said, turning to his mother. She didn't look surprised. I think she put the pieces together before any of us.

"You want me to campaign for her," she said, folding her hands calmly in her lap. "I think it will backfire. It's already suspicious that you two are romantically involved. I'm just speaking honestly."

She was right. That had always gnawed at me.

"I would agree with you, if you were the only one coming out in her support," Edward said. "But I hope you'll be persuaded to make a visit to the Rigbys."

My eyes went wide. Jacob Rigby would be, by now, my sister's husband or very close to it. She had left me to distance herself from my scandal.

"We can't get my sister involved in this," I stammered. "I have to respect her privacy and independence."

"Who are the Rigbys?" Lady Thomas asked Edward. Rebecca answered.

"They're a wealthy family with a home in Dawnhurst. Jacob's father is a solicitor, is he not?"

Edward nodded, urging Rebecca on.

"Their son, Jacob, has married Anna Winthrop, Luella's sister." Rebecca said.

"They are married, then?" I asked, eager to hear anything about her. Rebecca nodded.

"They announced it in the paper a couple of weeks past. I'm sorry I didn't tell you before. I wasn't sure how you'd take it, being Christmas and all. I know you miss her."

I swallowed a painful lump climbing my throat. So she'd done it. She got the husband she always wanted. I had chided her so much about immature love, but look at her now. I tried to imagine Anna's beautiful face in a beautiful home.

What if Edward's plan worked? Would I be willing to sabotage Cooper's reputation for a chance at reuniting with my most dear sister? I didn't dare hope that she might attend my own wedding, that we might visit at holidays or travel together, that we might—

"Edward, why don't you stop dancing around the issue and just lay the plan out clearly," his mother said. She picked up her glass again and took a deep sip of her wine.

"It's simple. If there's to be any future for Luella and myself, we have to deal with this murder allegation once and for all. To do that, I propose we arrange a meeting with the Rigby family at their home outside the city. While we're there, we can bring them into our confidence and win them over to our way of thinking."

"You mean convince them that Cooper isn't fit to lead the police," I said.

"Convince them," he continued steadily, "that Cooper has some improper motive for going after Luella and that he has targeted the Winthrop family unjustly. If we can convince them to help us, we can spread similar sentiments to other influential families and make a statement about it to the papers, all but exonerating Luella once and for all."

"What if they push for a trial?" Rebecca asked through a look of concern.

"Let them," Lady Thomas said. "What does Luella have to hide?"

"They wouldn't dare," Edward said. "By announcing Luella as my fiancée, she would enjoy the same privileges as the rest of our family. You don't lightly bring a lady of a certain status into court with no evidence."

The room fell silent. I felt as though everyone was staring at me, even though they were all avoiding my gaze at all costs.

"Is she your fiancée," Lady Thomas asked slowly. He looked at me with a pained expression.

"I'm sorry, Luella," he said. "I'd have wanted to do this differently, but given the circumstances, I don't know if we can delay."

He walked toward me and clutched my hands. My breath caught. This wasn't the way I had envisioned it. In my daydreams, his mother wasn't here.

"Luella Winthrop, if you'll have me, would you do me the greatest of honors and join your life with mine?"

It's difficult to communicate the feelings generated by a proposal from someone you love so dearly. Even if you know it's coming, even if the circumstances aren't ideal, there is nothing in the world like a man pledging his loyalty in the most permanent way possible. When you know the man to be scrupulously bonded to his word, it renders the proposal all the more meaningful.

What's more validating and intimidating than knowing someone else wants to make you his life's mission?

Of course, it's not just flattery and sweet feelings with proposals either. Doubt lurks behind everything. I thought I had cast out all doubts by now. Sure, Edward and I had our rough patches recently, but who wouldn't have given the circumstances. Still, the fear crept from its hiding place and irritated me like a thorn in a stocking.

I caused the death of this man's father.

His mother still harbored a healthy distrust toward me.

I was keeping secrets from him.

I was still magically ill, no one could even diagnose me, let alone cure me.

I was still dependent on Bram.

Edward might have enchanted me in the first place.

The list stretched on.

In the end, though, humans give themselves the benefit of the doubt when they see opportunities for happiness. At least, this human did.

"Luella?" Edward prodded. I snapped from my thoughts. Eight wide eyes from all corners of the room looked at me. "Please."

Perhaps it was the "please" that melted the tears from my eyes. It was a subtle reminder of just how sweet he was to me. That was enough. Steps of sweetness are enough to traverse a life of companionship.

"Yes," I said, closing my eyes. "So many times, yes. Oh, Edward."

The smile that lit up his face could never be taken from me. In bleak times, I would cling to it like fresh air.

We embraced, and I shut my eyes tight enough to forget the awkward circumstance and the others in the room. I squeezed him. He would be mine, and I would be his, and nothing else at all could ever matter. When we broke apart, Edward offered me a ring.

It was very simple, just an aged but polished band of gold, but I was the more happy for it. I had given little thought to the logistics of our engagement, but reflecting now, that the ring wasn't encrusted with giant gemstones pleased. It was simple, and that's all I wanted from Edward. Simplicity.

"It was my mother's first wedding ring," Edward whispered. "If you don't like it, I'll get you one however you prefer."

"I'll cherish it always," I whispered back.

"What the devil did we just watch?" Doug's raspy whisper to Rebecca was loud enough to snap me out of my reverie, and it made me laugh. Rebecca hit him as she wiped a tear from her eye.

Only Charlotte Thomas remained unaffected.

"Congratulations," she said calmly, as though Edward had just told her about finishing a good book. "Now, it would appear, I have no choice but to meet your sister. I'll send word to the Rigbys to inform them we are coming for a visit. Between our two families, hopefully we can sway the tide of public opinion in a town like Dawnhurst-on-Severn."

She approached Edward and me, taking one hand from each of us.

"So, the family grows," she said. She leaned in to whisper something so quietly to us it felt like a threat. "And I will protect my family until my heart stops beating."

She kissed my cheek before her eyes widened. A smile split her face.

"My word, Luella. We have so much planning to do."

"I agree," said Edward. "Convincing the Rigbys won't be difficult, but we want them fully invested—"

"Codswallop with the Rigbys. We have a wedding to plan." She looked down at my hand. "Edward, you gave her that old thing? Is that really the best you could do?"

I never imagined I would be torn so quickly from my fiancé, but before I could protest, Lady Thomas was whisking me out of the room for the first planning meeting regarding the union between Luella Winthrop, orphan, and Lord Officer Edward Thomas of Fernmount.

I remembered my time planning a wedding with Byron. He had wanted to put it all together in a week's time with as few guests as necessary.

This would be different. I could tell already. So very different.

Maybe it was the planning anxiety already setting in, or the compounding stress of Edward's plan, or the Bram-mandated abstention from the crimson ink, but even in this what-should-have-been-happiest of moments, my fingers twitched on the way out of the room.

Chapter Twenty-Five

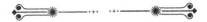

Strategy and Social Dance

Things moved much more slowly than I would have liked. Lady Thomas dispatched a note to the Rigbys, asking if the Thomases might pay them a visit on their way to Dawnhurst, and left it at that. I thought the wording of the note was a little vague. Why not just be forthright and say I was marrying Edward, and we wanted our families to meet?

"Some things are best explained in person," she said to me as a local florist displayed her most extravagant decorations in the Fernmount front room.

"I apologize our stock isn't more colorful," said the florist, Bethany, I believe her name was. "Given the current season, I'm afraid we'll be limited to holly and evergreens boughs. It would be a festive affair, my lady. If you were to wait until March, we may have some early bulbs blossoming."

"Well, tulips and snowdrops would at least add some variety. Plus, evergreen boughs are always available," Lady Thomas said. They both looked my way, but my mind was elsewhere. It all looked beautiful to me. I'd never dreamed of having such an elaborate wedding.

"I'll talk with Edward, though I'm not sure he will want to wait two months," I replied.

"What's two months," Lady Thomas asked, "when compared to the rest of your life?"

I bit the side of my cheek. What was the next two months? If only she knew. I still had to determine who enchanted me, with what type of magic, how to cure it, and do all this while confidently pretending everything in my life was splendid.

I had divulged nothing more to Edward about my condition since the night of his proposal, and for Rebecca's doubling as my conscience, I felt no small degree of shame over it.

I once thought it'd be easier to share my wicked secrets with Edward as we grew closer, but the opposite was true. I was embarrassed over the extra burden my personal issues brought to our courtship. I still hoped to avoid telling him altogether, wagering I could work out a discreetly administered cure with Bram and Hirythe. Then, I could reward Edward's love with a clean, healthy woman that would cherish him for the rest of his life.

"You make an excellent point, Charlotte," I said, awkwardly fumbling her first name. "I'll see what I can do to persuade him." She clapped her hands together and shooed away the florist, advising her to take extra care with her bulbs as they would need to be the picture of beauty come early spring.

This is how the past several days had gone. Lady Thomas whisked me around from one bit of wedding planning to the next, without leaving me much time at all for the laid-back holiday I enjoyed before Edward's proposal. She did all this, I feared, with a healthy dose of speculation.

We didn't get a response from the Rigbys until the end of the week. Of course, they would be delighted to host Lady Thomas and her guests, and they were sorry for the delay, and when should they prepare for the arrival, and did we have any preferences regarding meals...

The dance among wealthy families is a sight to behold.

The evening before we left, I sneaked away from Lady Thomas to go for a walk with Rebecca. I needed it, despite the chill. Besides, Cyrus would relish some exercise.

"In all the books I've read about a poor girl marrying a prince, the authors left out the nauseating tedium of the social niceties that come with wealth."

"I doubt the kings and queens in those stories did any more than hire people to make decisions based on a little given direction." Rebecca said, her breath frosting in the air from under her hood.

"Is that it? The Thomases just aren't rich enough, then?" I asked with a smile.

"Too rich for me," she replied. "I'm the one tangled up with a pub owner."

"That's no less complicated, from the sound of it," I said. She harrumphed.

"At least I'm not wasting my days picking between napkin designs."

The conversation lulled into a heavy silence. The pointer trotted around, sniffing at tufts of grass and loose twigs. I wondered what the world would be like if I had the senses of a dog.

Rebecca and I both knew what lay ahead, what risks were involved for all. If we failed to convince the wealthy families of Dawnhurst to take up our banner, I wasn't the only one on Cooper's list.

"Are you sure you want to come with us?" I asked. She shrugged.

"We're part of the plan, aren't we? The Steely-eyed Detective is right. I have an important perspective to take down old Cooper's credibility, being his former secretary."

I winced at how plainly she put it.

"It doesn't feel right going after Cooper like we are," I said. "You and Edward were so close to him. Does he really deserve the betrayal of two old comrades?"

Rebecca took a deep breath in and let it out in an enormous puff of steam as if she were thinking over pipe smoke.

"Well, maybe you and Cooper should have remained closer. It's always the friends and family who suffer in those situations, isn't it?"

"I'm so sorry, Rebecca. I didn't want any of this."

"You played the game of love, fame, and wealth, Luella. Did you think there wouldn't be casualties?"

Her words reminded me of the fog monster. I had not encountered it now for some time, but its manner of thinking had lodged inside my brain. They sounded like words it might have told me. Hearing its logic from Rebecca resonated that part of me like a bell.

"Is it so wrong for a girl to improve her life?"

"In this world?" She raised an eyebrow at me. "I just wish you'd learn your lesson."

"I beg your pardon?"

"You're keeping something from Edward. You kept something from Byron. You kept something from Anna. You even kept something from me. Let him in if you don't want all of this repeating itself over."

I choked out a bitter laugh. We crested a small hill, and looking back, we saw Fernmount illuminated by torches and gas lights against a ghostly winter forest behind.

"You mean repeat a magical curse and accidentally kill Edward's father again?"

"It's not a joke. You once asked why I cared so much about you." She stared at the house, treating it as an anchor, refusing to look at me. "I see myself in you. I once lost someone because of secrets I kept. If I can help you avoid my mistake, that's worth something."

I stared at her. If I wasn't so confident in her affection, I would not have found the courage to ask my next question.

"Who?"

"My mother." Her eyes glistened like snow on the moonlit hillside. She didn't look so different from Olivia that night in the Netherdowns. "And before you ask, no. A person need not die to be lost."

I wondered what Rebecca had kept from her mother to create such a distance between them. It took nothing short of magic to lure me away from my sister. And now, I would see her again.

"Perhaps you can reconcile things with your mother one day," I said.

"For a woman in such a peculiar situation, you certainly have found hope somewhere. Do you think when we're done with Edward's plan, you'll be able to reconcile with Cooper one day?" She shook the tears from her eyes and started following Cyrus back toward the house.

We left the next morning, a procession of carriages overladen with more luggage than we could use in a month. We weren't sure how long Edward's plan would take, but I was under the impression there were still laundries in Dawnhurst.

Apparently, I was wrong.

I had stowed the diary and the inkwell carefully in a small bag under my seat. I didn't plan to let either out of my sight. What a disaster it might be if I lost them.

The week had passed, and though there wasn't much to provoke me other than wedding plans, my frustration slowly mounted. I caught my twitching fingers occasionally and knew that sooner rather than later, I'd have another episode. Such was Bram's plan. But things were different now. I wasn't sure I could face the fog creature right before going to see Anna. So, I didn't tell Rebecca to observe me by night as I agreed I would.

In fact, I used Bram's ink the night before we left. It was just a blot's worth. If an episode was coming, I wouldn't have it at the Rigbys. I felt the ink work its magic, and unravel some of my enchanted anger, though not all of it.

Now, I sat uncomfortably laced up in green, with more skirts than I knew what to do within the confines of a carriage. Rose had carefully curled and braided my hair early that morning. Evidently, my facial expressions showed my doubts over the necessity of being done up.

"A family of our status going to visit a member of the gentry is a very, very delicate situation. I understand that the Rigbys have done well for themselves, but it doesn't erase the awkward dance that must be performed," Charlotte explained. I still had a hard time getting accustomed to her first name.

Edward sighed loudly beside me.

"Mother, you're acting as though we're to attend court, and father didn't just buy a title from a failing estate. According to the rest of the aristocracy, we're black sheep."

"That may be true, but the Rigbys won't see it that way. Even if they have heard some line of gossip that we're the lowest regarded house in England (which we are not, by the way), we're still visiting the gentry, and that is not just another day in their household. We're lucky they could accommodate a group our size."

We heard a bark, and Charlotte glanced out the window toward the carriage behind us where Doug, Rebecca, and Cyrus rode in comfortable privacy. I had insisted the pointer come along. I hoped he would help make it easier to reconnect with Anna. She always wanted a puppy. Charlotte argued that it would be an imposition on the Rigbys, but when Doug volunteered as the official keeper of the hound, she didn't find it worth fighting over.

I envied them sitting in that carriage. I wished I had the chance to ride to the Rigbys with only Edward and Cyrus for company.

"That should work in our favor, then," I said. "Shouldn't your influence help persuade them to cooperate with our plan?"

Her lips curled into a devilish smile. "Therein lies the dance, daughter."

"That's bad luck, mother," Edward said. "She's not your daughter yet." Charlotte waved him off.

"I have the benefit of coming from a lower step in society, and I don't pretend to ignore the realities of envy. Don't think for a moment that because they know the dance steps, they are happy with the song. No. I fear our status will prove more a hurdle than a help."

The Rigbys lived about a half day's ride south of Dawnhurst, for which I was thankful. Between my elegant attire and my nerves at seeing Anna again, my patience was wearing thin as an old nightgown.

I wished we had sent word ahead, but Lady Thomas insisted we keep the identity of Edward's fiancée a secret. I wracked my brain trying to remember if I had told Anna the truth about my hopes at a relationship with Edward, but I couldn't recall a time in which I'd used his name. Even if I had, what reason did she have to assume Detective Edward Thomas was now Lord Edward Thomas of Fernmount?

I hoped she would be happy for me. The last time I'd seen her, she was furious. I was planning to marry Byron then. Well, I wasn't marrying Byron anymore.

Would she be jealous that somehow, at my greater age, I secured an engagement with a house more affluent than the Rigbys?

I smiled, wondering if she was receiving the same terse instructions from Mrs. Rigby about proper manners as I was from Lady Thomas.

Our pace was going more slowly than desired, and Charlotte made the unpopular decision of pushing through lunch.

"It is always awkward to arrive at a host's home after nightfall," she insisted to our group as we took a moment to stop and stretch. Doug threw a ball for Cyrus, who took off after it into the snow. "Please, Mr. Tanner, let's refrain from wetting the dog right before he gets back in the carriage. Heavens. We must continue. And please remember not to eat too much at dinner. It appears ungraceful."

She shot a pair of stern eyes at Doug, who reacted as though she accused him of something completely out of his character. Rebecca and I suppressed a giggle before climbing back in the carriages.

In the early afternoon, we pulled on to a quaint country road and traveled through rolling farmland dusted with snowdrifts before rounding a bend and seeing a large countryside home with wood-thatched roof and several smoking chimney pots.

As we crossed over a small bridge spanning a still-flowing river, a feeling of gratitude and joy came over me. This was my sister's home. Good for you, Anna. It was much lovelier than what Byron would have provided us.

When our carriages crunched up to the front of the house, the whole family greeted us outside.

My sister looked beautiful. Marriage suited her, as did money. Her hair fell in delicate curls from beneath a blue bonnet, and her cheeks, rosy from the chilled air, settled into a natural, unforced smile. It was such a different face than the angry, desperate one I had seen last. Next to her, Jacob stood, looking somehow years more mature than when I last saw him. He no longer appeared the boy that Byron had slapped in a crowded restaurant.

Our door opened, and Edward was first to step down. Doug was already at his elbow, helping Lady Thomas, who elicited deep bows and curtseys from our hosts.

Finally, Edward held his hand out to me, and I exited the carriage, trying my very best to look tall and confident.

I swept my gaze at the greeting line before allowing my eyes to lock with my sister's.

"Luella!" Anna shouted.

I don't recall her running from where she stood, or how the others reacted. I just heard my name, and I was in her arms in a familiarly warm embrace I'd missed for months.

The delicate social dance Lady Thomas had been fretting over for days had just been smashed to pieces.

Chapter Twenty-Six

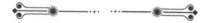

New Relatives

Anna didn't let go of my arm for hours.

At first, there was a great deal of confusion about how Anna knew me, what I was doing there, and other puzzlings over the implausibility of it all.

"Why didn't you tell us you were the fiancée of Lord Thomas?" Jacob asked with a wide smile.

"Please, call me Edward." Edward's familiarity caused no shortage of raised eyebrows from the Rigby family and his own mother.

"We wanted it to be a lovely surprise," said Lady Thomas, recovering from Anna's wrinkle in normal social protocol. "It appears quite soon our families are to be united."

"I can hardly believe it," said Mr. Rigby, a man of sharp nose and gaunt cheeks. He looked as though he had spent a good number of afternoons toiling at work while forgetting to eat. "Congratulations are in order! We're honored and delighted to receive you."

There were some formalities Lady Thomas had been expecting, but they came out in a jumble. Mr. And Mrs. Rigby looked as though a colossal weight had come off of their shoulders. I wondered with what reluctance they had accepted Anna as Jacob's betrothed. What story had they heard about me? Whatever it was, I didn't blame them for appreciating a turn in fortune.

May all who overlook others' shortcomings be so rewarded.

Mr. Rigby took an immediate liking to Cyrus, insisting that he kept several hounds for hunting. The pointer would be in good company.

They ushered us inside, where a long dining room waited, filled with wonderful smells of winter squash prepared with butter, parsnips and potato mash, and other delights I assumed were prepared from the estate's harvest. My mouth watered. I looked at Doug, who was white knuckled in his effort not to appear ravenous.

As I ate, Anna assailed me with a furiously paced monologue about her wedding, her trip away from Dawnhurst, life here at the Rigby home, the benevolent change in Jacob since he had committed to the wedding, and a hundred other things. It felt so much like being at home in our own kitchen that I wanted to cry with joy.

By the time dessert came around (a walnut cake that almost made Doug lose his composure completely), we had all settled into some naturally occurring social groups. Lady Thomas made polite conversation with the Rigbys. Edward and Doug were expanding their boys' club happily by jabbering with Jacob. Meanwhile, I sat enjoying nearly perfect company with Rebecca and Anna.

"Anna, I can't tell you how dear Rebecca is to me," I said.

"Then you will be my sister as well," Anna replied. "To think, I started today without the comfort of one sister, and now look at this. Luella has an outstanding husband to be, and I enjoy the bond of a new acquaintance."

"Now, ladies. Let's not get carried away in so much gratitude that we forget to enjoy the occasion," said Rebecca as she took a sip from her glass. Anna and I laughed.

The hours slipped away in good company and a quick tour of the home. As country homes went, the design leaned away from rustic toward refined and luxurious. The base home had appreciated with several expansions, a new wing here, an additional sitting room there... The way Mr. Rigby spoke, I could tell he took great pride in it.

"We are modest workers," said Mr. Rigby, "and have strived to improve upon our situation when fortunes allowed."

"I have the utmost respect for such wisdom," said Lady Thomas. "Mrs. Rigby, you are to be commended at turning what might have been a haphazard dwelling into an elegant and stately home."

Mrs. Rigby, a quiet woman with blonde hair just starting to gray at places, blushed and thanked her.

Later, Jacob's younger sister graced all of us with a performance at the pianoforte, while the gentlemen discussed whether a game of cards wasn't an awful idea.

"There is no rush on my account," Edward said. "I'd be happier to play tomorrow to tell the truth. I find my mind clouded after a day of travel."

"Let's not even mention the food," Doug chimed in after taking a breath for courage. It was clear to me that he felt uncomfortable in such distinguished company. "Is this your plan, Mr. Rigby? Provide guests with a dizzyingly good meal and then win at cards while we're still reeling?"

It wasn't the most graceful jest, but Mr. Rigby roared with laughter.

"There is a strategy I should try at the club," he replied. "My dear, I must bring your desserts with me next time I play cards in Dawnhurst!"

As the night wore on, Lady Thomas finally stood and made a rather formal showing of asking to retire.

"I wanted to inform you," Lady Thomas said to the Rigbys, "that I take the business of family very seriously. I'm encouraged to have found the relatives of my new daughter-to-be of such a high calibre. I hope that our bond can grow, and that we can bear one another's burdens, that they may be light."

The Rigbys returned a healthy dose of gratitude for these compliments, but I shared a shadowed glance with Edward. We both knew this was his mother's way of priming the pump for discussions to come.

As such, I thought the biblical reference of bearing one another's burdens to be in vulgar taste, but I wasn't about to share that opinion with anyone.

Soon the entire party dispersed, and Anna showed Rebecca and me to our room. She turned in the doorway and looked around.

"I'm not ready for the night to end," she whispered. "Why not pretend we're very young? I'll sneak back to your room in a few hours, and we can talk all night if we want."

The proposal made me grin. I turned to Rebecca.

"It's fine with me," she said. "If I get tired, I can sleep through anything. You might say I'm an expert at beauty sleep."

I nodded fervently, relishing in the indulgence. She giggled.

"Very well, I'll sneak away to you in just a bit. Don't worry. Jacob won't mind."

"Jacob isn't as I remember him," I said.

"He's changed since he proposed, but I'll tell you all about that later. Oh, Luella," she glanced cautiously at Rebecca and lowered her voice, "I was so afraid you'd hate me after my letter, that you'd blame me for leaving you."

I took her hands in mine.

"Anna, you were in the right. I'm just glad you left before the police tarnished our family's name."

"It's not true, though, is it Luella? You're engaged to the banker's son now."

I bit my cheek. There would be time to divulge everything to Anna, the way I did with Rebecca, but now we needed to convince the Rigby unequivocally that Sergeant Cooper had no basis to accuse me of foul play.

"I'm afraid the old Sergeant is using me to save face. Edward Thomas is the Steely-eyed Detective I wrote my stories about."

Anna's eyes went wide with excitement. I continued.

"I was there in the room when Edward learned about his father's suicide, and I suppose Cooper thought I acted strangely at the news."

"And that's it, then?"

I swallowed.

"That's all the evidence Cooper has against me."

She let out a heavy breath.

"I never wanted to doubt you. It's just that you were acting so unlike yourself before I left. You kept switching back and forth between wanting to marry Byron and wanting to leave him. You were two people in one."

I was ashamed of my behavior before months before. I shuddered, thinking about what Anna thought of me. Small wonder Byron wanted to recommend me for an asylum.

"That's behind me now. But I'll explain everything when you get back."

She nodded and swept off down the hall, leaving a smile in her wake. I closed the door and turned to see our room, which was modest by Fernmount's standards and lavish by the standards I grew up with. Rebecca was halfway out of her traveling clothes and into her nightgown.

"What?" I asked.

"I said nothing!" she protested while folding her blouse and depositing it on a dresser near the window.

"You're looking at me strangely."

"I'm not looking at anything."

"There!" I pointed. "A signature cocked brow from Rebecca Turner." She hid her face and smoothed her brow with her hand.

"It's none of my business."

"Oh, just out with it," I said.

"You're lying to her," she said matter-of-factly.

"I am not."

"You're hiding things again. That's all. We already talked about it."

"What should I have done? Tell her everything in the doorway and hope for the best?"

"No. You say, 'Anna, this is a long and complicated story, and I trust you to give me the benefit of the doubt. I'll explain everything, but don't worry.'"

"Then immediately she goes back to her husband an absolute wreck, and he connects that his houseguests, who have been here not one night, have deeply upset his new bride. You don't know Anna like I do."

Rebecca shrugged.

"I told you it was none of my business."

"You can't just back out of it now. Finish saying your piece."

She climbed into bed, pulling the blankets snugly over her torso.

"Fine, but this is the last I'll say about it. You just told your sister that the troubled and disturbed Luella Winthrop is a thing of the past. In reality, you're still magically ill—"

"—I have a treatment!"

"—you have a new condition you know nothing about, you're keeping things from Edward the same way you kept things from Byron, and now you plan to use the Rigbys to ruin a man for your own benefit."

My mouth fell open.

"What?" she asked. "If I'm not honest with you, who will be?"

Before I could gather a response, she turned over and nestled into her pillow.

She was right. But what could I do about it? Sergeant Cooper wanted me for murder. Only one of us would win this struggle. By now, it was a matter of survival. The Rigbys had a stake in this claim as well. If we could clear the Winthrop name, only good things would befall their new daughter-in-law's reputation. As for Edward...

That was complicated.

I changed out of my overly elegant traveling clothes and eagerly awaited my sister's return. I set my luggage next to a dresser and carefully took out the Mystic Diary and the crimson inkwell. I eyed them begrudgingly.

The inkwell looked emptier every time I saw it. I wondered why Bram still hadn't made more for me. He had mentioned it came at great sacrifice. But I was used to sacrifice. For Edward, I'd be happy to go through whatever was necessary.

I gingerly placed the book flat on the shelf and set the inkwell on top of it. It was there, easily accessible if I needed to get to it quickly. The remedy had worked to dispel my recent feelings so far, but I felt better having it near.

"What else am I supposed to do about Cooper?" I whispered at Rebecca's back as I climbed into bed. "It's not like he believes in magic. I can't just explain things to him. Besides, by now I doubt I can even get an audience with him outside of a cell."

"You could always trust the Queen's law will sort things out appropriately. Is there evidence to convict you or not?"

"You've seen the best evidence. It was the story I wrote about Luke Thomas's death before his death occurred."

I shuddered, remembering some details that made their way into my article about the arrangement of the room, the extent of the accompanying financial scandal—how had I ever let myself write something so incriminating?

"Luella," Rebecca said carefully, "have you ever wondered why Cooper is so convinced you're involved?"

"I constantly wonder that."

"Do you suspect there's a way he read a copy of that story?"

She turned to me, and I was about to respond, but three sounds occurred all at nearly the same time.

A book hit the floor, glass shattered, and Rebecca screamed.

I whirled around, and my breath caught in my lungs.

I'm not sure I could have designed a worse moment for Bram Lowhouse to emerge from his book of poetry.

Chapter Twenty-Seven

Too Close for Comfort

"Stay away from her!" Rebecca screamed.

"Rebecca, calm down!" I cried, trying to disarm my friend, who had grabbed a candelabra as a weapon.

"Come on, then. Let's not lose our sensibilities!" Bram said, retreating to a wall.

"Not a word from you. You stay silent right now. Both of you! You'll wake the entire house," I said.

"What do I care about that when some brigand has come to have his way with us!"

"Rebecca! This is Bram!" I grabbed her arms. She stopped flailing and looked at the two of us. Bram issued a sheepish smile.

"It's a pleasure to meet you. I'm sorry. I didn't realize Luella had company."

Rebecca looked at me, eyes full of a thousand questions. Before I answered even one, footsteps and creaked on the floorboards outside.

"You, hide now," I whispered at Bram with every ounce of menace I could muster. Bram took an exasperated look around the room before throwing up his hands in defeat. There weren't any hiding places.

"There," Rebecca said, pointing beside the door. "Luella, you get ready to open the door when they arrive."

"What about you?"

"Who do you think came up with the script for Mrs. Barker and Doug last year?" She hopped back into bed just as the footsteps arrived outside our room.

"Miss Winthrop, is everything all right?" That sounded like Mr. Rigby.

"Open that door, sir!" That desperately protective voice was Edward's. I put on my best smile, tried to ignore Bram flattening himself against the wall beside me, and greeted them.

"I'm so terribly sorry," I said. Nearly the entire house had come. Mr. and Mrs. Rigby, Jacob, Anna, Doug, and Charlotte.

"Unhand me! Unhand me this instant!" Rebecca shouted from behind me. I turned, and we all watched as she waved her arms in the air as if to fight off an unseen attacker. "I'm not that type of girl!"

I turned back to the group.

"She has terrible nightmares from time to time. They alarmed me as well, but as you can see, there's no genuine danger."

Edward's tense expression melted, but Charlotte's shrewd gaze shifted to the book on the floor and the shattered inkwell.

I did my best to contain a pathetic yelp.

The inkwell had broken! Its contents pooled uselessly on the rug.

"Shall I wake her?" Mr. Rigby asked.

"Mr. Rigby," I gasped, "I hardly think it's proper for you to enter our bedroom." I wrapped my arms protectively across my chest. Mr. Rigby choked on his concern.

"Well, I—I never intended, that is to say, perhaps Mrs. Rigby—"

"Not to worry, I'll do it," Charlotte said, taking a step forward. Before she made it in the door, Rebecca sat straight up, yawned, and turned to see everyone.

"What are you all doing here?" she cried, grabbing an armful of blankets and covering herself.

"You were having a nightmare," said Anna.

"Is that any excuse to peep on a woman in her nightgown?"

Doug blushed. "All right, everyone. It looks like there is nothing more to see here. Maybe make her a spot of tea to keep those nightmares from coming back, Luella," he said as he closed the door with his large arm.

As the door closed, I assured everyone that things would be be sorted and apologized for being a bother. When it clicked shut, I immediately held up my hand to ensure Rebecca and Bram remained silent until the footsteps and grumbling voices outside had faded away entirely. Then, I dropped to the floor, desperately trying to save any drop of the ink. Bram was beside me in a heartbeat, his face ghostly white.

"No. No no no," I said as I vainly tried to scoop some in my hand.

"This is bad," Bram said. My effort only dyed my fingers. The stains mocked me.

"We have to make more," I said, grabbing Bram by the shirt.

"It's not that easy."

"I don't care how easy it is. I need it."

"I said it's not that easy," Bram repeated, exasperated. "How were you so careless?"

"Me? What are you doing here? And at this time of night? Are you mad?"

"We hadn't heard from you in nearly a week. I needed some fresh air. Do you have any idea how exhausting it is living inside your memories without a word from the outside world? I was getting concerned. I thought you'd be alone."

He grabbed a piece of paper from a desk in the room and tried to sop up the ink.

"Because I'm always alone this time of night?"

"Aren't you?"

"No! I'm never alone anymore. I'm asleep and Edward is listening on the other side of the wall, or I'm with Rebecca. Sometimes both."

At mention of her name, we both straightened. She sat on the bed, hugging a pillow tightly.

"Rebecca, remain calm," I said.

"Did you come out of that book?" she asked, pointing at the diary.

Bram and I looked at each other before trying to explain at the same time.

"Yes."

"What an absurd notion—" said Bram.

"Wow," she said, inching forward. "Luella, you weren't jesting."

"You told her about the diary?" Bram asked, turning on me. I rolled my eyes. "What else did you tell her about?"

"Everything," I replied bluntly. "I was tired of keeping your secrets and bearing it all on my own. Don't change the subject! I told you not to come out of there."

He shook his head.

"Well, after Hirythe bonded a portion of his soul to the song he taught you, and you promised to come back with observations about one of your attacks, you might say we got anxious."

"Who are you, a doctor? I've been busy."

Rebecca rose from the bed.

"Would you two stop fighting? I'm sorry, Mister—"

"Lowhouse, but please call me Bram."

"Oh sure, you tell her your last name the first time you meet her," I said sarcastically. I felt my mood spiraling. Suddenly, I wished I had used a larger dose of ink the night before. I clenched my jaw.

"Bram, you need to go back into that book. Luella's sister may be returning this very moment."

I paled. If Anna discovered Bram, everything would be ruined. I grabbed the diary and stuffed it into his hands.

"Go back," I said. "I'll come visit tomorrow. I promise. You can't be here."

He looked wounded.

"Oh, stop," Rebecca said. "Don't act sore. You're in a bedroom with two women in their nightgowns, and you can't think of any reason Luella might not want you here when her sister arrives?"

Bram smiled.

"I like your friend," he said.

"Just go," I insisted.

"Very well," he flipped the book open, and I marveled despite my anxiety. He deftly handled the pages, flipping to a specific portion as if he had a hundred times. It was like watching Stradivarius tune one of his own violins.

What was I saying? The man was simply reading a book. He sat against the wall.

"What are you doing?" Rebecca asked.

"I'm going back," he said.

"Can't you read faster?" she replied. He grinned.

"I assume Luella explained how it works. I have to get lost in the words. Do you know a better way to travel to another reality?"

"Yes, yes. It's just like the sensation you get when you become so engrossed in a book you lose the world around you."

Bram beamed as I explained the workings of his enchanted book.

"High magic," he said. We shared a knowing glance. Letting someone else in on our secrets had a strange bonding effect between us.

Rebecca cleared her throat, shaking me out of the moment.

"Don't you have a shortcut or something?" I asked.

"It will go faster if I stop getting inter—"

There was a gentle knock at the door.

"Luella," Anna said softly. "It's me. I'm coming in."

I couldn't stop her in time. Bram couldn't read fast enough. Rebecca had no more tricks up the sleeve of her nightgown. Anna walked into the room, closed the door behind her, and all the trust she had in her sister vanished like smoke.

"What's going on here?" she asked, casting nervous glances at the mess and the man.

I wanted to explain, but words failed. I looked to Rebecca. She shook her head, eyes closed.

"This must look strange," Bram said, standing. "Allow me to introduce myself."

"I don't much care who you are, sir, but I can conjure up no possible business you can have for attending my sister or her friend at this hour or in this room."

She held a candle close. It flickered dangerously next to her face, like it would ward off evil spirits.

"Of course," he said. "In fact, I was just on my way."

"Luella, what is all this? You promised me you didn't bring scandal to this house. If the Rigby's knew what was happening under their roof!"

"It's not what you think, Anna. This is Bram."

"I think my sister, who came here to announce her engagement, is hosting a man other than her fiancé in her bedroom in the middle of the night."

Bram's back went rigid, and he turned to me.

"You're engaged?" he asked softly. His eyes darted to the simple ring on my hand.

"She is," Anna replied after a moment's pause. I must have taken too long to respond for her liking.

"Anna," I took a step toward her, "do you remember the old writing partner I told you about?"

"Not much," she replied. She had already developed the gentry's stuffy adhesion to ethics. Her chin jut out like a proud peacock. "I recall you coming home at another late hour on his account."

"It's not like that. It's hard to explain how things were before. It's largely because of Bram that I was in such a bad way."

Her nostrils flared.

"Not like that! My word!"

"Why did you come here, Luella? Didn't I make it clear in the letter I left you? I thought you'd be happy for me, that you'd want me to escape whatever business you're mixed up in."

Something inside of me snapped. I was sick and tired of debasing myself in front of every person around me.

"Oh, would you stop pretending like you're some goddess. You were the one slipping Jacob aphrodisiac pills just months ago!" I regretted the words immediately after I said them. Anna paled, while Bram and Rebecca both buried their taut faces in the floorboards.

"How did you know about that?" Anna asked.

"You had a loose-lipped confidante."

"That old gossip!" To Anna's credit, she didn't lose her temper or lash out at me as I would have done in her situation. She just slumped into a chair near the writing desk, embarrassed at being discovered.

"Did it work, by the way?" I asked. She ran a hand through her hair.

"It was the most humiliating moment of my life," she said. "Can you imagine if Edward had discovered you trying to slip chocolate covered flies into his potatoes?"

I tried to imagine it. He'd be embarrassed, flustered. Would he be flattered, even a little?

"I would have at least waited to sneak it into his dessert," I said. She laughed awkwardly. I joined in, eager to release some tension in the room.

"Do you have any idea what mother would say?" I said.

"Oh, don't bring her up," she said.

I sat on the floor beside her, head resting on her knee, Bram looked at the two of us curiously.

"Sisters," Rebecca suggested to him.

"Indeed," he replied. "Luella, have you tested her?"

The seriousness of his request alarmed me.

"Don't be ridiculous."

"I find her willingness to overlook our current predicament almost inhuman."

"That's because you don't understand the bond between sisters," I replied.

"Then what harm is there in testing her?"

"Test me on what?" Anna asked, her mouth slack.

"I wouldn't do her the dishonor," I said. Rebecca sat up rigidly on the bed.

"If you're as close as you say," Bram countered, "she won't have any problem forgiving you."

An unusual creeping dread filled me. Bram had me cornered, and not only was I running out of excuses, something dark within me agreed with him.

"Test me on what?" Anna asked again. I looked to Rebecca, who nodded at me grimly. "You look like we're about to raise the dead or something."

"Don't be ridiculous," Bram said with a cold smile. "I can't raise the dead. I've tried."

As if under a spell, I took Anna's hands in mine.

"Sister, what are you doing?" she asked, now more concerned.

"I'm going to sing you a song. Please don't take your eyes from mine."

She nodded haltingly, and I began. Singing to Anna felt different from singing to Rebecca. As the melody came out, distant memories of singing her to sleep from years ago distracted me.

Do you hear the echo
On the crags and in the meadow

The voices I'd heard when Hirythe taught me the song joined in immediately, insisting they add their voices to Anna's serenade.

I didn't even finish the lyrics before a hot, searing confusion tear through my heart.

"Luella, what was that?" Anna asked, gasping. Bram came forward at once and separated our hands.

"Well?" he asked. I was trying to breathe. This was all wrong. The magic was faulty. My dear sister could not have betrayed me. She couldn't have been my enchantress.

"What was that song?" she asked.

Rebecca's arms wrapped around me and gently pulled me to the bed. I don't remember sitting down.

"Luella, won't you talk to me?" she insisted. Bram grabbed a chair and sat down in front of her.

"What was the name of the enchantment?" he asked her.

"What?"

"What magic did you use?"

"What you're talking about. Luella—"

"How did you administer its effects? Do you care nothing about your sister?" Bram had a cruel twist on his lips.

"Who are you to talk to me about my sister? Luella, what is he talking about?"

My mind raced through the past six months. Was it even possible? Anna had been under significant stress. I knew things had gone poorly with Jacob at first. But what did that have to do with me? She would have had to enchant me before I met Edward. To what end?

But peculiarities of Anna's life wormed their way into my mind. She had purposefully tried to manipulate Jacob's feelings. She just told me the aphrodisiac had failed. Yet, he had married her. I still didn't understand why Jacob changed his mind and proposed. Did my sister know how to manipulate high magic?

Chilling memories of the fog monster promising to make Edward love me came to mind unbidden.

There were so many missing pieces.

Rebecca interrupted my thoughts.

"Luella," she grabbed me by the shoulders. "Focus. We must get a handle on this before our circumstance deteriorates."

"How could it deteriorate any more than it has already?" I asked.

"We're under the Rigby's roof. Edward, his mother, and Doug are here, all planning to move forward with a plot to unseat Cooper as head of the Dawnhurst police department. How does that plan change now Bram is interrogating your sister about magic? You could end up behind bars."

She was right, but there was hardly any fuel left in me for self-preservation.

"Your sister's life is in danger." Bram continued pressing Anna. "Whether you intended that or if it's an unfortunate coincidence, she's been infected by another high magic, and the combination is too much for her. If you care about her at all, you will divulge everything."

Anna's gaze shot around the room like a frightened animal. Was this all an act? Was she afraid because of her innocence, or was she afraid because of her guilt? Tears formed at the edges of her eyes.

"She won't speak," Bram said, standing up.

"Bram, enough," I hissed.

"She may be responsible for all of this."

"She is still my sister! You will not harm her." Bram recoiled as if I had slapped him.

"Harm her? I would do no such thing."

My jaw relaxed.

"Then what are you doing?"

Bram bent over and picked up the Mystic Diary.

"I'm taking her into the Netherdowns."

Chapter Twenty-Eight

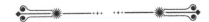

High Magic

"You mean you're taking her into the book?" Rebecca asked as she absent-mindedly unraveled a knit linen throw at the foot of the bed.

"No," I said, stepping in between Anna and Bram protectively.

"You heard the voices," he replied.

"The song has to be wrong," I insisted feebly. Bram rubbed the back of his neck.

"Luella, I'd understand if you doubted my, admittedly sometimes misguided, attempts at harnessing arcane powers." He looked at the shattered inkwell on the ground, damp ink now hopelessly soaked into the rug. "But, Hirythe put a part of his soul into that song. Do you realize how powerful that is?"

"Then maybe I sang it incorrectly," I stammered.

"If you heard the voices, it means she has the residue of high magic on her."

"I don't even believe in magic," Anna said.

Bram rolled his eyes.

"I'm taking her to the Netherdowns where we can do a better evaluation. Put the pieces together, Luella. She knew you well and well before your first encounter with the fog creature. She had ample opportunity."

"But, why would she do it?" I asked. "For what motive?"

"I'm not interested in a motive. I promised I would heal you, and this is the next step."

I wanted to scream. He was making sense, but I didn't want to believe it. If he was right, her betrayal would crush me. Why? Was she jealous knowing I was engaged to Byron while she couldn't seem to get Jacob to commit?

Doubt wriggled and squirmed from my heart. Dark feelings swirled, familiar feelings.

My fingers twitched, and my blood ran cold.

I looked at the shattered inkwell on the ground like an addict searching for laudanum.

"Anna," I said, turning to her, "don't read the book. He can't force you."

"Luella, what is all this? I'm so frightened."

Did she mean that? Or was she just trying to manipulate my feelings for her? I blinked back frustration. My emotions stirred, taking over my logical mind. I looked around, panicked. I could not slip into an episode now.

I grit my teeth and shut my feverish eyes.

Bram picked up the book again.

"You asked if I had a shortcut into the Netherdowns. I don't. But I made a way to bring others with me. Some of these poems, when applied in a certain way, have different effects than others." He cleared his throat and opened to a page.

"Bram, please stop," I said. "I need you—I need you to help me."

What colors follow briefly down,
  The woman who escaped me?
  The sea a maze of treasure coves,
  A graveyard meant to bait me.

Was it that simple? Could reading a specific poem from the book out loud to others draw them in as well? Leave it to Bram to come up with something hidden in such plain sight.

Helplessly, I cast my gaze around the room. Rebecca looked curious and excited. Anna clung to my arm.

Why had she left me months ago? I had spent my entire life caring for her, and she abandoned me at the first signs of distress. How could she possibly be so selfish?

No. That was the illness talking.

"Luella, what's happening?" Anna asked, pale-faced.

The air around us swimming by
  Container of the queerest wine
  To drink, to dance and decorate
  And live, not love or speculate.

I wanted to tell her not to listen, but I had doubled over in effort, trying to prevent the impending episode. It felt worse than before, stronger. And I had never been around so many people. Something inside of me wanted to let go. I couldn't trust them. I was in danger of being discovered, and if I was discovered, I would be lost, body, soul, and all.

"Luella, what are you doing?" Anna continued.

How then, red hen,
  Have you kept your frock so clean
  Explain, small brain,
  Lest casual jest
  Delays at best
  And worst makes red hens scream.

I shut my eyes. I don't know why, but in this bleak moment, my thoughts flew to fleeting memories of my father, not the false impression the fog creature had imposed on me, but the truest recollections of my childhood. I saw his ruddy, smiling face behind me at a park. He smiled as I ran off, chasing after birds, and laughed.

I missed the sound of his laugh so much.

When I opened my eyes, I saw the moondust trail. I almost gasped with relief. The trail of particles in the air looked like an old friend. They trailed through the room and directly into the Mystic Diary.

Curious.

Then it hit me. I'd be safe from the episode inside the Netherdowns.

How had I forgotten?

"Luella?" Anna cried.

I wanted to fall in love with the poetry. I wanted to dive into the words. I wanted its meaning to overwhelm me.

Who knows of death
  And sorrow more
  Then the pets of widows.
  Who lie at night
  beside the door
  With aching in the marrow?
  Who brim with love
  And selfless life
  Yet can't speak to their master.
  But doomed to silent
  Watching lie
  And silence ever after.

The world shifted, and rather than find myself on a hilltop, I arrived immediately in the middle of the Netherdowns' central square. Cobbled stones surrounded its running fountain, and the sound of merrymaking trickled to my ears from a nearby pub.

I breathed in fresh air like a woman saved from drowning. I was back, and the episode had not taken me. I sat down on the edge of the fountain and splashed water on my face before noticing Rebecca and Anna. Rebecca stared wide-eyed, running around and touching nearly everything to test its veracity.

"I thought you were crazy," she kept repeating. "I kept putting it off in my head, but when it came down deep into it, I thought you were crazy. How can this be possible?"

Anna, on the other hand, looked like her courage had been plunged into icy water.

"I'm dreaming. Please tell me I'm dreaming."

I took her hand and sat her down beside me.

"It's much like dreaming. Anna, you're in a place called the Netherdowns."

"No. No, no, no. I need to be with the Rigbys. I'm newly married! I must have fallen asleep. I don't remember the carriage ride. We must have gone far south. I don't see snow anywhere except in those mountains. Those mountains are exquisite!"

I shook my head.

"We didn't take a carriage. You came here through a magic book."

"Are we in the diary, then?" asked Rebecca.

"Not exactly inside of it. The diary is more of a doorway." I replied.

"A doorway to what?"

"A world made from pieces of combined memories." Bram said proudly. I didn't notice him appear, but that was the way of the book. You never saw a person just appear from thin air. They just so happened to turn up when no one is paying attention. "Come along. Miss—"

"Turner," Rebecca said with an overly theatrical bow.

"Miss Turner," Bram went on, "I'm sorry we have mixed you up in this. I'll need assurances of secrecy from you."

"Of course, my lord," she said. The three of us stared at her before Bram led us toward the familiar building made of fieldstone I recognized as Hirythe's office.

"What are you doing?" I hissed at Rebecca.

"What? Isn't he the lord of this realm?"

"Don't be ridiculous. This isn't an old fairy tale. It's just Bram."

"Ridiculous? Should I add that it's a little more ridiculous you are affording the person who created all of this little to no respect?"

"I'm afraid to go in that building," Anna said as we approached.

Bram bounded through the old weathered wooden door. The other two didn't know what was on the other side. Judgment awaited my sister in that study.

I eyed her critically, still trying to decide if the fear and confusion she elicited was just a way to cover up her genuine feelings.

I still could not come to grips with my sister bewitching me.

"Courage, Anna," I said. "What would father say?"

She nodded and took my arm. Rebecca took the other, and we followed the magician.

We walked through the door of the stone building, and I led them up the dimly lit staircase to the study. Hirythe sat at his desk, calmly reviewing a set of maps and parchments through a magnifying glass. When he looked up and saw Bram leading three women into the room, he froze.

"Bram, what is this?" he said, motioning toward us with the glass.

"I can explain—"

"Because it looks as though you've led two more women into the Netherdowns."

"The circumstances were a little peculiar—"

"And I remember you promising that Luella was a rare exception, and that it would never happen again."

"We're here on business," he said, folding his arms and gruffly setting a chair in front of the table. He motioned brusquely to Anna. "This is the woman your song identified." Bram leaned against the desk.

"This is my sister, Anna," I said. Hirythe set down the magnifying glass and stood to scrutinize her. He swooped smoothly around the table and peered at her curiously.

"Heavens above," Rebecca whispered, "but his skin is glowing a soft blue."

I hushed her, and Hirythe held out a hand.

"Anna, my name is Hirythe. Please, will you sit down a moment?"

Anna looked at me before nodding and taking her seat.

"I must be dreaming," she said.

"You are," Hirythe replied. "This is a most unusual dream. Do you know the woman behind you?"

"Of course. That's my sister, Luella."

"That's right. What about the woman beside her?"

"That's her friend, Rebecca,"

"They've only just met," I explained. Hirythe silenced me with a hand that sent a small gust of wind through the room.

"What about this man?" Hirythe pointed at Bram.

"Brad. Or Bram. Something like that. He was trying to seduce my sister."

Hirythe allowed a devious smile at the corner of his mouth. Bram rolled his eyes.

"Your sister told me she sang you a song earlier. Is that true?"

Anna wrung her hands in her lap.

"I can't remember," she said after a moment.

"Anna, it is very important you don't lie to me." Hirythe's voice was calm, but the menace he fit behind it amazed me.

"What are you?" she asked.

"I should ask you that same question. What am I?" Hirythe fished what looked like dust from his pocket and worked it in his hand behind his back. His image flickered, as though he were a reflection rippling in still water.

"My conscience?" Anna asked. Hirythe stopped fiddling with the dust and his form solidified once again.

"Why would you lie to your own conscience, Anna?"

"I don't want to be a wicked person." Anna's eyes were glazing over. She stared blankly forward.

"What is happening to her?" Rebecca asked me. I wondered the same, but I remembered conversations with Bram from months before. We sat in the audience for a hypnotist at the fair where I met him. He had once told me that hypnotism was real, even though what they did at the carnival was not.

"He's looking for answers," I replied, myself becoming entranced with the subtle, smooth motions of Hirythe's hands.

"Why not just use the song like you did?" Rebecca asked. I didn't have an answer.

"A human cannot lie to its conscience." Hirythe went on. "Did your sister sing you a song?"

Anna nodded. Tears welled in her eyes.

"What happened when you heard the song?"

"There were voices. They sang along with my sister."

"And, how did that make you feel?"

Bram paced the room by the hearth, one hand in his pocket, the other fidgeting relentlessly.

"I was afraid. I was afraid I'd be found out."

My heart skipped. Rebecca's grip tightened on my arm.

"What would be found out, Anna?" Hirythe prodded.

"I can't say. It's too hard."

"Then show me." Hirythe put a hand over her eyes, and the surrounding room shifted like water and mist. It rearranged into a building I was all too familiar with.

Byron's prized skylark sat whistling in its cage in the corner. We even saw a vision of Byron himself, sitting frozen at the desk in his office, door open as usual.

We were in a watercolor version of Langley's Miscellany print shop, frozen in a moment in time.

"You talked to this man?" Hirythe asked.

Anna nodded. "I hated him, but we had a mutual interest."

"Was that interest your sister?"

She nodded again. Tears ran alien and silent down her cheeks. "She'll never forgive me."

"What did you say to the man?"

"I told him she was crazy."

I unconsciously took a step forward, as if to hear more clearly.

"Crazy?" Hirythe asked. She nodded. Pain worked its way into her voice.

"She had been acting so strangely. One day she was the sister that took care of me my whole life. But the next she was so different. She railed back and forth like a madwoman, and I didn't want her to marry Byron. So, I visited him to confide that I had no assurance of her sanity."

A groan worked its way through me, but she continued. Oh, Anna.

"I thought if I convinced him, he would call off the wedding even if Luella would not. I didn't think he believed me, but when the papers came out later, and the Dawnhurst Police suspected her of murder, I was certain he'd reported her."

Her eyes glistened with the weight of remorse. Even if she weren't hypnotized, she'd have seen nothing through the tears.

"I ruined her reputation." She sniffed. "But now, she is engaged again, to a wealthy and important man."

Poor Anna. She had been living under the assumption that somehow her actions caused my downfall.

"Is that it?" Bram asked aloud. "There's no magic in that."

Hirythe glared at him, evidently peeved by his intrusion on the trance.

"It's good to admit these things out loud," Hirythe said.

"If Luella finds out, she'll never forgive me. I was afraid she would find out when she sang me the song. I couldn't hide anything when I listened to it."

I could withstand no more. That was my baby sister. She looked miserable. She would have never purposefully harmed me. Even if she did, I would never hold it against her.

I ran forward and threw my arms around her.

"I forgive you," I said. "I forgive you for all and any of it." I kissed her cheek. Hirythe backed away, and Anna snapped from the trance.

"Luella?"

"I'm here, sister."

"Did you hear?"

"I did. It's all behind us."

"Can you still love me?"

"I will always."

She threw her arms around my neck and wept. She embraced me the way mother used to. There was such a sense of family wrapped up in it, that I swear our parents present in the room. When we split apart,

Rebecca's eyes were wet.

Bram's were not.

"I don't understand," Bram said. "What about the enchantment? Why would the voices sing along if she didn't meddle with higher magic?"

Hirythe didn't answer, instead he looked curiously at a trail of moondust coming out of the skylark's cage and winding through the air through the door.

When Bram saw the trail, he also lost the edge in his posture.

"What is this?" he asked Hirythe.

"It's a moondust trail," I replied. "At least, that's what I call it. It led me here. It showed me the way to Cyrus. It led me from Fernmount. I've searched for it many times, but it just seems to appear for me at random."

Hirythe didn't take his eyes from the trail. It sparkled and glowed as it floated ghostly in the air.

"I don't believe Anna is the culprit we are seeking," Hirythe replied.

"I thought you said that only those touched by high magic would trigger the voices in your song," I said.

"She has been. You never mentioned that you might suspect a family member of enchanting you. The bond between family can be a high magic. When a family member offends that bond, have they not interfered with such magic?"

Hirythe followed the trail to the closed door of Langley's. He opened it, and we looked out into the courtyard where we had entered the Netherdowns.

"When that bond is repaired, it has a way of altering memory, or at least guiding us through it."

"But the Netherdowns isn't made of my memory."

"Yes," Hirythe said as he headed into the courtyard. "Peculiar, isn't it? You must have left your mark on the place."

"Luella," Rebecca said, "if Anna isn't culpable, then we should get back. As much as it pains me to leave a place like this, Jacob will notice if Anna is gone too long."

She was right. If we had any hope of continuing with our plan to push into Dawnhurst and test Cooper and Byron to discover who truly had enchanted me, we'd need to avoid suspicion.

Yet, the moondust trail had never led me astray.

"There's time enough," I replied and followed Hirythe through the door.

Chapter Twenty-Nine

Beyond the Mask

We followed a trail that led us out of the Netherdowns village, past the eclectic blend of architecture. Despite our hurried pace, a sense of calm possessed me. The town had quieted and nearly everything was dark. The usual lit torches or gas lamps on the outside of buildings sat extinguished. None of Hirythe's soldiers roamed the streets either.

The moondust twisted through bountiful farmlands. Iridescent moonlight bathed the surrounding terrain as farms became grassy fields. Beyond, the mountains stood like tall, silent sentinels guarding the horizons.

"My word," Anna said. "This is the most beautiful place I've ever seen."

The moondust trail wrapped around several stone outcroppings softened by coats of moss, and in the distance, I saw the foot of one of the three hills that served as entry points from the diary. By now, I began to perspire, and I could tell my sister unused to such effort. She puffed clouds of air. As we got closer to the base of the hill, the moondust faded away.

"It's stopped," Bram said. I looked up and traced the hillside up to its beautiful willow tree. Under the gently swaying branches stood Olivia, clad from neck to toe in her mirrored armor. Her face was uncovered, her hair tousled by the breeze.

"Is that an angel?" asked Anna.

"An angel of fury, perhaps," Rebecca whispered. "I have a strange feeling about this."

"What has she done?" muttered Hirythe. He tried grabbed Bram's arm, but too late. He had seen her face. It hit him at once. The memories he searched for in the Netherdowns for years stood atop the hill in front of him. He took off at a run.

"Olivia!" he shouted. She turned, and I watched as her features transformed from the stern and hardened soldier I knew to a dazzlingly beautiful woman. But that couldn't be. Was her face truly changing?

We chased after Bram, and the closer I came to her, the more flawless her features became. By the time I got to the top of the hill, I had a mind to agree with Anna. Olivia was an angel.

Bram raced forward to scoop her into his arms, his expression a mix of unbridled joy and bittersweet remorse.

Instead of welcoming him though, she held out her sword, Boudicca incarnate.

"Stay back, Bram," she said. "You're not meant to see me."

"Olivia? I'm sorry. I searched for you. I found your shadow everywhere, but I don't remember what happened. What are you doing here? I've missed you so much."

"I'm not what you think," she said.

"I know you're just a memory, but even your memory is enough to sustain me. Have you been hiding by Hirythe's side this whole time? How did I miss you?"

Hirythe ran between them, shielding Olivia with his body.

"Bram, this isn't smart."

"How dare you, Hirythe? You hid behind that mask this entire time? You told me Drycha was an old faerie warrior."

"She was. That's her mask. I knew her well."

"You lied to me," Bram said. He clenched his fists but looked more betrayed than angry.

"We had to, Bram." Olivia chimed in. She moved Hirythe aside with one hand. "My death was the only gift I could give you. When I knew I was too severely infected with Sraith to be cured, I decided. How could you live, knowing what you did to your wife?"

Wife? Rebecca and Anna drew closer to me. They were married. That amplified the solemnity of Olivia's ruse to fake her death tenfold.

Bram looked between his wife and the fae.

"What are you saying?" he asked at length.

"Both of you need to stop," Hirythe said more loudly. I thought I heard thunder, but as I listened more closely, it sounded like something else. Something awful. He looked out from the hill toward the town. "Olivia, put on your mask. You may need it."

"What are you saying?" Bram demanded.

"We faked my death, Bram. I'm sorry. It was the only way to free you from me."

"Are you telling me you're alive?"

I heard it more distinctly now, the sound of hundreds of hooves, growls, and other threatening animalistic rumblings.

I looked around us. Large grassy mounds surrounded our hill, rising from ample meadows. Appearing on the crests of those mounds, in all their terrifying glory, were legions of the monsters that plagued the Netherdowns.

"Luella!" Anna said hoarsely, grabbing my arm like a vice. Rebecca's eyes stretched wide as moons and just as pale.

Hirythe growled, his entire body erect.

"That can't be, Olivia. I saw you fall overboard," Bram said, blind to the monsters surrounding us while he put fragments of his memory back together. The creatures were terrifying. No enormous cats or angry bulls, but terrible beasts I'd never seen before. All of them shared the same curious hide made of white, gray, and black.

"Hirythe and I planned it. We staged it on the ship that day. We had a line already set out for me. I survived."

Bram scrunched up his face as he tried to remember. By now, Olivia was resplendent. Her face shone like the moon.

"Luella, what is happening?" Rebecca asked.

"Can't you do anything?" I said to Hirythe. "I hate to disappoint you, but my sister and I are not soldiers."

"You'd have to be ruddy good ones for it to matter against this many."

He set his jaw firmly and didn't respond. He just swept his gaze over the horizon, crawling with mirage monsters. They flickered in and out of view.

"Can't you send us back?"

"We need an anchor for them, something to tether them to the real world. Bram used the incense from his carnival for you. It'll take time to find them for your friend and sister."

"Where did your soldiers go? How did these creatures get so far into the Netherdowns?" I asked. Hirythe's eyes darted toward Bram.

"He was never meant to find Olivia."

"Why not? Bram isn't as weak as you believe. He infected me with Sraith just as he did Olivia. He's borne that burden all too well. Can the guilt of doing the same to his wife really be—"

Recognition settled over me. The Netherdowns were constructed from Bram and Hirythe's memories. I knew Bram well enough. When he discovered my enchantment, he vowed to find a remedy at any cost.

Surely, if he knew he was responsible for his wife's enchantment, the grief wouldn't overcome him, as Olivia suggested. It would fuel him. Besides, Hirythe told me that ridding myself of Sraith was simple enough, if not very painful. Why would they need to fake her death?

And why did so many dark memories congregate around us? If Bram discovered his living wife, wouldn't benevolent recollection spring up? It made little sense.

Unless Olivia was dead.

"What have you done?" I asked Hirythe. His eyes narrowed as he watched me the piece together his scheme.

"You really are as clever as he said," the fae replied.

Bram and Olivia now circled each other, Olivia's sword still separating them. I bounded toward Bram.

"Bram," I said, pulling his arm. The creatures advanced now, down the mounds of earth. "What happened to Olivia?"

"She fell overboard," he said, as though in a trance. "I thought she'd died."

I tugged at his arm harder, but he wouldn't take his eyes from her.

I turned to find Rebecca and Anna holding on to one another. The monsters reached the bottom of our hill. I could make out minute details in their terrifying appearance. Patchy fur, dripping fangs, scarred horns.

"What really happened? Don't listen to what she's saying. She did not stage her death. Something happened to her. Remember!" He didn't respond. I tried slapping him. I beat on his chest with my fists.

"What is happening to him?" I cried out to Hirythe.

"He's found her memory. In his mind, she's become infinitely more beautiful and lovely since her death. He's becoming a slave to the feeling of what might have been."

"Can you snap him out of it?" I asked.

"He hasn't seen me outside of the Netherdowns in too long. For all he knows, I'm a memory as well."

"I'm not a memory. He saw me in the real world an hour ago."

"He needs his own tether, a reminder of the present. Something potent."

"Luella!" Anna cried. Her lip trembled. She didn't look away from the advancing creatures. "I want to go home."

My mind raced. I searched for something. My eyes locked on Drycha's feathered horse. I'd hardly noticed it grazing peacefully on the slope behind the tree. I grabbed the reins and bounded toward Hirythe. "Can you ride them out?" I asked. He eyed the beast warily.

"More easily than I could defend them here," he replied.

"Then go. I'll do what I can about Bram."

"What if you can't help him?"

"Then you will at least have saved these two. Just go."

"Luella, no. We won't leave you here!" Rebecca called. Hirythe mounted the horse in a moment. He lifted my sister behind him on the saddle. He pulled on Rebecca's arm, but she resisted.

"Doug needs you. He loves you," I said. It was enough to distract her from the fae's strong arm for a moment. He slung her over the horse's neck and bounded down the hill. I watched after them only long enough to ensure he weaved through the first line of approaching monsters. They seemed to ignore them and continued crawling uphill, steadily toward Bram.

I turned back to the hilltop. How could I remind Bram of the present? What would detach him from Olivia's memory?

I didn't think. I grabbed Bram by the face and kissed him directly on the mouth.

He resisted before kissing me back. I held my eyes open to watch the furious jealousy in Olivia's face, darkening her features.

When we broke apart, she looked more like Drycha than ever.

"Luella?" Bram looked at me, confused.

"Olivia's dead, isn't she?" I said.

"I'm not," she stammered. Was that fear in her voice? "We staged the accident."

He looked between the two of us.

"Bram?" I asked.

A shadow passed over his brow.

"It was my fault," he said. His memory fill him like rainwater after a drought. "That night on the boat—I should have protected her."

Hirythe told me his soldiers fought against harmful memories. Was it possible that Bram's were all connected, even stemmed from one debilitating part of his past?

"In the Phantom Battalion, after Jeremy's brother died, he blamed us. He burst into fits of rage. Olivia was so afraid, but I assured her he would never harm her. They had been friends. We all had. She tried to tell me something taken him, but I insisted."

"Something unnatural lived in his eyes," Olivia continued. "Something evil enhanced his rage."

"A catalyst," Bram said. "She begged me not to travel back with him."

Olivia lowered her sword. Bram approached her. A sparkling tear dropped across her cheek. Around us, the monsters stopped their steady advance and stood like motionless witnesses.

"One night on the voyage back, I left our room to get some fresh air. I felt sick from the waves. The water was choppy and the deck slippery from a storm. She begged me to stay. I told her I'd be only a moment. I should have stayed. I took a quick walk around deck. When I returned, our cabin door was open. Jeremy had her, pinning her arms tightly to her sides. He pressed a knife to her neck."

I turned and saw Olivia's face, frozen with fear and sadness.

"He pulled her over the side of the ship with him. I ran to the edge, but it was so dark. I couldn't see anything, and I could only shout her name, over and over."

He reached forward, but Olivia stepped away from him.

"The look on her face," he said, gazing at her. He bent over and picked up her mask. "I tried to bury that expression."

I squeezed Bram's arm.

"You couldn't have known," I said.

"I should have listened to her. She was right."

"You said he was your friend."

"I meddled in things I didn't understand."

"But Jeremy's actions were his own."

He handed the mask to Olivia.

"Hirythe was right to hide her from me. I can't face her. She didn't die in an accident. It was my fault."

Olivia's face now sparkled with tears, bright as stars. She nodded and held the mask up to her face. In its reflection Bram stared back at himself.

I turned about, and the monsters began advancing again, slowly and menacingly up the hill. This was the Netherdowns, a tragically beautiful landscape plagued by the ravenous, venomous memories of the past. And by the looks of it, I would join the landscape. Rebecca and Anna may have escaped.

And yet, the monsters had frozen when Bram learned the truth. They were connected to him, connected to both of them. He couldn't ignore the past.

"You should have stayed with me that night. You should have listened to me about Jeremy," Drycha said. Her words stung Bram and confused me. Her perspective had shifted. She had been convinced she and Hirythe staged her death to fool Bram. Now, she compounded his misery with a fresh angle, and she didn't miss a step doing it.

I recognized that manipulation. The fog creature used it against me when posing as my father. It was dark and evil magic to turn memories of loved ones into weapons.

Perhaps that's why I lunged at Olivia.

She struggled, but surprise crippled her. We grappled back and forth, her strength returning quickly. She swung me around, nearly pulling me off my feet, but I wrapped my hands around her neck and held on as tightly. I felt Bram's arms trying to tear me from the memory of his wife, but I wouldn't relent.

Finally, I pried the mask from her face, and threw it hard against the ground.

The mirror shattered.

On impact, something washed over the Netherdowns, stretching out in a circle all around me and pushing outward, like a wave forced out in all directions.

Bram collapsed to his knees. Olivia stumbled back against the trunk of the willow tree, dropping her sword. The shining tears that clung to her cheeks fell to the dust and sprouted one by one.

I looked on in wonder. The plants grew impossibly fast into thin canes. Leaves sprang from the wood, unfurling like flags in a crisp breeze.

Olivia stood motionless and unsurprised. She looked longingly at Bram.

The plant developed into a small bush and grew still larger. Small flowers blossomed amidst the leaves, showing off pearly, luminescent petals, which quickly lost their lustre and fell from the plant one by one.

At first blush, it appeared to stop growing, but after a moment, I noticed a tiny currant dangling off of the tallest branch. It slowly grew more and more pale until it took on a metallic sheen.

"A silver currant," I said, breathless. Bram gazed on the plant with an intense curiosity. "Bram, isn't this what you've been searching for?"

I reached out to touch it, but he rushed to my side.

"Don't," he said, pulling my arm back. "It's not for you. Please."

I blushed as I had when I first met him, when I used to ask him rudimentary questions about magic.

This currant sprouted from Olivia's tears. There was no telling how very private a thing it was.

He looked hesitant to touch it himself. I looked between him and Olivia, the plant and currant between them like an altar.

"I'll leave you alone," I said. Bram nodded.

"Thank you."

I touched his arm before I left. "Bram, you don't have to fear her."

"It'll be all right. I'll be along soon."

I was four steps past him when I looked at the surrounding fields. I gasped. Instead of the leagues of monsters, hundreds of currant shrubs had sprouted.

I walked among them. None of them boasted a sterling silver fruit like the plant on the hilltop, but many still had their leaves and young, unripe currant berries. I allowed my hands to brush against them, soft foliage lapping against my skin.

I wondered what stories these plants waited to tell, what secrets they harbored. I looked back to the top of the hill. When I saw Bram and Olivia holding hands, resting their heads on each other, another wave of embarrassment turned me the other way.

I continued on without looking back again. It didn't take long for exhaustion to come on. After traveling most of the day, seeing my sister again, and all the excitement after dinner, it was a miracle I still stood.

My parting words to Bram stuck with me. I heard them over and over in my mind, second-guessing my intention. He didn't need to fear the past.

I was jealous that he had a chance to talk with Olivia. Even in memory, to have a clear opportunity to explore in depth the echo of a loved one...

All that remained of my father were the fog creature's twisted manipulations, and that creature waited hungrily for me back in the real world.

I hoped that whatever Bram found in his currant might lead him to my remedy.

The town lay ahead of me. I imagined Hirythe would have barricaded Anna and Rebecca in his tower, but the threat had dissipated.

I stopped walking and stared at the towers, standing tall above the rest of the town in the dark. What was there for me? Hirythe would send us back to the Rigby's home, and I'd be left defenseless against my attacks. There was no more ink. We still didn't know the full nature of my condition.

But I was sure coming into the Netherdowns had been correct. I'd seen the moondust trail. Was it all just to help Bram?

I turned and saw the dark stretch of forest that bordered Bram's world of memory on nearly all sides. As it had before, the deep within it had called to me, beckoned me. I had been afraid of what lay in the wood. Hirythe told me wild and dangerous memories roamed the trees.

Now, overwhelmed by a feeling of melancholy and reverence, I turned toward it. I had just told Bram that he didn't need to be frightened of the past.

I found myself at a run by the time I was halfway across the meadow, coming closer and closer to the dense tree line. I pushed down the thoughts of the menacing creatures that had already threatened me in this landscape. I was following a feeling.

As I pressed forward, I saw particles of moondust pick up beside my feet, except it wasn't a trail now. It looked like pollen, shining in the moonlight. It was all around me.

I reached the tree line but pushed through without losing a step. I squeezed between tree trunks and ducked under branches. It was dark under the canopy, but the moondust gave off a faint illumination, just bright enough to see.

That's the way it always had been with the moondust, just faint enough to see.

Ahead of me, I saw a break in the trees, a clearing in the forest. I tore through the branches and couldn't believe my eyes.

In front of me, stood the Church in Milford Square, the church I had frequented as a girl with my parents in Dawnhurst-on-Severn. It towered above me, its familiar grounds stretching out as though I had stumbled into the garden and not in the middle of a forest in the Netherdowns.

I walked around the side of the building to the graveyard. My parents were buried in this graveyard, at least they were outside of the Netherdowns.

As I approached my father's grave, my pulse quickened. There was movement beside his gravestone.

A verdant bush had sprouted and was just finishing unraveling its leaves.

I waited and watched as a shining silver currant ripened to maturity. As it did so, all of the moondust around me rushed into it, adding to its brilliance.

This was not Bram's. I didn't care how he had made the diary. This was mine.

I reached forward, plucked the berry, and put it in my mouth.

Chapter Thirty

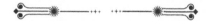

The Silver Currant

"Luella?"

I didn't want to turn around. I was afraid to look.

"Is that you?"

The fog creature had ruined him for me, perhaps beyond repair. If I saw him now, could I trust that he was real, the truest form of my father?

Sometimes I feared he didn't even look the way I remembered him, that over time his features had slowly slid like an eroding riverbed.

But there was more. I feared he wasn't the fog creature, that this was my true father. How would I face him in my current state? I had ruined so much of what he wanted for me.

"My darling girl."

I shut my eyes and turned around. I heard him breathing. When I found the courage to open them, I he stood on the steps of the church, wearing his old jacket and shirt, well-kept but worn, and a pair of handsome eyes.

"Papa," I said.

I rushed toward him, and he collected me in his arms as naturally and comfortably as if I were a little girl. I knew in a moment he was real, or at least pure, untainted by intervening magic. This was the memory of my father incarnate. The scratch of his whiskers, the smell of molasses and sawdust, the melody in his voice, all bore witness.

"Well, this is a surprise," he said.

I pulled back, and he assessed my face.

"Look at you. I always said you were beautiful, but this?" He touched the corners of my eyes. "Are those wisdom lines, as well?"

I patted his hand away and buried my face in his chest again.

"I've missed you so much," I said, his chest warming my cheek through his linen shirt.

"Of course you have. I'm your dad."

"But you don't understand. I thought we'd been meeting." I looked into his face, putting a hand on his cheek. "This was a mask before."

"All fathers' faces are masks."

"That was deftly poetic of you," I said, laughing.

"It didn't sound a bit clumsy?"

"I don't care."

He threaded my hand through his arm and led me around the churchyard, looking around at the ghostly visage of the Netherdowns' beauty.

"I always wondered what it would be like to go on walks with you like this, all grown, I mean. Truth be told, I dreaded you growing up. Once another man married you, what affection would be left for your old dad?"

"You'd have had mother," I said.

"I suppose that may be true," he said. "But that's a different type of love, I'm afraid. I don't remember there being a forest around this church."

"Papa, I've had a hundred things to ask you, but now that we're here, I can't remember any of them."

He patted my hand.

"Let's not fret over it. We can simply enjoy this moment together."

I furrowed my brow. I wanted to do as he said, but there was no telling how much time we had like this. I needed his insight. I needed his perspective.

"Do you think old Cooper would ever wish me harm?" I asked.

"Old Cooper? You mean the Police Sergeant?"

I nodded.

"Well, sure, if you'd committed a crime. A lot of my mates held that against him, but it's not often you meet someone so straightforward. Cooper's always been interested in one thing: upholding the law. He threw me in a cell once or twice."

"He did?" I asked, more surprised than I ought to have been.

"Obstruction of the law, he told me. Deep down he admired how I stood up for my friends, but at times I lost my respect for his authority. His words."

"He threw you in a cell for disrespecting his authority?"

"Well, there may have been a punch or two exchanged."

I laughed. My father was a mixture between Edward Thomas and Doug Tanner. Small wonder I liked both of them.

"Has Cooper harmed you, then?" he asked, concerned. He stopped walking, but I encouraged him on.

"I don't know. You won't believe me, Papa, but I've somehow been mixed up in a bit of magic. Someone enchanted me, and it's nearly ruined my life. The trouble is, I don't know who."

He nodded.

"I didn't believe much in magic before, well, afterwards." He gestured to the sky. "But I've come round since. The more I see it, the less I understand it. Why would someone care to enchant you, though?"

"That's what I don't understand. I've searched everywhere for a motive. That's what detectives do, don't they? Evidence. Motive. I have nothing."

"Can you let the issue lie?"

"I can't. I've ruined our family's name. Cooper's accused me of murder."

"Murder? My little Luella? What a sham. No one would believe it."

"They did because I ran. The enchantment's what caused a man's death. And I'm the one enchanted, so in a way, I am responsible This man's blood is on my hands."

"Is that right?"

"And not just any man, Papa, the father of my fiancé. Can you see the mess I'm in?"

Tears pooled in the bottom of my eyes. My father sat me down on a bench near the front of the church and cradled me into his chest again, rocking me back and forth. I soaked it in, and he began to sing.

There was once a songbird
  dreamed of travelin'
  All around the earth
  To share her ballad
  With all who felt
  That they had lost their worth
  Oft, she sang
  And oft discouraged
  By who refused her song
  But I count the winter
  Days until
  I'll listen summer long.

I smiled as his husky voice hummed out the lyric he'd sung to me as a girl, the same words I'd written on the blank page in Poems from the Wanderer.

"There, there, now. Life is always messy. Things never stay tidy for long. What's nice is messes can nearly always be cleaned up. Now, how can you go about becoming unenchanted?"

"We're not sure. To find out, first I have to discover who did this to me."

"Do you have a list of suspects?"

"A list of possibilities. Cooper. There's my friend Rebecca, but she's been proved innocent. Byron, my old fiancé."

"Old fiancé?"

"Not now, Papa. I even thought for a second it might be Anna, but she's since been proven innocent as well."

"Your sister can't hurt anything. I had to kill a mouse once, and she cried for weeks."

"Then there's—well, no, that's all."

He cocked his head to the side and squinted at me.

"Sounded like you had one more."

"It can't be him." I shook my head. I refused to include Edward in my list. It couldn't be him. I would not consider it.

"Right. Well, let's approach this systematically. Start by askin' why would Cooper want to enchant you?"

"I don't know. I can't think of anything he'd stand to gain."

"All right. What about Byron?"

"Perhaps he meant to make me more subservient? I always pushed his limits and went out of my way to make him uncomfortable. But he wouldn't wish this harm on me." I smirked. "Knowing Byron, he might have tried to enchant me and got it all wrong, released a tiger in the courtyard."

"So, it might be Byron."

"Possibly."

"And what about this other man you refuse to consider? Would he stand to gain anything?"

What would Edward gain from his father's passing? I swallowed. What had he gained since everything started? Fernmount. If our plan went well, possibly Sergeant Cooper's position. I shut my eyes tight.

"Nothing he wanted," I said. I swallowed a painful lump in my throat. I had pushed down suspicions of Edward, and I couldn't release them now, not while there was any other possibility. "It's not him, Papa, not my Edward. It can't be. I love him too much."

My reasoning made no sense, but my father's kindly eyes were full of sympathy and tenderness. He nodded and patted my arm.

"Now, now. If it can't be him, it can't be him. Which leaves Cooper and Byron."

"Yes," I said, wiping my eyes. "It must be on other others."

"What's your plan out of all this? You're my bright girl."

I nodded and explained Edward's idea to reenter the city and spread doubt on Cooper's competency. I explained the role Anna and the Rigbys would play and the reasons we felt it necessary to avoid a trial. He sat and listened quietly, pondering my words. When I finished, he stood and walked several paces away, looking into the woods.

"You're right to hope to avoid a trial. They're unpredictable. I have honest friends still in prison because of gifted solicitors."

"We're hoping that the unwavering support of the Thomas family will be enough to keep me from the same fate." He turned around. "But, Luella, you cannot carry out Edward's plan."

"Why not?" I didn't need to ask. I had reservations from the moment Edward gave his ideas a voice.

"Because Cooper doesn't deserve it."

"He accused me of murder."

"Is he wrong to?" He spoke softly, but his words hit me like sledgehammers.

"I didn't kill Luke Thomas."

"Luke Thomas is dead. His death was mysterious, and Cooper is investigating. You can't rail against him because he found out you're connected to his death. It's wrong."

"I'm not involved the way he says I am," I stammered.

"Sergeant Cooper has done a terrific job managing the police in Dawnhurst for years. You never knew the city without him. He made its residents' safety his life's mission. You can't dethrone him because you ended up on the other side of the law."

Suddenly, seeing my father again wasn't all warm feelings.

"You can't tell me what I can and can't do. You left us."

He stood struck dumb.

"I put it together, Papa. You spent the money on my lessons and a dress for Anna when you should have used it on medicine."

He stuffed his hands dumbly into his pockets and studied the ground.

"You weren't supposed to know about that," he said.

"I sat and puzzled over it for years Did you think I'd spend my entire life throwing my hands in the air and wondering? You should have bought medicine, taken a better chance on life. You didn't fight to stay with us. It was a fever. You could have beat it."

He smiled grimly.

"Could I have?"

I stuttered. I felt like a child, having put only a couple of the pieces together and holding them up as a trophy.

"The doctors said you had a fever," I said.

"I told them to tell you that. You weren't ready to hear the truth. I didn't want to hurt you."

I shut my eyes tight. Squeezing the tears out of them. Was I ready now?

"What's a man supposed to do when he wants to go home but no roads can take him? Some slow spreading poison called cancer. They told me they could try surgery, but it wasn't cheap, and few survived the treatment. There were ways to 'ease my passing.' We were poor. Those ways were expensive."

"But, would they have prolonged your life?"

He shrugged.

"Possibly. But what life would that be for you and your sister? I wasn't going to see you go hungry or your mother get desperate just to steal more time from fate."

"You don't know how hard it was for us." My lip quivered. "We still had bills once you were gone."

"Yes, but not doctor's bills on top. It's difficult to put a value on what it feels like to finish a story."

"I would have had my father with me a little longer. What's the value of even one day a little girl can spend with her dad? I'd have more memories to cherish, just more of you."

"Ah, but you've always had me, haven't you? Parents never leave us. Not really."

Bells rang in the distance, as they did when the bell tower in Dawnhurst worked. He looked up.

"It's time for church services," he said. He gave my hand a kiss. I wasn't ready to let him go, but the sense of closure was swimming in around us, like I was running out of air underwater. "It wasn't easy to leave you, Luella. I need to rest with the decision I made. Don't blame me for doing the best I knew how. I love you. Now you have to do your best."

My lip trembled.

"You mean about Cooper?"

My father turned and walked up the church steps. He grabbed one of the large handles on the door and turned back to me.

"Sometimes it's enough to do what we know in our heart to be right and hope that, one day, others will understand."

"If they don't?"

He smiled at me once more, then vanished into the dark chapel inside. The door closed behind him softly. When I tried to follow, they were locked tight.

Chapter Thirty-One

Tethered

I emerged from the wood in a trance, my thoughts stirring and twisting until I found myself back at the village. It was the middle of the night. We still had time to get back to the Rigbys and pretend none of this ever happened.

If Hirythe were in his tower, I was all but certain he'd see me. I sat down on the edge of the fountain and waited not more than a half hour before he, Rebecca, and Anna appeared on the back of a pair of feathered horses around the corner of a wooden cabin facing the courtyard.

"Luella!" Anna called. Rebecca nodded at me gracefully, eagerly enjoying her regal ride side saddle on such a steed.

"What happened?" Hirythe asked brusquely.

I raised my chin.

"What did you do to Bram's memory?"

He sneered.

"I asked first."

"I asked second."

We stared at each other for a moment, a battle of wills with little at stake. We'd both answer eventually. He sighed.

"Humans are so frustrating sometimes." He dismounted and helped my sister down behind him.

"Are you all right, Anna?" I asked.

She petted the horse gently.

"It was amazing. I've never experienced anything quite like it. The way those plants grew around us! It was like watching years in the garden all in a moment." She sat down next to me. "Are you sure this isn't a dream?"

"No. I'm not," I replied.

Hirythe offered a hand to Rebecca, who gently slid off her horse. She nodded her thanks and sat down next to me.

"I'm glad you're all right," she said. "We'd better get back."

"I altered Bram's memory," Hirythe confirmed. "I decided that if Olivia's true memory was running free in the Netherdowns, it would overcome Bram with grief and longing. You heard how he was at the top of that hill. He blames himself for the actions of a madman."

That much was true. Bram had felt so guilty he'd rather Olivia wear a mask than face her.

"I was afraid that Bram would become a thrall. He'd spend all of his time living in the Netherdowns, communing with his own memory to right a wrong he didn't commit."

I shuddered thinking about the conversation with my father. I had already considered ways I could find another silver currant. If he was as close as a book away...

"As he spent time with her, his memories of her goodness, beauty, forgiveness—they would feed on themselves. Her beauty would grow until he'd become a slave to her memory, like sirens that tempted Odysseus. You saw her tonight becoming more and more radiant."

I nodded.

"She looked like an angel," Anna said. Hirythe's eyes narrowed.

"If an angel could trap you into madness, then yes. So, I found Olivia first, and I convinced her she was real, that we had staged her death to absolve Bram from the guilt of seeing her alive but infected with magic."

"But if you convinced her she lived and had faked her own death..."

"It was a method of rewriting Bram's memory. So long as I kept Olivia hidden from him in the Netherdowns, he could go on living outside of the Netherdowns the way a normal widower might. He would struggle, work, and possibly discover love again."

Hirythe looked at me too astutely at the end of his sentence.

"I broke the mask," I said.

The horse whinnied.

"You what?" Hirythe replied.

"I broke the mask. That's what made the monsters vanish and the currant bushes sprout up."

"Did Bram find a silver currant?" Hirythe asked, trying to mask his eagerness. I was finally starting to recognize his emotions.

"He ate one at the top of the hill, next to Olivia."

Hirythe sat down beside us, looking like he was grappling with the implications.

"Perhaps you were wrong to underestimate him and hide her memory," I said.

He shook his head.

"Perhaps someone on that hill that gave him new strength."

I blushed. As usual, Hirythe was right. Bram's resolve failed him on the hill. Had it not, I would have never lunged at his late wife. Or kissed him. Did I really do all that?

Anna edged closer to me.

"Luella, does Edward know about Bram?" she asked.

Like a bell, thoughts of Bram, Hirythe, and the Netherdowns scattered.

"Hirythe, I need you to send us back."

"Nothing would please me more," he replied sarcastically. "We successfully found some tethers in the tower."

Rebecca nodded with a strange smile on her face. I wondered how Hirythe ascertained them.

"What are they?" I asked, curious.

"The smell of Mrs. Barker's iced buns," Anna replied. Rebecca blushed.

"I don't want to say mine," she said.

"It's Doug's soap," Anna whispered. Rebecca hit her in the arm.

I stood up, pulling them to their feet beside me.

"It was such a pleasure meeting you, Mr. Hirythe," Anna said. He rolled his eyes and produced a small cloth bag tied with a string.

"We're lucky I could recreate these," Hirythe muttered. "The buns were easy, Bram's tasted them, but the other…"

"Rebecca was quite detailed in her description," Anna said. Rebecca blushed.

He waved the bag in front of my sister, and I lost track of her.

"Your turn, Relcavitch," he said, rubbing some large leaves together and held them out for Rebecca. She inhaled indulgently, and a dreamy look came over her, and somehow, I missed the moment she vanished.

Hirythe opened the bottle of perfume that had sent me back from the Netherdowns on many occasions. He turned to administer the scent, but stopped, an expression of concern crossing his brow. He peered deeply into my eyes.

"What is it?" I asked.

"Peculiar. For some reason, I can't see your enchantment."

"What?"

"Curious." Before I could inquire further, he sent me back.

Chapter Thirty-Two

Unveiled

I opened my eyes to the unfamiliar walls of the Rigby residence, lit by the light of a candle. Compared to the dark courtyard in the Netherdowns, it looked bright as a roaring fireplace.

I immediately sensed something wrong. This wasn't my room. The color was different, and I didn't recognize the armoire next to me.

Where had Bram left the Mystic Diary?

No wonder Hirythe felt so uncomfortable about who had custody of the book. To go in from one place and return to another was disorienting.

"Rebecca?" I called out. My eyes were adjusting now. "Anna?"

"Here," said a voice. It didn't sound like either of them. I turned and saw Anna and Rebecca sitting sheepishly on the bed.

"What's the matter with you two?" I asked.

"Don't mind them. They've just been caught out of bed."

I knew that voice. Seated across the room in a chair beside the door was Lady Charlotte Thomas, with a stiletto cradled in her hand, no less.

"Charlotte," I started.

"Don't you Charlotte me," she hissed, curling her hand around the handle of the weapon. "I knew something strange was happening. Evil always has a palpably sinister aura around it. I made myself sensitive to that long ago. To think I welcomed you in my own home. You're wearing my wedding ring, for heaven's sake!"

"I can explain," I said.

She motioned toward a writing desk beside the bed. The diary sat there, innocently. "You mean to tell me you haven't been practicing black magic."

I took a step toward the diary, but Charlotte stood up and pointed the blade menacingly.

"Don't go near that," she said.

"What are you going to do with that? Stab me?"

She pursed her lips. "I will defend myself."

"There's nothing to defend yourself from."

"Answer me plainly. Is this a magical book or not?"

I looked at Rebecca and Anna. My poor sister. A day ago she was probably working at needlepoint with her mother-in-law. They both stared at me helplessly.

"Yes," I admitted. "It is." What was left to say? She had us sticky-handed in the larder.

My admission set something like relief off in Lady Thomas. She gasped and stumbled back down into her chair.

"So, I was right," she said. "This whole time."

I was struck dumb. Questions about my future with Edward or even the police would come later. Now, like a common thief, I wanted to know where I went wrong.

"The young think they are so clever," she said to herself. "You and Edward were painfully obvious to one who knows how to identify the signs."

"The two of us?"

"He always showed such an interest in the supernatural in his youth. I hoped we'd all but beat it out of him by adulthood. It just took the right woman to cause a relapse."

Edward. My accomplice and protector. I remembered the old musty tomes from Oxford library and the clumsy attempt at a spell for Bram.

Was my gallant knight not so different from Bram after all?

"Plus, it was odd how protective you were of that dog and that book. The way the two of you snuck around our suite in Oxford after I'd gone to my room… I didn't just close the door and fall asleep immediately? You mysteriously disappeared in the middle of the night."

My mouth fell open.

"You looked in my room?"

She waved a hand at me like I was speaking nonsense.

"Don't act like your sense of privacy is so delicate. Earlier tonight you had no qualms about welcoming about anyone into your room, male or female."

I sat down beside Anna, grateful that my time in the Netherdowns seemed to have calmed whatever episode was coming on earlier. I didn't want to imagine how this interaction might have fueled my Sraith-powered paranoia.

"How did you know?"

"While everyone else was so distracted by your friend's playacting, I had the common sense to glance through the crack in the doorframe where a man stood clear as night."

Now the tumult of emotions began. She knew it all, about the book, the episodes… It was only a matter of time before she assumed my dark magic had something to do with her husband's death, if she hadn't already. Edward was right. His mother took this very seriously.

Was this the end of my hope at a marriage with Edward? She'd turn me into the police.

"Lady Thomas, you don't understand. It's not evil," Rebecca said, standing up. "If you had seen what I saw tonight… It was extraordinary. A marvel! It was divine!"

"How dare you, Miss Turner? After I welcomed you in my home. You suggest I sink to your level?"

She didn't even have to use the stiletto to skewer Rebecca's courage. My friend sat back down sheepishly. I felt terrible to have mixed her up in this, even more so for Anna.

If only she'd confronted me alone. It would have been so much easier to bear.

An idea struck me.

"You didn't say anything," I said.

Lady Thomas raised her eyebrows.

"You said you knew about Bram in my room earlier tonight. You said nothing to the others. Why? Was it just to avoid a scandal? If so, why confront me now?"

She peered at me relentlessly, like she was trying to fit a piece of thread through a needle, and I was the eye of that needle.

"I trust I don't have to convey the severity of my request that you two stay silent about all this." It took a moment for Anna and Rebecca to realize she spoke to them. They nodded vehemently, like schoolgirls avoiding a whipping. "Then I imagine you are both tired."

Rebecca looked puzzled. "Are you kicking me out? I'm meant to sleep here," Rebecca protested.

"You'll figure something out, Miss Turner. I'm sure Doug could help you," Charlotte quipped.

Rebecca blushed, but they both quickly scurried out of the room.

When they'd gone, I looked across the room at my once future mother-in-law. She studied me carefully before starting to speak in low, even tones.

"When I was a young girl, my family moved for a spell to a small hamlet much north of here. When we attended church at the quaint chapel close to our new home, my parents noticed some subtle differences between the way the local parish conducted services."

She sat back down in the chair beside the door.

"We thought nothing of it until we noticed peculiar customs in my father's line of agricultural work. Offerings left out after harvest. Figures of speech uttered only in certain circumstances. That sort of thing. One day, my mother came home from the market breathing heavily, her face flushed of color. She had offended one of these bizarre customs and received a warning by several local women."

"What type of custom?" I asked, curiosity overcoming me.

"She didn't know. My father took it as a threat and wanted to have a talk with the husbands of those women, but when he did, he got an altogether different impression. It wasn't a threat. The locals were afraid for my mother. My father shrugged it off, but things started going wrong. The crop failed. The livestock perished. One evening, my father caught a small fire in the corner of our home before it became a blaze."

As she spoke, my mind raced for explanations. My enchantment had affected me from the inside out, but from what Hirythe and Bram had told me, magic could also work from the outside in.

My expression must have betrayed these thoughts. Lady Thomas nodded in acknowledgment.

"You understand what my father would not admit," she said. "Our new friends in the village, even the local priest, urged us to follow the customs and leave out a generous portion of our harvest. My father followed this advice one time. The next day, our last cow died without warning."

She took a breath before continuing.

"Eventually, we left. We lost the small savings my family had, and the experience turned my father hard. He never smiled like he used to. He looked like a man with a grudge against a king, perpetually bitter and entirely unequipped to retaliate."

I nervously played with the edge of a blanket on the bed.

"You're afraid of magic," I said. I assumed she was trying to explain something to me.

She shook her head.

"I hate it. I won't have it at Fernmount."

"You're not alone. I've had my fill. I want nothing to do with it," I said, eager to agree about something.

"Then what are you doing, Luella? Why was there a man in your room? Why are you using that devilish instrument? Tampering with these powers can ruin your life."

I couldn't stop the rueful smile forming on my lips. If only she knew.

"Is this funny?"

"No. Forgive me."

"Good heavens, girl. Why did you have to do this? Especially now that I was—"

She cut herself off and buried her head in her hands. I wondered what words were coming out next. Was it possible that Charlotte Thomas had grown to like me?

"Charlotte?" I asked. She didn't respond, so I knelt beside her. "Charlotte, I love your son. I want to make him unconditionally happy." I swallowed down a lump of nerves. "I hope you don't mind me saying that I've come to care for and respect you as well. I lost my mother a long time ago, you see."

She raised her face. Tears streaked her cheeks.

"Then why?"

I had expected a scolding when she sent Rebecca and Anna from the room. I expected spiteful words and personal attacks. I did not expect a tired, beaten woman with pleading eyes.

And that's why I told her.

"I am enchanted," I said.

"Enchanted?"

"Cursed might be a more appropriate classification. Your father had his fortune stolen from him. My sanity is being leeched from me."

I explained my situation in Dawnhurst-on-Severn, how I'd been engaged to Byron and desperate to find a long-term income for the benefit of my sister.

I explained how I stumbled foolishly into questionable company and how that company introduced me to what looked like a shortcut to happiness.

Charlotte nodded along. She hadn't been born into wealth. Her husband had accumulated it. She likely remembered the same hungers for comfort and stability.

When I explained about the pen, she nearly gasped aloud. She stood up and turned from me all the same. I didn't explain about the final story I wrote for Langley's. She had already understood. She held the stiletto in her hand tightly.

"You lost control of the instrument," she said.

"Yes."

She shook her head.

"Payment," she muttered. She squeezed the handle of the blade so tightly I feared she might hurt her hand.

"What?"

"Ever since my family left our farm in the north, I've been afraid that the debt wasn't settled, and some devil still has a ledger with my name on it."

"Your name on it?" I asked.

"I told you my father tried to leave a portion of our harvest to appease whatever was out there." She took a big breath. "Well, his cynicism had worn off on me. Little girls worship their fathers. To prove him right and the locals wrong, I drank the milk he put out on our step when he wasn't looking." She tried to blink back tears, but they fell. "I've never a living soul."

I stood up.

"Don't be ridiculous. Your husband died because I was reckless. I tried to control the magic."

"Whether you had a hand in it or not, my husband is gone."

I had no rebuttal.

"So, what's wrong with you now?" she asked.

"I'm trying to find a cure. Edward tried to propose after your husband died, but I refused. I didn't want to take advantage of his grieving, and I wanted to be whole before uniting myself with him."

"But you've accepted his proposal now."

"Because a cure is within reach. I've been traveling into that diary to find my remedy. But I'm so tired of all of it, Charlotte. Please. All I want is to be a faithful and devoted member of your family."

She had walked to the armoire and gently touched a porcelain teacup that rested there. She looked like a rendition of Lady Justice, a stiletto in one hand, a teacup in the other.

"Have you told Edward?" she finally asked.

"Yes. He left Fernmount with me to track down the people who could help me." People. Perhaps it was best not to mention it was one man not all that much older than myself. I also left out what Rebecca had been scolding me over.

Why was it so easy to lie about how close I was to finding a cure? Was this wishful thinking or flat denial of circumstance?

"Good heavens! And Edward still came up with a plan to defame the Police Sergeant? Cooper is right to suspect you. Edward knows that."

I saw the face of a disappointed parent. The Edward I'd known had always been a beacon for the truth. The plan was underhanded. All who understood the true details of my situation must agree.

"I've had a change of heart regarding that plan," I said. "I felt uneasy when he unveiled it to me, and its outlook never improved."

"So you'll be turning yourself in?" she asked. I stared at the empty air, trying to form a response. I hadn't considered it yet. I just knew my father didn't want me to defame an honest policeman.

"I suppose I will. I can hope the lack of evidence will acquit me." I studied her face, looking for any sign of acceptance or refusal. "Or, I will take my place in prison, which in many ways would be just."

She put down the stiletto.

"How did you manage to secure such loyal friends? What is it about you that inspires so much fidelity?"

I shrugged. "I hardly deserve it."

"That is true." She pursed her lips. "And yet, I'm not ready to see my future daughter-in-law eaten alive by the courts or rotting in a prison cell."

I blinked. Twice. Three times.

"What did you say?"

"If you arrogant children would have come forward in the first place, I could have come up with a better plan than a defamation campaign."

"Did you say future daughter-in-law?"

She folded her arms and turned away from the teacup.

"I don't know who is to blame for Luke's death, but if what you're saying is true, I can only hold you accountable for actions you intended. I've seen what magic can do to a human being. But I will only accept you into this family if we can clean up this mess."

I couldn't help myself. I crossed the room and embraced her.

"Thank you, Charlotte." Tears flowed from my eyes. I felt like a dirigible inflated near bursting. I hadn't dared hope for this. In the best most fantastical outcome, I imagined I would keep my secrets from her for the rest of my life.

"Luella, please. How old are we?" she asked in a stuffy sort of way. But when I released her, she didn't hide the gloss in her own eyes. Forgiveness is a harvest, the more you take the more you receive.

"Now, if you'll listen for a moment, I have a plan to rid you of your charges."

I stumbled onto the bed and landed with an ungraceful plop.

"I'd be eager to hear it."

"You're going to need that ability to inspire perplexingly strong faithfulness. You mentioned that some others got you involved with your magical item."

I nodded.

"Then it's simple. You only need to convince one of them to confess to my husband's murder."

Chapter Thirty-Three

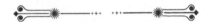

Bending and Breaking

My relief about confessing to Edward's mother was palpable. And, seeing as it came so quickly after my encounter with my father's memory, my spirits soared quite high, despite the difficulties that lay ahead of me.

Charlotte wanted me to go to Edward immediately and explain the shift in our plan, but I convinced her to give me a little time to ensure her plan would work.

I had my doubts.

She wanted me to convince Bram to submit to a trial for murdering Luke Thomas.

Instead of dragging Sergeant Cooper's name through the mud, we would respect his intuitive police work. But Bram pushed me to write more daring stories with the ink, it was only fair he should shoulder the weight of justice for Luke Thomas' death.

That made sense. A heavy, dreadful type of sense.

But she quickly pointed out that if the whole affair was as magically affected as I claimed, he stood a good chance of walking free, anyway.

Since Lady Thomas was the widow in the case at hand, I considered this almost inhumanly reasonable.

"Something feels wrong," Rebecca told me when I'd finished explaining it to her.

She returned to our room, with many grumpy words about hiding in the halls in her nightgown, the night before right after Charlotte left me. We woke improperly late in the morning, tender and achey as if we spent the night being dragged in a sack at the bottom of a river.

"Don't say that," I replied.

"It's not normal. Her husband died, and she's willing to overlook your involvement?"

I swung my legs from the bed and tested the joints in my knees. One night parading around the Netherdowns and now I was fifty years old. I stood up and went to assess myself in a mirror. That took courage.

"What about her family's story? If she's really believed all this time that some spirits in the highlands had it out for her, her husband's death may seem an inevitability. It's almost as though the person responsible was just a vessel."

The looking glass was not kind. I prayed Anna did not forget all of her beauty tricks now she was a married woman. I would need a whole different sort of magic before seeing Edward that morning.

"But, Luella, doesn't something seem wrong? How are you so scrupulous about defaming Cooper only to turn around and put Bram's life in jeopardy?"

I bit my lip.

"It won't be."

"How do you know?"

"Because he'll never get to the trial. I have an idea."

Rebecca threw her head back on to her pillow.

"Do you have any idea how exhausting you are? Why can't we just have a lovely day with some tea and some baked goods and some quaint strategy at cards or needlepoint or something?"

I threw a brush at her, gently.

"And this comes from the woman filled to the brim with a lust for adventure. Has Doug made you soft?"

"Lust for adventure? I was a typist that enjoyed a good novel. I ate at the same restaurant four times a week. What adventure are you talking about?"

A gentle knock at our door preceded my sister's face. Looking at her, you'd have never supposed she had enjoyed a maximum of two hours' sleep.

"Well, that isn't fair," Rebecca said. "She looks beautiful."

"Is everything all right? Luella, I woke this morning and thought it was all a dream. Do you know what I'm talking about?"

I motioned for her to close the door and ushered her over to me.

"It wasn't a dream, but everything is all right. In fact, it's even better than we could have hoped."

She took a deep breath, like she just woke up after an enchanting night at a ball.

"So it's all real? The magic?"

"I better hope so, seeing as only your magic can make me look presentable for my Edward," I said with a smile.

"And me for my..." Rebecca paused. "Well, in the case I should develop a 'my'." She scrambled from the bed so as not to get left behind from being made up.

Anna was adept with her restorative powers, and by the time we made it to the dining room, Rebecca and I did not look fifty years old after all.

The Rigbys had set aside a bit of breakfast for us. It was homey and hearty, filled with fluffy scones and savory sausages, and dinner seemed so very long ago.

We lathered butter on the bread as gracefully as one can lather anything.

"I was so worried about you after Rebecca's fright last evening," Edward whispered to me at the table. Across from us, Doug nibbled on some extra scones beside Rebecca, despite insisting he ate enough already. Everyone else had moved on from breakfast. We enjoyed a private dining room.

"Rebecca's fright?" I asked.

"Yes, when the entire household came rushing to your room."

"Of course. I'm sorry, Edward. I'm so distracted this morning."

He nodded.

"I'm sure reuniting with your sister has been emotional for you," he suggested.

"It's not only that." I struggled to tell him everything that happened the night before. I was tired of yanking Edward's emotions in different directions. If there was nothing wrong, or nothing I couldn't handle on my own, I didn't know why I needed to share every little thing with him. And I didn't want to explain everything again, not right now. I was tired.

"I dreamed about my father last night," I said, uncovering only a small bit of truth. He tensed.

"You told me you've been using the ink to prevent that."

"Not that type of dream. It—it felt real, pure. I talked to what I can only assume was the unadulterated version of my father's memory."

Edward stared at me.

"What did you talk about?" he prodded.

"Much. My life. Anna. You. And, honestly, our plan to defame Cooper."

Edward set his jaw firmly.

"What did your dream father have to say about our plan?"

I swallowed a piece of potato.

"He didn't like it. He said Cooper has done anything wrong."

"It isn't wrong to ruin a woman's life without evidence to support an arrest?" Edward asked, coldly. His answer came quickly, and I understood that there may have been some professional, ethical lines on which Edward disagreed with the Sergeant.

"But his intuition led him down the right path. Even if I wasn't responsible, I was involved in your father's death."

Edward took my elbow, gently and firmly, and turned me toward him.

"That may be true, but this is the plan we have. If I saw another plausible option, perhaps we could take it, but I don't see how else to clear your name. I won't have you in prison, I won't have you in an asylum, and I won't have you in a trial."

His eyes blazed with intensity, and I realized that although we were now engaged, we had drifted apart. The secrets I kept from him piled high, and they stung like thistle spines. Even if I concealed them with the best intentions, I wondered if some high magic went to work when people kept secrets from each other.

I missed him. I missed seeing him carefree. Memories of his laughter before his father's death drifted through my memory. I saw him standing bright-eyed and eager to perform his work as a police officer.

Had I dimmed his eyes? Could I rekindle them?

I put a hand on his.

"Can you give me one day, dearest?" I saw his defenses fall immediately. I needed that. I needed to feel like he put up walls for the rest of the world, but not for me. "Let me enjoy a day with my sister's family. We can get back to our plan tomorrow."

"Of course," he exhaled. "I'm sorry. I don't mean to push you. It's no secret I've been anxious over this. I'm just eager to see it put to rest."

"And eager to be married," I said. He smiled and blushed, handsome and boyish. "As am I. And I hope to enjoy every step of our journey, even this one."

"What about my mother?" he asked.

"I'll talk to her." He raised his eyebrows incredulously. "I mean it. Let's enjoy our engagement. Today, we're spending time with our future relations."

He didn't expect such tenderness at the breakfast table. I watched a smile infuse his entire body.

"We're fortunate in that department," he said. "I quite like the Rigbys."

We spent the rest of the morning in light-hearted joviality, and I knew what I said was true: I couldn't wait to marry him.

I just had to do a few things first. Namely, I needed to convince Bram to go along with my plan to take the fall for Luke Thomas' murder, find out who enchanted me, and restock the treatment for my magical condition while we managed a cure.

All these obstacles seemed insurmountable as early as the day before. But since I ate that silver currant, my perspective was overwhelmingly positive.

After all, my conscience about slandering Cooper was now clean. And I'd narrowed down my list of suspects considerably. It had to be Byron, and I was confident he did not intend to unleash something quite so powerful.

Byron Livingston received more than he bargained for after proposing to me. When he discovered his wife-to-be was full of ambition and dreams and all those other traits that make women difficult, he must have fallen prey to some questionable street peddler, perhaps at a carnival. His path may not have been so different from mine, tinkering with a magical trinket and accidentally unstopping a malignant spirit.

He might not even be aware of all he did.

Or, it may have been Cooper, though at this point I doubted it. I still had no motive to assign him.

And, even if I suffered attacks from my illness, Edward was aware of those, and now I was confident his mother would understand. Marriage was possible for me. It would be difficult, but it would be possible. I could be Lady Edward Thomas.

The idea sent chills through me.

We spent the rest of the day exactly as I'd asked. Doug and Edward insisted on helping chop wood, a request the Rigbys found charmingly out of character for someone of his station. As Doug split a log, he would toss smaller bits of it to Cyrus and a few other hounds that congregated on the side of the yard.

The women stayed in and chatted pleasantly about whatever was available for idle gossip. Someone broke out a deck of cards and before the men came back red-cheeked and damp around the collar, I had lost at three games I'd never learned before.

It felt not unlike the Christmas holiday I'd enjoyed with my friends, except now I enjoyed it with my sister.

By the time Rebecca and I retired to our room again, I had all but convinced myself life was relatively normal.

But I knew that, despite how tired I felt from the night before, I would back into the Netherdowns. I didn't bother changing, and I hoped whatever Anna did to me that morning still had some potency left.

I had a favor to ask, and Bram wouldn't like it.

"Do you want me to accompany you?" Rebecca asked.

"No. I will need to do this alone."

She nodded.

"Just remember, you're an engaged woman," she said, straightening my coat. I scoffed.

"What?" she stammered. "You told me about Bram before last night, but you never mentioned he was such a handsome man."

"Is he? I didn't notice."

She rolled her eyes.

"Rebecca, I'm not only engaged. I'm in love with Edward."

She took a breath in as though she were about to voice an objection or a critique but shook her head.

"Right. Well, don't stay too long on any account. You're exhausted."

She settled into bed and produced a novel from her bag.

I took the diary off the shelf and settled into a chair beside our writing desk.

"Luella, do you think all magic is real? Even the stuff we read in books?"

I flipped through the pages and found a poem I particularly enjoyed, one of Bram's best.

"If it's not, what keeps us reading?"

She smiled, and I lost myself in some poetry.

Chapter Thirty-Four

Crimson Ink

"I don't like it," Hirythe said. We watched a group of mirrored soldiers in the courtyard from the second story of his study. They set small candles in paper lanterns that illuminated their armor in curious ways.

"You always talk like that, Hirythe," said Bram, who leaned dreamily on his hand.

"Is it possible, though?" I asked.

"Possible? Yes. In some ways, it's more secure than using the entire diary, but that's not what I'm worried about." The fae played with a deck of cards absent-mindedly.

"Then what concerns you?" I prodded.

"Apart from having me locked up as a murderer?" Bram added.

"An alleged murderer!" I corrected. "It's not the same."

He cocked an eyebrow in a way that reminded me of Rebecca.

"You're telling me a Dawnhurst court wouldn't love to throw a vagrant carnival worker in a cell after blaming him for the death of one of their wealthiest bankers?"

Bram rattled this off nonchalantly, as though he wanted to probe how well I'd thought through my own plan. He looked different now, more mature somehow. His encounter with Olivia had changed him. My silver currant changed me.

"Well, that's why we don't let you get to the trial," I replied. "If a single page torn from the Mystic Diary can get you to the Netherdowns, it's as simple as making sure we hide a folded piece of paper on your person."

"And what happens to the paper after he's gone? What's stopping a prison guard from reading it and getting to the Netherdowns?" Hirythe asked.

"I could float it in a water bucket or something while I read," Bram suggested. "By the time the guards realized I was gone, the paper would be useless."

I shrugged and looked at Hirythe.

"What if they find the paper and take it from him? What if Bram can't lose himself adequately in the writing if it's only a single page? But that's only half of my problem. If Bram wants to lock himself in a prison for the rest of his life, I've always thought he was part idiot. But neither of you appreciate the ripple effect all of this back and forth is causing. Weeks ago, Bram would quietly come into the Netherdowns occasionally."

"Occasionally. You make me sound like a relative that's forgotten to write you letters or something."

"Now," Hirythe continued ignoring Bram, "we have used this magic so frequently and so often, I'm afraid bending it like this will defeat the purpose for creating the book in the first place."

"To hide from Jeremy," I said.

Hirythe scowled.

"To put it crudely, yes. He never was a fool, Bram, and he's had adequate time to find a way to detect magic like this, what with the trinkets he stole from you. What if this is the thread he needs to unravel the Netherdowns?"

Bram played with a ring on his hand, one I'd never seen him wear before.

"You overestimate him, Hirythe." Bram's stare locked on to the festivities outside the window in the street below. "Jeremy was never brilliant. He was just vindictive and desperate. You and I haven't been able to come up with a way to trace magic across England. If you haven't, I doubt he has."

"What if you're wrong, Bram? I know that seems impossible, but what if you are? All of this damnable hiding would have been for nothing, and if I die so does my race, or worse."

I knit my eyebrows.

"Worse? What could be worse?"

They both ignored me, which made me realize how solemn my question was.

"I promised you a long time ago," Bram said. "There will be no more blood on your hands."

An eery chill went up my back. I looked at Hirythe and old questions about what happened to the other fae came back to me. I had no idea who Hirythe was, how old he was, or what he had been through. I knew him as merely an almost comically judgmental friend of Bram's.

If I knew him as Bram did, or better, would I sit beside him so comfortably?

"Hirythe, let me do this. It's only right, after everything I've put her through."

Hirythe curled his lip and sneered out the window where some paper lanterns floated in the air.

"Are you seeking my blessing or my permission?"

Bram nodded grimly.

"It's settled, then." He stood up.

"Where are you going?" I asked.

"I promised Olivia I would help set off a lantern with her," he said. "You two will get along, I trust?"

He clapped Hirythe's shoulder, but the fae didn't look at him. He smoldered looking at the living memories congregating outside the window.

When Bram had gone, the silence grew thick. I was uncomfortable, fearing for the first time the being beside me. Before, he seemed so human. Human with enhancements, perhaps, but I regarded him as human all the same.

"You don't have to be afraid of me," he said wearily. Could he read thoughts, or was my body language that obvious? "I hope you know what you're doing, Luella Winthrop. Bram is the only human I've ever really liked. Well, Olivia wasn't bad either."

I swallowed.

"Why are they celebrating?" I asked, nodding at the lanterns out the window.

"Bram and Olivia have reconciled. Positive changes are coming to the Netherdowns," he replied. I watched the lights lift gently into the air, wondering what it would be like to come to terms with your past.

"You had a silver currant," Hirythe said. "How was it?"

I hesitated. Hearing him bring it up so casually sounded sacrilegious.

"How did you know?"

"They say that women expecting a child have a certain something about them that can almost distinguish them physically from others. The afterglow of a silver currant experience is similar."

I pondered this. I had felt remarkably better about my life since communing with my father.

"Before, you said there was no such thing as a silver currant," I said. He smiled.

"Before, I was trying to hide Olivia from Bram," he replied.

I screwed up my courage for my next question. His smile had set me a little more at ease.

"Have you ever had one?" I asked.

The corner of his mouth twitched.

"Come here." He stood and led me over to his sturdy wood desk. Silently, he touched an intricate lock on a drawer with the tip of his finger. The lock slid apart organically. A glow emanated from the drawer from the moment he cracked it open and displayed within as if they were a collection of meticulously catalogued insects, were rows and rows of silver currants.

It took my breath away.

"I've never had one," he said.

"How can you bear the curiosity?" I asked.

"I'm afraid of what they may inspire me to do. A silver currant is the fruit that grows from your purest, most potent memories. It goes beyond conscious recollection and builds something from the perfect fossilized version of a person or a place or an event. Many people would be uncomfortable with that idea. Can you imagine why?"

I resisted the urge to touch them.

"It's not a memory, really. It's just your mind creating something from stray pieces."

"You've come a long way since you were a petty journalist, Miss Winthrop. You're correct, though you would be wrong to fear them.

Although they're not a true memory, a silver currant can't deliver falsehood. Who did you see when you ate one?"

"My father."

"Do you understand? You may wonder if you only heard what you wanted from him. You didn't. You can trust that conversation as though it had truly transpired between you and your living father."

I stared at his collection in reverence. They were so bright. I fell into a trance looking at them.

"The memories of your father were strong enough to create one of these fruits. You loved him. Your currant was made of love. Bram's was as well."

He looked at me intently, like he had just asked me a riddle.

"What are yours made of?"

"Nothing I want to remember," he replied. He closed the drawer, and the lock slid back into place, before vanishing under the desk's solid wood like as if it dipped underwater.

"How did my father's memory come into the Netherdowns?" I asked.

"You must have inserted it somewhere along the way, like the cat or the bull."

My father's song. I had written it on a page in the book when I first started investigating it. I smiled, wondering what had prompted me to do such a thing.

Hirythe nodded at the ring on my hand.

"I didn't notice it last night," he said. "What's his name?"

I pulled my hand closer to me as if I could protect myself with the ring.

"Edward."

"Does he know about your condition?"

I nodded, somehow embarrassed this was coming out now. I felt a rushing need to explain myself.

"He's been with me through thick and thin, through all of this mess. He's protected me even during my most violent episodes."

Hirythe didn't respond. Instead, he just quietly sat back down in his chair by the window.

"And, now that I know the crimson ink can ward off my attacks, I simply have to find a way to make it in regular batches."

Hirythe laughed quietly.

"What's funny?" I asked, a wave of defensiveness manifesting as tension in my shoulders.

"You can't make the crimson ink in batches."

"Why not?"

"Didn't Bram tell you what it was?"

I shook my head. I'd tried to get an answer from him before, but he'd brushed off my questions.

"He bottled distilled years of his life."

I choked. My heart plummeted.

"What?" My knees lost their strength, and I fell into a chair. Hirythe shook his head.

"I suppose if he'd told you, you'd have never used it."

"He first insinuated the pen was magical." I remembered him fishing out the heavy pen from his chest that first night we met.

"A bit of intelligent misdirection."

"He said that it would turn my fiction into fact. That's what it did when I wrote with it."

"It does that, yes. That distortion of cause and effect infected you with Sraith. But Bram made the inkwell to treat his wife. He hypothesized that sacrificing a portion of his life would realign Olivia's natural understanding of cause and effect. It's nothing less than years of Bram's life. To make more, he'd have to distill more."

"Can they be mine?"

Hirythe shook his head.

"Not if you're to use them. Someone else must make the sacrifice. Bram's the only person who knows how to do it. You've just asked him to be arrested for murder, do you amend your request?"

My memory ran wild, recalling every conversation we'd ever had about the ink, recasting his intentions all over again. I felt nauseous remembering the sound of the inkwell shattering on my floor, Bram's life literally seeping into the rug.

"Why would he want me to use it in the first place?" I asked, choking back guilt and remorse. I never wanted him to do that. If I'd only known…

"If a decade of your life sat in a bottle on your shelf, would you be interested in using it?" Hirythe leaned over conspiratorially. "He didn't get to it much with Olivia. Maybe he saw something in you."

It wasn't right. I felt wronged, like I was responsible for Bram's choice.

"That's not fair." I shook my head, balancing indignation and sadness. "I didn't want anyone to do that for me."

"Yet you're about to be married. Isn't that the same thing?" Hirythe asked, his words like lemon juice in a paper cut. Edward. How much of his life had I taken already? True, it wasn't distilled in a bottle, but he had put everything on hold for me. For me. Why was everyone doing so much for me?

"I should leave," I said. "I'm exhausted."

"Quite right, Miss Winthrop," he said. "But first, please write down what time you'll need Bram out of the diary."

He handed a pen and paper to me. Did I imagine things, or did it look like the pen Bram had offered me in his tent at the carnival?

I took it numbly and scratched out a date and time. He took the paper back, as casually as though it were instructions for tea. Then, he produced the bottle of strange fragrance that served as my anchor to the real world.

"If the plan changes, notify us immediately," he said before the anchor took me back.

Chapter Thirty-Five

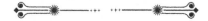

Worlds Colliding

I hardly wanted to share the news with Charlotte. I'd done what she'd asked and solidified a pathway to my union with Edward. Not only would I have her blessing, but we had a way to clear my name without dragging Cooper unjustly through the mud.

She would be thrilled. True, I had no intention of letting Bram see time in prison, but I had a feeling that Charlotte expected justice to cheat her. It was in her ledger.

When I woke the next morning, any semblance of the euphoria gifted to me by the silver currant had vanished, blanketed over with anger at being falsely induced into wasting so much of Bram's life. It was wrong of him.

I grappled with guilt and fury all at once. Stupid man. My foolish, foolish Bram.

Charlotte responded graciously, even commenting that Bram was doing an honorable thing. We had a private family gathering (which somehow included Doug and Rebecca) to debrief her updated plan.

"So, we will leave the poor Sergeant well enough alone," Charlotte said when I had finished explaining.

Edward looked at me and took my hand.

"You're sure that Bram will go along with this?"

I nodded. I imagined a twisted part of Bram was excited about it.

"That's good. It's time he stood up and accounted for what he's put you through."

"You don't know a thing about him," I snapped. Edward flinched. The rest of the room stared at me, surprised how I had spoken so harshly. I shook my head. "I'm sorry. It's just hard to have so many people sacrifice on my behalf."

Doug patted me gruffly on the back.

"We're not doing it for you alone," he said. "I, for one, am eager to get back to my pub."

"Then it's settled. We leave for Dawnhurst tomorrow, and soon we'll put this entire thing behind us," Charlotte said.

She was wrong, though. This would never be behind us. I would still have bouts of madness. I would still live with the guilt of wasting Bram's years.

If there were solutions, they weren't behind us.

The day passed more quickly and less joyfully than the one before. The Rigbys expressed their regret that we couldn't stay longer. Anna looked particularly rueful.

"Come now," I said. "This will be our new routine. We'll visit again soon, and after the wedding, we'll host you and Jacob at Fernmount."

She hugged me tightly.

We left the next morning. I sensed the excitement brimming in the rest of my party and a general sense of levity in the carriages as we rattled along to Dawnhurst-on-Severn.

I spent most of the trip quietly looking out the window, lost in thoughts about Bram, the fog creature, Sraith, and my father. My trance was broken by Charlotte Thomas' voice.

"Ah, there it is, Edward. Your father's mistress, Dawnhurst-on-Severn."

I craned my neck and saw the forest turn into farmland, and soon I felt my home in my bones. The humidity and sound of the rushing Severn River wafted into me like a missing piece of my soul.

Soon the buildings grew more and more familiar as we ventured deeper into the city. Before I knew it, we were passing through the streets of my childhood. It was strange being back, seeing that despite my absence the city had barreled on through time, ruthless and uncaring. The Church in Milford Square looked less welcoming now than it had in the Netherdowns.

"What time is it?" I asked.

"Nearly three o'clock," Edward said, after checking his pocket watch. I sighed.

"Are you ready to meet Bram?"

"What do you mean?"

His mother's eyes narrowed at me.

"I thought we'd have arrived by now," I replied apologetically.

Right at three o'clock, we crossed Dawnhurst's central bridge, and I looked out the window. We were close to the lot that had housed the carnival where Bram and I met.

When I glanced back into the carriage, Bram was there, sitting next to Edward's mother.

"Hello, Bram," I said. It took him a moment to orient himself, and when his gaze swept across the interior of the carriage, I saw Bram grow more tense than I'd ever seen him. A fresh understanding of what I had asked him to do sprang up in my gut. He was a calf at the slaughterhouse, and he hadn't even confessed to the police yet.

Charlotte didn't jump, nor did she betray any weak emotion, but something in the air was like a razor's edge. Edward bristled beside me, and I feared he might lunge at the meddler.

"You must be Edward," Bram said.

Edward nodded.

"Luella is very fond of you," Bram continued.

"I would hope so. It's a shame you won't be able to attend our wedding."

This was a mistake. I never wanted Edward and Bram to meet, and it was becoming evident why at an alarmingly fast rate.

"She will make a beautiful bride." Bram smiled sadly and looked into his lap.

"Do you know who I am?" Charlotte asked him.

"I'm afraid I can assume. I'm here to take responsibility for your misfortune."

Charlotte wrangled up all the regal posture of the status her husband left her.

"Do you accept that you were responsible?" she asked.

"I accept that I was negligent when I ought to have been more careful. But I can't accept responsibility for what I did not do."

"Will you still submit yourself to the police?" Edward asked.

"I will. And I hope that some justice may bring you comfort. It's a terrible thing to lose a father or a spouse."

"What would you know about losing a father?" Edward asked. He was struggling to maintain his composure, and Charlotte stretched a hand across the compartment to comfort him.

"Mr. Bram, it's important to me that you understand I bear you no ill will. You have been very foolish, and I can't take away the consequences you're facing because you chose to meddle with magic."

He nodded rhythmically and looked to me. I turned to avoid his gaze, to studying the passing city I'd called home my entire life.

We sat in silence until we arrived at a building in the heart of the city's west side. The facade looked ornate and expensive. I recognized it as one of the gaudiest buildings in Dawnhurst. Lady Thomas was the only one who exited, assisted by a man in a smart coat and top hat.

"Aren't you all coming?" she asked.

"It's best to deal with all of this as soon as possible, mother. I don't like having Luella in the city while the storm is still overhead."

She clasped her hands together.

"Of course. I'll see that Doug and Rebecca are comfortable."

The door closed, and before Edward could signal the driver to set off, Rebecca's face was at the window, Doug followed close behind with Cyrus on a leather lead.

"Cyrus? Is that you?" Bram asked, bewildered. I saw his face brighten, and I found myself thankful that he had at least a moment of comfort after the awkwardness of the carriage.

The pointer barked and whimpered.

"He seems to like you," Bram said to Doug. The pub owner shrugged. I winced.

"You will protect her, won't you?" Rebecca asked.

"Of course," said Edward and Bram at once. They eyed each other like posturing animals. Rebecca looked at me and gripped the edge of the door tightly.

"Doug," I said, "I know you're eager to get back to your pub, but—"

"Don't worry. I'm not half as bad at being patient as people think. I'll wait for the signal from this louse."

He tipped his hat toward Edward, who inclined his head conspiratorially. Then, Edward gave the roof of the carriage a few distinct taps as he had done when he rescued me from this city what felt like ages ago.

But everything was different now. My arms and legs might as well have been filled with iron.

I kept trying to remind myself Bram wouldn't truly face trial if everything went to plan. And, even if he did, there was very little evidence to condemn him, apart from my word and his confession.

That was the root of my unease. I wasn't dragging Cooper's name through the mud, true, but I was throwing Bram in the line of fire to save myself.

It was cowardly. I'd never consulted with my father on this new plan. What would he say?

But the wheels clattered along all the same.

"Will I need to secure irons?" Edward asked Bram.

"No need," Bram said. "My word is my bond."

"How comforting," Edward muttered.

The carriage pulled to a stop, and there it was, standing like a ghost from the past. The brightly painted door of the Dawnhurst Police Force.

"I'm ordering the driver to continue circling the avenue. Don't leave the carriage until you see me again. I want to make sure old Cooper will not be brash and arrest both of you on sight."

He looked at me, and I recognized the smallest traces of fear in his eyes.

"I hope this works," he said. I gave his hand a squeeze, and he kissed me boldly on the cheek before hopping out of the carriage and disappearing into the building. As we drove on, I heard muffled applause from inside.

"I understand why you'd want to marry him," Bram said.

"Bram, please. Not now."

"Darling of the police force. Extravagantly wealthy. Unjustly handsome. It makes sense."

I took the diary and opened it across my lap.

"Do you have a preference about which page you take?" I asked. My words were mechanical.

He took the book and flipped to a certain poem before handing it back to me.

"This should do fine," he said.

I glanced at the words on the page, ensuring not to get lost in them.

* * *

I don't know where the wind comes from
Or where trees hide in seed
The origin of the running stream
Is mystery to me
I can't explain the pendulum
That undulates the sea
But at least I know to find you
Where dreams meets memory.

I looked at him with a puzzled expression.

"For Olivia?"

He managed a smile for me.

I bit my lip, trying to find graceful words to form the question that brooded inside of me. I ripped the page from the book, folded it tightly, and handed it to him. He tucked it in a hidden pocket inside his trousers.

"Why did you ask me to use the ink? Why didn't you tell me what it was?" I blurted out.

"It was my ink, Luella, and we used it just about the best way I could imagine. All, I suppose, except for the last bit."

I set my jaw. I wanted to disagree, to call him a fool for wasting his life.

"Should things not work out the way we hope," he continued, "I'd like you to know that, somewhere in the Netherdowns, I expect there's a new silver currant for me. And for that, I thank you."

The carriage came to a halt, and Edward reappeared at the door. He swung it open.

Beside him were four other officers and, standing at the building's entrance, the old bear of a Sergeant himself.

"It's time," Edward said.

Bram gave me a wink and exited the cab. When his feet hit the ground, they grabbed him roughly, put him in irons, and led him through the door.

I watched him disappear and choked back tears.

My feelings toward Bram Lowhouse were complicated and frustrating, but it twisted my conscience watching him walk away in bondage like that. I regretted agreeing to Charlotte's idea. There was too much risk.

I didn't have long to ruminate, though. Sergeant Cooper joined Edward at the open carriage door.

"Miss Winthrop, I understand we have some things to discuss."

Chapter Thirty-Six

Old Friends

"Take a seat, Miss Winthrop," Cooper asked, motioning to a chair in his office.

Walking into the station felt like wandering through one of the memory-distorted dreams that haunted me by night. I had shuffled by the lanky redhead at the front desk without exchanging a word. I thought back fondly to when he asked if I was there to report a missing person. Instead, he looked at me like I was a wild animal being escorted by its handler.

But what shocked me more than anything else was the plump, gray-haired woman sitting primly at Rebecca's desk, typing her way through a stack of papers.

Seeing Rebecca's replacement felt like the desecration of a holy place. This was where I had met my closest friends. It was a place of treasured memories, and yet the building cared so little about me.

We walked into Cooper's office. Edward took a seat and held my hand to put me at ease. It didn't work. I bristled as I sat in the chair facing the Sergeant. Cooper sat across from us, both hands placed on his desk, spread wide apart, forming a pyramid.

"The last time we spoke, you exchanged heated words with me," he said. "We were both concerned for Lieutenant Thomas. Now, I may see why that was the case."

"How do you mean?" I asked.

"I should have recognized the defensive posturing of a woman in love."

I blushed at his words, but he delivered this line with a stone-carved face void of conviction. I wondered if he still suspected I aided Luke Thomas' demise.

"Congratulations on your engagement," he said stiffly.

"Thank you, Sergeant," Edward said. "You'll afford my fiancée the same respect you give me. After all, if I'm convinced that she's innocent in my father's case, you would be hard-pressed to disagree. I have no thanks to offer you for the spectacle you made over her, though. Do you have any idea how difficult it was introducing her to my mother with the backdrop you set?"

Sergeant Cooper's eyes barely peeked out from under his leveled brow.

"Lord Thomas, surely you remember the pursuit of justice cannot afford to be bashful. Your fiancée," Cooper took his time on the word, "ran from the police."

"I ran because I was frightened!"

"Her, then-fiancé also told me, in confidence, she wasn't of sound mind. I wanted to question her, and she obstructed that aim, interfering with an official investigation."

Edward tensed beside me, but Cooper held out a hand.

"But, if what you're saying is true, I'm willing to overlook all of that. My interest is bringing criminals to justice. If you believe me to have harbored ill feelings toward Miss Winthrop, you are wrong. If she's innocent, she will have my esteem."

I gulped. Was I innocent? Could I let Bram take the fall for this? Even if he escaped to the Netherdowns, he'd be a fugitive for the rest of his life, however long that was.

"So, Miss Winthrop, Edward tells me you've located the party responsible for his father's death, and that your testimony serves to convict him. Is that true?"

I was sweating. I didn't want this for Bram. I looked all around the room for an idea, some backup plan, but there was no way out.

Edward squeezed my hand.

"It's all right, Luella," he said. "It's time to put this all to rest."

I looked in the eyes of my Steely-eyed Detective. It seemed like we met so long ago, when he took the breath out of me just for being so unapologetically valiant. His eyes filled now with weariness. I had put him through so much.

I don't know how I ever thought I'd be able to avoid this moment. At the same time, I never imagined the stakes would be so high. It was finally time to choose between Edward and Bram.

How bitter, to realize that, in love, a choice between two people was not only about who would be the exclusive recipient of my romantic affections. Loyalty went beyond kisses and holding hands.

"Luella, please," Edward said as if reading my thoughts. It's difficult to gauge how others manage perceived infidelity. I always imagined that if my husband had suspected me to be unfaithful, he would simply cast me out.

But looking at Edward, the tired pleading in his eyes, the echoing of his words to "put this to rest" in my ears, made me realize not everyone grieves the same way. How could Edward believe nothing had happened between Bram and me? Yet, he had not left me or turned against me. He just asked that I come home.

Bram had agreed to this.

"It is true," I said after a deep breath. "I met Mr. Lowhouse at a carnival after writing my first story about Edward for Langley's Miscellany. He tried to convince me he had a magical instrument that could turn my imagination into reality. After he guided me through writing several unlikely but frivolous stories, he persuaded me to write a piece about Luke Thomas, financial scandal, and suicide."

Cooper raised his eyebrows. He hadn't expected this.

"And he did all of this to deflect blame for a murder?"

"A murder of one of the wealthiest men in the city," Edward added. "Perhaps someone paid him." He folded his arms.

Cooper eyed Edward over the rim of his overly small glasses.

"That may be true, but aren't there easier ways to frame someone? Why choose a female reporter who had almost no connection to your father?"

"He will confess," I said.

"That's what I find most difficult to believe of all. Why come forward now?"

I tried not to look at Edward as I spoke.

"Because, as he lived out his plan, he... well, he fell in love with me."

Cooper leaned back in his chair, eliciting a generous creaking noise, the wood refusing to break. He folded his arms.

"Miss Winthrop, I mean no offense by this, but I don't understand how these men keep falling in love with you."

Edward stood and threw his gloves on the table.

"Sergeant, I won't have you talk to her that way!"

I put a hand on Edward's arm and sat him back down.

"Trust me, Sergeant. No one is more surprised than me."

At least this comment perked up a solitary corner of Cooper's tight mouth. He sighed a mighty sigh and uncrossed his arms.

"Well, I don't suppose this is the strangest thing to have ever happened in criminal history."

If only he knew. We had gone back and forth about telling Cooper about the magic, but ultimately decided his reaction would be too unpredictable to rely on. I'm glad he took this version of the story well enough.

"If you two are telling the truth, I'm afraid I will owe you a hefty apology, Miss Winthrop," Cooper said, standing.

"That settles it," said Edward, standing as well. "Once Mr. Lowhouse confesses, you will drop all charges from Luella and issue a public apology. And you won't pursue Rebecca Turner or Doug Tanner, either. They were only protecting her from a false arrest."

Edward extended a hand. Cooper stared him down before taking it professionally.

"This color doesn't suit you, Edward."

"One can only hope it will fade with time," he replied. "Are you ready, Luella?"

I hesitated. Cooper was still on my list. I had him here now. There would be no better opportunity to discern if he was my enchanter.

"Actually, Edward, would you give me a moment alone with the Sergeant? You can wait in the carriage, I'll be there directly."

Edward furrowed his brows, but I patted his hand reassuringly.

"I'll only be a moment."

He nodded and turned warily from the room. Cooper sat back down at his desk.

"Why do I suspect I'm about to hear a slightly different version of the story?" he asked. I had to hand it to him. He had a nose for police work, but I didn't stay behind to confess.

"Nothing of the sort," I said, folding my hands all ladylike. Hopefully, my time around Charlotte was paying off.

"Do you wish to lash me out, then? Luella, listen, I only wanted to do my job—"

"Nothing like that, either." I smiled weakly. "It's just, when I ran from the city, it was like running away from my home and my family. I'd never left Dawnhurst before. You are one of the few people I know that knew my father."

"Your father was a good man," Cooper said. "Even those who think differently from us can be good people, don't you agree."

"The best people think differently. That's why I want you to know that I don't harbor any ill will toward you. I had a dream about my father, and he told me you were always straightforward, solely interested in upholding the law. You were right, in the end, that I had information. I can't begrudge you for being right."

Cooper almost looked like he might cry.

"You don't think I'm a ruddy poor excuse for a Police Sergeant?"

I shook my head.

"No." I offered a handshake. He looked at it solemnly before he clapped both of his giant paws around it. "I expect if I break the law in the future, you'll come find me."

"I must. It's my calling."

He released my hand, and I stood to go.

"Do you mind if I sing you something?"

He leaned back in surprise and a small measure of embarrassment.

"What, here?"

"It's a song my father used to sing," I lied. Cooper looked around the room for an excuse, but apparently found no reason to object.

"If it's not a long song."

"It's very brief."

My heart beat faster. I didn't believe Cooper to be guilty, but in moments of trial, the world has a pattern of surprise.

I began singing.

Do you hear the echo
In the crags and in the burrows.
Do you see the moonlight mellow
In the cracks and in the barrow

But where have the hill folk gone?
And where have the wood folk gone?

When I finished the room was quiet.

Quiet. I heard nothing. Cooper had not enchanted me.

I smiled. Of course, he didn't.

"That was, uh, very nice. A bit of an odd lyric, if I'm being honest, but you have a passable voice."

I stifled a laugh of relief.

"Thanks for listening. Farewell, George Cooper."

"For the time being, Miss Winthrop."

We rode back to the Thomas' apartment in quiet. I think we both appreciated the solemnity of the occasion. I also imagined Edward was processing my confirmation of what he might have suspected for some time. Bram was in love with me.

It was an unusual love, though. A widower's love lives suspended in midair, like clothes on a line. I had seen the way he looked and pined after Olivia. I had seen the apex of whatever his devotion, and I doubted that what he felt for me could ever grow as grand.

But, then again, perhaps love isn't a contest of size or strength. Maybe each relationship is like a lock, and two people have to pick their way through it. The reward on the other side being what we call love, not a pile of gold to be spent, but a state of being, a room of exquisite beauty.

At the end of the day, one need not answer if Bram would have chosen Olivia over me, because there never existed a world with both of us in it.

I wrung my hands. I should debate this with Rebecca later.

Charlotte met us when we arrived.

"Is it done?" she asked.

"It's up to Lowhouse to keep his word now," Edward said, hanging his hat.

"He will," I said, bitterly. "He will confess."

Charlotte instructed the cook prepare a fine dinner. My friends ate enthusiastically, albeit quietly, but I had no appetite. My thoughts kept returning to Bram. Bram, who risked the gallows in my place. Bram, who had literally given me years of his life in liquid form.

That night, in the comfort of a room all to myself, I went back to the Netherdowns. I walked my way through the meadows, knowing that

Bram would not yet be there. Although not as powerful as the crimson ink to remedy my outbreaks, a simple visit to the Netherdowns had a similar effect on me. And an outbreak was the last thing I wanted at present.

Instead, I wasted hours slowly meandering through the desaturated flowers, wondering if I might not bump into Olivia somewhere. I didn't.

When I appeared at Hirythe's study, we hardly spoke to one another, but he offered me a cup of tea and we watched the fire in his heart until it burned to a pile of cinders. He sent me back unceremoniously.

Despite the late night, I rose early the next morning, and set out into the familiar streets of Dawnhurst. Time marched on, but not much of substance changed in a few quick months. It was cold, the winter chill off the river accentuated by the morning air, but it was home. I saw memories of my family in these streets.

I wanted to meander as I had through the Netherdowns and sip in the nostalgia, but I business called. Cooper had passed Hirythe's test. There was one man left on my list.

I turned a corner and saw the familiar front door of Langley's Miscellany. Through the front window, beside a pathetically small fire in the hearth, I found Byron Livingston, my old editor and fiancé. He read a stack of papers, comfortable in his natural habitat.

A smile arrived on my face unbidden. Byron had betrayed me, but he had fought for me afterward. That was my old Bryon. He always presumed he knew what was best for me, and he was never quite right.

I walked through the door.

"We're closed until 9," he called without looking up.

"Perhaps just a cup of tea, then."

He looked up at me, and a terrible mix of surprise, joy, regret, and sorrow wash over his face in quick succession.

"Hello, Byron," I said meekly.

"Luella," he stuttered. He stood up and papers slid everywhere. "I never expected to see you again." His voice broke. "I'm glad you got away. The way the papers got on after you, what Cooper said, it was all rubbish. All of it. I didn't stand for it for a moment. Oh, please forgive me. It was all my fault."

He slid back into his chair and buried his face in his hands. "How can you even look at me?" he cried.

I strode forward, gingerly stepping around the stray papers, and pried his hands away from his face.

"How about that tea?" I asked.

We spent the better part of an hour talking. The months of my absence seemed to have aged him. Then again, I wondered if it was the clarity of distance that gave me fresh eyes.

It took a good amount of time for me to convince him that everything ended up for the best. I told him about how I convinced Bram to step forward as the responsible party and Cooper's promise to acquit me.

This had the effect of unloading at least a partial weight from his shoulders.

"Thank goodness," he said.

"Byron, I heard that you fought for my reputation once I'd left. I'm very grateful. I feared that as soon as I left, you'd turn in the story I wrote."

He put his teacup down.

"Well, of course I would fight for you. I was heartbroken, Luella, but I still cared for you. I don't know how you wrote that story so quickly, but I trust there is a reasonable explanation. It looks as though everything has worked out. Would you like a biscuit?"

I smiled. I did not want a biscuit, but I took one anyway.

"And I'm marrying Edward Thomas," I added. "I hope that doesn't make you upset."

"No," he said, breathing out relief. "I always suspected you fancied him, from the moment you shared your first story about the Steely Eyed Detective. Back then, I still believed I deserved you."

"Don't talk like that. You deserve someone who will make you very happy."

He blushed.

"Well, in all honesty, I may have found her."

I gasped and tried to fight off a feeling of offense. After all, it had only been a few months. Humans are walking hypocrisy.

"So soon?" I asked.

"Carolina Drake, from the committee for the Golden Inkwell. She is a tremendous woman, many admirable qualities, easy to talk with, tall I'll admit, though she does have a nasty jealous streak about you."

We both sipped our tea awkwardly for a moment that seemed as long as it was slow.

"Well, I wish you every happiness," I finally said.

He raised his teacup to me.

"Livingston," a voice cried from the front door, "Storm's last story was an absolute wreck!" A man bounded forward. I turned and saw Brutus wrapped in a red scarf and tall hat.

"Luella Winthrop!" he said. "What a surprise to find you in Dawnhurst!"

"Hello, again. To be honest, I'm surprised you made it back so quickly. Didn't you stay in Oxford long?"

"No," Brutus replied, leaning against a desk. "I only stayed for a few lectures and some assorted business."

"Jeremy Evans! Is it nine thirty already?" Byron said as he stood and checked his pocket watch. "Carolina will be along!"

My tea practically froze in its cup.

"What did you just say, Byron?"

"We've been talking for over an hour. That's what happens when you get chatting with old friends. It's like I've always said, life is better when viewed over the rim of a teacup."

"If you're busy, I can come back another time," Brutus said.

"If you would be so kind. Luella here has set me back. I'm not prepared for you."

Their words ran over my head as if I were underwater.

Jeremy Evans. J. E. Surely it wasn't such an uncommon name. Small wonder it had sounded familiar when Bram used it. I hadn't used Brutus' real name in years, but that was hardly an excuse to forget. My pet name for him had encapsulated him.

It wasn't possible.

"I'll see you in a few hours," Brutus said, heading out the door. "Miss Winthrop, it's always a pleasure. I hope this is a sign that I might read more of your writing soon." He tipped his hat and vanished. I stood, instinctively, as though to chase after him.

But for what? Would I knock him down and ask if he knew Bram Lowhouse and a fae name Hirythe?

"Luella, I don't mean to be a fuddy dud, but I must get back to work. I would love to set up a time for us to all get dinner. You, me, Edward, and Carolina. Would it be terribly awkward?"

My mind raced, and I was being ushered at the front door. I came here for a reason.

"Can I sing you something?" I blurted out.

He blinked at me. His skylark had woken up and started chirping.

It probably wasn't the best way to ask him, but remembering Brutus' first name was like getting punched in the gut.

"I didn't know you sang," he said dumbly.

"It's a surprise for Edward. I just need some honest feedback from someone." It was a sloppy fib, but I couldn't focus. "I need someone to tell me if singing this for him at our wedding is a terrible idea."

Byron screwed up his face.

"Well, all right. Do you want me to sit down? Then, I really must get back to work. It probably wouldn't be wise to have you around when Carolina comes soon."

He looked for a chair and sat.

"That would be wonderful," I said, forcing myself to remember my purpose. This was Byron. I expected that he inadvertently hexed me. This had to be right.

"Very well, I'm ready," he said, sitting tall as though he were out for a night at the theater. His eyes darted awkwardly around the room. This wasn't ideal. I was supposed to have his undivided attention, maintain strict eye contact, but I'd take what I could get. I took a deep breath and began singing.

Do you hear the echo—

I hadn't even finished the first line when a shower of melancholy voices joined in. Even after I stopped, they continued, and they sounded angry.

I was right. Byron Livingston had dabbled in high magic. I gaped at him.

"Is that the whole song?" he asked, timidly.

I blinked.

"What?"

"It's just a bit strange, is all, especially for a wedding surprise. I'm just trying to be honest. You'll understand."

I nodded. "Of course. I must come up with something else," I said, numbly.

I turned and walked out the front door without so much as a glance backward.

Chapter Thirty-Seven

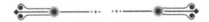

Mending the Sail

I tried searching for the man I called Brutus for twenty minutes without success. After wandering the streets, my previous warm nostalgia replaced with acute anxiety, I gave up and headed back to the flat.

I tried piecing everything together in my mind. The revelation about Brutus' true name hit me like a sack of sand, stealing all sense of triumph from learning I was right about Byron being my enchanter. After all this time...

Hirythe told me the first step to curing myself of the magic that plagued me was to determine who caused it. Bram had tangled me up with the ink. We knew that. But Byron, of all people, had somehow unstopped a terrible power that ruined my life.

I filtered through our memories, trying to discern when a magical bond might have attached. But it was fruitless. Byron was boring.

There. I said it. We sat down each morning to the same cup of tea, talked about the same things, and read new editions of the same papers.

Perhaps it had something to do with the tea. Maybe Byron infused it with magic somehow, and cup after cup, day after day, my illness was the price for living something so dreary.

Or maybe Jeremy talked him into doing something. But what sense did that have? Why would Jeremy want Byron to enchant me, if Jeremy even was the same Jeremy from the Phantom Battalion? I needed to insist on learning surnames from now on.

By the time I stumbled into the dining room at the Thomas flat, I had more questions than answers.

There was a morose welcome party waiting for me. Doug and Rebecca had gone to see how his pub fared in his absence, leaving Edward and Charlotte, looking gloomy and grim, to usher me into a seat.

"Where did you go?" Edward asked gently.

"An early morning walk," I said, slathering my piece of toast with regret and guilt. "I needed to clear my head."

"You're worried about Bram," Edward suggested.

I swallowed.

"It would be inhuman to feel otherwise," I replied. Charlotte put down the saltshaker she had been toying with.

"You're right. This is dark business. Edward, you were the one to tell me that when administering the law, one should rejoice in success but never forget the severity of the consequence." She looked at me. "It's no easy thing to watch a man go to the noose. You need not be ashamed of that."

Charlotte's words were intended to comfort me, but mention of the word noose made me sick to my stomach. Edward noticed. I put down my toast.

"It may not come to that, mother. They don't have any evidence. Even if Cooper's intuition was correct, that's the curse of many policemen. We need evidence to do away with criminals. Evidence can be slippery in the easiest cases, let alone the magical ones."

He put a hand on my back.

"I doubt he'll hang over this."

He wouldn't. Not if I could help it. He still had the page from the Mystic Diary. That would work. Then, I would meet him in the Netherdowns and tell him and Hirythe about Jeremy. He had only to spend a few days in a cell.

I wanted to go over the plan again in greater detail. Remind him it would be best to vanish before going to trial and being sentenced, that way he would walk around as a fugitive but at least not a condemned murderer.

The silence became deafening, maddening, in that somber dining room decorated with trinkets worth so much. These two would shortly become my family, yet I was leagues removed from the lifestyle surrounding me.

"Excuse me," I said. Charlotte nodded graciously as I pushed away from the table and headed directly to my room. I needed to escape.

I closed the door behind me and reached for the diary. I needed to busy myself. I should tell Hirythe about Byron. And it's possible he'd have insight on Jeremy. There was a ripped photo on his desk. Perhaps he still had the other piece locked away behind one of the odd mechanisms on his drawers.

At the very least, he could tell me what Jeremy looked like. I needed to know if my greatest literary critic was the same man who worked alongside Hirythe, Bram, and Olivia.

"What are you doing?" Edward asked.

I had already flipped the book open. He entered so quietly.

"Edward," I said, startled. "I didn't hear you come in."

"I was worried about you," he said. We stared at one another. In the place of the magnetic attraction that so often connected us lay a void. Did he sense the same? "Are you leaving again?" He motioned toward the book with his chin.

I froze like a drunk caught with a bottle of liquor.

"I just need to do something," I said, hating how pathetic my answer sounded. Edward sauntered in the room and leaned against the edge of the door.

"I hoped, maybe, since Bram was no longer inside that book, you might not be spending as much time there." His voice was sheepish. He was once a sheepdog.

Rebecca's voice sounded off in my brain. What would she say if she were here? She'd urge me to talk, to lay bare my secrets and open up to him. I smiled to myself. She was hardly one to give romantic advice, however.

"Did I say something amusing?" Edward asked, noting my expression.

"No," I blurted out. "Of course not. It's just—"

I trailed off, trying to manage my emotions. Something was pulling me into the Netherdowns, tugging at me from the pages of the diary. Yet, something else pushed me toward the void between me and my fiancé. I had the power to fill that void.

Why didn't I?

"Edward, are you jealous over Bram?" I asked. Edward didn't hesitate.

"Yes. Yes, I am. I've tried not to be, but he is many things I'm not."

My heart wrenched, and I welcomed it. If it took sympathy to reconnect me to Edward, then I'd happily open the gates and let it in.

"What are you talking about? You're Edward Thomas, Lord of Fernmount, my Steely-eyed Detective."

"And I cannot rescue you." He shrugged sadly. "I've tried, but I'm not smart or savvy enough, and I can't learn fast enough. I can only watch as another man makes the sacrifices for you."

"Don't say such things. You envy Bram because he's going to the gallows in my place?"

"I'm not proud of this, Luella, but I watched my father shut my mother out for years. I don't want the same between us. It shames me, but yes. How can I ever compete with what he's doing for you now?"

He shook his head and avoided my eyes. What happened to the man who wasn't afraid to look even a complete stranger in the face?

"It's not a competition."

"Then perhaps fate has dealt him a playable hand, while I have to fold and sit out the most important round of the game."

I stood, closed the book, and shut my eyes.

"Edward, I'm engaged to you. What more do you want from me?"

He swooped across the room and cradled me into his arms before kissing me. I was so surprised that at first, I went rigid as a board, but it took less than five seconds for me to lose track of everything.

I reciprocated, wrapping my arms around his neck, not caring whether it was proper or if his mother might come upstairs or about anything at all. For a moment, felt no guilt or anxiety, only the moment around me. I drank in the passion, the desperation, the call to come home.

I don't know how long we kissed. It might have been a minute or an hour. When we broke apart, I felt like I was reentering the world from the Netherdowns. But, when I opened my eyes, Edward was there and a crushing comfort and sweetness settled over me again, springing tears from my eyes.

The truth hit me at once. I had been so afraid that Byron wasn't my enchanter. I never let myself consider what it might mean if Edward turned out to be my villain. It was too awful to contemplate. Yet, the doubt lurked within me as sure as my heartbeat.

I was afraid it was him. I had my greatest resource and friend beside me the entire time but refused his help.

"I'm sorry," Edward said, looking appalled. "I shouldn't have done that."

I needed my Edward back. It was time for me to eradicate the barriers between us.

I stepped forward and kissed him again.

Something about the kiss cast down the walls we'd spent months putting in place. We passed the rest of the morning in my room talking. I spent the time opening up to him about everything at last.

At first it was hard to remember all the small secrets I kept, and each new truth hurt him. At times, I was afraid he would recoil, but Edward wasn't that way. Instead, he gripped my hand tighter.

I started by explaining how Bram worked out my double malady, and how that malady was traced back to the fog creature, the same fog creature Edward had seen in an alley so long ago. I told Edward about my dream the night of that attack. Then, I explained about the Netherdowns, Hirythe, the Phantom Battalion, Olivia, everything.

Once I started it was difficult to stop. There is something cathartic about letting so much pent up hardship out to someone who so clearly cares about you.

Edward, meanwhile, rejected nothing I had to say. He already believed in magic, but it was still surprising to see someone calmly accept the reality that took me some time to come to grips with.

I was about to explain all about Hirythe's song to detect someone who had meddled in high magic when a brusque knock and throat clearing interrupted us.

"Are we interrupting?" Rebecca asked coyly.

"Becca, let's leave them alone." Doug was red in the face at seeing Edward and me sitting so close together in my bedroom.

"No, no, Doug." Rebecca entered the room and sat down beside me. "It's our duty to chaperone these two until the wedding. We are the guard against lascivious feelings."

"Rebecca!" I gasped. Edward turned beet red, but he was smiling so handsomely that even Doug joined in poking some more fun at him.

"It's tradition," she continued, "to make the betrothed couple as uncomfortable as possible. If you can't run the gauntlet, how can you handle the stress of marriage?"

We all laughed, but it didn't prevent me from mulling over Rebecca's words. Run the gauntlet? Edward and I could check that box. I looked at him, taking comfort and warmth from his gray eyes. He smiled at me and squeezed my hand. I'd have to share the rest later, but I already sensed the bond between us had changed.

I was such a fool for having doubted him.

"Come along, then," Doug said. "We've got a bit of a surprise."

"A surprise?" I asked. My mood improved every moment, and I was tired of feeling guilty over it. I was gloomy all morning, and rightly so, but that wouldn't help Bram.

"Doug needs some poor target dummies to make sure his kitchen is still working properly." Rebecca smiled.

"The sooner we can get the pub running again, the sooner I can bring the lads back on. Heaven knows how they've been faring without the income."

Edward stood up and clapped Doug on the back.

"We'd be delighted. It'll be like old times."

Rebecca put her hands on her waist.

"Who thought we'd ever say that again?" she asked.

"Lady Mother is invited as well," said Doug. "Where did she end up?"

I blushed. I hope she hadn't seen Edward and me in our more comfortable moments. Then again, if she didn't hate me by now, she never would.

"If she's not in the dining room, then she's likely sleeping. The poor woman hasn't slept well in days," said Edward.

"Best not to wake her, then. She'll have to see what real fish and chips taste like another time."

We all started toward the stairs.

"But she's had your chips already, Doug," I said. He scoffed gruffly.

"A master craftsman without his tools can still impress, little Luella. But a masterpiece requires the artist's workshop." Doug strutted out the front door, and the four of us made our way, arm in arm, to Doug's Fish and Chips Pub.

By the time our troughs were empty, and Doug had put away a couple of pints of his favorite beer, I was happy to have a moment to push aside Bram's current predicament or Brutus' true identity as a man named Jeremy Evans.

Doug was rattling off a story about some trouble one of his friends ran into with two women, one loaf of bread, and a goat. He hardly even cared if we were listening, and I drifted into my own thoughts.

It felt natural for the four of us to sit together at "Rebecca's table" next to the window in Doug's pub. A warm joy spread over me, more than the euphoria of a full stomach. I saw glimpses of the future. How many meals would the four of us enjoy here together?

If I closed my eyes hard enough, I almost dared to see children running among the aisles, bothering patrons and working Doug into a fit.

Edward gave my hand a gentle squeeze under the table. I turned to him.

"Are you all right?" he asked as our friends bickered on. A smile crept into my lips.

"I'm home," I whispered. Edward nodded.

Rebecca now contradicted a point in Doug's story. Apparently, the goat was impossibly large. Doug started huffing and puffing over his questioned integrity.

"We don't have to spend all our time at Fernmount," he replied quietly to me. "We have the lodgings here, and we—"

"No, I mean here, at this table. The four of us."

Edward stared into my eyes as if he might kiss me again. Instead, he just nodded gently.

"Home," he said.

I wished I could have frozen the moment forever. Instead, the door swung wildly open.

"There you are!" A man in a familiar heavy coat and hat rushed to the table.

Byron Livingston nearly knocked over our empty mugs.

"Luella, I'm so sorry. She's not thinking straight. I swear. She promised me she'd leave you alone, but she gets so jealous!"

Byron was practically frothing like a lunatic.

"This establishment is closed, sir," Doug chided, standing to show his girth.

"What are you talking about, Byron?"

"It's Carolina. She found out you came by this morning, and we quarreled. Oh, did we quarrel. She said it was improper."

Rebecca raised an eyebrow, and Edward stood as though to escort

Byron out.

"I told her not to, but she took it while I wasn't looking."

"Took what?" I asked, bewildered. A sense of terrible unease crept into my bosom.

"The article," Byron said. "The article describing the death of Luke Thomas."

My three friends must have understood the implication at once, but I doubt they experienced the same vertigo as I. The room stretched before me like a nightmare.

"What have you done?" Edward asked Byron.

"Why didn't you destroy that story? How did she even know about?" asked Rebecca in rapid succession.

Everything slipped away from me. It was as though color somehow was bleeding backward into whatever source it came from.

"She said we should have turned it into the police months ago," he said.

"We need to go," I croaked out.

"That's why I came," Byron insisted. "I wanted to warn you."

"Luella, we already told Cooper about the article," Edward said, urgency and panic straining through his composure. "What difference will it make?"

"It's the only piece of evidence they'll have, and it's linked to Luella. Bram's confession will be all but worthless," said Rebecca.

"We need to go." I stood up, shakily, and knocked over a chair by accident. But it was too late.

Sergeant Cooper filled the frame of the door's entrance, dressed neatly in a freshly starched uniform. The man wearing it drooped like a wilting flower. Behind him, I saw at least four other officers.

"Cooper, you devil," Edward shouted. "You gave us your word!"

Cooper ignored my fiancé and turned his sad face to me.

"I'm sorry, Luella."

I swallowed hard, trying to stem panic in my throat.

"As am I, George."

Chapter Thirty-Eight

Brick, Iron, Parchment

Edward ran beside the police carriage until his lungs gave out, shouting threats at Cooper, reassurances to me, prayers to God... I hardly heard any of them.

After all this time, Cooper had me in a locked wagon. I should have known better than to come back to Dawnhurst. But the plan was working. We were so close. I had it all lined up and worked out. Bram would have escaped, and I would have had my happy ending.

I should have stuck with Edward's plan to discredit Cooper. My father had been wrong in the Netherdowns.

I wrung my hands, trying desperately to ward off the barrage of thoughts and paranoia that swarmed me. I had to take my mind off of it, but the carriage ride to the jail dragged on slowly, and my wrists were in irons. There was not much to distract me, no sweet Edward to melt away my fears.

The jail sat on the far east side of the city. It wasn't much, but it was only meant for temporary holding. Edward once explained that the Dawnhurst police force had an arrangement with some other localities. After trial, criminals were either transferred to a larger jail in another city or disposed of outside of the town's limits.

When the carriage came to a stop, two officers escorted me roughly to the ground and marched through the gates of a plain brick building. Inside, past the back door of a bland office, were a few rows of cells, each with a wide wall between them. They weren't luxurious, just rectangles of brick, stone, and a wall of iron bars. Two cells branched off a row at a time, so as to face one another.

The grim officers escorted me down one aisle and unlocked a cell towards the middle.

"In there," Cooper said, pointing from behind them.

"What would my father say about this?" I asked him. He didn't respond or look at me. The two officers led me into my new home and closed the door behind them. They walked with Cooper back to the front of the building. "What do you gain from this, Cooper?" I asked. "The Thomas family believes in me. You had a culprit. Why arrest me?"

He stopped and turned around.

"I don't care about the Thomas family," he mumbled. "I'm the Police Sergeant of Dawnhurst-on-Severn. I am a servant to my duty. Your father understood that. I don't know how you're involved in this, Luella, but don't you dare use your dad as a shield."

I seethed. Anger welled inside of me, along with helplessness and fear. What if I had an episode in the cell tonight? I'd be sent away a lunatic. Which was better, the asylum or the noose?

He turned on his heels and marched from view. The door to the front office slammed behind him and echoed with a metallic clang, leaving me alone, the evening light straining through small windows toward the ceiling. I saw no other prisoners.

I touched the cold, solid bars in front of me, but didn't have much time to ruminate before Edward's muffled voice sang through the jail making terrible threats. I strained my ears but failed to decipher Cooper's response. Whatever words they exchanged, Edward burst through the door.

"Luella?" he called feverishly.

"I'm here, Edward!"

He hurried over to my cell, followed closely by a prison guard.

Edward grabbed my hand through the bars.

"I don't have long. One of the guards owed me a favor. This is madness," he said. His voice wavered. His hands trembled. "They can't take you like this."

"Edward, please, it will be all right."

He nodded and kissed my fingers.

"No one can convict you. I'll bear testimony. So will my mother."

"And how will your mother respond to the details of the evidence they bring forward?"

"You're a member of our family." Since I had met Edward, he had been the picture of poise and composure. Even in his darkest moments, he kept his head level and tried to second-guess himself. I had often wondered if anything could unravel him, but seeing him fall apart at the seams now laid that curiosity to rest.

"Of course," I said. It was hard not to see the manic lustre in his eyes. He didn't deserve any of this. "Let's keep hope then. It will be as you say. Do you have a family solicitor?"

"Of course," Edward said. "I'll summon him at once. But, Luella, I don't want it to come to that." His voice had dropped to a whisper.

"What do you mean? What other choice is there?"

"Bram Lowhouse."

"What about him?" I asked. I hadn't told Edward about hiding a page of the diary on Bram's person. Rebecca had interrupted us before I had a chance. "He is locked up as sure as I am."

"Something seemed suspicious about him. I suspect he has another plan, perhaps a way out. Doesn't he have a vast understanding of magic? Surely he can do something."

I bit my lip. How did Edward's mind work so quickly? I hadn't even considered alternatives to my imprisonment. If Edward retrieved Bram's page of the diary and bring it to me, I could use it to escape. Then, I could rip out another page and get it to him somehow.

"You might be right," I whispered. "If you can find where they're keeping him, he can help."

The guard approached Edward and tapped him gruffly on the shoulder.

"That's time, Edward. Come on. You know the rules."

Edward shook him off.

"Edward, go. It'll do no one any good if they lock you in here with me. Besides, you need to summon your solicitor."

He kissed my hand again.

"You'll be free again. I promise."

"Of course, I will. Now go."

"I love you," he said. I blinked back tears, my insides melting, my whole body aching to be wrapped safely in his arms. I opened my mouth to respond.

"Goodbyes are easier if you don't drag them out," the guard said, yanking Edward away from the cell. Then the panic set in as I watched him leave. He didn't take his gaze from mine until he left my sight.

The door clanged shut again, leaving me truly alone. Bitterness, fear, and anger simmered beneath my skin. I sunk to the crude bench attached to the wall with rough iron fittings and cried.

I had promised my father I would clear our family name, but I hadn't. Instead, one of his old friends had arrested his daughter. Now I'd be tried for murder. Where would I end up? In a cell like this for the rest of my days? Perhaps when the evidence came out and no reasonable explanation behind it came forward, they'd put me in an asylum.

Or what if the worst were to happen?

Tears ran hot down my cheeks. A wave of shame enveloped me as I considered that Bram had willingly subjected himself to these fears by choosing to go along with my plan. Now, I had the audacity to send Edward to retrieve his only way out?

I was so foolish walking directly into Langley's as I had that morning. That morning? Would this day never end? But how was I to know that Byron was already engaged to a jealous mistress, or that he so recklessly kept a copy of my article?

Had the past several months been worth anything? Had I ever escaped with Edward from Dawnhurst the first time? Byron still betrayed me to the police. The same evidence hung over my head.

I lay down on the bench and tortured myself, looking for an answer to this question.

Nothing happened for hours. The block of cells was silent, and the guard at the front sat quietly on a chair. I had almost forgotten he existed until his gentle snores whispered through the dark.

It occurred to me about an hour before that Bram was, in all likelihood, somewhere in this building. Dawnhurst didn't have any other prison I was aware of. Once I settled on that conclusion, a growing need to talk with him consumed me. I welcomed the obsession. I wanted something, anything, to distract me.

I wished we had come up with a signal a long time ago. I imagined he had a signal with Hirythe or Olivia. A certain bird call or a series of taps on a wall would have been handy. Instead, I found myself risking a loud whisper, trying not to wake the guard.

"Bram?" I called hoarsely. Silence followed. "Bram, it's Luella." Still nothing.

"Bram, please!"

"I'm here," replied a calm, resigned voice. The sound had come from wall opposite the door to the office. The wall reverberated with it.

"Is this some type of magic?" I asked, putting my hands on the bricks.

"No," Bram said. "I'm right here. They put you in the cell beside mine." I heard a thump through the wall, then another closer to the bars.

I scrambled to the door of my cell and strained at the corner.

"You've been here this whole time?" I asked.

"Your fiancé is passionate," he said.

I snorted.

"Not usually."

"Out of curiosity, did you ever sing him Hirythe's song?" Bram asked lazily.

"I didn't need to."

"Why not?"

"He would never do that to me," I replied. "I'm sure of it."

"Is that you didn't simply ask him to retrieve the diary and bring it back here?"

My face flushed.

"Byron hexed me. I doubt he meant to do something so severe, but the song worked. The voices confirmed his guilt."

I heard nothing for a while, just some skittering down the hall. My stomach turned as I considered the rodent might be making the noise.

"The way you talked about Byron, I must say I'm surprised," said Bram.

"What does it matter now?" I asked.

"It's good news. You should tell Hirythe."

I balled my hands into fists. I wanted to ask him how that was possible, try to lead him into giving me the page from the diary. I'd never experienced such a fervent desire for self-preservation.

But no. I had already endangered his life. I wouldn't take his only escape route.

"Luella, just take the page. Let's not make a thing of it."

"What are you talking about?" I stuttered.

"I heard what you said to the Steely-eyed Detective. You will insist I use it and escape, and I will insist you be the one to go free."

I shook my head.

"No, Bram. I told him that so he'd stay busy. I got you into this mess."

"Did you?" Bram asked.

"Yes. I used to blame you, but you should blame me."

"I convinced you to use the pen," he replied.

"And, as we're both aware, you could not have known I would react at such an accelerated rate."

I picked at the dirt beneath me, nervously. All I had to do was choose not to accept the page from him. I held the power. We sat in silence for several minutes, and it scared me. Silence waited everywhere, reminding me that after everything finishes, silence waited to welcome me home.

"What did Olivia tell you?" I asked.

"What?"

It was a deeply personal question. I understood that all too well, but I needed something to distract me from the fear. Fear would lead to desperation. Desperation would make me take the page from him.

"When you ate your silver currant." My hands shook.

"How do you know she said anything?" he asked.

"Because I also found a silver currant," I confessed.

"Where?" he asked quickly. "How? Your memories don't make up the Netherdowns."

"I filled the blank page you left in the diary. After I left you on the hill, I wandered into the wood. I found my parents' church inside. My father came and spoke with me." The memory was bittersweet. Part of me still wanted to blame my father for discouraging the plan to take down Cooper, but it was a desperate remorse.

"What did he tell you?" Bram asked.

"I asked you first," I replied. He sighed.

"It's just a little personal," he said. I snorted.

"Now's a good time, don't you agree? One of us heading to the noose and all."

There was a pause.

"That's a good point," he said.

"Well?" I asked. He let out a long-sustained sigh.

"Olivia told me she was happy I fell in love again."

I froze.

"What?" I asked, forgetting myself.

"I feel stupid saying it now that Lord Thomas told you the same thing a few hours ago."

"You fell in love with me?"

"You didn't sound so surprised when he said it."

"He's my fiancé."

Bram laughed. It sounded hollow in the jail. The guard stopped snoring suddenly, and we both fell silent. But the snores resumed quickly.

"When I met you, you had a different fiancé, one you were not in love with."

"If you're planning to convince me to use the page by insulting me, it won't work." I slumped against the brick.

He said he loved me. I'd said as much to Cooper, but it was very different to have it confirmed. I wondered if I manipulate those feelings and convince him to enter the Netherdowns.

"What use do you I have in escape, Bram? If I ran, I couldn't marry Edward, not openly anyway. What would I do? Live as the hidden wife of Lord Thomas, rumored but never seen, locked up somewhere in Fernmount?"

"Incredible. I admit feelings for you, and you just go on about marrying Edward?"

"You're impossible."

Silence.

"It's not because he's wealthy, right?" Bram asked. I rolled my eyes.

"How dare you," I said, trying to sound as offended as possible.

"It's just when we met you wanted to be a successful writer so badly. Perhaps to you that meant financial freedom. Now, if you were to marry the aristocrat—"

"He's not an aristocrat," I countered, but when he mentioned my writing, my mind quickly caught hold of Jeremy. I gasped. Jeremy. Maybe if Bram knew Jeremy was so close, he'd rush back to the Netherdowns to warn Hirythe. "Bram, wait. I need to tell you something. I found Jeremy."

"Jeremy?" Bram's voice echoed harshly off the brick.

"This whole time I've known him. He's my largest critic. The one that wrote about my work in his column."

"That must be coincidence."

"You tell me, then. Is the Jeremy Evans from your circle of adventurers gaunt, tall, with inclinations toward academia?"

"What academic is not gaunt and tall?" Bram asked.

"Isn't it strange, though? Are you willing to risk it? You need to tell Hirythe."

I toyed with the hem of my skirt. We played a game of chess. The winner reluctantly avoided the gallows.

"Devil take me," Bram said. "Luella, if what you're saying is true, then you have to take the page." He stretched his arm through the bars and reached the page out to me. If stretched enough, I thought I could reach it.

"What are you talking about? Why should I be the one to—"

"Please, just stop talking for a moment. This is serious. If you're right, we may all be in danger. If Jeremy finds a way into the Netherdowns, or can lure Hirythe out of the Netherdowns, I'm not sure what the old fae might do. He is much more powerful than you realize, and you are not the only one who has to fight off magical urges."

My pulse quickened, hammering in my neck.

"Go tell him what you saw. You can show him the way your sister did. He can't see that from me. Please, I need you to do this."

I searched for words. The timbre of Bram's voice sounded broken, desperate.

"Bram, can't you read the page aloud like you did to bring Anna and Rebecca to the Netherdowns? We can both go."

"This is the wrong page for that. Plus, I'd never several more. I didn't want any other eavesdropping criminals to follow me back."

I rested my head on the iron bars, eyeing the paper.

"Can't you tie it on a string or something?" I asked.

"What string do you think I have?"

"Rip some thread from your clothes or something!"

"The cells are just too far apart. Please, Luella. I made him a promise that I wouldn't allow the last of his kind to turn into the type of monster that used to torment men. I promised him. If he has to fight Jeremy—please, Luella do this for me. If you care about me at all, please do this for me now."

Slowly, my hand reached out from my cell, and my fingers barely trapped the corner of the paper between them. I was hypnotized by his request. I cared for Bram, deeply. Desperation dripped from his voice. Maybe with Hirythe's help, we could still rescue him. Or, I would urge

Edward to hire solicitors on his behalf. Or... I would think of something.

Bram's resources were only magical and thus limited in the modern world.

My eyes scanned the page before I even realized.

I don't know where the wind comes from
  Or where trees hide in seeds

The words absorbed me. Was this Olivia's poem, or mine?

The origin of the running stream
  Is mystery to me

I wouldn't leave him here alone. I would rescue him. Hirythe was the first step.

I can't explain the pendulum
  That undulates the sea

The magic pulled on me. The Netherdowns shuffled into the peripheries of my vision. I wanted to shout something to Bram, tell him not to fear, that I'd make it my life's mission to save him, but failed. I was too late. There was no turning back now.

But at least I know to find you
  Where dreams meets memory.

Chapter Thirty-Nine

Critics Are Evil Monsters

I appeared on Walnut Hill. It was dark, but the moon was out and bright, shining through the branches of the tree above me. I missed seeing the Netherdowns during the daytime.

Rainwater dripped through the leaves, splashing on my head in little cold drops. That was odd. I'd never seen it rain in the Netherdowns before. But here it fell, and I was getting wet quickly. Lightning streaked across the sky, illuminating the grassy climbs and meadows outstretched before me. Wind whipped through the lawn, giving the illusion of tempestuous waters.

The storm set off a greater sense of urgency in me. I needed to find shelter, and I needed a plan to save Bram by the morning.

I picked up my skirts and set off as quickly as I dared toward town. Firelight and torches set off a misty glow in the distance.

Bram's warning about Hirythe had me on edge. Hirythe had shown me his collection of private silver currants hidden away in his desk, made from memories he dared not revisit. I was afraid to imagine what the fae might become when provoked.

It was strange to watch the storm pass through the landscape. Small rivulets had become streams, and missteps in hidden puddles occasionally soaked me up to the knee.

It took me about a half hour to get to the village, and when I arrived, painful cramps flared under my ribs. I couldn't distinguish between rain and sweat. But when I got to the central courtyard, as fortune would have it, a light was on in Hirythe's study.

I pounded on the door, my wet stiff hands ineffective against the aged wood. I tried kicking it, but there was no response.

"Hirythe!" I called, but the buffeting rain muffled my voice adeptly. I didn't have time to wait. I tried ramming it with my shoulder.

When I made contact, the door gave way to the weight of my body. On closer examination, the metal fittings on the lock had scorch marks and the ends of it had melted into odd, goopy shapes.

My breath caught in my throat. Something was wrong. I knew the dangers of the Netherdowns. They didn't manifest in storms and melted locks.

I rushed in the building and bounded up the stairs, the cramp in my side like a knife. It was dark in the stairwell, but a roaring hearth shot streams of light through the cracks in Hirythe's closed door.

"Hirythe!" I called. "It's Luella. Bram's in trouble."

I pushed the door open, and the first thing I noticed was an enormous portrait of Charlotte Thomas hanging over the fireplace. I had never seen a portrait there before, nor could I understand what such a portrait was doing in the world of Bram and Hirythe's shared memory.

Hirythe stood beside the hearth, face screwed up in anger and concentration. His shirt was largely undone, and his hands were balled into aggressive, dangerous fists.

Across from him, sitting in one of the tall lounge chairs and wearing a sick smile, was Brutus. The fire illuminated his features in venomous contrast. I froze.

"Luella Winthrop," Brutus said, "aren't you supposed to be in prison?"

I put a hand to my head. This made little sense.

"How are you here?" I spit out.

"Courtesy of the stately Lady Thomas. Doesn't she look radiant? She was under the impression you had destroyed the diary. You can imagine her disappointment when she found it lying out in your room."

Fear crackled through me like thunder. The weight of my wet clothes was suddenly too heavy to bear.

"She was quite distraught when I came by, and it only took some mild persuasion to discover the cause. How relieved she was when I reluctantly explained my willingness to destroy the book."

"You're lying. Charlotte Thomas would have never willingly admitted you," I said. She was too proud to divulge family indiscretion like that.

"Perhaps you're right," he replied with a twisted smile. "But how will you know what caused the effect? I hear you struggle with that."

I wanted to apologize to Hirythe, get some form of acknowledgement from him that I was even there, but his eyes remained locked on his adversary. He had an elbow on the hearth, as if lost in concentration.

"You destroyed it?" The implications had me swimming. If he destroyed the book, how would I save Bram from his fate? How would I ever come back here? Worse. How would we leave in the first place?

"Not yet," Brutus replied. "But soon."

"I need that book," I replied.

"Why? So that Bram can escape justice again?"

Dread weighed down my already tired limbs. Charlotte's portrait stared eerily down at me.

"Hirythe?" I asked.

"Not now, woman," Hirythe barked at me. He rubbed his thumb and forefinger methodically without taking his eyes from the gangly man sitting in his chair.

"What have they told you about me?" Brutus asked. I shook my head.

"Very little. They said your brother died of an accident on one of your expeditions."

He nearly choked.

"Accident? Is that what you told her, Hirythe? You accidentally killed him? You accidentally turned his mind into gruel? Did you accidentally use him as the guinea pig whenever you had a new epiphany about one of those damned trinkets Bram made?"

I looked at Hirythe. I wanted to dispute the claim, but I knew Bram persuaded others to use magic. Hadn't he done that to me? Hadn't he admitted to doing the same to his wife?

"That's right, Miss Winthrop. You owe this beast no loyalty. I trusted it once, as well."

"Luella, you need to leave," Hirythe muttered.

"What did they promise you, Luella?" Brutus asked, noting the apprehension on my face. "Tell me. Was it untapped potential? A chance to surpass what would have otherwise taken years to accomplish? Did they promise you Dawnhurst's oh-so-coveted Golden Inkwell?"

I found the courage to move toward Hirythe.

"Don't go near him," Brutus said. He motioned to a table beside him, where I noticed Hirythe's drawer of currants removed from the desk and lying askew.

"Or what?" I asked. "You'll destroy his memories?"

"Oh, no," he replied. "We'll all enjoy them together. Perhaps then you can see what a monster you've been dealing with." Brutus picked up a currant. The silver shimmered in the firelight.

"I'm sorry, Hirythe," I said. This was my fault. I left the diary in the open. Edward distracted before I started reading. "I should have come back earlier to warn you."

Hirythe's eyes darted in my direction, as if to raise a question.

"You've been spying on me," I said to my old critic.

"That's a harsh word," he said. "You're a journalist. Let's use terms you'd appreciate. I was investigating. It's a shame you got mixed up in this lot. I meant what I said about your writing."

"This is ridiculous," I said. "You're a literary critic!"

"Don't pretend you know anything about me. Here I was, all this time, on pins and needles, wondering when you'd put together that I was the same Jeremy from the Phantom Battalion. I didn't realize until our sit down in Oxford that you didn't even remember my name. Imagine my relief and hurt pride."

"How long?"

"That's a hard question, actually," he said. "I first started keeping a closer eye on you after your first article about the Steely-eyed Detective, when you wrote about Roberto's death in that alleyway."

"Roberto?" I stammered.

"The Italian," Hirythe said.

"The other member of our Phantom Battalion. It's amazing how willing people are to ignore what they can't understand. Mysteriously missing in that first fateful article were any facts about the victim.

That's selfish reporting, Luella."

"The police never discovered anything to identify him. Hirythe, I didn't know. I'm sorry." I pleaded.

"How did you kill him?" Hirythe asked Brutus. His eyes were wide with understanding.

"I used the song you were always so afraid of. You had a right to be. That song woke up something very dark, very difficult to control. It was master of fog and shadow. Powerful. It promised me great things. I think I disappointed it when it learned all I wanted was revenge. It kept going on about my weak ambition. Imagine! Killing three people and the magic called it weak ambition."

"Bid me do, I will obey," I muttered to myself. "Byron never meddled in high magic, did he? You triggered the voices." I said. How did I miss it before? My question made Brutus laugh.

"Byron? He can't even put together a balance sheet."

"That's impossible, Luella. Not if you administered the test correctly," Hirythe said.

"I didn't, though. I couldn't get him to maintain eye contact." I eyed Jeremy. "So, what is it? The fog creature was your creation?"

"Creation, no. But I woke it up. It killed Roberto under my instructions, then abandoned me, and ended up attached to you, Miss Winthrop."

"Why me?" I asked.

"I think it sensed a more delicious type of hunger in you."

The dream I had the night after talking to Edward. The fog. It all came to me like words to a song.

"When you wrote that article, at first I was paranoid. I decried it as sensational with the hope to persuade you to stop chasing similar stories. I wanted the magic back under my control. I hoped it would lead me to rest of the team. I suppose it did, just through you."

"You can't control magic that way, Jeremy. You never understood," Hirythe growled. "Let her go. If you wanted me, here I am."

"Here you are, and Bram will hang for a crime committed by the woman infected with the monster I awakened. It's poetic."

"What was your next step, old friend?" Hirythe asked. "I don't see the fog demon with you now, you are in unfamiliar terrain, and I have the power of many of my fallen kin inside me."

A terrible storm brewed in Hirythe's eyes.

"I brought a few trinkets with me, some of Bram's oddities. Enough to keep you busy for a while. There are many theories about how to harm your kind, and I'm interested in trying all of them. Where better to do it than here? Any unpredictable clashes of magic might make this whole little world unstable. And what would happen to you if it destroyed the world you inhabited? There go the fae, trapped in their own memory, forever."

Hirythe's face darkened, calculating, trying to predict what Jeremy had brought with him and how to counter it in as surgical a way as possible. I had experienced firsthand what a fragile world the Netherdowns was when confronted with the outside. Hadn't I wreaked havoc with a simple letter and a defunct spell?

"Do you plan to kill me, then?" I asked.

"If you die, it's the fault of Bram and Hirythe. If you don't, I imagine you'll have a difficult time escaping blame for the disappearance of Lady Thomas," he said. "After all, Bram was locked up when she vanished, and who else would take the blame other than the escaped fugitive Luella Winthrop. You're already accused of making her husband disappear, after all."

I looked at the painting. Was Charlotte trapped there? If high magic existed in music, it most certainly existed in other art forms. Brutus must have distorted it for an evil purpose.

"You've thought of everything," I said. "And I expect once you're finished you plan to get back to your cozy critic's corner?"

His head twisted like on a spindle, a sick grin plastered on his face.

"It's unlikely. I expect I will also perish when this world falls apart. But first, I think I will have a grand old time with the memories here. Even if Bram doesn't hang, I wonder if you'd recognize him by the time I finished."

Suddenly, a devilishly powerful gust of wind swept through the room, knocking items from their shelves, moving furniture, and making the fire in the hearth sputter like a candle. Brutus, chair and all, flew backward and into a tapestry behind him. It crumpled over him on the ground.

Hirythe swooped forward and collected his drawer of currants before rushing me out of the room and closing the door behind us.

"You can't stay here," he said, pulling me down the stairs by the hand. "We have to get you back, now."

"What about Charlotte?"

"We may find a way to restore her, but I need Bram to face Jeremy. There are many misguided myths about how to harm my race, but not all of them are without merit. If Jeremy stole some of Bram's trinkets,

I'll need his help to unravel them."

We burst through the door and sprinted for a stable at the foot of the hill by his tower. One of the magnificent feathered horses waited. It stamped its feet impatiently, sensing our anxiety.

"How will I set Bram free? Hirythe, our plan fell apart. They arrested me. I used the page to get out of prison. It's sitting in my cell out of Bram's reach."

"Then you must find another way."

He pulled a bottle of incensed perfume from the saddlebag.

"Where that will send me?" I asked, eyeing the bottle fearfully. He glanced back at his office window.

"Wherever Jeremy left the diary. Find it. Keep it safe. Don't return without Bram. In the meantime, I'll do what I can to prevent him from defacing Bram's memory."

"And your own," I said. He just nodded and unstoppered the bottle.

"Luella, you should know that night you found the silver currant, I saw no magical ailment inside you."

My heart, beating rapidly, plummeted into my feet.

"What?"

"I can't explain how, but you're healed."

"Why didn't you say anything? How could you keep that from me?"

"I didn't want to tell you because I feared you would abandon us and run off with your fiancé. I didn't want that for Bram. Or myself. I suppose I might know one more human who isn't so terrible."

It wasn't time for heartfelt moments, but his words elicited a swell of emotion from me just the same.

"Don't trust anyone but Bram. Do you understand?"

"What about Edward?"

The door from the old stone building swung open, giving me little time to protest.

"No one," he repeated, and he waved the bottle beneath my nose, throwing me into darkness.

Chapter Forty

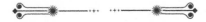

Drowned

My breath rushed from my lungs in a flash. All around me, icy hot needles plunged into my flesh. My fingers and toes numbed. My skin was on fire. I tried to breathe in only to gulp a bucket of liquid down my throat.

I flailed, sinking in freezing water.

I thrashed my arms, fighting its sluggish resistance all around me. I didn't know which direction was up or down. The cold threatened to pluck my eyes from their sockets, but finally, I saw moonlight above. I kicked and reached, straining for the surface.

Just as my vision blurred and my limbs fell limp, my face broke the surface. My skin screamed anew from the sting of the night air. I took huge gulping breaths as I tried to keep my head above water.

I had to gain my bearings, collect myself, but the cold was all encompassing. My strength would fail me in minutes, and I'd drown. I looked around me and found I was in the middle of a river, floating chunks of ice congregating on eddies nearby.

Was this the Severn? I looked to my left and discovered buildings and the top of a bell tower. I knew that tower. I knew this river. I was still in Dawnhurst.

Near me, the sounds of churning water called my attention. I spun round on my back and discovered a small ferry. Two men exchanged blows on its deck. One looked like a veritable giant. I blinked away river water, disbelieving my eyes. In the other, I recognized Edward's dark form, as if he was brawling with Big Bill. If only I could call out to him, but the cold took my voice from me.

My legs grew weaker, and soon I couldn't keep myself above water. So this was my end. A watery grave welcomed me, leaving Bram, Hirythe, and Charlotte to their own devices. The regret weighed as heavy as my waterlogged raiment.

Well, at least I would see my father again. I hoped that, despite everything, he'd be proud of me. Anna would carry on the family legacy, even if she was a Rigby now.

The water folded over my head. I raised up my arm, trying to touch the surface as I plummeted down.

Suddenly, a monster brush past me. Wet fur. Something had followed me back from the Netherdowns. No. That was impossible. Not a monster.

I flexed my fingers and grabbed the creature. I knew this feeling. Thoughts of lazy autumn days under linden trees flashed across my memory. I groped and found a small strap of leather, and soon I was being pulled upward.

Cyrus.

I surfaced again, sputtering, and saw him paddling as hard as his little canine heart would permit toward the ferry.

"Good boy, Cyrus," I croaked. I coughed, dislodging pockets of water from my mouth and throat. Edward looked over the side of the boat.

"Luella! Oh, my sweet Luella!" A rope ladder rolled off the side of the hull, and he shimmied his way down quick as an arrow. He tugged my skirts free, and I enjoyed an immediate ease of movement. I struggled as he helped me up the ladder, my numb legs all but useless.

He set me gently on the deck before going back over for Cyrus. In a moment, the pointer lay beside me, panting and shaking. Edward dragged us both to the small engine room, where a fire burned. He shut the door behind us and cradled me in his arms, massaging my limbs, trying to warm me.

"Cyrus, you wonderful boy. You blessed mongrel!" Edward said. I tried to burrow my entire body into Edward's chest, desperate for more warmth. He positioned us as close to the furnace as he dared and found a blanket to wrap me up.

"How did you escape?" Edward asked.

"Bram was in the cell beside me. We tore a page from the diary before they arrested him. It was his backup plan to escape before his trial. I managed to enter the Netherdowns from it." I talked in quivering half sentences. "But Hirythe is in trouble there. Bram is in trouble. We need to save him."

"Luella. I'm so sorry. We've lost the diary," Edward said.

"It's all right. Jeremy stole it, but it must be close by if I returned here."

"No. Luella, that's why I'm on this boat. When I left the prison, Cyrus blocked my entrance into our apartment. He was an animal possessed until I followed him to the docks. He nearly ripped the throat from a man setting off."

He wiped the dripping water from my face before continuing.

"I had to go on deck and separate them. I saw the book as I stepped off the deck. By the time I realized what was happening, the man had already thrown the diary into the river."

Where I must have emerged from it into the water...

"It'll be impossible to find by now, and even if we did, I imagine it's ruined. I'm so sorry."

I laid there in his arms, riding the rise and fall of his chest.

"Where's the man now?" I asked.

"Unconscious," he said remorsefully, "but I think he'll come to."

I focused on my breathing and trying to warm up. I tried to ignore all the thoughts and fears. I tried to ignore that my only way back to the Netherdowns had just been destroyed. I tried to ignore that Edward's mother was trapped there. I tried to ignore that I was again a fugitive.

But above all else, I tried to ignore Hirythe's parting words to me and how unlikely it was that Edward had been ready to rescue me right when I emerged from the book.

Don't trust anyone.

"It'll be all right," Edward repeated.

I wanted to tell him about his mother. I wanted to tell him I was healed, that we could run off and leave everyone behind. I wanted to return the comfort he tried to offer me now. Instead, when I opened my mouth, the fae's song came to my lips.

Do you hear the echo
  In the crags and in the barrow

"Luella," he hushed, putting a hand to my lips. "Just rest for now."

I closed my eyes and held him tighter. This was my Edward. He was mine. He promised me.

I had only sung two quick lines, but the sound of the powerful, sorrowful chorus was all but deafening.

END OF BOOK 2